ULTERIOR MOTIVE

DANIEL ORAN

☆ ☆ ☆ ☆ ☆

ULTERIOR MOTIVE

Kensington Books
http://www.kensingtonbooks.com

KENSINGTON BOOKS are published by

Kensington Publishing Corp.
850 Third Avenue
New York, NY 10022

Library of Congress Card Catalog Number: 97-075387
ISBN 1-57566-302-3

First Printing: July, 1998
10 9 8 7 6 5 4 3 2 1

Printed in the United States of America

To my parents,
Marilyn and Frederic Oran

ACKNOWLEDGMENTS

My agent, Emilie Jacobson, generously put her faith and enormous expertise behind a first-time novelist. Without her help, my manuscript might never have become a book.

My editor, John Scognamiglio, contributed the title and offered dozens of great suggestions for improving the story. He helped me make this book vastly better.

For their advice and encouragement, I'm also grateful to:

Marty Fahey
Nancy Nearing Go
David Hilzenrath
Michael Hirschorn
Meryl Kessler and Julia, Rebecca, and Scott Oran
Jake, Nikki, Susan, and Sam Klepper
David McLaughlin
Lorraine Shanley
Mike Shatzkin
Julie and Marvin Simms
Wesley Strick
Joshua Thayer
David Wehner
Pat and Norman Zashkoff
Sylvia Zashkoff

Prologue:
Tuesday, October 10

☆ ☆ ☆ ☆ ☆

He'd been doing talk shows for nearly a year now, but Jack Malcolm was still a little nervous just before the red light went on.

All the political consultants he'd hired were full of hints for looking good on TV. Really helpful hints like, "Smile!" Or, "Just be yourself!" What morons.

But Malcolm couldn't blame them. He was raw meat. A billionaire and his money are soon parted, he'd taken to saying in stump speeches. Especially when that billionaire is running for president. It was a great applause line, but the truth of it made him wince.

The makeup made Malcolm wince, too. Gritty, powdery stuff in some weird shade of brownish orange. At first, he'd resisted wearing makeup on TV. As far as he was concerned, he looked pretty damned good for 59. Sure, his face had some lines, and his red hair wasn't very red anymore, but he knew that the younger guys at Megasoft still had trouble keeping up with him.

Every year, he led a company expedition to the summit of Mount Rainier. At some ungodly hour of the morning, a whole busload of eager beavers would start out from the corporate campus in Woodside, across the lake from Seattle. On the way south to Rainier, Malcolm would hold court, regaling them with stories from Megasoft's early days. He'd even wax nostalgic about his first career, as a physics professor at the University of Colorado.

The kids ate it up. More stories to swap about their legendary chairman, JackM. In the Megasoft jargon, he was always JackM, which was his address for electronic mail. Walk by any conference room in any of the twenty-odd Megasoft buildings, and you'd hear someone invoking JackM's name. Well, JackM was pretty clear about this point, someone would say. No, would come the reply, I was at the last JackM project review meeting, and he was totally against that.

Marathon project reviews with JackM were a rite of passage for Megasoft managers. A dozen people would file into his office mid-morning, usually after staying up the night before trying to get the software demos to work properly. Nobody wanted to crash and burn at a JackM review.

Malcolm would sit behind his empty desk, which was just a long expanse of plate glass balanced on four metal poles, and fire questions at the crowd. Half of them had to sit on the floor. There was never enough room. Working without notes, he'd mercilessly drill them on the fine points, by turns prosecutor, teacher, and preacher. JackM knew his audience.

But tonight was different. Yes, there was a crowd in his office—television technicians, campaign staff, security people—but they weren't his real audience. They were off-camera. They were only distractions.

Sitting behind his desk, staring into the TV camera, Malcolm felt as if he was on the wrong side of a one-way mirror. Millions of people were watching him, but he couldn't see a single one of them. Even his interviewer, Lou Silver, was present only as a disembodied voice in his earpiece.

Malcolm tried to focus completely on the camera. He tried to imagine that he was talking to a person, not a lens.

But that didn't make him feel any less nervous.

Ten minutes into the talk show, after a call from a viewer in Texas who wanted to know the specifics of Malcolm's policy on water conservation, Lou Silver finally brought up what was on everyone's mind.

"So, tell me, Mr. Malcolm, do the death threats scare you?"

Damn, the Cincinnatus question again, Malcolm thought. The whole freaking campaign was being overwhelmed by this thing. A band of home-grown American terrorists holding the country hostage. Not to mention the campaign. First, there were the bombings. Nearly a hundred passengers killed on a rush-hour New York City subway car. A 747 blown up on the runway in Chicago, with 83 people on board. Two oil refineries in Houston demolished. And now these lunatics had him in their crosshairs.

They called themselves the New Society of Cincinnatus, some kind of twisted reference to George Washington's original Society of the Cincinnati. Well, old George must be turning over in his grave, because these guys were anarchists, pure and simple. They weren't interested in less government, or in limited government. From the rambling treatises they mailed to newspapers every few weeks, it was quite clear that only the complete absence of government would make them happy. Their credo, lifted straight from Henry David Thoreau, was simple: "That government is best which governs not at all."

Malcolm had become their target in the campaign, if only because his two opponents had so little to say about Cincinnatus. They were scared. It was just that simple. President Boyden had barely survived a primary election challenge, finally collecting the delegates he needed for re-nomination at the Democratic convention in Nashville. Since the New Society of Cincinnatus had begun its reign of terror two years before, the Administration had tried a series of totally ineffective measures. They'd blown it, big-time. So Boyden wanted to ignore the issue at all costs.

When Bob Duncan, the Republican Governor of New Hampshire, had announced his candidacy eighteen months earlier, he'd taken a strong stand against domestic terrorism. "The American people will not be pushed around by a band of thugs," he said. Then, a week after his speech, his security people discovered a bomb in a limousine the Governor was to ride in during a campaign stop in Iowa. No one was hurt, but Duncan was clearly shaken by the incident. Rumor had it that he'd received threats from Cincinnatus against his family. When he returned to the campaign trail two weeks later, his speeches included only passing references to domestic terrorism.

At first, Malcolm had focused his campaign almost exclusively on futurist themes. How technology was changing society. The role of government in the Information Age. For a few months, he was the news media's darling, with his picture on the covers of the newsweeklies and long, respectful pieces on the inside pages. President Boyden was too busy fending off a primary challenge to pay any attention to Malcolm. Duncan and his Republican brethren kept their distance from Malcolm, uncertain of his intentions—and even his party affiliation. But when it became clear to the Republicans that Malcolm had no intention of seeking their nomination, all bets were off. They baited him with attacks on his business dealings and his character. Gradually, reluctantly, with visible irritation, Malcolm was drawn into a political firefight.

Grasping for ammunition, he turned to the Cincinnatus issue as a glaring emblem of the entrenched parties' ineptitude. "They may not like what I have done," he said in response to Republican criticism of his business record, "but the fact is that I do get things done." In the same speech, he outlined an aggressive plan to contain and to crush the New Society of Cincinnatus. The death threats against him began soon after. Cincinnatus was brazen enough to place a $1 million bounty on his head. Malcolm tried hard to detach himself from the terror issue, to return to his initial themes, but the toothpaste was out of the tube. There was no going back.

"No, I'm not scared." Malcolm paused. He wanted to get this right. "Let me just say I'm concerned. And my personal safety is the very least of it. What concerns me most is that we're allowing ourselves to be intimidated. The times demand courage, but all I see is cowardice. Since I made that speech about this whole issue back in February, my opponents have had ten words to say about it combined. Frankly, I think that's pathetic. The American people deserve better than that. And when folks stand in the voting booth next month, well, I think they're going to choose the candidate who's confronted this very serious issue head-on."

It was a good answer. Out of the corner of his eye, in the back of his office behind the camera, Malcolm saw a campaign staffer give him a thumbs-up. Maybe Lou Silver would go to some viewer calls now.

No such luck. Silver had another question.

"Sir, why has your running mate, General Constanza, not spoken out more forcefully on the Cincinnatus issue? As a former Chairman of the Joint Chiefs of Staff, wouldn't you say that he has some unique insight into the terrorism issue?"

Malcolm hated answering questions about Constanza. The General had been a disappointment as a campaigner, no doubt about it. When Malcolm first asked Constanza to join the ticket back in June, the pundits called them the Dynamic Duo. Peter Constanza, the first Hispanic Chairman of the Joint Chiefs of Staff, was a genuine hero. The son of Puerto Rican immigrants, he had fought his way out of the barrio to West Point, to a Medal of Honor in Vietnam, to the Pentagon. After stepping down as Chairman, Constanza accepted Malcolm's invitation to lead the Center for Technology Policy, a Megasoft-supported think tank headquartered on the corporate campus. Less than a year later, he was Malcolm's choice for VP.

But the General was out of his element. Despite all of the coaching, he never got the hang of the ten-second sound bite. Instead of telling the time, he would laboriously build the listener a watch. Where simple words would do, he found arcane acronyms. And he antagonized members of the press, treating them like dimwitted recruits in basic training.

"Lou, I would disagree with the whole premise there. Pete Constanza is 100 percent behind the proposals I've made. I think he's made that very clear in his speeches. If you're asking, are we going to see the General making a whole bunch of flashy speeches, full of flowery rhetoric, then the answer is no, we're not. I think Pete acknowledges that's not his great strength. And frankly, that's not why I asked him to be my running mate. As most Americans know, Pete is a born leader. He led in Vietnam, he led at the Pentagon, and if, God forbid, something should happen to me as president, I can't think of anyone I'd rather have a heartbeat away from the presidency."

"As you know, Mr. Malcolm, some of the polls seem to be indicating that General Constanza has been a negative for your ticket, particularly among women. Any regrets now on choosing him?"

Malcolm forced a smile. Yeah, like I'd really tell you, he thought.

"Oh, no, nothing of the kind, Lou. Nothing of the kind. The general is going to be the most extraordinary vice president this country has ever seen. I'm certain of it."

"The latest polls haven't had much in the way of good news for you, Mr. Malcolm, isn't that right? You're ahead of the president, but Governor Duncan seems to be pulling away from you. Is there enough time left in this race for you to catch him?"

"Lou, I don't pay any attention to the polls. Never have, never will."

"But you must be concerned by the trend."

"No," Malcolm said curtly. He peeked at his watch. The minute hand had barely made any progress.

"Okay, we have to take a break here. Back in a moment with Jack Malcolm and your questions. The number is 1-800-555-CALL. That's 1-800-555-2255. Stay with us."

The red light was off. Malcolm exhaled slowly and surveyed the scene in his office. A few years back, he'd let his wife, Ruth, redecorate the place. He didn't much like the modern chrome-and-leather furniture she'd picked out, but he didn't want to hurt her feelings either. So he said nothing, and grimaced every time he banged his shin on the glass coffee table.

Tonight, they'd moved the coffee table to make room for the TV camera. There was a maze of cables on the carpet. Soft-drink cans and fast-food wrappers on the bookcase. What a mess. Malcolm liked things neat, orderly. He hated clutter. Rarely did a sheet of paper survive on his desk for more than a few hours. At the end of the day, papers went into his briefcase or into the trash can.

"Jack?"

Malcolm squinted past the bright lights. It was Herb Abernathy, the campaign press secretary.

"Just wanted to remind you that we've got you booked on another talk show in the morning. We need you back here at seven-thirty."

"Maybe I'll just sleep right here at my desk, Herb."

He turned to look out the long picture window on his right. Beyond his own reflection in the glass, he could make out the meandering peaks of the Cascades in the moonlight. It was a clear night, unusual for Seattle in October. Ruth Malcolm was probably already in bed, curled up with a book.

Waiting for the red light on the TV camera, Malcolm shifted uncomfortably in his dark blue suit, which had been selected by a consultant for its "presidential" appearance. He hated the suits almost as much as the makeup. Until the consultants had intervened, Malcolm had bought his suits off the rack at a local big-and-tall men's outlet. He usually wore jeans. Dressed-up for him meant wearing an old tweed jacket from his academic days.

"Mr. Malcolm?" It was a voice from behind the camera. A technician.

"I'm all set here," he said, sitting up straight. He felt a familiar tension in his chest.

"Ten seconds, sir."

Lou Silver cleared his throat. "We're talking with Jack Malcolm, independent candidate for president. He joins us from his office in Woodside, Washington. Jennifer, from Camden, New Jersey, what's your question for Mr. Malcolm tonight?"

"Hi, Lou," Jennifer said with a little giggle.

"Hi, Jennifer. What's on your mind?"

"Hi, Mr. Malcolm."

"Hi, Jennifer."

"How are you?"

"Fine, fine, thanks." Malcolm wanted to roll his eyes, but resisted the impulse. People watch ten-thousand hours of call-in shows, and they still don't know what to do.

"So what's your question, Jennifer?" Silver flashed a toothy smile.

"Mr. Malcolm, every year, thousands of innocent animals are subjected to horrendous experiments, just to satisfy some sadistic scientists' curiosity. I mean, even the cosmetic companies—"

"Let's get to the question, Jennifer." Silver smiled again, but less enthusiastically.

"Okay, so, Mr. Malcolm, what's your position on this?"

For a long second, Malcolm couldn't think of anything to say. He suddenly felt exhausted, and he really didn't want to answer any more questions. Not now. Not tonight. What if he just stopped it all here, he wondered. Got up and walked out and went back to being just JackM, king of his own little mountain. But it was too late for that now, he thought. So he switched on the old autopilot.

"Interesting question, Jennifer. You raise an important point. There definitely needs to be a sensitivity here on this. There's no need to abuse the laboratory animals. No one wants that, I'm sure. So we have to make sure that the proper controls are in place, that all the regulations are followed."

"So you're in favor of animal testing, then?" Her voice had a harsh edge.

"I think—"

Malcolm stopped. There was some kind of commotion behind the camera.

"What the—" In the dim field beyond the lights, he saw the glint of a gun being drawn from beneath a suit jacket. One of his security guys, he thought. Then it all happened so quickly. It sounded like firecrackers, like the Fourth of July. There were small bright flashes. Malcolm saw the security man with the gun snap backward and crumple to the floor.

"Oh my God."

A set of the bright TV lights toppled forward, smashing in front of Malcolm's desk. When he looked up, the scene was clear. Three dark figures with black ski masks and submachine guns advanced toward him.

Malcolm heard Lou Silver's voice in his ear.

"Mr. Malcolm, what's happening there?"

But there was no time to answer. One of the figures in black stepped to the very edge of his desk, where so many Megasoft projects had lived or died, and pushed his gun toward Malcolm's torso. His eyes met Malcolm's for a brief instant. Then he pulled the trigger.

Malcolm and his chair tumbled backward to the carpet.

Two Weeks Later:
Monday, October 23

☆ ☆ ☆ ☆ ☆

1

☆ ☆ ☆ ☆ ☆

At night, the Megasoft campus reminded Jonathan Goodman of an ant farm. One of those clear plastic things you got as a kid, with a maze of chambers and walkways and bridges. That was Megasoft. A collection of modern, low-rise glass and concrete buildings, intricately interconnected, and nestled in a dense evergreen forest. In the misty darkness of a Seattle night, amid the ancient trees, the buildings appeared to glow. With light and with pure energy. At a thousand windows, you saw young people at keyboards, staring intently into the cool blue light of computer screens. On his very first day at Megasoft, six years earlier, Jon had learned the company credo: "The best way to predict the future is to invent it." So letter by letter, line by line, the worker ants painstakingly created the software that defined the future as Megasoft saw it.

Jon joined the company right out of college. It all started as a mistake. He was an English major, a true liberal arts guy, with no skills, no idea of what he wanted to do with his life. Maybe he'd apply to law school. Or maybe he'd go to Europe for the summer and think about it in the fall. Who knew? The folks at the career office encouraged him to take a standardized job aptitude exam. After dulling a few No. 2 pencils filling in the little ovals, he was handed the computer's verdict: he'd be happiest as a hairdresser or a gardener. His parents were not amused. Not after all the hard-earned money they'd paid for higher education.

Out of desperation, Jon decided to sign up at the career office for interviews with the companies that recruited on campus. Mainly banks and accounting firms. Accounting sounded mindnumbingly boring to him, so he chose a few banks. On the appointed day, he arrived at his first interview, dressed in a stiff new blue suit. To his surprise, the interviewer was wearing jeans, a T-shirt, and running shoes. Hey, he thought, this banking stuff might not be so bad after all. They made small talk. About the weather, sports, movies. When the interviewer mentioned a recent movie he'd seen, Jon told him about a filmmaking course he'd taken in college. The coolest thing he'd ever done. The interviewer was fascinated. They ended up talking about it for fifteen minutes.

Finally, the interviewer asked him a serious question. "So, tell me, how'd a computer science major like yourself end up taking a course in filmmaking?"

"Computer science," Jon said, laughing. "Yeah, right."

The interviewer wasn't laughing. "Isn't this your résumé?" he asked, passing it to Jon.

He took a quick look, and realized immediately what had happened. "Actually, that's not mine."

"So you're not John Goodman."

"No, I'm *Jon* Goodman."

"Wait, so you are John Goodman?"

"No, no. I'm *Jon* Goodman."

When they both stopped laughing, the interviewer offered him a job on the spot.

Jon had a question. "What kind of bank are you, anyway?" he asked.

Grinning, the interviewer, Ted Nesbitt, head of the digital imaging group at Megasoft, said, "The craziest bank you'll ever work for."

It was already past midnight, and Jon still wasn't finished. As project manager, he was responsible for the software's "spec," the basic specifications for the way it should look and work. Codenamed "Hollywood," the project had been the subject of wild speculation in the trade press for months. First, the rumors suggested it was an entirely new operating system for handheld computers. It wasn't. Then, certain unnamed sources insisted that it was an incredible new video-game platform, complete with 3-D holographic displays. It wasn't. More recently, the articles claimed that, whatever Hollywood was, it would most certainly revolutionize television. And, on that point alone, there was the ring of truth.

Hollywood was Megasoft's entry in the anticipated market for interactive television, or ITV in the industry jargon. Since its inception, television had been a passive, one-way experience. The networks produced programs and everyone else sat at home watching. ITV would change that. It would turn monologue into dialogue, couch potato into involved citizen. That was the theory, at least. Replace the ordinary cable-converter box with a powerful microcomputer. Then transform the existing cable system into a national computer network. Suddenly, along with ordinary television, consumers would have access to a grand "information superhighway," taking them electronically wherever they'd like to go. Shopping. Banking. Sightseeing. And, of course, the movies.

It was this notion of "video on demand" that captivated the experts. They imagined never again having to trek all the way to the video store. Being able to watch any movie at any time of the day or night. The pundits were certain that video on demand would be ITV's "killer app," a software application so compelling that it would cause common folks to rush out and buy the hardware. Word processors and spreadsheets had done that for personal computers. Now video on demand would do the same for ITV.

Jon and his team, though, weren't convinced. Their market research revealed that most consumers weren't willing to pay very much for video on demand. So it would be hard to charge them enough to repay the massive investments required to install the new technology. It seemed clear to Jon's team that video on demand was a risky investment at best. Instead, after months of fierce internal debate and countless JackM review meetings, they convinced the company to bet on an entirely different approach: *personal video.*

Just as computers had revolutionized the publishing business, they argued, so would computers revolutionize the broadcasting business. Before personal computers, most people were only consumers of publishing. Only large companies could afford to own the expensive equipment required to produce publications. Inexpensive laser printers and easy-to-use publishing software changed all that. In a few years' time, consumers were transformed into producers. Jon suspected that the same thing would happen with video. Add inexpensive video camcorders and easy-to-use editing software to the burgeoning ITV network, and pretty soon people who never dreamed of producing their own videos would be doing just that. In schools, kids might learn videomaking along with reading and writing. Instead of writing about their summer vacation, they'd create a video report. It just might change the meaning of literacy itself.

Hollywood was the linchpin technology for personal video. It provided the easy-to-use editing, storage, and retrieval software for videomaking. JackM liked the idea enough to invest millions of dollars and dozens of the company's top programmers in the effort. Jon lobbied hard to get the project manager position, which usually went to an ex-programmer. Ted Nesbitt, now VP of the systems division, went back and forth on the decision for weeks before finally tapping Jon. "Welcome to the Big Leagues," he told Jon. "Screw this up, and you'll be back looking for a job at a bank."

Jon looked at his watch. 1:03 A.M. He wasn't making any progress. He pushed aside some empty soda cans, and put his feet up on his desk. He was barefoot. He'd taken off his shoes hours ago. He studied the hole in the knee of his very worn jeans. This time of night, he often caught himself staring at the cursor on the computer screen, just watching the thin black line blink. It was mesmerizing, and he found his eyelids feeling heavier and heavier. But he had to stay awake. He'd promised TedN that the spec would be done by the end of the week.

His eyes wandered around his office, searching out something to keep him awake. Except for a withered green cactus plant and a few skiing posters that had previously hung in his college dorm room, the office was all Megasoft standard-issue. One desk, with genuine simulated wood veneer. One ergonomically correct chair that allowed the office's occupant to spend far too many hours behind the desk. One steel bookcase loaded with technical manuals and plastic company-supplied mementos commemorating previous projects. And two somewhat uncomfortable guest chairs, which discouraged visitors from wasting the office occupant's precious working time.

Then there were the computers. Always at least two of them. Having just one computer at Megasoft marked someone as inexperienced at best, or some kind of useless, non-technical marketing bozo at worst. Ideally, there were at least three computers in an office. One for development, one for testing, one for e-mail. But the more, the better. Over the years, Jon had acquired four machines, even though he had never developed or tested a single line of programming code. He really only used one of them, but he left all of them on, twenty-four hours a day. Everyone did that. So, at moments like these, late at night, he could watch the screen savers, animated computer graphics in garish colors that danced upon the dominant displays. One screen showed falling leaves. Another had the flashing lights of a city skyline at night. The third displayed a virtual ticker tape of stock quotes and news headlines.

Sometimes, when Jon got tired of watching the screen savers, he just stared out the window. As a grizzled veteran with six years of experience, he was entitled to an office with a window. During the day, he could watch the lush green lawn being carefully manicured by the Buildings and Grounds Department, the only Megasoft employees who regularly ventured outside during daylight hours. And at night, even while the rest of the world slept, he could look out across the dark lawn and pick out dozens of lighted windows on neighboring buildings. There was something reassuring about knowing that he wasn't here alone. It was either reassuring or depressing, sometimes he wasn't sure which one.

Time for a break, he thought. Maybe Kenny was still around.

Kenny Alden was the hotshot programmer on the Hollywood team. Just 21, he was already two years out of college. At 15, he'd made it into the Hacker's Hall of Fame by breaking into computers at a top-secret National Security Agency facility. He might have gone to prison, but for his age and an enlightened judge who ultimately decided to "sentence" him to early enrollment at Cal Tech.

Kenny's office was next door to Jon's. Over time, they'd developed a kind of Morse code. Two knocks on the wall meant, "Still there?" Three meant, "Nesbitt's on the way over for a demo."

And four meant, "Francine's on the warpath." Francine was the curmudgeonly head of the technical writing group, which churned out dense instruction manuals. She was known to be chummy with JackM and prone to tantrums when she didn't get her way.

Jon knocked twice. Back came two knocks. Come on over.

When Jon went next door, he was surprised to find that Kenny's office was dark. Weird. Where he'd go? Jon took a step inside, reached for the light switch—

He felt something hit him above his left ear. What—

He felt a blow to his stomach. Hey—

And then the lights came on, and Kenny Alden was laughing uproariously, with a toy gun in his hands. The FoamBlaster 2000, the latest addition to his quite extensive arsenal.

"You little juvenile delinquent," Jon said, massaging his stomach. "Give me that thing." Kenny put up a struggle, but Jon, who played varsity lacrosse in college and outweighed him by at least fifty pounds, quickly wrested away the red plastic contraption.

Jon unloaded a volley of foam rubber pellets at Kenny.

"Okay, okay!" Kenny cried, putting up his hands to protect himself. "You got me."

"Do we have a truce here?" Jon asked, lowering the plastic barrel.

"Yeah, all right," Kenny said, smiling. "At least for tonight."

Jon started to put the FoamBlaster on the desk, but when he saw the mischievous gleam in Kenny's eyes, he thought better of it. Kenny looked disappointed.

"Where'd you find this thing?" Jon asked, still holding on to the FoamBlaster for security.

"Toy Town, bud," Kenny said, pouring some Froot Loops directly from the box into his mouth. "EricT and I made a run over there last night after we finally got V-File to run." Eric Torricelli, another Hollywood programmer, was Kenny's habitual partner in crime.

The image of Kenny at Toy Town made Jon chuckle. Every now and then, Kenny would drag him along on one of his toy-buying sprees. The clerks always gave them strange looks. Kenny, with his blond ponytail and tie-dyed T-shirt, looked like some hippie surfer from hell. Jon, with dark slicked hair and fashionably black attire, usually wore sunglasses, just in case the two of them ran into anyone he knew.

"V-File? You really have it running?" Jon asked. V-File was the video manager component of Hollywood. It worked like an electronic filing cabinet, with enough room for thousands of video clips.

"Well, we thought we did," Kenny said. "Then Francine came in this morning and complained that the colors on the screen were all wrong." He shook his head.

"The *colors?"* Jon asked incredulously.

"Yeah, the background of the screen actually, where we list the names of the video clips. It's black type on a *light gray* background."

"So?"

"Well, she told me that it's Megasoft company policy to have black type on a *white* background," Kenny said with smirk.

"You gotta be kidding."

"I kid you not, bud, I kid you not."

"Fine, whatever. But we're not going to waste development cycles on that kind of stuff now, right?" According to the organizational chart, Jon could make this decision. But no one paid any attention to org charts at Megasoft. Authority was in the eye of the beholder.

"I've got some bad news for you," Kenny said, ducking his head.

"You didn't." Jon clenched his jaw.

"Yup, we did. Took EricT and me all day, because we'd hardwired the colors. I mean, who thought we'd ever have to change them?"

"I can't believe you'd do that," Jon said. "Why didn't you come find me? I could have dealt with it for you."

"Jon, I tried. Really. Everyone said you were in a meeting, but nobody knew where."

He had a point, Jon knew. A meeting that was supposed to take half an hour dragged on for most of the morning.

"I tried to stall," Kenny said, "but you know the kind of crap she pulls. I start disagreeing with her, and the next thing you know, she's back with TedN, who doesn't know anything about this color stuff. And doesn't want to know anything. So he just told me to fix it. And that's what I did."

Jon sighed. "I've got to talk to Ted about this. If Francine has a problem, I don't want her coming over here and distracting the programmers. We need you guys focused on the important stuff." Damn, he thought, there goes the whole development schedule.

"What's the deal with you and Francine, anyway?" Kenny asked. "You know, every time she just mentions your name, she makes this face, like she's constipated or something."

"I don't know," Jon said, shaking his head. "I think she's still pissed at me about Astro."

"Wait, I thought she wasn't even involved in that project. Didn't you guys use outside contractors for the manuals?"

"Yeah, and that's exactly what pissed her off. She went crying to TedN that it wasn't fair her team was left out. Well, he sided with me, and she never forgave me for it."

"Beautiful," Kenny said. "Well done. You really are quite the suave one with the ladies."

"Yeah, thank you, Dr. Freud, for the analysis."

Laughing, Kenny pulled a neon orange yo-yo out of his desk drawer and started playing with it.

Jon asked, "What's so funny?"

"Nothing," Kenny said, with a huge grin.

"What?"

Kenny smiled and kept on playing with the yo-yo.

"What?" Jon nearly shouted

Kenny put the yo-yo down. "Bud, you come on too strong. You're too intense. You never finesse anything."

Jon sat down on the sofa. "That's not true. Give me an example."

"Okay, who's that marketing babe you were going out with? Tracy? Stacy? What was her name?"

"Tracy."

"Right, Tracy." Kenny picked up the yo-yo again. "You were always arguing with her about these piddling little things. I mean, I remember one time you got into some crazy argument on whether Bogie ever really says, 'Play it again, Sam' in *Casablanca.*"

Jon was shocked. "How do you know that?"

"Jon, we share a wall."

"You could really hear that?"

Kenny threw his head back. "Yeah, of course I could hear that. I hear *everything* over here. Like that time after the Christmas party last year with Donna what's-her-name. I could hear that too."

"You're a total pervert, Kenny. Anyone ever tell you that?"

"Yeah, you, about two weeks ago. You always tell me that." Kenny went for another gulp of Froot Loops. "But you're changing the subject. We were talking about old Bogie and 'Play it again, Sam.' "

Jon sat up. "Hey, I was right—"

"You see, you see!" Kenny said gleefully. "That's the problem. You always want to be right. Always." He paused to think about it. "And, you know, mostly you *are* right. And that pisses people off, too."

Jon stared off into the hallway.

Kenny put the yo-yo back in the drawer. "C'mon, Jon. Look, all I'm saying is, lighten up a little. Don't start World War III over some stupid detail. Go along sometimes. Even if you don't totally agree."

Jon slowly exhaled. The little twerp was probably right. "Okay, doc. I'll work on it."

Kenny poured the last few bits of Froot Loops into his mouth. "I'll believe it when I see it."

"Me too." Jon got up. "You ready to go? I've had enough therapy for one night."

Kenny shut the lights. "Next time we'll work on your sarcasm."

Jon's car was the last one in the parking lot. He waved as Kenny roared by on a motorcycle, then he slid behind the wheel of his car. It was an orange 1971 Volkswagen Karmann Ghia convertible he'd painstakingly restored over two summers during college. In the moonlight, he could see the chrome on the dashboard shine. Even the clock worked, Jon noted with some satisfaction. Clocks in old cars never worked.

He looked at the time. About one-thirty. Let's see, he started calculating, he'd be home in ten minutes, in bed by two, set the alarm for eight, and back here at nine for the staff meeting. Then, he suddenly felt uneasy. Was the staff meeting at nine tomorrow or eight? He remembered running into Suzy Chu, TedN's assistant, in Building 7 during the day and her saying something about the meeting time. He fished in his pocket for his appointment book. Damn, it wasn't there. Where'd he leave it? He visualized where he'd been. His office. No, it wasn't there, he was pretty sure. Kenny's office. No. The cafeteria. No. The conference room. Yeah, in Building 7, that's where he saw Suzy. Now he had a clear image of the appointment book lying on the long conference table. What a drag. Maybe it was still there.

Two minutes into Jon's walk over to Building 7, the perpetual Seattle drizzle turned into a real downpour. With just a sweater on, he soon felt like he was wearing a cold, wet blanket. He thought about going back for the car, but he realized that he was already halfway to Building 7. Then Jon saw a short cut. A nice dry short cut. The parking garage under Building 9. At the other end, he could just take the stairs up to Building 7. Brilliant.

Jon walked down the ramp into the garage. He ran his hands through his hair to get out some of the water, then he folded his arms across his chest. He was shivering. Great, he thought, I'm going to be on time to this stupid meeting tomorrow, then I'm going to be in bed with pneumonia for six weeks. Jon looked around the garage. It was empty, but for a lone car near the Building 9 entrance to his left. Heading toward the stairs at the far end, he started thinking over what Kenny said. Maybe he did come on too strong sometimes. Maybe he could patch things up with Francine. This was going to be a long project. Two years of skirmishes with her over these picayune details would be unbearable. And maybe she really was right about some—

A sound startled Jon and he instinctively turned toward the source. He saw the door to Building 9 slamming against the concrete wall as it opened. As the sound reverberated through the garage, he watched a man run madly, frantically toward the lone car. His arms were pumping, his legs flailing. Jon froze. What was going on? A wide concrete pillar now blocked his view of the man. The heavy footsteps abruptly stopped and Jon heard the soft jangle of keys. He slowly moved his head to the left, to get a better—

Jon jumped as he heard the steel door slam open against the concrete wall a second time. He ducked back behind the pillar.

Now he heard another set of feet, lighter than the first he thought, echo in the garage. Jon looked from behind the pillar and could see the first man at the car door, fumbling with his keys. Then the other set of feet came into view. He was taller, thinner than the first man. In business clothes, a dark blue suit. His arms were thrust in front of him.

He was holding a gun.

Finally, the first man was able to fling open the car door, but his pursuer was now no more than ten feet from the car. Jon saw the gunman's arms jerk backward. Instantly, the driver side window in the car shattered. Jon snapped back behind the pillar. There was a series of short popping sounds. He heard broken glass cascading to the hard concrete floor, and a dull, heavy thud.

Then there was silence. All Jon could hear was his own breathing. Short, shallow breaths. Gasping for oxygen. He pressed his body against the pillar and squeezed his eyes shut. Please, he prayed to whoever was listening, let me live. Please. He strained to hear something, anything, but he heard nothing. He slowly opened his eyes. Staring at the concrete, he waited. His mind was racing as fast as his breath and he tried to think of what he should do. Run? No, that would be crazy. Don't be a fool, Jon, he told himself. Think this through. There's a man with a gun. You wouldn't get ten feet before—

He heard footsteps rasping on the pavement. Calm, deliberate footsteps. Then a cough, short and hoarse. There was a pause. Jon heard a familiar swishing sound and a beep. A magnetic pass card, used to unlock the door. With a squeak, the door opened. There were more footsteps, now muffled, then he heard the door snap shut.

Jon exhaled. Was he safe? He couldn't hear anything, couldn't see anything. He waited. He wanted to look at his watch, but he was afraid to lift his arm. So he counted. To 100. And then to 200. He had no idea of how much time had passed. A minute? Five minutes? He couldn't tell.

Gradually, his breathing steadied. He unclenched his jaw. Jon decided that he had to move. He had to see what was happening. He had to get out of the garage.

Slowly, deliberately, he leaned to his left to look past the pillar. Then he gasped. What he saw was grotesque.

The driver's side of the white car was splattered with blood. Irregular splotches, large and small. On the pavement, blood coated a thick carpet of glass shards. The driver's door was open, its window entirely missing, blown away. The open door blocked Jon's view into the car. But where was the driver? He had to see.

He warily crept toward the car. The garage was still, silent. Halfway to the car, Jon finally made out the driver. Or at least his legs, which stuck out from under the door. They sat in a puddle of blood. Jon moved closer, closer, until he heard glass crunching underfoot. He took one more step and finally saw the driver.

Jon felt sick. It was a horrifying scene and he wanted to look away. But he couldn't look away. He couldn't stop staring. The man sat on the pavement beneath the open car door, his head resting against the driver's seat inside the car. He was covered with blood. His eyes were fixed open, unblinking, unseeing. He was older than Jon had thought. Maybe past sixty. His gray hair was still neatly combed. It was hard to make out his features. His face was round. He was heavyset. His light blue shirt was taut around his belly, which spilled over his belt.

For an instant, Jon thought the man was moving. But he wasn't. It was only an illusion. Jon wanted him to move. Wanted him to get up and walk away. Wanted this all to be just a nightmare. A sickening, terrifying nightmare.

But the man did not move.

Jon got a little closer. On the man's belt, pressing into his belly, was a Megasoft pass card. Sealed beneath the plastic lamination, now sprinkled with drops of blood, the man smiled at Jon from a tiny photograph. His name? Jon squinted to read it from a few feet away. The first name was "Walter." And the last name? He bent yet closer. "Kaminski." Walter Kaminski. Jon was certain that he had never heard the name before.

Jon's hands trembled as he dialed 911 from the reception desk in Building 7. What did the gunman look like? He tried to remember. Blue suit. Tall. Dark hair? He wasn't even sure. The face was a total mystery. He'd barely gotten a glimpse from the side. His mental picture of Walter Kaminski, meanwhile, was indelible. He couldn't clear it from his mind.

"Megasoft Security," he heard in his ear.

Jon opened his mouth to speak, but no sounds emerged. He cleared his throat. "The police," he managed to mumble. "Call the police."

"Sir," the female voice said, "you'll have to speak up. I can barely hear you."

He tried to calm down. "Call the police," he said slowly. "There's been a shooting. A man was shot."

"Okay, sir," she said evenly, as if she were reading from the dictionary. "Okay, take it easy. I need some information from you. What's your name?"

"Goodman. Jonathan Goodman."

"Mr. Goodman, what is your location now?"

"The lobby. The lobby of Building 7. But it happened in the garage. He's in the garage. That's where he is."

"*Who* is in the garage, Mr. Goodman?" she asked.

Anger welled up in Jon. Who is in the garage? Santa Claus is in the garage, he wanted to say. I'm calling to tell you that Santa Claus is in the garage. He took a deep breath. "The dead man. The dead man is in the garage. In Building 9. He's in the Building 9 garage. He was shot."

"Okay, sir, the Building 9 garage. I'm dispatching a unit there now."

When Jon got back to the garage a few minutes later, he was surprised to find that three Megasoft Security cars were already on the scene. The revolving red lights on the tops of the cars created a surreal disco-like atmosphere. One blocked the ramp into the garage. A second was near the entrance to Building 9, obscuring his view of Kaminski's white car. The third was parked right in front of him, at the base of the stairs to the garage from Building 7.

A uniformed officer got out of the car when he saw Jon.

"Sir, I'm sorry. The garage is closed. I'm going to have to ask you to leave."

"No, you don't understand," Jon said. "I'm the one who called."

The officer looked confused. "Called, sir? Called about what?"

Was this man a moron? "About that," Jon gestured toward Kaminski's car. "About the shooting. I was there. I saw what happened."

The officer stared at Jon for a second. "Okay, sir, I'm sorry. I just arrived on the scene. Can I ask you to wait here for a minute?"

"Yeah, I'll wait."

The officer took a few steps and then turned back. "I didn't catch your name, sir."

"Jonathan Goodman."

"Okay, Mr. Goodman. Just bear with me a minute."

Jon watched him walk to the patrol car parked nearest Kaminski's car. He stood talking with three other men in uniform, occasionally gesturing back to Jon. Finally, a different officer walked back to talk to Jon.

"Mr. Goodman," he said, extending his hand, "I'm Jerry Hayes, deputy chief of security at Megasoft. I'm sorry to keep you waiting. There was just a slight miscommunication with the dispatcher on this. It wasn't clear to us that there was, uh, that you were an eyewitness. Can you tell me what you saw, sir?" He pulled a notepad from his back pocket.

Jon tried to stitch a jumble of disjointed memories into some kind of coherent narrative. Going back for his appointment book. The sudden downpour. The short cut through the garage. Seeing the man running toward the car. The gunman in the blue suit. And then the grisly aftermath.

While Jon spoke, Hayes focused mainly on his notepad, only infrequently looking up from his writing to nod. When Jon finished, Hayes continued to write for another minute or so without saying a word. Jon guessed that he was in his fifties, from the finely wrinkled skin and flecks of gray in his dark mustache. As Hayes hunched over to write, Jon was left to stare at thc top of the officer's head, noticing the gray roots peeking out from his very black hair.

"Okay, now, I think I have that down," he said, tapping his pen twice on the final period. He furrowed his eyebrows. "You know, maybe you can help me with a detail here, Mr. Goodman,'' he said, flipping a few pages back in his notepad. ''You said that the gunman was wearing a blue suit. I guess you probably got a pretty good look at him. I mean, you'd recognize him if you saw him again, am I correct?''

Jon tried once more to conjure up some image of the gunman's face. But nothing came to mind. ''I don't know, I just saw him for a second.'' Jon paused and concentrated on the memory again. Nothing. It just wasn't there. ''No, I remember the blue suit. I remember him being on the tall side. But his face? I don't think I ever really saw his face. I mainly *heard* him. I mean, the footsteps and the shots and all.''

Hayes exhaled. ''I see. Well, you know, under the circumstances, that's not surprising. Here you are walking through a garage late at night, not expecting anything out of the ordinary, when, pow, all hell breaks loose. No, now that I think about it, I'd be surprised if you could've seen very much.'' He nodded his head a few times, apparently agreeing with his own analysis, then went back to writing.

Jon looked at his watch. 2:07. This was going to take all night. ''When are the police going to be here?''

Hayes looked up. ''Pardon?''

''The police,'' Jon said. ''The Woodside police. They've been called, haven't they?''

Hayes smiled. ''Oh, yeah. I'm just trying to make their job a little easier here. I was on the force over there twenty-seven years. Just took retirement last year, and decided to give the private sector a try. It's been a nice—''

''Jerry?'' It was one of the officers near Kaminski's car.

Hayes waved to the officer, then turned back to Jon. ''Sorry about that. Would you excuse me for a minute?''

Jon watched him walk across the garage to the patrol car. Another officer handed Hayes a cellular phone. Hayes put the phone to his ear and walked a few paces away from the other officers. He stood there for a few minutes, speaking occasionally, but mainly listening. Finally, he returned the phone to the officer and walked back over to Jon.

''Okay, here's the deal,'' Hayes said. ''Just spoke to Chief Ashby from the Woodside police. Brought him up to speed on the situation and he agreed with me that there's no reason to keep you standing around in the middle of the night. Especially after what you've been through and so forth.

"I've got your statement right here," he said, patting his back pocket, "and I'll pass that along to the Woodside boys when they get here. Silly to have you go ahead and repeat yourself a million times. No need for that. You're right on campus here, got your office number and all, so if the Woodside PD has questions, I'll send them by in the morning. Meantime, you get yourself some sleep."

Jon nodded. He felt exhausted.

"Oh, and one more thing, Mr. Goodman," Hayes said. "I'd like to ask a favor of you. We obviously don't know exactly what took place here tonight, but we do have a pretty strong suspicion. Looks like the classic drug deal gone wrong. And this is confidential, but we've been working with the Woodside PD for a few months now investigating a drug situation right on campus.

"Anyway, what I'm asking is that you keep this to yourself for now. A whole mess of publicity now would foul up the entire investigation. And, I gotta say, one Megasoft shareholder to another, don't quote me on this or anything, this kind of thing doesn't do much for the stock price." He chuckled. "Stock options weren't too big a deal over at the old Woodside PD. What a difference a year makes."

Jon labored to move the corners of his mouth into something that looked like a smile. Whatever. He just wanted to go home.

"Mr. Goodman, would you like one of my guys to give you a ride home?"

"No, thanks, I'm fine."

"Okay, then," Hayes said, turning back toward the other officers, "you drive safely now. And you have yourself a good night's sleep. Put this crazy thing behind you. Shame a nice guy like you has to be exposed to this type of incident. But that's the world we live in, my friend. That's the world we live in."

Jon started to walk back up the stairs to Building 7 when he heard the officer's voice again.

"Mr. Goodman, this totally slipped my mind. You weren't familiar with the deceased, were you? I mean, never saw him around campus or anything like that?"

Jon shook his head.

Hayes smiled. "No, I didn't think so. And that's what I told the Chief. A guy like you wouldn't run into that type of individual."

It wasn't until he sat on the edge of his bed, setting his alarm clock, that Jon realized that he'd never retrieved his appointment book. The perfect end to a perfect evening. Was the meeting at nine or at eight? He still couldn't remember, so he set the alarm for seven, just to be safe.

Lying in the darkness, exhausted but wide awake, Jon found himself replaying the events in the garage over and over. He thought about how Hayes had described it. A drug deal gone wrong. Jon wasn't convinced. The actors seemed so badly miscast. The killer looked like a stockbroker. Or maybe a lawyer. And Jon couldn't picture Walter Kaminski as either a dealer or a buyer of drugs. The man looked like a kindly clerk at the shoe store. Or a rumpled academic, but that was pushing it. A member of the drug scene? No way.

Then Jon remembered Kaminski's Megasoft pass card. Of course. That's how he'd known the man's name in the first place. Jon didn't have to guess about what Kaminski did for a living. He'd just look up Kaminski in the employee directory.

Jon turned the light back on, went over to his desk, and flipped on his computer. He stared wearily as the computer loaded the basic system software. The machine was on loan from Megasoft. Mostly, it collected dust. After using computers all day at the office, Jon didn't much feel like sitting in front of one at home.

When the machine was finally ready, Jon dialed the Megasoft mail server. He heard a familiar series of touch-tone beeps, a few rings, and a burst of the distinctive static that signaled a successful connection. On the main mail screen, he selected *Search For . . .* from the menu of commands, then typed "Walter Kaminski." A few seconds later, the answer appeared.

Name: Walter Kaminski. Office: 9-207. Phone: 3241. Title: Research Associate. Group: Advanced Projects. Division: CTP. Manager: Alan Block.

Jon scanned the entry for some clue. Well, Kaminski's office was in Building 9, so it was no wonder why he parked there. Research Associate in the Advanced Projects group? Pretty vague. CTP was the Center for Technology Policy, the think tank that Megasoft funded. Jon thought the whole thing was a boondoggle, the kind of highminded thing big companies do to make themselves seem more public-spirited. Maybe Kaminski was a rumpled academic after all.

His manager was a pretty senior guy, Jon noticed. Alan Block was VP of research and development at Megasoft, and he also served as assistant director of the CTP. An administrator, basically. Jon imagined that he took care of handing out research grants to the academics while General Constanza, the director of the Center, hobnobbed at conferences. Or did whatever else. Constanza kept a low profile on the Megasoft campus. No one was sure what he did.

Jon was about to shut down the computer when he had a slightly morbid impulse. He copied down Kaminski's phone extension, wondering what the man sounded like on his voice mail message. For good measure, he also scribbled down the office number. If he was in the neighborhood, maybe he'd swing by. Just out of curiosity.

Before getting back into bed, Jon dialed Kaminski's extension. One ring. A second ring. Jon listened carefully for Kaminski's message.

"Hey, I just told you, if you keep on interrupting me, it's going to take longer," a brusque male voice barked into Jon's ear. "He's got stuff everywhere. I don't want to miss anything."

Jon was dumbfounded. "Um . . ." he stammered.

"Charlie?" asked the voice, tentatively.

"I'm sorry, is this Walter Kaminski's extension?"

There was a click, and Jon found himself listening to a dial tone.

When he dialed again, after four rings, he heard Kaminski's

message. "You've reached Walt Kaminski at CTP," said the recorded voice in an unremarkable monotone. "I can't take your call right now. Please leave a message after the beep, and I'll get back to you as soon as I can."

Jon hung up before the beep.

Tuesday, October 24

☆ ☆ ☆ ☆ ☆

2

☆ ☆ ☆ ☆ ☆

For once, Jon awoke long before his alarm sounded. Usually, he hit the snooze button again and again, staying in bed so long that there was barely enough time to shower and shave. Then he'd shove a piece of bagel in his mouth, gulp down some orange juice, and hop in the car, only loosely adhering to the prevailing speed limits.

Not this morning, though. At six o'clock, Jon found himself fully awake, staring at the ceiling. Briefly, in the hazy zone between sleepiness and alertness, he considered the possibility that the unsettling events of the previous evening had never occurred. Was it just one of those weird nightmares that seemed so real when you first woke up, but completely evaporated only moments later? Maybe. Then he spotted the scrap of paper with Kaminski's phone extension and office number on his night table, and he knew that he hadn't been dreaming.

It was still dark outside. Jon desperately wanted the night to end. He got out of bed, and went around the apartment turning on lights. Every last one of them. In the bedroom, in the bathroom, in the living room, in the kitchen.

The place looked even worse with the lights on, Jon thought. Unlike Kenny Alden, who was still living out of cardboard boxes, Jon actually had some furniture. But just the bare essentials. There was a sofa, a coffee table, a cart for the TV, and a kitchen table. The kitchen table only had two chairs. On the walls, there were three framed photographs of the Seattle skyline at night, all gifts from an ex-girlfriend who had gotten tired of staring at blank walls. The only other wall hanging was a Malcolm campaign poster that Jon had sheepishly asked JackM to autograph at the last project review meeting. Above his signature, Malcolm had graciously scribbled: "Jon, you worry about Hollywood, and I'll worry about America."

The apartment itself wasn't old enough to have charming details like ornate window moldings or parquet wood floors. And it wasn't new enough to have modern touches like recessed ceiling lights or high-tech kitchen appliances. Instead, the backdrop of graying stucco walls and yellowing linoleum floors gave the place a dingy, generic feel, more like a motel room than an apartment.

The two-story, motel-like building was in the heart of suburban Woodside, a sprawl of strip malls and gas stations and fast-food restaurants that had grown ever more sprawling as Megasoft had grown ever larger. Even now, through his window, Jon could see a bright yellow Denny's sign lit up against the dark sky.

He suddenly felt hungry, truly ravenous. The refrigerator was a disappointment. He was down to orange juice, ketchup, grape jelly, and two eggs. In the cupboard, he saw only a can of baked beans and a box of instant pancake mix. The beans were strangely alluring, but he thought better of it. This was breakfast. He'd make the pancakes.

A few minutes later, Jon sat down at the kitchen table and slathered some grape jelly on his burnt pancakes. He tentatively took a bite. Not bad. Then, listening to himself chew, he decided that it was too quiet in the apartment. So he flipped on the TV and immediately spotted a familiar face. JackM, live from Washington, D.C. It was a news conference, his first public appearance since the assassination attempt. He looked a little pale, Jon thought.

For months, the Megasoft campus had been completely consumed by the Malcolm campaign. Employees had taken to following JackM's poll numbers as avidly as they tracked Megasoft's stock price. Politics had replaced programming as the favorite subject of discussion at lunch. There were always a few TV news crews wandering around campus now, and an informal e-mail early-warning system had evolved, ensuring that semi-spontaneous JackM rallies erupted in the halls whenever the cameras went on.

The official policy was that Megasoft was totally neutral when it came to the Malcolm campaign. There was no corporate endorsement of JackM's candidacy. No company resources were to be used on the campaign. Employees could only work on the campaign on their own time.

Unofficially, though, the official policy was a charade. Jon couldn't think of a single coworker who wasn't fervently pro-Malcolm. There was a minority sentiment that Megasoft wouldn't be the same without JackM, so they'd all be better off if he lost. But most people agreed that the country would be better off if he won, so they were willing to take a chance on a Megasoft without JackM at the helm.

As the election neared, product schedules were slipping more dramatically than usual. People just weren't focused on their work. The campaign was a huge distraction. With committees set up in every building on campus, there was always some new volunteer activity to siphon off time. Web sites, petitions, voter lists, posters. But no one was ever rebuked for electioneering. When TedN had walked in on a campaign Web site design meeting in Jon's office last week, right in the middle of the business day, Jon had worried that he was in for a scolding. But instead, to Jon's amazement, Ted had lingered for over an hour, offering his suggestions for the on-line JackM advertisement.

Malcolm had been absent from public view for two weeks, but he'd reappeared on-line at Megasoft within two days of the assassination attempt. Jon heard that Malcolm had infuriated his doctors by insisting that a computer be installed next to his hospital bed. And within hours, there was the usual stream of e-mail from JackM, reviewing strategies, suggesting product features, and arbitrating disputes, now from the comfort of his hospital bed.

JackM was legendarily plugged in to e-mail, no matter where he was in the world. The morbid joke going around campus was that even if Malcolm had been mortally wounded, the e-mail would have continued, but with a return address of jackm@god.com. A handful of cynics speculated that the address actually would have been jackm@hell.com, but even they were convinced that he would have found a way to stay on-line.

There'd been a rumor in the last few days that Malcolm was

going to throw his support to one of the other candidates and drop out of the race. But Jon didn't believe it. JackM wasn't a quitter.

Jon pushed aside his pancakes and turned up the volume on the TV.

Malcolm stood behind a lectern, surrounded by volunteers representing each of the fifty state campaign organizations. The stage was decorated with red, white, and blue streamers. A huge banner proclaimed, "America is Malcolm country!"

It was hot under the lights, and Malcolm was sweating. He pulled a handkerchief out of his pocket and dabbed his forehead. When he saw the brown makeup that had rubbed off onto the white cotton, he wanted to curse. But there were fifteen TV cameras pointed at him, so he just shoved the handkerchief back into his pocket and tried hard not to frown. He felt tired. Back home in Seattle, it was still early in the morning.

"I have a short statement," he told the auditorium full of reporters, "then I'll take some questions." He paused. "If you have any, of course," he added, to much laughter.

Malcolm didn't like crowds to begin with, and it had been a few weeks since he'd been in front of one. He felt rusty. And the butterflies were ferociously knocking around in his stomach. He considered himself a private person. What others perceived on the outside as arrogance, he felt on the inside as shyness. He generally felt uncomfortable around people. Some days, it was an effort for him to put on the blustery mask he'd created over the years.

"I'd like to begin by thanking the people to whom I literally owe my life. Some of them work at a small company in San Diego by the name of Protective Armor Corporation. They make a product called the PAC-Lite vest, a product that saved not only my life, but also the life of one hell of a brave man, Peter Devlin." Malcolm gestured to a burly man seated in the front row. "Going far beyond the call of duty, Pete stopped one of the bullets intended for me. It's hard for me to find the words to express . . ." His voice trailed off as his eyes welled with tears. There was an awkward silence as he looked down, aimlessly rearranging his papers on the lectern.

Malcolm felt nauseated as he recalled the assassination attempt.

Nauseated with guilt. His campaign had consequences he'd never anticipated. A man who had served him loyally for years was nearly killed by a stray bullet. In the Megasoft world, JackM could control everything. In the real world, Jack Malcolm worried that events were spinning out of his control.

He blinked a few times to clear the moisture from his eyes, then he swallowed hard and plunged back into his speech.

"I owe a debt of gratitude to the doctors and nurses at Woodside General. When I arrived at the emergency room on that incredible night two weeks ago, I was not in good shape. Thankfully, I had some extraordinarily talented medical people working on me."

The experience in his office that night had been almost surreal. Lying on his back behind his desk as dozens of faces swirled around above him. There was shouting, shoving, pandemonium. The air was heavy with the harsh smell of gunfire. Then, almost immediately, the shrieking sound of sirens growing ever nearer. Racing through the hospital corridors strapped down on a gurney, watching the ceiling tiles fly by. The next morning, from his hospital room, it looked like half the journalists in America were camped out in the parking lot.

"Finally, I want to thank the American people, who have sustained Ruth and me during this so very difficult time with their words and their gifts and their love. We've been overwhelmed by the outpouring of good wishes. Something like 100,000 letters. Truckloads of flowers. And a quart of chicken soup from Bernice Lerner of Brooklyn, New York. Thank you, Bernice, it worked like a charm." He smiled unhappily at this point, angry that he'd allowed the speechwriters to leave in such a cornball line. They insisted that it was the kind of endearing comment that was sure to make it onto the TV news. Sadly, he thought they were probably right.

"I'd just like to say to everyone who wrote or sent a gift or just remembered us in their prayers, Ruth and I will never be able to thank you adequately for what you've done for us. You know, when I first got into this race, I said that it was, in part, to repay this country for all it had given me. Well, today, I don't know how I could ever repay you for what I've received. But that won't stop me from trying. So, in case there was any doubt, I am very much in this race and I intend to remain in this race until Election Day. I've received what few men do: a second lease on life. And I pledge whatever time I have left to serving this great nation of ours."

Malcolm took a sip of water. "Okay, now, on to the fun stuff. You people think of any questions yet?" Every reporter in the room leaped into action. "Whoa, hold on now. Not all at once. Let's start way in the back there, with the young lady in the bright red."

She cleared her throat, then read from her notepad. "Mr. Malcolm, there's been a veritable sea change in the polls since the attempt on your life two weeks ago. Most of the recent ones give you a ten-point or more lead over your opponents. Do you think that's a margin you can hold on to?"

A mischievous impulse almost persuaded him to say no. But then he decided to stick with the script. "Well, as you know, I've often said that I never pay any attention to the polls." He took another sip of water. "But, hell, that was when I was behind." After the laughter subsided, he said, "In answer to your question, I believe we're going to win this election. And you can quote me on that."

3

☆ ☆ ☆ ☆ ☆

Jon got to work about seven-thirty. The whole building was quiet. Most of the programmers didn't straggle in until ten or so. Kenny Alden was known to arrive as late as three. Jon sat down at his desk, flipped on the computer monitor, and scanned the subject headings on the morning's batch of electronic mail. One of them was marked HIGH PRIORITY. From Suzy Chu, TedN's assistant. The staff meeting was indeed at eight this morning, but the location was changed, due to a scheduling snafu. The only available conference room large enough for all the participants was in Building 7. Jon had to smile. It was the room where he'd left his appointment book. At least he'd finally get it back.

It was a sunny morning, a nice change from the usual Seattle gloom. In the sunlight, the lushly landscaped Megasoft campus looked like a botanical garden, with inviting wrought-iron benches beside serene man-made ponds. It amused Jon that the benches were only rarely occupied, even on the sunniest days. The Megasoft corporate culture generally frowned on such public displays of idleness.

The sun energized Jon this morning, recharged him, as he retraced his route from the previous evening. In the light and the warmth, he felt any lingering sense of unease dissolve within him. He had been through a strange, unsettling experience. But it was behind him. It was just a memory, already fading rapidly. Feeling emboldened as he walked by the entrance to the Building 9 garage, he decided to confront his memory head-on. He would see the crime scene again, and it would look different this morning, he was sure. Smaller, less threatening, less ominous. Sort of like going back to some childhood place years and years later.

Jon walked down the ramp briskly, confidently. Immediately, he saw a pleasant difference. There were a dozen or more cars. The place was hardly deserted. He made a left turn, and walked over to the entrance to Building 9, where Kaminski's car had been parked. Jon had wondered whether he'd find the area roped off, with a chalk outline on the floor, but apparently that was only on TV. The spot was empty, Kaminski and his car tidily removed. Where there had been bloodstained glass shards, there was now an immaculately clean concrete floor. Initially, this efficiency annoyed Jon. With a fresh perspective, he wanted to see things as they had been. As he stood there, though, he gradually felt reassured. Now the only remnants of his nightmare were some unpleasant memories and maybe a few police Polaroids.

By the time Jon got to the meeting, a few minutes before eight, there was only one seat left at the long conference table. Right next to Francine. What a way to start the morning. To fortify himself, on the way to his seat, Jon grabbed a cinnamon roll and a bottle of apple juice from the tray by the door.

"Hi, Francine," Jon said as he sat down. "How's it going?"

"Jonathan," she said, acknowledging him.

Francine was the only person at Megasoft who called him "Jonathan." In fact, he couldn't think of anyone else who had ever consistently called him "Jonathan." Except maybe Mrs. Harris, his third-grade teacher. She'd hated him, too. "Jonathan demonstrates inadequate respect for authority," Mrs. Harris had noted gravely on his report card. Perhaps not coincidentally, Jon thought, Francine had worked for years as an elementary-school teacher before getting into technical writing at Megasoft. Even after spending a decade in the torn-jeans-and-a-T-shirt environment at Megasoft, Francine still favored formal, frumpish blouses and jackets. Her schoolmarm's demeanor made her seem significantly older than her coworkers. Behind her back, the programmers called her "Aunt Francine." When Jon gave her drafts of his Hollywood spec to read, she often handed them back with corrections written in red pen. "Run-on sentence!" she wrote reproachfully in the margin on one occasion.

Jon made an attempt at small talk. "So how's your gardening going?" he asked. He knew that gardening was one of her passions.

"It's a little late in the season for serious gardening," she said, ending the small talk right there.

"Oh, yeah," Jon said, trying to sound wistful. Before he could think of another clever conversational gambit, TedN opened the meeting.

"Okay, boys and girls," he said, adjusting his gold granny glasses, "we've got a lot of territory to cover today, so I want to get started." He spread out his notes on the table. "But before I do that, let me just make a quick award presentation."

In a phony baritone voice, Nesbitt pretended to read an inscription from his conspicuously blank yellow pad. "For wasting the most company time on non-company activities, the JackM campaign volunteer award goes to . . ." He paused dramatically. Then he stared directly at the recipient.

"Jon Goodman."

For a brief moment, Jon was afraid that Ted was going to make an example of him. After all, Nesbitt had walked in on that campaign meeting in Jon's office last week. It really had been a flagrant violation of company policy.

Then Nesbitt was leading a round of applause, and Jon realized that it was all just one more TedN joke.

"I actually do want to congratulate Jon," Nesbitt said, "on the way the campaign Web site is coming together. I know he and KennyA and a whole bunch of other folks have worked very hard on it, and the effort really shows. It blows the other guys' Web sites out of the water."

There was some cheering around the table.

"In fact, I've heard from some reliable sources that JackM is incredibly impressed by what you've accomplished. So keep up the good work."

Jon was relieved.

Nesbitt looked over his notes. "Number one on the agenda today, some news from the exec meeting yesterday. We reviewed the current state of the development schedule, and it's been decided to refine the target release date for Hollywood."

There were snickers from around the room. The development process at Megasoft always began with a wildly unrealistic schedule. Inevitably, it was only a matter of weeks before the programmers fell behind. Just six months into the Hollywood project, there had already been three major overhauls of the schedule. This was the fourth.

"Look," Nesbitt said, "the execs realize how tough it is to predict these things. They just want to be reassured that we're doing everything we can to keep the project on track." He consulted his notes. "Which brings us to number two on the agenda. JonGo's truly pathetic management of the schedule."

There was a mock serious gasp from the crowd, which was long acquainted with TedN's antics.

Nesbitt grinned and raised his hand. "Just kidding, just kidding. Boy, you people have no sense of humor this morning. Goodman's doing just fine. BruceK, though, is another story," he said, gesturing to the lead programmer. "Now that he's going out with JackM's secretary, Mr. Kroll here thinks he can do no wrong." Nesbitt thought about it for a moment. "And you know what? That's probably true. Bruce, dude, put in a good word for me, will you?"

He paused for the laughter. "No, no, Bruce is doing okay. I just wish he'd work a little harder." Even Francine smiled this time. Bruce Kroll spent so many hours programming, he basically lived in his office.

"Anyway," Nesbitt continued, "number two on the agenda. I just want to get an update from Jon on what's happening with V-File. Kenny gave me a little peek at it yesterday, and it looked pretty good. So, Jon, what's the scoop?"

Jon held up a finger as he gulped down the large piece of cinnamon roll he was chewing.

"Jon, we're not interrupting your breakfast, are we?" TedN asked, before Jon could speak.

"Well, as a matter of fact . . ." Jon said, furrowing his brow.

After the laughter subsided, he continued. "Okay. V-File is in surprisingly good shape at this point. KennyA's been a wild man on the coding the last week or so. Believe it or not, I think we're actually ahead of schedule on V-File right now."

"Incredible," TedN interrupted. "This may be a first in the entire fabled history of the Megasoft Corporation."

Jon rolled his eyes. "Don't worry, Ted. We'll find a way to fall behind again."

"Yeah, tell me about it," Nesbitt replied.

"So, anyhow, the bottom line right now is that V-File is pretty solid. Kenny finished up the search engine, so you can just type in what you're looking for. Obviously, that's pretty important when you have thousands of video clips in the library. You don't want to look at every book on the shelf."

"Jon, how are the search times?" Bruce Kroll asked.

"Not bad," Jon replied. "With a thousand or so video clips in the library, I think we're in the under five seconds range. And that's without any optimization. Kenny says he can get it down to under three seconds once he improves the disk caching."

"Cool," Kroll said.

"It's impressive," Jon said. "The search engine was really the last big piece of work we had to finish under the hood. Now the focus shifts to the user interface. For most of our customers, the user interface is the software. It's the whole look and feel of the product. The bad news is that the UI is still kind of a question mark. I'm just about done with the spec, so most of you should see a copy in your mailbox in the next few days."

"Jonathan," Francine interrupted, "could you make sure that I'm on the distribution list for that? I really need to be in the loop on the UI."

"Absolutely, Francine."

"Because I'm already concerned by some of the things I've seen."

"Like what?" Jon said, his jaw tightening.

"Like the failure to conform to some basic Megasoft corporate user-interface standards. I served on the committee that developed those standards, so I should certainly know," she said testily.

Jon raised his eyebrows. "Francine, if you—"

"Time out," TedN interjected, making a T with his hands. "Why don't you two take this discussion off-line, after the meeting?"

"That's fine with me," Jon said.

"Yes, let's do that," Francine said, avoiding Jon's eye.

"Anyway," Jon continued, turning to TedN, "that's the story on V-File. So far, so good."

Nesbitt called on Bruce Kroll for an update on his area. Jon tuned out, rehearsing what he planned to tell Francine about distracting his programmers. If she had problems with what they were doing, she should be talking to him and not—

The meeting was over and TedN was speaking to him. "Jon? Earth to Jon."

Jon looked his way, smiling sheepishly. "Sorry."

"I was just saying that, if you have a minute now, I want to chat with you and Francine. You're free, right Francine?"

She ran her finger down the page in her appointment book, then nodded.

Seeing Francine's appointment book jogged Jon's memory. He'd never looked for his. "Hey, before you leave," he called out, as people started to stand, "anyone find my appointment book? I left it on the table here, I think."

No one had seen it.

"All right," Jon said, "thanks. Must be somewhere else, I guess."

Most visitors from outside of Megasoft were surprised by how small TedN's office was, considering he was a division vice president, with a thousand people below him on the org chart. In fact, his office was exactly the same size as every other employee's at Megasoft. Except JackM's. But people were quick to note that JackM's office doubled as a project-review conference room, so it wasn't really a departure from the corporate policy at all.

All offices were created equal at Megasoft, but not all views. Sitting on the sofa in TedN's corner office, Jon admired the view of a Japanese-style garden. He stared out the window mainly to avoid making eye contact with Francine, who sat at the opposite end of the sofa. They were waiting for TedN. Jon had a feeling he knew what this meeting was about. He felt a little like he'd been summoned to the principal's office for being naughty.

TedN poked his head in the door. "I'll be right with you folks.

Suzy's trying to get AdamL on the phone for me from Taipei.'' Adam Levine was Nesbitt's boss, the senior VP for worldwide products.

Jon and Francine both looked up and nodded. Then Jon went back to staring out the window, and Francine returned to flipping through her appointment book.

Sitting there, staring out the window, Jon suddenly decided that the whole situation was ridiculous. He and Francine were both adults, professionals. They should be able to work this out themselves.

He wasn't sure exactly where to begin. ''You know, Francine, on this UI stuff—''

''Jonathan,'' she said, turning to him, ''let's wait for Ted.'' She looked down at her appointment book.

Jon's impulse was to laugh, but he controlled himself. So much for both of them being adults, he thought.

A few minutes later, Nesbitt came back into his office, shutting the door behind him. ''I'm really sorry about that. Adam's working on this massive licensing deal, and I just wanted to make sure he had all the info he needed.'' Nesbitt sat down at his desk, and briefly glanced at his computer monitor, scanning the electronic mail.

''Okay now,'' Nesbitt said, leaning back in his chair. ''Look, this is no biggie. I just want to clear the air, that's all. I saw the sparks fly at the meeting before, and obviously it wasn't the first time.''

Francine sat forward. ''Ted—''

He raised his hand. ''Francine, hold off for a sec. Let me just make a few observations, then I'll let you two jump in.'' Nesbitt rubbed his hands together, thinking over what he wanted to say. ''Both of you are doing great work. That's what I said in your quarterly reviews last month, and I really mean it. The problem—no, it's really more an issue. The issue here is that you're doing great work separately. But I need you two working together more often. As a team. And it's not happening that way now.

''I started to try to think of ways to get the teamwork going, but then I realized that it's really up to you two. You know best how to work this out. So what I'd like to do is add this to your performance objectives for this quarter. It'll be a line item like any other, and we'll review it in January the way we review everything else. How's that sound to you?"

Glumly, both Jon and Francine nodded their assent.

Nesbitt smiled. "Good, I like the enthusiasm there. We'll work on that. And maybe that's a good segue to my second observation." He put his hands behind his head. "There's a certain hostility, I guess you could call it, between the two of you, that worries me. I get the feeling that this thing is personal at some level. And that's bad because it affects not only you two, but the whole morale of the project.

"Look, I'm not asking you to be pals. But maybe you need to make more of an effort to get to know each other better." He chuckled. "I don't know, maybe that's too touchy-feely. Well, whatever. Anyway, spend some time thinking this over. You're both bright folks. You'll figure it out."

There was a gentle tap on the door, then Suzy Chu opened it a crack. "I'm really sorry to interrupt," she said. "Ted, it's Adam on the phone. He has a question for you, and I knew you—"

"No problem," Nesbitt said, getting up. He turned to Jon and Francine. "We're done here, right?"

Francine started to speak, but Nesbitt was already at the door. She closed her mouth and collected her appointment book.

Jon followed her out the door, and started down the hallway.

"Jon?" It was Nesbitt. "You know, I bet Adam's going to want some Hollywood numbers. Wait up a minute."

Jon went back into the office, and TedN closed the door.

Nesbitt wasn't smiling anymore. "Goodman, I'm only going to tell you this once. You're screwing up, big-time. Yeah, Francine's an idiot and she's totally obnoxious. I've noticed. Look, if I could have, I would have gotten rid of her when they made me her boss. But she and JackM have this mutual admiration society going, and he'd get rid of both of us in a flash before he'd ever think of letting her go.

"So you better learn to live with her, buddy. Because if it comes down to choosing between you and her, I'm telling you right now that you're not going to like the choice I make. You're a good guy, Jon, but, hey, I've got a family to feed. Do we understand each other?"

“Yeah,” he said, nodding grimly. He wanted to say more. He wanted to vent his anger at Francine. He wanted to catalog her numerous and flagrant faults. But he knew it wouldn’t make the situation any better.

“Fine,” Nesbitt said, reaching for the phone. “Now get out of here. I have a call from Taipei to take.”

4

☆ ☆ ☆ ☆ ☆

When Jon got back to his office, he noticed that the red light on his phone was flashing. Voice mail. He picked up the phone, dialed into the voice mail system, and typed in his password.

"You have two new messages," intoned the computerized voice. "Press the star key to—"

Jon jabbed the star key to hear the first message.

"Hi, Jon. Sorry, dear, this isn't one of your very important business calls. It's only your Mom, in case you don't recognize the voice." She chuckled. "No, I guess it really hasn't been that long, but Dad and I just wanted to see how you're doing. Everything's fine back East, everyone's well. So give the old folks a call when you have a chance. Bye, honey."

Jon made a mental note to call them, then pressed the pound key. "Message erased. Next new message."

"Good morning, Mr. Goodman, this is Tom Carroll, Detective Tom Carroll of the Woodside PD. I'm following up on the incident yesterday night. I'd appreciate if you could give me a call at your earliest convenience. My number here is 886-2311. Thanks very much."

Out of habit, Jon pressed the pound key. "Message erased. End of new messages." Then he realized that he hadn't copied down Carroll's phone number. "8-8-6-2-3-1-1," he repeated to himself, rummaging through his desk drawer for a scrap of paper. He couldn't find one. Welcome to the paperless office, he thought. "8-8-6-2-3-1-1." Damn. He turned to his computer, opened the word processor, and typed in the number. Whew.

Jon dialed Carroll's number and got him on the first ring.

"Carroll, Woodside PD."

"Hi, this is Jon Goodman from Megasoft, returning your call."

"Would you hold on a minute, Mr. Goodman? Let me just grab the file." Carroll's voice was vintage cop, Jon thought. The kind of gruff, unemotional voice that says words like "perpetrator" and "assailant" for a living.

After the sound of some paper shuffling, Carroll was back. "Jeez, this file is already a mess. Some of these guys have no respect for the process." He shuffled a few more papers. "Here's what I'm looking for. Okay, well, first of all, Jerry Hayes already passed along your statement to me, so that takes care of almost everything. You know, let me just say, so you don't get the wrong idea, if it were anyone else besides Jerry, I'd want to go over everything again. But Jerry's a pro. A helluva cop. The day he retired, there were a lot of tears over here. The man was really a cop's cop, that's what it comes down to. You folks over at Megasoft are lucky to have him. That's all I'll say. Lucky to have him."

Carroll coughed. "All right, anyway, I just want to follow up on two points. Number one is the gunman. I need to know whether you think you can ID him. Jerry seems to indicate here that you didn't get a good look at him. What do you think this morning, after getting some rest and maybe thinking about it a little more?"

"No," Jon said, trying to visualize the killer's face. "I've really been racking my brain trying to remember what he looked like. But, you know, I think I never really saw his face at all. I just got a quick look at the back of his head. And that's not much to go on, I guess."

"Definitely makes it difficult," Carroll said. "Too bad." He shuffled some papers. "Okay, Mr. Goodman, second point is the victim. Jerry has down here that you weren't familiar with the deceased. Had never seen him before. Even on the checkout line at the supermarket or something like that."

"He got that right," Jon answered. "The guy was a total stranger to me, as far as I know. I'm bad about remembering names, but I always remember faces. So I'm pretty sure I'd never seen him before."

"Fair enough," Carroll said, going back to his paper shuffling.

There were some voices in the background. Carroll finally said, "Mr. Goodman, let me put you on hold a minute."

While Jon listened to the Muzak, he thought about Kaminski, wondering what he did at the Center for Technology Policy. One of these days, Jon decided that he'd wander over to Kaminski's old office and—

"Okay, Mr. Goodman, I'm back live here. Just had a word with the Chief on this. Here's the situation. The Chief has reviewed the file, and he's been in contact with Jerry, and with Burt Seely, your chief of security over at Megasoft. I don't know whether Jerry mentioned this to you or not, but we're in the middle of an investigation of a drug situation on your campus, and it seems pretty clear to us at this point that the incident you witnessed is related. So I think it's safe to say that we're very close to breaking this case. Very close."

Jon was tempted to offer his opinion that Kaminski hardly seemed like the kind of guy who was involved with drugs. He decided not to. It's none of my business, he thought.

"Now, Mr. Goodman," Carroll was saying, "this is highly irregular, you should know, but your Mr. Seely has asked the Chief to keep this incident private for the time being. He says it wouldn't be fair to Mr. Malcolm to have this become a distraction in the campaign. Hell, we'd have a media circus down here. And there's really no need for that. No need for that at all. So we'd like to ask you to treat this as confidential while the investigation is going forward. That'd really be the best for everyone concerned. That makes sense to you, Mr. Goodman, doesn't it?"

Jon felt uneasy. He wasn't a lawyer, but it sounded strange, maybe even illegal to him. Wasn't this sort of a cover-up? Then he imagined having to answer reporters' questions. Microphones shoved into his face. Who needed that? And if it helped out JackM, well, all the better.

"That makes sense to me," Jon told the detective.

"Good," Carroll said. "If you have any questions about any of this, or you happen to remember something more about what you saw, I want you to give me a call. You have my direct number, my personal line. That's the number you should use."

"Okay."

"Don't you worry, Mr. Goodman," Carroll said before hanging up, "you've got the full resources of the Woodside PD on this case. And we're just like the Mounties. We always get our man."

The Hollywood spec still wasn't done. Jon had spent most of the morning staring at his computer screen, and he had about fifty words to show for it. At one point, he'd actually had seventy-five, but then his computer crashed. The screen just froze. After waiting two minutes for the system to re-boot, he couldn't remember the other twenty-five words. Writing specs was an ordeal. Every little detail had to be considered, every possible scenario anticipated. Jon liked to think in broad strokes. He found it painful to cover every square inch of the canvas. Hey, you asked for this job, he reminded himself. Just get it done. He typed a few more words.

Then the phone rang. Saved by the bell.

"Jon Goodman."

"Hi, Mr. Goodman, my name is Karen Grey. I'm the Seattle correspondent for *Business World* magazine." She raised her voice at the end of the sentence, as if to say, You've heard of us, right?

"Uh, yeah, *Business World.*" He had a subscription.

"How are you today?"

"Fine, thanks," he said, wondering why people he'd never met bothered to ask how he was.

"I'm sorry, am I like the twenty-third reporter who's called you today?"

What was she talking about? "Uh, no. Why?"

"After yesterday's news? No one's been calling you about it?"

I can't believe this, Jon thought. Those Woodside PD guys are bozos. The story's already out.

"Look, I really can't talk about this," he said. "You're going to have to call the Woodside police for more information."

"I beg your pardon?"

"The police. They're investigating the murder. That's really all I can say."

"Murder?" She sounded surprised.

"Yeah," Jon said irritably, "I was the witness in the garage. I saw it happen.'' For a reporter, Jon thought, she seemed pretty dense.

There was a long silence.

''I'm a little confused here,'' she said. ''You're saying you saw a murder?''

''I was the witness,'' he repeated. ''I was the one who called the police.'' Clueless didn't begin to describe her, he thought. How did she manage to report anything?

''Mr. Goodman, I'm calling about the press release.''

''Press release?'' Jon was furious. Why didn't anyone tell him about this stuff? First they're keeping everything all hush-hush, now they're issuing press releases. He had to call back Detective Carroll.

''It's from Megasoft public relations,'' she was saying, ''with the headline, GOODMAN NAMED HOLLYWOOD PROJECT MANAGER.''

''What?''

''It says you were promoted to project manager as of yesterday. That's why I'm calling.''

Jon slumped back into his chair. He finally got it. She wasn't calling about last night. ''What's the date on that press release?''

''Well, yesterday, I think,'' she said. ''I just got it this morning. Let me find it. Yeah, Monday, Septem—'' She stopped reading. ''Oh, I see what you mean.''

Jon sighed. She was calling him about a month-old press release, and he tells her about the murder. How was he going to get out of this?

''I'm sorry,'' she said, ''this is kind of weird. I guess we weren't talking about the same thing.''

''No,'' Jon said quietly. ''No, we weren't.''

''Now, you said this happened in the garage. The Megasoft garage?''

''I really don't have anything else to say,'' he said. I've already said too much, he thought.

''Can you at least tell me who the victim was? A Megasoft employee?''

''You're going to have to call the police.''

"I see. Well, congratulations on your promotion, Mr. Goodman."

"Thanks," he said. "Thanks a lot."

Karen Grey hung up the phone, then leaned back in her chair to adjust the blinds. The sun was shining on her computer screen. She didn't have to lean back very far because the office was so small. On bad days, she felt like she was working in a large walk-in closet. A closet with a view. She was on the fifth floor, overlooking a plaza with a fountain. It was actually a nice building, an unusually tasteful modern tower from the 1970s, with a prestigious downtown Seattle address. She just had the smallest office in the building.

The *Business World* masthead listed her as Seattle bureau chief, but that wasn't saying much, since she was the only person in the Seattle bureau. Back in New York a year ago, her editor had tried to sell it to her as a promotion, but she knew what it really was. A punishment. An exile. A convenient way to get her out of the New York office. At the time, she'd thought about leaving the magazine and making a fresh start somewhere else. She'd made some calls, put out some feelers, but there were no takers. Suddenly, she was damaged goods. So she accepted her "promotion" and moved to Seattle. With some luck, maybe she could write her way back to a job in New York.

Karen mulled over what the Megasoft guy had told her. Had he said what she thought he'd said? That he'd witnessed a murder in some company garage? It sure sounded that way. There was a chance this Goodman guy was out of his mind. But there was also a chance that her luck was changing. That this could be her ticket back to New York. She pulled off her sneakers and slipped on a pair of black heels. There was work to do.

Where was that number? Jon knew he had scribbled down Detective Carroll's number somewhere. Then, staring at the computer screen, he remembered. He'd never written it down at all. He'd typed it on the screen. Jon was pleased with himself until he realized that the computer had crashed an hour before, and he'd never bothered to save the number.

He called information for the number of the Woodside police, carefully wrote it down this time on a real piece of paper, and dialed.

"Woodside police."

"Hello, Detective Carroll, please."

"Who?"

"Tom Carroll."

"I'm sorry, sir. We don't have anybody by that name. Can someone else help you?"

This was pathetic, Jon thought. First he forgot the meeting time. Then he forgot his appointment book. Then he forgot the detective's number. Now he even forgot the guy's name. Jon, he told himself, get some sleep.

"Is there a head of detectives or someone like that?" Jon asked.

"That would be Vic Oppenheim. I'll connect you, sir."

The phone rang a dozen times. Jon was about to hang up when someone finally answered.

"Oppenheim," growled a man with a hacking cough.

"Hi, my name is Jon Goodman."

"So what can I do for you?"

Jon felt like an idiot. "I got a call from a detective before, and I seem to have forgotten his name. I thought he said 'Tom Carroll,' but—"

"Tom Carroll?"

"I'm pretty sure that's what he said. Do you—"

Oppenheim chuckled. "Billy, is that you?"

"I beg your pardon?"

"This is a joke, right?"

"No."

"C'mon, Tom Carroll has been dead for ten years at least."

This was turning into a very strange morning, Jon thought.

"I'm sorry, I just have the name wrong. I'm trying to get in touch with the detective who's looking into the incident at Megasoft last night."

"Incident? What kind of incident?"

Jon hesitated. Then he decided that if *Business World* had the story now, it could hardly be confidential anymore. "The murder," he said. "I was the witness."

"You were the witness to *what?*" Oppenheim asked with surprise.

"The murder. In the Building 9 garage last night."

There was silence on the phone line.

"Let's back up here a second," Oppenheim finally said. "What did you say your name is?"

"Jonathan Goodman. I work at Megasoft."

"Okay, Mr. Goodman, so you're telling me that you were the witness to a murder last night. Is that right?"

"Yes."

"And where did this happen?"

"In the Building 9 garage."

"At Megasoft?"

"Right."

There was another long silence.

"Mr. Goodman, did it occur to you to contact the police last night?"

"I did," Jon said quickly. "I mean, I called Megasoft Security and they contacted the police."

"Well, I was on duty last night and I don't know anything about it."

"Maybe another officer is handling it."

"No, I don't think so."

"Why?"

"Because I'm the only detective on the force. And I'm the only one who would investigate a homicide."

This was weird, Jon thought. Why didn't the police know anything about Kaminski's murder?

Then he realized what had happened. Carroll, or whatever the guy's name was, had explained it to him.

"You know," Jon said, "I think this is being kept confidential for now." What was the police chief's name? Oh, yeah. "Maybe I can talk to Chief Ashby. I know he's been involved in this since last night."

Oppenheim didn't say anything. He just started to laugh.

"What's so funny?" Jon asked.

"Very good," Oppenheim said, still chuckling. "You got me.

You had me going there for a while. Who is this? Did Billy put you up to it?''

Jon was totally confused.

''What are you talking about?'' he said.

''A confidential murder investigation? Yeah, right.'' He started laughing again. ''And Billy should have warned you not to bring up Ashby. The Chief's been on vacation for two weeks already. Camping down in California. Billy knows that. But other than that, not bad. Tell Billy that we're even now.''

''Look, officer, I don't know who Billy is. And this isn't a joke. A man was murdered last night.''

''Uh-huh,'' Oppenheim said breezily. ''And where's the victim now?''

''I don't know. I went back to the garage this morning, and everything had been cleaned up. Nothing was there.''

''So the murder victim disappeared.''

''Yes.''

Oppenheim guffawed. ''I love it. The Case of the Mysterious Disappearing Body. Tell Billy that I owe him a beer.''

''Is there someone else I could speak to, please?'' Jon asked. ''I don't think—''

''I have to go now,'' Oppenheim said. ''But thanks for calling. You made my morning.''

Then the detective hung up.

Sorting out the possibilities made Jon's head ache. Who knew what was going on? And, maybe more important, what was going on anyway? He thought about the players involved.

Walter Kaminski. Just some academic type, it seemed. Hardly a likely murder target.

The killer. Nameless, faceless, and dressed like a stockbroker. A complete question mark.

Jerry Hayes. The Megasoft Security guy. Was he a total phony? Says he talked to Chief Ashby and worked out everything with the police. But the chief was camping in California. Or was he really? And the police didn't know anything about the murder. Or did they?

Tom Carroll. The cop from central casting. He did sound like a cop. But the Woodside police operator had simply never heard of him. And Vic Oppenheim said a Woodside cop by that name had been dead for years.

Jon tried to think of what to do next. He decided that he had to talk this over with someone. Someone he could trust. He knocked twice on the side wall of his office, waiting for a reply. But there was silence. Jon looked at his watch. Just before noon. Kenny probably hadn't gotten to work yet.

How about Jerry Hayes? Jon was thinking of the names on his mental list. Aside from Detective Oppenheim, Jerry Hayes was the only person who was both alive and reachable by phone.

Jon pressed 0 for the Megasoft switchboard.

"Thanks for calling Megasoft Corporation. How may I direct your call?"

"Jerry Hayes, please. In corporate security."

"Thanks. I'll connect you."

Great, thought Jon, at least Jerry Hayes was a real person.

The phone rang four times, then Jon heard the voice mail.

"Hi, this is Jerry Hayes, deputy director of security at Megasoft. I can't take your call right now, but if you—"

Jon hung up. He didn't want to leave a message. He'd try Hayes again later.

Okay, now what? Jon drummed his fingers on the desk, considering his next step. Then it came to him. Kaminski. He had to find out more about Walter Kaminski. Jon decided to start with a visit to Kaminski's office in Building 9. Maybe he'd run into someone over there who could tell him what Kaminski was working on at the Center for Technology Policy.

All Jon needed was the office number. He turned to his computer, and ran the electronic mail program. After selecting the *Search For . . .* command, he typed in Kaminski's name, and pressed the enter key.

The answer was nearly instantaneous. *Name not found.*

Jon tried again. Kaminski. K-A-M-I-N-S-K-I. *Name not found.*

Okay, maybe that wasn't how it was spelled. He searched for "Walter." A few seconds later, he was looking at a list of fifteen employees whose first or last name was "Walter." None of them had a name that looked anything like "Kaminski." None of them worked in Building 9.

Jon knew that the central directory for electronic mail was updated over the weekend. New employees arriving on a Monday had to wait until the following Monday for their names to appear in the directory. Ten hours ago, at two in the morning, Kaminski had been listed in the directory. Now he was not. What were the chances, Jon calculated, that (a) someone is killed at 1:30 in the morning, and that (b) the bureaucrats who run the mail system find out although the police apparently don't, and that (c) they happen to reschedule the weekend directory update to a Tuesday morning? Zero. A big fat zero. Someone was working overtime trying to erase not only Kaminski's death, but also his life.

How about the switchboard? Did they have a listing for Kaminski? Jon pressed 0.

"Thanks for calling Megasoft Corporation. How may I direct your call?"

"Walter Kaminski, please. At the Center for Technology Policy."

"How are you spelling the last name, sir?"

"K-A-M-I-N-S-K-I. Kaminski."

"I'm sorry, sir. There's no listing."

Déjà vu, Jon thought. There was an unsettling pattern here. "You know, I may have the wrong spelling. Could you give me Human Resources, please? Maybe they'll be able to help."

"Certainly, sir. I'll connect you."

After a few rings, Jon heard a pleasant female voice. "Human Resources."

"Hi, I'm trying to find the phone number for a Megasoft employee I met at a trade show a few months back. I can't find his number in the on-line directory, and I'm wondering whether he might have left the company or something like that."

"Sure, no problem. I can help you with that. What's the person's name?"

"Walter Kaminski. The last name is K-A-M-I-N-S-K-I."

"Okay, let me just get into that screen. All right. Kaminski. Well, I don't see a current listing, so it doesn't look like he's an employee at this point. Let me search the database of former employees. Let's see. Kahn. Kaiser. Kalb. Kane. No, sorry, no Kaminski. Doesn't look as if Megasoft has ever had an employee with that name. But I guess it's kind of an unusual one.''

''Yeah, I guess it is.'' He paused. ''You know, this is a strange question, but if someone dies, do they stay in your database?''

''Well, you're right, that is a strange question. Hadn't heard that one before. The answer is yes, though. Once you get a job at Megasoft, even if you only last the morning, you're in this database for life.'' She chuckled. ''And for death, too.''

''That's reassuring,'' Jon said. ''Thanks for your help.''

5

☆ ☆ ☆ ☆ ☆

It was nearly one o'clock, and Jon's stomach was growling. Usually, a group of programmers stopped by around noon, on their way to one of the cafeterias on the Megasoft campus. But today, Jon had his door closed, so they went without him. Maybe it was just as well, Jon thought. He wasn't in the mood to make light lunchtime conversation about 32-bit memory addressing or object-oriented programming or whatever happened to be the topic of the day.

He was trying to decide where to go for lunch, when the phone rang. It was the receptionist.

"Jon, just wanted to let you know that your visitor is here," she said.

"Visitor? I don't think I'm expecting anyone." He looked around in vain for his appointment book. Oh, right, that's where this all started, he remembered. "I'm sorry, did you get a name?"

"Yup. Karen Grey, from *Business World* magazine. You are expecting her, aren't you?"

Wonderful, Jon thought. Exactly what he needed. Some reporter grilling him on what he knew. He was about to send her away, when he had a sudden change of heart.

"Yeah, must've slipped my mind. I'll be out to the lobby in a minute."

There was a certain logic to this, Jon decided. This Karen Grey already knows something is up. A murder at Megasoft. There was no way for Jon to take back what he'd said. And maybe someone should know his side of the story. Just in case, Jon thought. In case of what, he still wasn't exactly sure.

On the way to the lobby, Jon ran into Kenny Alden, who looked like he had just woken up.

"One o'clock," Jon said, glancing at his watch. "What brings you in so early this morning?"

Kenny smiled. "I don't know, bud. I got out of bed and I was just raring to go. It happens every once in a while." He yawned. "Hey, wanna grab some lunch?"

"Nah, I can't. I've got an appointment with this, uh, person who's waiting—"

"This person?" Kenny laughed. "Do you mean that babe in the lobby? She's hot. Who is she, anyway?"

"Just a friend," Jon said, smiling in surprise. How did Kenny figure out these things?

"Right. That's what you always say, Jon."

Grinning, Jon started down the hallway. "You gonna be around later on?"

"Yeah, why?"

"I want to get your opinion on something."

"My door's always open."

"I'll be by," Jon said before rounding the corner.

"Hey, Jon," Kenny called out. "If it's the first date, don't bring up *Casablanca.*"

Before Jon got to the lobby, he tried to imagine what a female *Business World* reporter would look like. She'd probably be wearing a conservative blue suit and a white blouse with one of those frilly tie things at the neck.

But then Jon turned the corner into the lobby, and he realized that, as usual, Kenny was right on the money. Karen Grey was a babe.

Jon found himself smiling. One of those silly, totally involuntary smiles. And he found himself staring. It was hard not to.

Karen Grey was indeed wearing a suit, but it wasn't conservative or blue. The suit was form-fitting, and what a form it was. The fabric was black, which made her blond hair look all the more luminous. Her blouse was barely visible beneath the deeply dipping lapels of her jacket. And her skirt ended well above the knee.

Karen got up from the sofa.

"Mr. Goodman?" she said, extending her hand.

"Please," he said, shaking her hand, "call me Jon. Mr. Goodman is my father."

She smiled. "I'm Karen Grey. Thanks for seeing me. In my line of work, I get a lot of doors slammed in my face."

Jon looked at her. "Somehow, I find that hard to believe."

"That's very nice of you, but you'd be surprised." She picked up her briefcase. "Is there someplace we can talk?"

"Sure," Jon said, and started to turn back toward his office. Then he stopped. "Have you had lunch yet?"

"No."

"Like Japanese?"

"Love it."

"Let's go," Jon said, heading for the front door.

After the waiter took their order, Karen pulled a notebook out of her briefcase. "I know you said that I should talk to the police, and I hate putting people on the spot, but I think there's something a little odd going on here."

"Why's that?" Jon asked, still uncertain of how much he should tell her.

"Well, after I got off the phone with you this morning," Karen said, "I obviously was pretty curious. I mean, a murder at Megasoft. In a garage somewhere. Sounds like a great story." She reached out and touched his hand. "I'm sorry, that's what happens when you've been a reporter for too long. You start thinking that a murder is good news. Anyway, you know what I mean. It's the kind of story that makes headlines.

"So, of course, I went right over to the Woodside police station. But I couldn't find out anything. The sergeant at the desk told me that he didn't know of a murder in Woodside in the last year. I was still curious, so I called the coroner's office. And I got the same story. No murder

"At that point, I was thinking, Karen, you've been had. It was a joke. This guy doesn't want to talk to you, so he makes up this ridiculous story to be funny, but you're too dumb to even get the joke. Wouldn't be the first time. Then I started thinking about our conversation again, and I wasn't so sure. When you spend all day interviewing people on the phone the way I do, you get pretty good at cutting through the bull. And I just had this feeling that you were telling the truth.

"So, anyway, I decided to call the Megasoft PR people. Usually public relations is totally useless. All they want you to do is write these fluff pieces. But I don't have any contacts at Megasoft, so I called. And, I know I'm starting to sound like a broken record, but they also said they didn't know anything about a murder.

"I was about to give up, when I had one last idea. I called back the Megasoft switchboard and asked for the head of security, and I got transferred to this Burt Seely's office. First his secretary said he was in a meeting. But then I mentioned I was working on a story about a serious crime that took place on the Megasoft campus, and he was suddenly available right away to chat."

Karen smiled. "Funny how that works. Well, I told him immediately I was calling about the murder, and I heard that magical silence. I think journalists and psychotherapists are the only people who really listen to silences. That's a shame, because you sure can learn a lot from what people don't say. And exactly when and for how long they're not saying it. This Burt Seely didn't say anything for maybe five seconds, which is an eternity on the phone. I just knew something was up, because it doesn't take that long to be surprised if you really are surprised.

"No, I don't think he was surprised in the least. It sounded like a calculating silence to me. The wheels were spinning. He was trying to think of a lie. Of course, when he finally opened his mouth, he tried to sound surprised. Said he didn't know what I was talking about and all that. But he was a lousy liar. I wasn't convinced. So I told him that a source—I didn't use your name—said that the murder took place last night in a Megasoft building. Now—"

Karen paused as the waiter put down the appetizers.

"Now, this is the interesting part," she said. "We were going back and forth for a few minutes. He was denying that there was any murder and I kept saying that my source said there was. Then, he got all indignant, and said something like, 'If there was a murder in a Megasoft garage last night, Ms. Grey, I'd certainly think that the chief of security would know about it.' And that's where I got him. I never mentioned anything about a garage. I just said building. Now I remembered that you'd said garage, too, and I knew it couldn't be a coincidence. I mean, if someone told me that a murder took place in a building, I don't think the garage would pop right into my head."

Jon smiled. He was impressed.

Karen took a sip of her miso soup. "I pounced on that. I told him, I didn't say anything about a garage. Is that where it happened? Well, he didn't like that. Not one bit. He basically started screaming at me. The whole story is ridiculous. I'm being irresponsible. He's going to call my editors. And on and on. They always do that when they're lying."

Jon asked, "Did he calm down eventually?"

"No, actually, he hung up on me," Karen said. "The liars usually do that, too."

By the time the waiter cleared away the plates, Jon had shared with Karen everything he could remember about the previous twelve hours. The murder and its aftermath. The call from the nonexistent Detective Carroll. The unsettling information from the Woodside PD. And the rapidly evaporating victim, Walter Kaminski.

Karen flipped to a clean page in her notebook. "Okay, let me ask you about a few things. Let's start with the gunman. I think you're right. I totally agree that he doesn't sound like your typical drug dealer or whatever nonsense they were trying to sell you. This wasn't some random drug murder. It sounds like a professional hit. An execution, really."

"Maybe," Jon said, "but who'd want to execute Kaminski? What'd this guy do?"

"The question could be, what'd this guy know? You said that he worked at the Center for Technology Policy. This may sound crazy, but do they do any classified research? Military stuff, maybe?"

Jon shook his head. "It's very academic, as far as I know. They study things like the adoption of new technology by consumers. Not something you'd kill for, I don't think."

"No, definitely not." She looked through her notes. "You know, let's hold off on Kaminski for a minute. I'm still curious about the gunman. Did he say anything to Kaminski before he fired?"

Jon tried to visualize the scene again. "No, I'm pretty sure that he didn't. As soon as he got close enough, he just started shooting."

"What happened afterward? When he stopped shooting, did he immediately leave? Or did he go over and have a look?"

"Well, he didn't leave right away. That much I know, because I could hear him. But I'm not sure what he was doing, because I was behind the pillar."

"When he finally did leave, did he run? Was there a real getaway? I mean, did you hear tires squealing somewhere a minute later?"

"You know, it's funny," Jon said. "I never really thought about what happened to the gunman. I heard him walk back over to the door to Building 9. I heard him swipe his pass card and open the—"

"His pass card?" Karen interrupted. "What do you mean his pass card?"

"Well, you need one of these to open the door," Jon said, pulling his pass card from his pocket. He showed it to Karen. "Every Megasoft employee has one of these. It's coded to work on all the outside doors to your building."

"How about other buildings?"

"Nope, doesn't work on those."

"So we know at least one thing about the gunman, right?"

Jon thought it over for a second, then realized what Karen was getting at. "He works in Building 9."

Karen smiled. "No wonder why that Hayes guy on the scene and this imaginary Detective Carroll both made such a big point of asking whether you could ID the gunman. He's one of them. He works for Megasoft. They wanted to make sure that you couldn't identify him. You might run into him one day on the Megasoft campus. They couldn't take that risk."

The prospect of seeing the gunman again gave Jon the chills.

Karen drew a line across the page in her notebook. "Okay, back to Kaminski. You said he worked in Building 9, too? Or at least that's what this electronic directory thing said when you first looked?"

Jon nodded.

"So maybe these two guys knew each other," she said. "Who knows, maybe their offices were next door to each other."

"Could be. Maybe he's also a direct report of Alan Block's at CTP."

"Alan Block?" Karen asked.

"I forgot to mention that before. When I looked up Kaminski in the directory, Block was listed as his manager."

"So do you know anything about this Alan Block?"

"Not really," Jon replied. "I mean, I know his title. He's VP of research and development, and he's also assistant director of the CTP. But that's about all I know. There really isn't too much connection between the product teams and the research groups at Megasoft."

Karen tapped her fingers on the table. "A vice president. Kaminski reported to a vice president. So he clearly wasn't some entry-level guy. He must have had some responsibility."

"I agree," Jon said. "Now, I wonder what Block is going to say about Kaminski. Will he just say that he never heard of him?"

"There's only one way to find out."

"You know, on second thought, maybe it's kind of a waste to just ask him point-blank, did Walter Kaminski work for you? Because once he says no, and he's probably going to, we won't get anything else out of him."

"Good point," Karen said. "So how do you handle it?"

The waiter brought the check.

"I think I have an idea," Jon said, picking up the check.

Lying on the sofa in his office, Kenny Alden pressed the framed picture against his nose, then slowly moved it away.

"Damn," he said, "I can't see it." He repeated the process a few times, staring intently at the picture only a few inches from his eyes, then gradually pulling it away from his face.

"Eric!" he shouted across the hall. "Bud, what is this thing? Give me a hint at least."

But Eric Torricelli wasn't parting with the secret so easily. "Tell you what, Kenny," he called back, "you finish the V-File user interface for me, and I'll tell you." The programming for the user interface was assigned to EricT.

"You're a total slime, Eric. No way. That's extortion."

EricT laughed. "Yeah, maybe I'm a slime, but at least I can see it."

"C'mon," Kenny pleaded, "give me an idea of what I'm supposed to be looking for."

"Okay, dude, it's easy." He paused dramatically, heightening the suspense. "You're looking for a 3-D image." Then, laughing, he kicked closed the door to his office.

"A 3-D image," Kenny repeated derisively, as Jon entered the office. "What does he think I'm looking for?"

Jon shook his head. "Kenny, you're turning into an addict, you know that? Every time I come in here, you've got one of these 3-D things in your face."

Kenny put down the picture. On first glance, it appeared to be a colorful, but largely random, scattering of tiny dots. When the viewer relaxed his focus, though, looking through the picture as if it were a window, he magically saw a three-dimensional object.

"Maybe I have been a little obsessed about it," Kenny said sheepishly.

Jon picked up the picture and looked at himself. "Cool," he said, after adjusting the distance a few times. "I've seen this one before." He put it down. "Anyway, what I wanted to—"

"Wait, wait," Kenny said, sitting up. "You know what it is?"

Jon shrugged. "This is an old one. It's been around for months."

"So . . ." Kenny began.

"So what?" Jon replied, smiling.

"So what is it?" Kenny asked, already knowing the answer.

"Aw, sorry, Kenny, I'd love to tell you, but—"

"C'mon, give me a break. I'm not getting any work done. V-File is never going to get done, at this rate. And that's going to make you look bad, too."

Jon made a big show of thinking it over for a minute. "Okay, I'll make a deal with you. You help me out, and I'll help you out, too."

Kenny nodded. "Sounds fair, I guess. So what do I have to do? Your laundry or something?"

"Nah, nothing like that," Jon said, smiling. "This is inside work, no heavy lifting."

"What?"

"It's easy. Remember last year, for April Fool's—"

"The e-mail," Kenny cut in, laughing.

"Yeah, the e-mail. You sent that e-mail from the Facilities department about my office, right?"

"Me and EricT, actually. How'd you know?"

"We share a wall, right? Well, I heard you laughing a little too hard when I was on the phone with Facilities."

"It was pretty funny, you have to admit."

"Funny for you. For two days, I was convinced that they were on their way over at any minute to move my office to Building 12."

"We were dying over here when you were on the phone with Facilities. Screaming at them. You bought it, hook, line, and sinker."

"Well, every time I hung up with them," Jon said, "after they'd just told me that I wasn't scheduled to move, I'd get another piece of e-mail saying the movers were on the way.''

''It was a great prank. We haven't done anything that cool since.''

Jon sat down on the sofa. ''So, how'd you do it?''

Kenny smiled. ''Uh-uh,'' he said, shaking his head. ''Top secret.''

''Okay,'' Jon said, starting to get up, ''you can figure out the picture your—''

Kenny grabbed his arm. ''All right, all right, you win. I'll tell you.'' He slumped back on the sofa. ''It was pretty simple, actually. Devious, but simple. Everyone's e-mail account is protected by a password, right?''

Jon nodded.

''So it's basically impossible for somebody else to go in and read your mail. Or to send mail from your account. Unless, of course, that somebody else is the mail system administrator.''

''The administrator's password can unlock anyone's account,'' Jon said.

''Exactly. So the question is, how do you get the administrator's password? You can't call him up and say, 'Mr. Administrator, may I please use your password to send mail from someone else's account?' That generally doesn't work.''

''So what'd you do?'' Jon asked.

''Who makes the electronic mail software we use, Jon?''

''We do. Megasoft does. We use Megasoft Mail, don't we?''

''Yes, we certainly do. And wouldn't you think that certain individuals who may have worked on that type of project would have some special knowledge of—''

''EricT,'' Jon said, smiling.

''Yup. Eric worked on Monarch, which was the first release of Megasoft Mail. And luckily for us, Mr. Torricelli was kind enough to leave a back door.''

''Back door?''

''A way into the system that bypasses the administrator's password. Eric put it in to make testing easier. Then, he never got around to taking it out before the product shipped. What a shame.''

''So you can send mail from someone else's account with this?''

''Send mail, read mail, create new accounts, delete existing accounts,'' Kenny recited. ''Anything the administrator can do. And actually a little more.''

''Like what?''

Kenny smiled. ''Some other time, bud.''

''Like April Fool's Day next year, huh?''

''We'll see, we'll see.''

Jon laughed. ''Okay, whatever. So how do I use this back door?''

''Just log in as JackM.''

''Yeah, right. How do I figure out JackM's password?''

Kenny put up his hand. ''No, no, you don't want to use JackM's password. Just type in our ZIP code for the password, then follow the instructions.''

''The ZIP code? That's it?''

''EricT said it was easy to remember. You can't forget the ZIP code.''

''True,'' Jon said, getting up. ''Well, thanks. You're right. It's easy.'' He headed for the door.

''Hey, wait,'' Kenny called. ''Aren't you forgetting something?''

Jon remembered. ''Oh, yeah. The 3-D image.'' He took a look at the picture. ''It's an airplane, I think. Or maybe a rabbit.''

Kenny jumped to his feet. ''What? You don't know for sure?''

''Sorry, bud,'' Jon said from the hallway, ''I've never been able to see those things.''

Jon looked up Jerry Hayes's phone number in the electronic mail directory and dialed.

''Jerry Hayes.''

''Hi, this is Jon Goodman.''

''Oh, uh, hello, Mr. Goodman,'' Hayes said after a brief silence. ''How're you doing today?''

''Fine, thanks. But, you know, tell you the truth, I'm still a little shaken up by what happened last night.''

''That's a helluva thing to come in contact with. Very unfortunate.''

''Just bad luck, I guess. Well, any news yet on the investigation? Do the police have any leads?''

"You know, I haven't heard anything myself. Did Detective Carroll have a chance to call you?"

"Yes, he did. He called this morning. It was nice of him to call."

"Tom Carroll's a real professional. An outstanding cop. Everything's in good hands with Tom on the case."

Jon smiled and shook his head. This Hayes is brazen, he thought. "I guess you must have worked pretty closely with Detective Carroll when you were on the force."

There was a pause. "Sure, Tom and I go way back. Great guy."

"Is he the head of detectives or something like that? Seemed very knowledgeable to me."

"Tom pretty much runs the show over there. He's the top guy." Hayes cleared his throat. "Anyway, Mr. Goodman, appreciate your call, and—"

"Have you been talking to Chief Ashby about all this? I guess he must be pretty closely involved, too."

"Absolutely. Hal keeps tabs on everything. He's really a hands-on chief."

Jon wasn't sure what to do next. "I'm sorry, do you mind if I put you on hold a second? Just have to answer a quick question for someone here."

"Sure," Hayes said unhappily. He clearly wanted to get off the phone.

Jon punched the hold button and tried to collect his thoughts. Was this the right time to challenge Hayes's apparent lies? Then there'd be no doubt he was on to something. Or should he say nothing? But maybe they'd already surmised that he was Karen Grey's source.

After pondering the choice for a moment, Jon pressed the hold button again.

"Sorry to keep you waiting."

"No problem," Hayes replied without much enthusiasm.

"A strange thing happened before," Jon began.

"What's that?"

"Well, I wanted to give Detective Carroll a call back, and couldn't find the number he gave me. So I just called the main Woodside police number. But it was really odd. They didn't have a number for him. Had never heard of him, actually."

Hayes laughed nervously. "That happens all the time. Probably the girl's first day on the job. Yesterday she was flipping burgers, and today she's answering phones. Tell you what, I don't have Tom's number handy, but I'll hunt it down, give him a call, and ask him to get in touch with you pronto. Anyway, if that's all, Mr—"

"You know, then they finally connected me to a detective, this Vic Oppenheim. And, believe it or not, he said there was no Tom Carroll working at the Woodside PD."

Hayes coughed. "Well, I'll be darned, Mr. Goodman. Vic Oppenheim should be ashamed of himself, pulling your leg like that. He's a real kidder, that Vic. A real kidder. Next time I talk to Chief Ashby I'm going to mention that. It's really not something that should happen to citizens who call in."

"So you think he was also just kidding when he told me that Chief Ashby is on vacation? And that the Woodside police have no record of the murder last night?"

"You asked him about the incident?"

"Yeah, but he said he didn't know anything about it."

"Did he say he was planning to follow up on your conversation?" Hayes asked quickly.

"No, he actually thought it was all some kind of prank."

Hayes exhaled. "Well, like I told you, old Vic is a real kidder. A laugh a minute. Very funny guy. Used to have us rolling on the floor with those whoppers of his." Hayes cleared his throat. "But I have to say that this seems like a very inappropriate situation for that type of humor. Very inappropriate. And I'm going to have a word with Chief Ashby about it."

"Thanks," Jon said. "I knew there had to be a simple explanation. It all makes sense to me now."

"Oh, sure. This kind of thing can be unsettling, if you're not used to it. Well, now that we've cleared that up, why don't I let you get back to work. I'm sure an important guy like you has a lot to do."

EricT had included a little bit of humor in the Megasoft Mail back door, Jon discovered.

Following Kenny Alden's instructions, Jon opened the mail program and typed in JackM's name instead of his own. When the system asked for his password, he responded with the ZIP code. Instantly, the screen was filled with a grainy, but clearly recognizable, photo of JackM. And then, much to Jon's surprise, his office was filled with a scratchy recording of JackM's voice.

"Son, you just haven't thought this through!" JackM roared from the tinny speaker inside the computer.

Jon smiled. He'd heard those words more times than he cared to remember. EricT had no doubt recorded them at a JackM project review.

After a few seconds, a menu of options appeared on Jon's screen:

1. Log in to an existing mailbox
2. Delete existing mailbox
3. Create new mailbox
4. System parameters
5. Housekeeping
6. Exit

He couldn't figure out options 4 and 5. Probably the mysterious functions Kenny Alden had mentioned. He'd have to wait until April Fool's Day to find out. Jon decided to play it safe and simply create a new mailbox. He entered his choice.

Jon was staring at a whole screen of questions. First name? Last name? Office? Phone? Title? Group? Division? Manager? He lingered a second on the name. It was hard to pull a name out of thin air. Okay, Tim . . . Smith, maybe Smith is too generic, Jon thought. All right, Tim Schmidt. Fine, sounds a little more ethnic.

Now, where does Tim Schmidt work? Easy, Building 12, home of the computer-repair folks. The phone number was trickier. Jon decided to take a chance and use the repair department's main number, which he found on a page of phone extensions tacked to his wall. Title? Support Technician II. Sounded official. Group? Hardware Support. Division? Operations. Manager? Jon tried to remember who headed the computer-repair department. Lou Crowley? No, not anymore, Jon remembered. What was the new guy's name? Terry Sanders. Jon pressed the return key.

A new screen asked for the password to Tim Schmidt's mailbox.

Jon paused. He always had a hard time thinking up passwords. Then he spotted a bright yellow pencil on his desk. Ticonderoga, it said. He typed in "Ticonderoga" as the password, and pressed the return key once more.

After a few seconds, a confirmation message appeared on the screen: *Mailbox created. Press any key to continue.* Jon tapped the space bar, and was back to the main menu. He chose option six, *Exit,* and he soon saw his usual workspace on the screen.

Jon went back to the mail program, this time logging in as the new employee, Tim Schmidt. Password? Ticonderoga. Jon smiled when the familiar mail screen appeared. He'd have to thank EricT.

Okay, let's try this thing out, Jon thought. He selected the command for sending a new message. Recipient? Alan Block. Subject? Kaminski status. In the box for text, he typed:

> In Repair Request #71-8734a, your direct report, Walter Kaminski, specified a faulty hard drive in his system. In response to his request, a new drive was ordered and arrived yesterday, at which time I sent e-mail to Mr. Kaminski informing him of the installation this Thursday at 3 PM. Due to a team meeting during that time slot, however, I need to reschedule. But Mr. Kaminski's e-mail and phone extension now appear to be disconnected. If he has been transferred from your group, please advise. I will need to file a Capital Asset Reallocation form on the drive if it cannot be installed in Mr. Kaminski's computer. Thanks for your help.

Jon read over what he'd typed, chuckling when he got to the mention of the "Capital Asset Reallocation" form. He had no idea what that was, and hoped that Block wouldn't have any idea either. But it did have a pleasant bureaucratic ring to it. Jon selected the Send command, launching the message off into cyberspace.

As Jon approached the entrance to Building 9, he tried to recall the last time he'd been inside. Definitely before the Center for Technology Policy even existed. The corporate library used to be on the second floor, he remembered. When he first arrived at

Megasoft, he was often overwhelmed by the nonstop immersion in technical details. So, many an afternoon, he'd sneak over to the library and thumb through the little-read issues of popular magazines. It was a refreshing respite from his work. Six years later, Jon couldn't remember the last time he'd been to the library. In fact, he wasn't quite sure where the new library was.

The lobby of Building 9 had changed dramatically, Jon noticed when he opened the front door. A receptionist's station had sprouted up in the center of the lobby. And, unlike the lobbies in other Megasoft buildings, there was a glass wall with a single door behind the station, limiting access to the rest of the building. Very inviting place, this Center for Technology Policy, Jon thought. Who were they trying to keep out?

Jon avoided making eye contact with the receptionist, who appeared to be busy with a computer game, and walked directly to the glass door behind her. He tugged the handle. Locked. Damn.

"Sir?" It was the receptionist.

Jon turned around and pulled out his Megasoft pass card. "Hi, I'm running late for a meeting," he said breathlessly. "I guess you need to open this." Then he put his hand back on the door handle.

"I'm sorry, sir," the young woman said to Jon. "May I have your name, please?"

"Goodman. Jon Goodman." He looked at his watch. "Jeez, it really is late. I've got to get up there."

The receptionist typed something into her computer. "Goodman? No, I don't see you on the visitor list. Who are you meeting with?"

Good question. He looked at her blankly for a second, then decided to take a chance. "Walter Kaminski," he said, searching for any sign of recognition in the woman's expression.

But there was none. "Walter Kaminski? I don't think we have anyone by that name at the Center, sir, but let me check." She did some more typing. "No, I'm sorry, there's not a Walter Kaminski here in Building 9."

"Did you say Building 9?" Jon asked, feigning surprise.

"Yes," she said coolly, "this is the Center for Technology Policy."

"You know, it's just been one of those days," Jon said, shaking his head. He looked at his watch again. "I was supposed to be in

Building 8 ten minutes ago. Have any idea which one Building 8 is?''

''Building 8 is right across the parking lot,'' she said, gesturing toward the front door.

''Thanks so much for your help,'' Jon said on his way to the door. ''They really should label these buildings more clearly.''

7

☆ ☆ ☆ ☆ ☆

"You have one new message."

Jon pressed the star key.

"Yes, hello, Mr. Goodman, this is Burt Seely, chief of security here at Megasoft. I've been meaning to catch up with you all day, and it's just been one thing after another for me. Hope I haven't missed you. I'd really like to have a quick meeting with you before the end of the day. I'm at extension 2189. Give me a call, and if I'm not here, ask for Cindy Hall. She'll be able to track me down. Thanks. Look forward to talking to you later."

Jon dialed.

"Burt Seely's office," said a cheery female voice.

"This is Jon Goodman—"

"Oh, Mr. Goodman, thanks for calling. This is Cindy Hall. I'm Burt's assistant. He's actually not here right now, but he told me you'd probably be calling. Let me just look at his schedule a sec, here. Okay, let's see, Burt's free at 5:30. How's that work for you?"

"Sure, that's fine."

"Great. I know he really wanted to see you today. You know, I'm just looking at the schedule, and I see that Burt has a six o'clock on this side of the campus. Would you mind meeting over here?"

"No problem, I could use the exercise. What's the office number?"

"Burt's in 2-178."

"Okay," Jon said, scribbling down the number, "5:30 in 2-178."

"Super. I'll let him know."

* * *

Karen first noticed the car on the way back from lunch. It looked like a rental car, a boxy four-door model in some hideous shade of purplish brown. It was in her rearview mirror when she left the Japanese restaurant. Then she noticed it again when she stopped to buy some cough drops at a shopping center a few miles down the road. So when she spotted it behind her on the bridge back to Seattle, Karen started to feel a little uneasy.

She took the first exit after the bridge, and headed toward the University district. The brown car stayed with her. While she waited at a traffic light, Karen peeked in her side mirror and got a look at the driver. He looked like a businessman. In his fifties, probably. Dark suit and tie. Aviator sunglasses. Talking on a cell phone. Not really very threatening, she had to admit. Maybe you're just imagining it, she told herself. There must be a million ugly brown cars on the road. Maybe it's not the same one.

At the next intersection, she made a U-turn to get back onto the highway. The brown car didn't follow. She felt a little silly for being so paranoid.

Now, back at her desk, two hours later, Karen didn't feel so silly. From her window, she could clearly see a brown sedan parked across the street. She was too far away to be certain, but it definitely looked like the same car. She wasn't sure what to do.

The ringing phone made her jump. She stammered when she said hello.

"Karen, is that you? It's Jon."

"I'm sorry, I was just a little distracted here."

"Is everything okay?"

She looked across the street. The car was still there. "It's probably nothing," she said.

"What's nothing?"

"I think I'm being followed." She told him what had happened after she'd left the Japanese restaurant. "Do you think I'm nuts?"

"No way. I think you're probably right."

"What do you think I should do?"

Jon looked at his watch. His meeting with Seely was in a half hour. There wasn't enough time to make a roundtrip downtown.

"That Seely guy called me. He wants to meet at 5:30. If you can sit tight until seven, I can pick you up." Then he had second thoughts. "You know, maybe I better just cancel the meeting and come over now."

"No, no, don't cancel the meeting. I'll be fine. There're plenty of people around here."

"Okay, so I'll pick you up at seven then."

Karen peeked out the window again. The car was gone.

"You know, Jon, maybe I am nuts. He's not down there anymore. Look, why don't I just meet you later. I don't think there's anything to worry about."

Jon hesitated. Some weird things had been happening. "Really, Karen, I don't mind driving into Seattle. We could—"

"No, I'm sorry I even mentioned this. I'm sure it's nothing. I was going to head home now anyway. Why don't you come over when you're done with your meeting? I'll pick up some Chinese food." She gave him her address, then hung up the phone.

A few minutes later, before leaving her office, she took one last look out the window.

The brown car was back.

Tim Schmidt, the conscientious Support Technician II, had already received a reply from Alan Block.

> In response to your message, the individual you mention has been reassigned. But the Capital Asset Reallocation form is not required because I believe the Center for Technology Policy is still entitled to the hard drive that was requested. We have a limited budget for computers, so it is essential that each one function properly. Please contact my assistant, LauraSi, to arrange a time to perform the hard drive installation. Thank you in advance for your cooperation.

Reassigned? Yeah, right. Well, at least Block wasn't claiming to have never heard of Kaminski. Jon typed a message to LauraSi.

> Alan Block asked me to contact you regarding the installation of a new hard drive in the computer that belonged to Walter

Kaminski before he was reassigned. The installation will have to be performed this week in order to avoid forfeiting the drive to the general pool. The next available installation time is tomorrow at 7 PM. In the past, technicians have had difficulty gaining access to the Center in the evening. I would appreciate if you could make the appropriate arrangements so that we can keep to our schedule. Thank you in advance for your cooperation.

Boy, this Tim Schmidt is obnoxious, Jon thought. Then he sent off the message to LauraSi.

The decor in Burt Seely's office was certainly unique by Megasoft standards. There were no snowboards on the floor or 3-D pictures on the wall, common artifacts for the company's mostly twenty-something employees. Instead, Jon quickly decided that Seely's office reminded him of a war museum. An entire bookcase was filled with antique military helmets, some with bright ribbons, others with intricate camouflage paint. On one wall, there was jungle netting and stark black-and-white photographs of soldiers in uniform. And a table behind Seely's desk held a collection of vintage handguns.

Jon was a few minutes early, and Seely hadn't arrived yet. The door to the office was open, but the lights were off. The orange glow of a setting sun filtered through the windows, casting long shadows and faintly illuminating the helmets and the handguns. Jon waited at the threshold, rehearsing what he planned to say to Seely. He didn't want to tip his hand entirely, but he did want to know more. There was something strange going—

"Hope you haven't been waiting too long, Mr. Goodman."

He turned to see a compact man with a crew cut.

"I'm Burt Seely," he said, extending his hand. "Nice to meet you."

Jon shook Seely's hand. "Jon Goodman," he said. "Perfect timing. I just got here a minute ago."

"Please, come in," Seely said, putting his hand on Jon's back. "I hate to keep people waiting." He flipped on the overhead fluorescent lights, which revealed a leathery complexion and abundant gray hair. "I'm an old military man," he said, looking around the office, "just in case you couldn't tell."

Jon smiled. "Great office you have."

"Thank you very much. It's really a labor of love." He gestured to a sofa, covered with a Mexican blanket. "Why don't we sit down over here." He kicked away a doorstop. "And let's shut this so we don't have a whole bunch of interruptions."

Jon sat down next to the handgun collection. "You really have quite an assortment here," he said, looking it over.

"It's funny," Seely said, sitting down on the sofa, "some people travel and bring back seashells or pottery or whatever. And I have this habit of finding new guns for the collection. I tell you, it always wreaks havoc at customs." He laughed.

"I could imagine," Jon said.

"Well, actually," Seely said, "a few of these are from my military days. See the one in front? I pulled that baby off a Vietcong in '67. What a day that was. Straight out of hell. Oh, man."

"How long were you in Vietnam?"

"I was over there about three years altogether. One tour would end, and I would be crazy enough to sign up again. But I was serving with some pretty exceptional men. Most of them truly unsung heroes, especially the ones we had to leave behind over there." Seely got up, reached over his desk, and pulled a photograph off the wall.

"Here I am outside of Saigon," he said, holding up the photograph for Jon. "Must have been around '66, I'd say. I guess the only other face you'd recognize is the fella behind me. That's General Constanza." He chuckled. "Well, Pete wasn't a General then. But this was just around the time he became our commanding officer. Hell, I guess I've been working for this guy my whole life." He put the photograph back on the wall. "I mean, up until we both retired from all that good stuff a few years back. Now, of course, JackM's the boss."

"So you and General Constanza served together after Vietnam, too?" Jon asked.

"Oh, yeah," Seely said, sitting down. "When Pete went off to the Pentagon, I followed him. And when he became the Chairman of the Joint Chiefs, well, old Burt Seely was there, too. But, to tell you the truth, I never expected to follow him into the private sector. No, sir. I thought I was a lifer in the Army. Then I visited him out here after he joined the CTP, and my wife and I just fell in love with the Northwest. We've always been outdoors people, so this place is just paradise for us. Well, next thing you know, we're packing up, and moving from Washington, D.C. to Washington State. And here I am back in the same organization with Pete again. Can't get away from the guy."

"It really is a small world," Jon said.

"Certainly is. Anyway, Mr. Goodman, I didn't invite you here to bore you with this old soldier's war stories. My wife always goes into the next room when I start with this stuff. You're very kind to listen."

"My pleasure," Jon said, with as much enthusiasm as he could muster under the circumstances.

"Thanks, you're a good audience." Seely shifted on the sofa. "Now, obviously, I wanted to chat with you about what you saw last night. Must have been a pretty scary thing, I imagine."

Seely leaned closer. "The first time I saw a man killed, and mind you, this was on a battlefield, I just about threw up. Nothing prepared me for that moment. Nothing. I felt physically sick. For days, really. And here I was in the middle of a war. You were just strolling through the parking garage." He shook his head. "This is a crazy time we live in, Mr. Goodman. A crazy time. I have two grandchildren, and I have to tell you, I worry about the kind of country they're going to grow up in. It really makes me angry."

Jon nodded.

"I gather that Jerry Hayes and Detective Carroll have filled you in on the investigation we've been pursuing?"

"A bit," Jon replied.

"Well, why don't I give you a little background on this so you can understand what's happening here." Seely exhaled. "About three months ago, it became apparent to us that there was some serious drug business going on at Megasoft. Now, I don't mean a few kids just out of college buying marijuana. No, I'm talking high-volume, wholesale drug distribution. Mainly these new so-called designer drugs.

"You see, you have an unusual combination of resources and

talents on this campus. With all the stock options we hand out, there are plenty of guys well under thirty who have half-a-million bucks in the bank. And these are smart folks, no doubt about it. Unfortunately, they tend to see this drug stuff as one big game. You put some chemicals in at one end, and take your money out at the other. It all seems very simple. Too simple.

"The problem comes when they start rubbing shoulders with the rest of the drug world. Guys who may not be so smart, but sure as hell are a lot more ruthless. It's not a game for them. You get in their way and they kill you. No tears. And that, I'm sorry to say, is what you ran into last night."

"Some kind of drug deal?" Jon asked.

"Apparently. The victim was a janitor in the building. Probably a go-between. And something went wrong, so they killed him."

Jon squinted at Seely. "Walter Kaminski was a janitor?"

Instantly, Seely's faced hardened, his nostrils flared. "I thought you said you didn't know the victim," he snapped.

"I didn't," Jon said, surprised.

"So how do you know his name?"

"I saw it on his pass card."

"His pass card?"

"It was right on his belt."

Seely stared icily at Jon for a few seconds, then regained his composure. "Of course, that makes perfect sense." He took a deep breath. "I'm sorry, Mr. Goodman, it's been a long day. You'll have to forgive me."

"No problem." Then he decided to try again. "So, you were saying that Walter Kaminski was a janitor?"

Seely cleared his throat. "To the best of my knowledge, the victim was a janitor."

"You know, that's odd," Jon said, watching for Seely's reaction, "when I looked up Walter Kaminski in the employee directory last night, he was listed as a research associate at CTP."

Seely swallowed. Jon had him, and Seely knew it. "Research associate," Seely said slowly, as if hearing the words for the first time. "Well, that is odd, Mr. Goodman. Very odd. Probably a mistake, I imagine." He forced a smile. "You know how those computers can foul up things."

Jon didn't smile back. "Here's another odd thing for you. When I called Walter Kaminski's voice mail last night, his message said he worked at CTP."

Seely looked down. "It's possible I could have that detail wrong, Mr. Goodman. Yes indeed. Why don't I double-check with Chief Ashby and—"

"According to the Woodside police, Chief Ashby is on a camping trip down in California."

"Is that so?" Seely asked calmly. "Well, I'm sure Detective Carroll can—"

"The Woodside police say they have no Detective Carroll on the force."

"Gee, I'm certainly surprised by—"

"And they have no record of the murder. None. According to them, it never happened."

Seely's eyes narrowed. "You really are a font of knowledge, Mr. Goodman. But what's that they say? A little knowledge is a dangerous thing."

"Let's cut to the chase, Mr. Seely," Jon said sharply. "What, exactly, is going on here?"

"Mr. Goodman, I think I've already explained that to you."

Jon shook his head. "A drug deal?" he asked derisively. "Do you really expect me to believe that? I was there. I saw what happened. Those were no drug dealers. And that was no drug deal."

Seely stood up. "I don't like your tone of voice, Mr. Goodman."

"We're even, then, because I don't like your lies," Jon said, getting to his feet.

"I think our meeting is over, Mr. Goodman," Seely said, opening the office door. "I was hoping we could reach some understanding, but—"

"I think we understand each other just fine, Mr. Seely," Jon said, then he walked out the door.

General Constanza had his feet up on his desk, and he was admiring his new cowboy boots. There was a knock at the door.

"Come on in."

It was Burt Seely.

"Pete, I think we've—"

"So what do you think of the boots?" Constanza asked.

"The boots?" Seely took a quick look. "Very nice, Pete, very nice. Now—"

"Genuine alligator skin," Constanza said, lifting up one leg. "A gift from Jack Malcolm. Says this stuff plays well out West. But what the hell do I know? I'm a city boy from back East. You don't wear boots in the barrio." He laughed. "I should have had a pair of these babies when I was back at the Pentagon."

Seely smiled at the thought. He tried to imagine Constanza in uniform, with alligator cowboy boots, but he couldn't. He still wasn't used to seeing the General in civilian clothes. Constanza looked like he belonged in uniform. At 62, he still worked out at the gym regularly, occasionally getting into the boxing ring to spar with opponents half his age. And aside from a slightly bent nose, the casualty of a West Point boxing match, Constanza's face had the classic lines of the little faces on the athletic trophies he'd accumulated by the dozens as a young man.

"So what's up, Burt?"

"We've got a problem, Pete," Seely said, closing the office door. He sat down in a chair in front of Constanza's desk.

"The Kaminski situation?"

"Yes. Specifically, the witness."

Constanza raised his eyebrows. "I thought you had that under control."

"I thought we did, too," Seely said quietly. "But I just had a very disturbing conversation with this guy. I'm telling you, we've got problems. He knows more than we thought. And he's not buying the cover."

"Damn," Constanza said. "This is turning into a mess. I'm not happy about the way this has been handled, Burt. I wanted a clean operation. Take out Kaminski. Period. But obviously the whole thing was botched. Now we've got a witness walking around."

"And not just the witness, Pete. That could be the least of it."

"What else?"

"This guy has been talking to a reporter."

Constanza slammed his hand down on the desk. "Jeez. I can't believe it. What is this, amateur hour? I thought we were hiring professionals. And all I'm seeing here is amateur hour. This is unacceptable, Burt. I want this fixed. And I want it fixed now."

"Pete, this isn't going to be easy."

"I don't care. Just get it done. Whatever it takes."

"I've already got the two of them under surveillance. If we need to make them disappear, we've got assets in place to do that." Seely raised his eyebrows. "If that's what you're suggesting."

Constanza shrugged. "Do we have a choice?"

"Maybe. Let me look into it some more."

8

☆ ☆ ☆ ☆ ☆

On the way into the kitchen, Karen took another look out the window, scanning the cars parked on the dark street below. Her loft was in a renovated leather tannery, not far from historic Pioneer Square, on a block of long-dormant factories and warehouses. Until now, she'd loved the wall of ceiling-high windows in the loft, with the panoramic views of downtown skyscrapers and Puget Sound. But tonight she felt exposed. She wished there were drapes to pull shut, some way to seal the place from observation.

Jon looked up from setting the table. "See anything out there?"

"Nope, no brown car. I just saw it for that minute when I got home, then it disappeared."

"Karen, maybe you really should call the police. Maybe they—"

"No, it's too soon for that. I'm still not really even sure." She started taking the Chinese food out of the bag. "I mean I'm sure I saw it. And I—" Her elbow smacked a plastic container of soup. She caught it just before it toppled over.

Karen, calm down, she told herself. You're making yourself crazy.

"Jon, you know what? Let's talk about something else. This is getting me too stressed."

"Okay." He finally noticed that she looked different. She'd traded her suit for jeans and a white polo shirt with a little *Business World* logo on her chest. Watching her in the kitchen out of the corner of his eye, he also noticed that the shirt was tight enough so that the logo stretched and jiggled as she—

"Hey, I forgot to ask what kind of Chinese food you like."

"What'd you get?"

"Nothing too exotic. Wonton soup, eggrolls, moo shu pork, sweet and sour chicken. Sound okay?"

Jon laughed.

"What's so funny?" Karen asked, coming out of the kitchen with the soup.

"I usually don't eat meat," Jon said sheepishly.

Karen smiled. "You're a vegetarian? No way."

"Why do you say that?" he asked, sitting down.

"I don't know, you just don't seem like the type."

"Thanks. That was a compliment, right?"

"I'm not sure yet," she said, ladling out some soup. "Well, do you want to try some?"

"Sure," Jon replied.

"Because I could just make you something else. I've got plenty of stuff in the fridge. I just thought the Chinese food would be easier."

"No, no, this is fine. Really."

"I don't want you dying on me here or anything. I mean, you have eaten meat before?"

"Of course. I've only been a vegetarian for a couple of years."

"Okay, then I don't feel so bad."

Jon stared at the huge abstract paintings on the wall behind Karen. Each of the canvases was at least six feet tall. There were bold swirls of reds and yellows and greens. He looked up. High above their little bistro table, a mobile of white steel clouds floated below massive wood ceiling beams.

"Your place is amazing," he said. "Is all of the art yours?"

"No, I wish. I'm just subletting. A friend of a friend is an artist, and she's spending the year teaching in Paris. So I just lucked into this place. Otherwise, I could never afford it."

He surveyed the cavernous space. "God, it's enormous. It's like living in a gymnasium. Do you have any roommates?"

"No, it's just me and the cat," she said, after a sip of soup. "Back in New York, I had a roommate, but I got tired of doing her dishes after a while. When I moved out here, I vowed to get my own place. Which really has been great. It does get a little quiet sometimes, though, I have to admit."

"I know the feeling. I've got my own place, too, which I really like. But I come home some days and the place seems so—" He tried to think of the right word.

"Empty?"

"Yeah, empty. That's it." Jon smiled. "Maybe I need a cat."

"Maybe. But you can't share Chinese food with a cat."

"Very true." He ate a piece of wonton. "So, anyway, what do you think, did I make a mistake confronting Seely?"

"No, I don't think so. You really had to at some point. And it wouldn't surprise me if he'd already figured out that you were my source."

"I think you're right. We'll see what happens." Jon picked up his soup bowl. "Done with yours?"

"Yeah."

Jon took the bowls into the kitchen. "Hey, what did you find out about Kaminski?" he called, grabbing the cardboard containers on the counter.

"I think we know where he lived, for one thing."

"Did you find him in the phone book?" Jon asked, putting the food on the table.

Karen smiled. "I wish it'd been so easy."

"How did you find the address, then?" Jon asked, taking a seat.

"Sorry, that's a trade secret."

"C'mon."

"Okay, simple. His credit report."

Jon put down his fork. "His credit report? How'd you get that? Aren't credit reports supposed to be confidential?"

"In theory," Karen said.

"In theory?"

"The reality is that anyone can look at them."

"How do you do that?"

"Just have some totally lame story," she said. "The easiest one is that you're screening a prospective employee. Believe me, no one checks."

"That's devious," Jon said, shaking his head.

"Oh, you know us evil, muckraking journalists."

Jon smiled. "Okay, Ms. Muckraker, where'd Kaminski live?"

"Right in Woodside, actually, not too far from the Megasoft campus. An apartment complex." She looked around for her notebook. "I think the name was Briarcliff Square or something like that."

"Briarcliff Place," Jon said. "I know where that is. They're furnished apartments. Megasoft puts up new hires there for a month or two, until they find their own apartment."

"Looks like Kaminski was there longer than that. His address changed as of about six months ago."

"Where'd he move from?"

"The Washington, D.C. area. A couple of addresses in Maryland. The last one was in Bethesda, I think."

Jon took a bite of the chicken. "Hey, this is pretty tasty."

"You'll see, I'll break you of this vegetarian nonsense."

"You're a bad influence," he said. "So do you get employer information from this credit report scam?"

"I almost forgot. Very interesting."

"What?"

"Well, Megasoft is listed as Kaminski's current employer. But can you guess who he used to work for?"

Jon shrugged. "I don't know. Some university?"

"No, the U.S. Department of State. The Foreign Service, actually." She noticed that there was a pitcher of water on the table, but no glasses. She got up and headed for the kitchen.

"The Foreign Service? Kaminski was some kind of diplomat?"

"I don't know. I guess so."

"Well, that's weird," Jon said. "What's an ex-diplomat doing at the Center for Technology Policy?"

"Beats me," Karen called from the kitchen.

"Hey, so is it worth going over to Kaminski's apartment complex tomorrow?" Jon asked. "Maybe someone knew him there."

"I agree. It's definitely worth—"

Jon jumped when he heard the smashing sound. He turned to see Karen by the window, holding one glass, and another broken on the floor.

"Are you all right?"

Karen stood there dazed, looking at the shattered glass on the floor. "Jon, now I'm really scared."

"What's wrong?"

"The brown car is back."

Wednesday, October 25

☆ ☆ ☆ ☆ ☆

9

☆ ☆ ☆ ☆ ☆

It was already almost 9:30, and Jon was getting worried. He was sitting in his car in the parking lot at the Briarcliff Place apartments, trying to focus on the thoroughly mundane reasons why Karen could be so late. The usual morning rush-hour traffic. A stalled truck on the bridge from Seattle. A mistake in the directions he'd scribbled down for her last night. But he was finding it easier to come up with more frightening explanations.

He was suddenly sorry that he'd left her alone last night. He should have stayed over. Or insisted that she stay with him. But Jon hardly knew her. And she said that she'd be fine. At his urging, she'd called the police. But by the time they'd shown up, around ten, the brown car had pulled away again. Then he'd stayed with her until midnight, and there'd been no sign of the car.

Jon flipped on the windshield wiper to clear the fine mist from the glass. Another gloomy gray day in Seattle. He counted the months on his fingers. November, December, January . . . Wonderful, only eight short months till summer. God, he was feeling cranky this morning. And paranoid. On the ten-minute drive from his apartment, he was convinced someone was following him, too. A green minivan. He looked around now, but didn't see it.

Where was she? He checked his watch again. 9:32. Time flies. He wondered whether she could have parked somewhere else. But he couldn't see where. This was the only parking lot. Briarcliff Place was a tangle of attached two-story town houses, clad in weathered redwood. It reminded him of his apartment complex, which also looked like a motel.

What was he doing here, anyway? What was he thinking? He'd be better off just keeping his mouth shut. Seely was right. This wasn't any of his business. And who did he think he was all of a sudden? Sherlock Holmes? This wasn't some computer game. One guy was already dead. And that was how he was going to end up if he wasn't careful.

He never should have talked to Karen. He had been selfish. He needed someone to talk to, and she was convenient. Now they were after her. What right did he have to screw up someone's life like that?

Then he thought about Walter Kaminski again. Slaughtered like an animal, left to die in a pool of blood on the concrete floor. It was murder, pure and simple. How could Jon turn his back on it? How could he let them get away with it? He knew that he couldn't. He wasn't that kind of person. A few years ago, he'd driven six hours roundtrip to fight a $75 speeding ticket he'd gotten on vacation. He could have just sent in his check, paid the fine, and been done with it. But it was a scam, a speed trap, and he wasn't going to let them get away with it. Now, how could he seriously consider walking away from the blatant cover-up of a cold-blooded murder? He just couldn't. As far as he was concerned, if he did nothing, he was an accomplice to—

He was startled by tapping on the fogged driver-side window. When he rolled down the window, he was delighted to see Karen.

"First there was an accident on the bridge," she was saying, "so when I got over to Woodside, I tried to save time by taking a short cut. But then I got totally lost. I'm so sorry, I—"

Jon wanted to throw his arms around her and tell her how happy he was to see her. But it just didn't seem appropriate at the moment. She was dressed for work, in a pale blue suit. She looked totally stunning, he thought, but very professional. And he didn't think that a hug would be very professional.

"No problem," he said, trying to sound matter-of-fact. "I just got here a few minutes ago myself.'' It was a lie, but he didn't want to make her feel bad.

''Should we take a look around?'' she asked, heading for the entrance to the apartments.

''Let's go.'' He wasn't sure whether to ask about the brown car. She hadn't mentioned anything so far. Maybe she didn't want to talk about it. But he really wanted to know. ''That car from last night didn't come back, did it?''

''No, fortunately not. When I got up this morning, I was honestly dreading looking out the window. But it wasn't out there. And the whole way over here, I had one eye in the rearview mirror, and I didn't see anything.''

''Good.'' He decided not to mention anything about the green minivan.

''You didn't see it, did you?''

''No.''

She stopped walking. ''You know, I hope I didn't freak you out last night. I probably overreacted.''

''Overreacted? Don't be crazy. Someone was following you. That's scary.'' He couldn't believe it. He'd gotten her mixed up in this thing, and now she was apologizing.

They walked up the steps to No. 237.

Karen knocked on the door and waited. No answer. She knocked again, louder this time. Nothing.

''Want to try the rental office?'' Jon asked.

She twisted the doorknob. It was locked. ''I guess so. I'm not sure who I expected to find here anyway.''

''He could've been married,'' Jon said, turning to walk down the stairs. ''He definitely looked like the family man type of guy.''

Karen knocked one more time. Still no answer ''All right, let's try the rental—''

The door to No. 238, the adjacent apartment, swung open. ''If you people are looking for Mr. K, he moved,'' said a small woman with pink hair curlers. She looked well past eighty.

Jon stepped back onto the landing. ''Moved?''

''Just yesterday. The movers didn't get here till dinnertime, and they were in there making a racket till past midnight. Nice young fellas, though. I came out once or twice to check on them, and they were all polite as could be. Clean-cut, too. None of that wild hippie hair you see nowadays. I have a grandson who plays in one of those rock-and-rolls bands, and I don't understand how his parents allow him to wear his hair like that. I'm telling you, it just isn't right."

Jon nodded sympathetically. "So you knew Mr. K?"

The woman eyed him suspiciously. "Who are you two anyway?" she asked, tightening the sash of her bathrobe. She looked at Karen. "You're not Helen, Mr. K's daughter, are you, hon? Mr. K was always talking about his Helen."

Karen shook her head. "No, we're just—"

"Cousins," Jon said. "We're visiting from back East."

"Isn't that nice," the woman said, smiling. "Family. I love to see families stay tight. Blood is thicker than water, I always say. There's nothing like having your family around. It's a blessing, really. But, these days, people just don't think like that anymore. If you ask me, it's a darn shame what goes on today. A darn shame."

"How true," Jon said. "How true. You know, we were supposed to be visiting last week, then our plans changed, and we were never able to get in touch with Mr. K. But he never said anything about moving."

"That's awful, dear," she said. "You know, I was surprised myself when the moving men came in yesterday. It was the first I heard of the move. I saw Mr. K last Thursday or Friday, and he didn't say anything about it. If I'd known he was moving, I'd have whipped up a batch of my famous chocolate-chip cookies. Everyone loves those cookies. And they're really so easy to make. The secret is putting them into a hot oven. But no one bakes anymore. Folks just don't eat right, and that's terrible for the children. Do you do much baking, hon?"

"Sometimes," Karen said. "The movers didn't say where Mr. K was moving to?"

The woman adjusted her curlers. "That's a good question. Well, you know, I just never thought to ask. I did ask why Mr. K was packing up so suddenly. They said it was for work, and then I wasn't so surprised. From what Mr. K told me, it sounded like he was always moving. His whole life. Foreign places, too. As far away as South America, he once said. Personally, I could never do that. I'm the kind of person who puts down roots and stays. Harry, my husband, God rest his soul, always had a touch of wanderlust. But not me. No, I'm really a homebody."

"What kind of work was cousin Walter doing these days?" Jon asked.

"He was with that big company right here in Woodside. What's the name? Megaphone or something like that?"

"Megasoft?" Jon asked.

"That's right," she said, smiling. "Megasoft. The one Mr. Malcolm owns. I like that Mr. Malcolm. What an ordeal, his being shot and all. A terrible strain on his wife, I'd say. But she's quite a lady. Tough as nails. Going to the hospital every day to be by his side. And what lovely clothes she has. I watched it all on the news. I tell you, it's just a miracle the way he pulled through the way he did. It's a real miracle, that's what it is. And then to stay with his campaign and all. For the sake of the country. Well, he certainly has my vote."

"What did cousin Walter do at Megasoft?" Karen asked. "Sounded like he was pretty important."

"He was a real big shot over there, I think," the woman said. "I'm not sure whether he knew Mr. Malcolm, but he said that he'd met that other fella a load of times. Oh, I'm so bad with names. You know, the handsome fella who's running with Mr. Malcolm. The general."

"General Constanza?" Jon asked.

"That's the one," she said, nodding. "Mr. K met him plenty of times. And that general is a real hero, I understand. With all those commercials on, you learn a lot about these candidates. So I know that general is a real hero. Served in Vietnam and all. My Harry was a big booster of Vietnam. He had no patience for those protesters. Communists, he called them. America, love it or leave it. He'd shout that at the TV when the protesters came on."

"You know," Karen said, "you mentioned cousin Walter's daughter. Maybe she could help us get in touch with him."

"Now, that's a good idea, dear," the woman said. "The only thing is, I got the feeling that Mr. K and his daughter weren't very close. I think Mr. K only visited Helen once or twice in all the time he was here. And she never came by here. I'm pretty sure of that. Considering that she lives twenty minutes away, in Seattle, I just didn't understand that. As a parent, I know that you don't want to force yourself on your children. But it hurts when they don't keep in touch. I have a son and a daughter, and my son is like that. Calls me once a year on Mother's Day."

"Is Helen still Helen Kaminski?" Karen asked. "Does she have a married name now?"

"Well, I know she got divorced recently. But she's one of those artist types, so I don't think she ever changed her name in the first place." The woman smiled. "So how long have you two been married?"

Jon and Karen looked at each other and laughed.

"We're not married, ma'am," Jon said.

"Really," she said, surprised. "I usually can tell these things. Well, you kids make the sweetest couple." She winked at Jon. "Why don't you make it legal, dear?"

Jon smiled. "Thanks so much for your help," he said, quickly heading for the stairs.

"Anytime," the woman said. "You say hi to Mr. K for me when you see him."

"She was kind of scatterbrained, but she actually told us a lot," Karen said.

They were standing in the Briarcliff Place parking lot.

"Finding out he had a daughter," Jon said, "that's an incredible lead."

Karen took out her notepad and started to scribble. "She said the name was Helen Kaminski, right?"

"Uh-huh. We should talk to her as soon as we can. Do you want to try to find her or should I?"

"I'll do it." She wrote another note.

"What do you make of what she said about Constanza? That Kaminski knew him so well?"

"I don't know. She said Kaminski had met Constanza a lot of times. Does that mean they worked together?"

"She was pretty vague."

"Well, let's assume for a minute that Kaminski really did work with Constanza. That changes everything. It makes you wonder whether this is somehow related to the campaign."

"That would be some story," Jon said.

"It sure would be." Enough to get me back to New York, she thought.

As Karen was getting into her car, Jon caught a glimpse of the green minivan again, parked across the street.

"Should I try you at the office later on?" she asked.

He was looking straight at her, but trying hard to see the minivan out of the corner of his eye.

"Jon?"

"Huh?"

'Are you okay?"

"Yeah, I'm sorry. What did you ask me?"

"Can I catch you in the office later?"

"Yup, that's fine," he said, deciding in a split second not to mention the minivan.

There was no reason to worry her.

10

☆ ☆ ☆ ☆ ☆

"Hey, bud, got a minute?" Kenny called out when he saw Jon go by. It was only eleven o'clock. Jon was surprised to find Kenny in the office so early.

"What's up?"

"Have a seat," Kenny said. "I think you're going to like this."

"Like what?" Jon asked, sitting down.

"You haven't finished the user-interface spec yet, have you?" Kenny turned his computer monitor so that Jon could see it.

"Nah, it's still a work in progress. And, you know, at the rate I'm going, it'll always be a work in progress."

"Well, bud," Kenny said, typing at his keyboard, "you owe me. Because I just did your job for you."

Jon smiled. "How's that?"

"I just came up with the perfect Hollywood user interface."

"Cool," Jon said, sitting up. "Let's see what you've got."

Kenny swiveled in his chair. "Okay, but I just want to warn you that this is still pretty rough. I mean, don't go asking me about all kinds of details at this point because—"

"Kenny, c'mon, just show it to me already."

"All right, here goes. Prepare to be amazed." He tapped a few keys, then sat back. "I've been thinking about this for a while, and I've finally realized why V-File is so hard to use. There's no easy way to preview the video clips."

"What do you mean? Give me an example."

Kenny adjusted his ponytail. "Well, say you're putting together a little movie on your last snowboarding trip. You've got something like fifteen minutes of video you shot. Maybe that's fifty different scenes, or what we're calling clips, depending on how long each one is. So how do you organize it all?"

Jon shrugged. "You just read down the list of clips you have and—"

"Hold on right there," Kenny interrupted. "There's the problem. First of all, you have to type in a label for each clip. In ten words or less. That's tough. Then, later, when you read those ten words, you have to imagine what the whole scene looked like. If you have fifty clips, that's impossible. You can't keep all those clips in your head at the same time. The words just aren't enough."

"I agree," Jon said. "In my spec, I've been playing around with some way of having a little picture for each clip. That would help a lot."

"True," Kenny said. "A picture is worth a thousand words. The only thing is, where do you take the picture from? Is it the first frame of the clip? The middle frame? The last? If the clip is twenty seconds long, an awful lot can happen. One little picture isn't going to tell you enough."

Jon nodded. "So what else can you do?"

"I'm glad you asked that question," Kenny said, moving back to his keyboard. "Here's what you can do." He pressed a key, and the words on the screen were replaced by a checkerboard of sixteen miniature movie screens, each one playing a different video clip. There was a bright green number in the upper left corner of each clip.

"That's very cool," Jon said. "You're showing all the clips at the same time. Now, what happens when a clip gets to the end?"

"It just loops back to the beginning. So if you stare at any one square on the screen long enough, you'll see the whole clip, from beginning to end."

"How do you organize the clips? You know, put them in the sequence you want for the movie."

"Simple," Kenny said. "See the number in the corner of each clip? Just type in the number, and the clip drops down to the bottom of the screen, right into your movie. So, for example, here we are arriving at the ski lodge in clip 3. So I type in 3, and, boom, the clip drops down to the bottom. Then, in clip 7, you can see us putting on our equipment. So I type in 7, and there it goes down to the bottom. And you just keep on doing that till your movie is done.''

''Amazing,'' Jon said. ''What made you think of doing it this way?''

Kenny laughed. ''I bought a new TV last week, and one of the features is just like this. You can see eight channels at the same time on the screen, to help you figure out which one you want to watch. I really just adapted it from that.''

''Kenny, this is a great idea. Thank you. Once more, dude, you've saved my butt.'' Jon got up. ''Maybe I'll try to get TedN to come by and take a look at this later on. I'm going to bring him and say, 'Ted, you're looking at the new user interface for Holly—' ''

''New user interface? I still haven't received the spec, Jonathan.''

Jon turned to the door. It was Francine.

''Hi there, Francine, how's it going?''

''What's this I heard about a new user interface?'' she asked, walking into Kenny's office.

Jon sat down on the edge of Kenny's desk. ''Well, actually, Kenny's just showing me—''

''Let me take a look at this,'' Francine said.

''Sure,'' Jon said, ''but it's really just something Kenny—''

''I'd like to see it, if you don't mind,'' she said, positioning herself behind Kenny's chair.

Kenny looked at Jon, who shrugged back at him. ''Okay,'' Kenny said. ''The idea is to give users an easier way to preview the video clips. I put together this mock-up of one possibility.'' He pressed a key, and the checkerboard of video clips flickered back onto the screen.

Francine slipped on her glasses, which were dangling from a cord around her neck, and leaned over Kenny's shoulder toward the computer monitor. She wrinkled her nose. ''I'm confused already,'' she said. ''What am I looking at here?''

''Those are all the video clips you can choose from,'' Kenny said.

Francine frowned. ''I don't understand. Where's the list of clips, with all the descriptions?''

"This would replace the list, Francine," Jon said. "Kenny pointed out that it's hard to visualize an entire clip from just a couple of words."

She took off her glasses. "Well, I happen to disagree, Jonathan. Ten words is plenty to describe most clips. And the whole reliance here on pictures instead of words, that's a mistake. A very serious mistake."

Kenny twisted around in his chair. "But, Francine—"

"The more I look at this," she said, "I get the feeling that you're turning the user interface into something out of one of those atrocious music videos. It's a complete mishmash on the screen. Totally incoherent. Looking at this gives me a headache."

"Francine, this is still really rough," Jon said. "Kenny just threw this together to—"

"And what are those hideous green numbers?" she asked, bending closer to the screen.

"They identify the clips," Kenny said. "I put them there to—"

"Well, that color is completely unacceptable," she said. "Completely unacceptable. Why do you think we bother to develop company standards for colors? You just can't invent a new color any old time you please. That's not the way we do things at Megasoft."

"Look, don't worry," Jon said, "we're definitely going to get all the colors approved before we finish programming this."

"Finish programming this?" she asked. "I don't think you should even start programming this."

Jon took a deep breath. "No, no, I just mean that if we pick something like this for the user interface, then we'll be sure to go ahead and get approval for—"

"Picking something like this would be folly," Francine said, walking toward the door. "And I want to go on record as being opposed to it. Adamantly."

"Francine," Kenny began, "why don't you wait until I clean up the—"

"Jonathan, may I have a word with you?" she asked from the hallway.

"Sure," he replied, heading for the door. "Let's go into my office."

Jon followed Francine into his office, and closed the door behind him.

"What's up?" he asked, taking a seat behind his desk.

"I am very disappointed, Jonathan," she said. "After yesterday's meeting with Ted, I had hoped that you would make some small effort to keep me informed about the user interface."

"Francine, I am making an effort to keep you informed. But there hasn't been any big change since yesterday. I still haven't completed the spec."

"Do you think I'm blind?" she asked angrily. "I know what you're doing. The spec never gets done, but here you already have the programmers working on the user interface. So I never have a chance to give any feedback on it."

Jon shook his head. "Francine, that's not true. I told you, what Kenny did was his own idea. It's just a prototype. It's not final code. And the spec really isn't done yet. No one else has seen it either. It's just taking longer than I thought to—"

"You're insulting my intelligence," she said, getting up. "I don't believe one word of that. These programmers don't design user interfaces. They're obviously getting instructions from you." She opened the door. "I'm going to have to talk to Ted about this."

"You do that," Jon said to the closing door.

He sighed, leaned back in his chair, and put his feet up on his desk. This was just what he needed. In the middle of everything else.

He already knew how it would play out. Another stern reprimand from TedN. Another insincere apology to Francine. And then a few weeks of uneasy peace until the next blowup.

One of these days, he was going to tell Francine exactly what he thought of her.

11

Karen drummed her fingers on her desk. It was already time for lunch, but she wasn't going to give up so easily.

She'd called directory assistance, called the credit bureau, paged through old phone books, searched an on-line database of newspaper stories, and she still couldn't find a trace of Helen Kaminski.

Maybe the old lady at Briarcliff Place had gotten it wrong. Maybe Kaminski's daughter lived somewhere else. Or maybe her last name wasn't Kaminski. Or maybe Kaminski didn't have a daughter at all.

Karen was about to head out for lunch when she had one last idea. She went back to her computer, opened the Web browser, and typed in the address of a search engine. When the page appeared on the screen, she typed "Helen Kaminski."

After a few seconds, she saw the results.

Nothing found.

So she tried just plain "Kaminski." After a short delay, she was shocked to find that 521 Web pages contained the word. So it wasn't such a rare name after all.

She added "Seattle" to her search criteria, and tried again.

One page found.

A moment later she was staring at the home page of Ellen Kaminski, a Seattle-based sculptor. There was a phone number.

Karen smiled, wondering how many times Kaminski had tried to correct his elderly neighbor. Not Helen, Ellen.

She picked up the phone to make an appointment.

* * *

At a little past 2:30, Karen and Jon were standing on Ellen Kaminski's front porch, which was gently swaying with the waves.

The little Victorian-style cottage, painted in shades of pastel purple, floated on a concrete barge that was moored just a few feet off a downtown Seattle dock. It belonged to a community of several dozen floating homes, linked by narrow wooden piers.

"She told me on the phone that her number's still listed under her ex-husband's name," Karen whispered while they waited. "That's why I couldn't—"

The front door opened, and Ellen Kaminski greeted them with a warm smile. She was a tall woman, with a long, angular face. Native American jewelry in silver and turquoise adorned her neck and wrists.

"Please, come in," she said, ushering them into her foyer. "It looks miserable out there. I guess yesterday was a gift. Now we're back to the usual rain and gloom."

She led them into her cozy living room.

"I really find this weather depressing," she said. "I grew up in Southern California, and I've just never really gotten used to the winters up here. The rain gets to me after a while."

Karen smiled. "I know exactly how you feel. I'm from Miami originally, so this weather drives me crazy. After a few months of rain everyday, I just lose all my energy. I think I must be solar-powered or something."

"Definitely," Ellen said. "You know, I'm sorry, I'm forgetting my manners here. Can I offer you a cup of tea? I've got some great herbal blends. I know this is sacrilege in Seattle, but the truth is that I don't drink coffee."

"That makes two of us," Jon said. "But it really can be hard sometimes."

"It sure can. Talk about peer pressure." She laughed. "Any takers for the tea?"

"No, no," Karen replied, "we're fine, thanks."

"I have to say I'm flattered that *Business World* thinks I'm important enough to send two reporters to interview me." Ellen rolled her eyes. "I shouldn't tell you this, but I didn't even know that *Business World* covered the art world. You know, I'm amazed you found out about my show. I think there was just one small ad in the local newspaper.

"Your show?" Jon asked.

"At the Louis Henry Gallery in—" Ellen stopped. "Uh-oh, I'm seeing some confused-looking faces. You are here to talk about my sculpture, aren't you?"

"Actually, no," Karen said.

"I have to apologize, then," Ellen said. "I guess this proves that you have to be a little self-centered to be an artist. When Ms. Grey called, I just assumed—"

"No, that's my fault, really," Karen said. "I was very vague on the phone,"

"Business World," Ellen said, thinking out loud. "Of course. You probably want to talk about that new waterfront development plan. I've been circulating petitions against it for months now."

"No, really, it's nothing like that," Jon said. "We're actually here to talk about your father."

"My father?" Ellen asked with disbelief.

"Yes," Jon replied. "Your father is Walter Kaminski?"

"Yes," she said, "my dad's name is Walter. But—" She shook her head. "Gee, you've really thrown me for a loop. What do you want to know about my father?"

Jon looked around the living room. "Do you have a picture of your father somewhere?"

"Sure, let me go find one for you." She left the room for a minute, then came back with a small cardboard box. "You know, it's funny that you should ask for a picture. The last time my dad and I got together, I was complaining that I only had about three pictures of him. This was the beginning of the summer, around the Fourth of July. Well, last week, totally out of the blue, I get this box of photos from him in the mail."

She rummaged through the box. "There's some great stuff in here. Great-aunts and cousins that I never met. Pictures of my parents before they got married. Even a couple of old home movies. My dad had them transferred to video." She picked up the videocassettes and laughed. "The only problem is that I don't own a VCR.

It's really embarrassing. I must be the last person in America without a VCR. Maybe now I'll finally get around to buying one."

Ellen pulled a photo album from the bottom of the box. She found a picture of her father on the first page. "Here he is."

Jon recognized him immediately. Amid a crowd of people at some family gathering, there stood a younger, slimmer Walter Kaminski. It was clearly the same man Jon had seen murdered.

"What's this about?" Ellen asked. "Is my father in some kind of trouble?"

Jon's eyes met Karen's. "I think—" He took a breath. "You know, maybe I could ask you something. Have you been in touch with your father recently?"

Ellen shook her head. "No, I haven't. I've been meaning to give him a call to thank him for the pictures, but—" She looked down at the photo album wistfully. "You see, we don't have that kind of relationship. Our lives have been pretty separate over the years. My mom passed away when I was only three. And my dad, well, I guess he couldn't handle it. But that was a long time ago. Who knows?

"I was raised by my grandparents, my mother's parents. And I used to see my dad a couple of times a year. Always for Christmas. Then maybe for my birthday. He traveled a lot for his business. So there were long stretches when we just never heard from him."

Ellen gave a faint smile. "I'm sorry. You asked me a simple question, and here I am dredging up old memories. Let me think. I'm almost certain that the last time I saw my dad was the Fourth of July. And I know for sure we haven't spoken since then."

Jon nodded. "You mentioned your father's business. I understand he was with the State Department at one time?"

Ellen looked down. "That's right. The Foreign Service. But he's retired from that now. He's some kind of consultant." She closed the photo album. "Is that what this is about? I mean, his work as a diplomat?"

Jon looked at Karen, and then back at Ellen. "Well, I know this sounds strange, but we're not really sure."

"I'm just wondering," Ellen said, looking puzzled, "why are you talking to me, and not my father?"

"I'm not sure how to tell you this," Jon began.

"Tell me what?"

"Your father passed away on Monday night. I was with him when it happened."

"Oh my God," Ellen said softly. "What happened? Was it his heart?"

"No, no, nothing like that," Jon said.

Ellen was confused. "Then what was it?"

"Your father was murdered, Ellen," Jon said. "I was a witness."

"Murdered?" She brushed away a tear rolling down her cheek. "Where did this happen?"

"In Woodside, on the Megasoft campus."

Ellen covered her face with her hands, sobbing. "I'm sorry," she said, accepting a tissue from Karen, "I'm so sorry. This is just such a shock."

After a minute, she looked up, wiping away her tears. "Forgive me. I'm really embarrassed. I never thought I'd cry this way for that man." She shook her head. "Tell me, how did it happen? Was it a robbery?"

"No, I don't think so," Jon replied. "I'm pretty sure it wasn't a robbery." He shifted uncomfortably on the sofa. "Ellen, was your father involved in anything, or with anyone who, uh—"

"Who would want to kill him?" she asked.

Jon nodded.

She sighed. "My father led a very complex life. He was a very complex person. You know, I'm forty-six years old, and I still feel as if I never knew him very well. He kept everything inside, and all he showed the world was this poker face, this mask. You just never knew what he was thinking. Maybe that's why he did the kind of work he did. I'm not sure which came first."

"You mean his work as a diplomat?" Karen asked.

Ellen smiled sadly. "Diplomat," she said, shaking her head. "I guess that's what his passport said for all those years. But my father was no diplomat. He was a spy. And a very good one, from the little he told us over the years. It was really his life. I was surprised when he retired from the Agency last year."

"The Central Intelligence Agency?" Karen asked.

"Yes, they recruited him out of college, and he made a career of it. You know, it's funny, most people think of James Bond when they think of spies. But my father was nothing like that. He was ordinary-looking, really unremarkable. He blended in. Maybe that's why he was so successful.''

''Did he talk much about the assignments he had?'' Jon asked.

''Bits and pieces,'' Ellen said. ''When he came home for a visit, we would hear about some of the places he'd been. In the sixties, he was in Vietnam, at the American Embassy in Saigon. Many years later, he told us that he'd actually been the CIA station chief. So you have some idea of the kinds of things he—''

Through the living room window, Jon saw a green minivan slowly circling in the parking lot at the end of the pier. Was it the same one he'd seen earlier?

''In high school,'' Ellen was saying, ''I was active in the whole anti-war scene. I was just devastated when he told me he worked for the CIA. As a little girl, I always had this image of him as a great diplomat, making peace between countries. That somehow made it okay that he was never home. Then, to find out that it was all a sham. And that he was involved in the war. It shattered all—''

Jon leaned forward on the sofa to get a better view of the parking—

''Is everything all right, Mr. Goodman?'' Ellen asked.

He jerked his head away from the window. ''I'm sorry. I thought I saw a meter maid out there.'' He smiled lamely. A meter maid? Couldn't he think of anything better?

Karen looked at him quizzically. He shrugged.

Ellen was craning her neck to see the parking lot. ''Well, I don't see anyone. Do you want to go out and—''

''No, no,'' Jon said. ''Forgive me for interrupting. Please, go on. You were talking about. . .''

''My father's assignments. You know, I think the final straw for me was Chile in '73 when Allende fell. My dad was posted to the embassy there. I was in college at the time, quite the radical, and I just hated him for it. He never said he was involved in the coup, but what else could he have been doing in Santiago at the time? Our relationship really changed after that. I was finally old enough to understand what he did, and I didn't approve of—''

Jon was trying unsuccessfully to peek out the window without turning his head. Damn, he couldn't see anything. Was the minivan still out there?

"For a couple of years," she was saying, "I didn't see him at all. But then my grandfather died, and my grandmother not too long after. And he was suddenly my only family. Well, I guess we'd both mellowed a little by then, to the point where we could spend an afternoon together without a fight. So that's what we'd do, a few times a year, spend an afternoon together. Maybe it doesn't sound like much of a relationship, but it's all we had."

Ellen bit her lip, holding back the tears. "I'll miss him," she finally said.

Jon pulled over across the street from Karen's downtown office. "How do you want to handle this?" he asked.

"I need to talk to my editor at some point." She looked at her watch. "It's already past six in New York, so there's no way I'm going to catch him today. Besides, we need to work out some details."

"Like?"

"Well," Karen said, "like whether you really want to be a named source or not. As a reporter, I'd love to have the name in the story. But, as a friend, I don't know." She paused, looking across to her office building. "We really don't know who we're dealing with here, Jon. And to tell you the truth, the CIA connection gives me the creeps. It could just be a red herring, for all we know. But from what Ellen Kaminski said, it's pretty clear that her father wasn't just some low-level guy in the CIA. He was senior. And then he goes and leaves this thing that she says he basically loved more than his family, and he takes a job at Megasoft. Pretty strange career move, if you ask me. Then, although he apparently survived Vietnam and Chile and who knows where else, at Megasoft, at some corporate think tank, he gets killed.

"Jon, you're the only witness to this murder. Without you, the murder never happened. Without you, Kaminski never even worked at Megasoft. That makes me pretty uncomfortable about building this story around you. Because the same people who killed Kaminski may read it and conclude that, without you, there isn't much of a—''

Jon was peeking in the rearview mirror. Was that the green minivan parked across the—

''Jon, what are you looking at?''

She started to twist around to see for herself, but Jon put his hand on her shoulder.

''Karen, hold on, I don't want them to know we've seen them.''

''Who?''

''Look in the side mirror. Can you see the green minivan?''

She glanced discreetly. ''With two guys in the front seat?''

''Uh-huh.''

''I see it. Have they been following us?''

''I think so.''

''Wait, is this why you were staring out the window at Ellen Kaminski's?''

''Yeah, I thought I saw them in the parking lot.''

She glared at him. ''And when were you going to get around to telling me this?''

''Karen, I—''

''How long have they been following you?''

He hesitated. ''I just noticed them at Ellen Kaminski's.''

She studied his face for a second, then shook her head. ''Bull. I know you're lying.''

He sighed. ''Okay, this morning. I spotted the minivan on the way to Briarcliff Place.''

Karen stared straight ahead, fuming.

''Look, Karen, I didn't want to worry you. I thought that—''

''What else haven't you told me?''

''Nothing.''

She didn't say anything.

''Karen, I swear, that's the only thing I haven't told you.''

They sat in silence.

Finally, she looked at him again. ''Listen to me carefully. We're partners in this, and—''

''Karen, I was just—''

''No, let me finish. I don't want to be patronized. I don't want to be protected. I'm not some damsel in distress. I'm your partner.

We're going to figure this thing out together. Am I making myself clear?"

He nodded.

"Good," she said, flipping through her notepad. She cleared her throat. "Okay, we need to figure out what Kaminski was working on at this Center for Technology Policy. Where do we start?"

"His office," Jon replied. "I'm going to try to get in there tonight, if I can. There's probably nothing left, but who knows? Maybe someone was careless."

"Fine. What time are we going?"

"We? We aren't going to Kaminski's office. I am."

Karen slowly closed her notepad and carefully tucked it into her coat pocket. Then she opened the car door and started to get out.

"Wait, where are you going?" he asked.

"Jon, I think you haven't been listening. Because I just got done telling you that we were going to do this as a team. I don't want to be treated like—"

"Karen—"

"—some glorified secretary. And—"

"Karen—"

"What?"

"You win. I'll meet you at six."

12

☆ ☆ ☆ ☆ ☆

There was a yellow sticky note on Jon's office door when he got back.

"Jon," the note read, "Please call me ASAP. Very important." It was signed by Suzy Chu, TedN's assistant.

As he dialed Suzy's extension, Jon wondered what could be so urgent.

"Hi, this is Suzy."

"Suzy, Jon Goodman. Just got back and saw your note. What's up?"

"Jon, can you hold on?"

"Sure."

While Jon listened to the canned music, he swiveled around to his computer and logged into the electronic mail system. He typed his password, and waited to see his new messages. After a few seconds, though, an error message appeared. *Log-in failed. Invalid address and/or password.* He smiled. A truly user-friendly computer. He started to re-type his password, when Suzy came back on the line.

"Jon, Ted needs to see you before the end of the day. He'd like you to come by right now."

Jon looked at his watch. Four o'clock. He still hadn't done any real work today. Oh, well.

"That's fine. What's so important, anyway?"

There was a pause. "Jon, why don't I let Ted go over that with you."

"Okay, I'm on my way."

As he walked up the stairs to the second floor, it finally occurred to Jon what the meeting was about. Francine. After she'd stormed out of Jon's office earlier, she'd no doubt rushed right over to TedN's to complain. Jon isn't giving me his spec. Jon isn't following the corporate color standards. Jon isn't listening to my insightful user-interface analysis. Blah, blah, blah. What a drag. Jon just wasn't in the mood for Francine's nonsense. He prepared himself for a scolding from TedN.

The door to Nesbitt's office was closed. Jon knocked.

"Come in," Nesbitt called.

Jon opened the door and found a full house. There were two people he didn't recognize sitting on the sofa.

"Excuse me," Jon said, stopping in the doorway. "I'm sorry, Ted. Didn't know you had visitors. I'll catch you later." Jon backed out of the office.

"No, no, Jon," Nesbitt said, standing up behind his desk. "Come on in." He gestured to the chair in front of his desk. "Please, have a seat." Nesbitt walked over to the door and closed it behind Jon.

"Jon, do you know Chuck and Barbara?" Nesbitt asked, looking at the rather solemn man and woman on the sofa.

Jon shook his head. "No, I don't think we've met."

Nesbitt sat back down at his desk. "This is Chuck Nakayama, from Legal, and Barbara Hanover, from Human Resources."

"Nice to meet you," Jon said, nodding.

"Personally," Nesbitt said, "I would prefer to handle this myself, but I'm told that there's a corporate policy on this type of situation now. That's why Chuck and Barbara are here."

Jon frowned. "What type of situation is that, Ted?"

Nesbitt took a deep breath. "An incident occurred today that was very unfortunate. I was surprised when I learned of it. And extremely disappointed. Let me say, I realize that Megasoft can be a pretty freewheeling place. But even so, there are definite bounds on our behavior. The most important one is that we respect the rights of other employees. That's an absolute. That's not something we can bend. Which is why what happened today is simply unacceptable. It's not something that we can tolerate."

"What was it that happened today?" Jon asked, having no idea where the conversation was heading.

Before Nesbitt could respond, Nakayama spoke. "Ted, before you go into that, I assume you're going to do the employee handbook?"

Nesbitt nodded. "Yeah," he said, shuffling a few papers before finding the right one. "Jon, I just wanted to review with you two sections from the current employee handbook." He handed Jon a copy. "I'd like to direct your attention to page thirty-four, and the section titled, *Interpersonal Conduct.* Could you read for us the sentence that's been highlighted there?"

Jon squinted at Nesbitt. "You mean, read out loud?"

"Yes, please," Nesbitt replied.

"I'm sorry, I think I missed something," Jon said, putting down the handbook. "What's this all about?"

Nesbitt looked down. "Jon, I think we all just want to get this over with quickly. It would be a lot easier for everyone if—"

"What would be a lot easier for everyone?" Jon interrupted.

"Please, just read what's been highlighted there."

"Fine," Jon said, picking up the handbook. "It says, *Threats, aggressive language or behavior, and all other forms of coercion or intimidation are strictly prohibited.*"

"Okay, let's go to page fifty-one," Nesbitt said. "Please read the sentence that's been highlighted in the section, *Employee Use of Electronic Mail.*"

Jon flipped to the right page. "All right, *The electronic mail system shall not be used to convey messages containing obscene, profane, perverse, or otherwise offensive material.*" He closed the handbook. "What is this? Could someone please tell me what's going on here?"

Barbara Hanover cleared her throat. "Ted," she said, gesturing to the papers on his desk, "the blue sheet."

Nesbitt picked it up and started reading. "This exit interview has four purposes: First, to inform you of the termination of your employment by Megasoft Corporation. Second, to explain—"

"Termination of my employment?" asked Jon, shocked. "You're firing me?"

"Mr. Goodman," Hanover said from the sofa, "you'll have a

chance to ask questions later in this meeting. I think it would be in your best interest to—''

''Ted, is this a joke?'' Jon asked, shaking his head. ''I can't believe this.''

Somberly, Nesbitt looked up at Jon. ''No, this is not a joke, Jon. In fact, I don't think there's anything funny about this at all. Now, these people say I have to read this. So why don't you just let me get this over with.''

Jon suddenly found himself sweating profusely. His chest felt tight. He labored to breathe. So many feelings, so many thoughts, occurred to him at once, that he had trouble focusing on any one of them. Calm down, he told himself. Get a grip.

''Go ahead,'' he told Nesbitt.

''Okay,'' Nesbitt said, picking up the blue sheet. ''Second, to explain the reasons behind this termination for cause. Third, to outline the effect of this termination on your medical benefits, profit sharing, and stock options. And fourth, to offer you the opportunity to ask questions and make comments regarding this termination.'' He put the paper down, and looked over at Hanover.

''The yellow sheet, Ted,'' she said softly.

''Right,'' he said, picking it up. ''Jon, I wish to inform you that your employment with Megasoft Corporation is being terminated, effective immediately. Here is a letter notifying you of this termination.'' He handed it to Jon. ''At the conclusion of this meeting, you will be asked to return any property of Megasoft Corporation now in your possession, including your employee pass card. In addition, under the supervision of security personnel, you will be permitted to retrieve from your office any personal items you have chosen to store there. Please note that Megasoft Corporation will not be held responsible for the safekeeping of personal items that are not removed today.''

Jon had trouble following what Nesbitt was saying. The whole thing just seemed alien, surreal. In a daze, Jon felt as if he was watching it happen to someone else. It surely couldn't be happening to him.

Nesbitt continued reading. ''Megasoft Corporation is terminating your employment today for cause. Specifically, you have grossly violated rules regarding interpersonal conduct and employee use of electronic mail, as set forth in the employee handbook. Your behavior is unacceptable. As a result, you can no longer effectively carry out the job responsibilities that have been assigned to you. For this reason, Megasoft Corporation is terminating your employment."

Barbara Hanover stood up and handed Jon a green sheet of paper. "Mr. Goodman," she began, sitting down again on the sofa, "I want to go over briefly how this termination will affect your medical benefits, profit sharing, and stock options. This sheet summarizes the—"

"Hold on," Jon said brusquely. He felt his face flush with anger. "I don't care about the medical benefits. I just want to—"

"Mr. Goodman," Hanover interrupted, "it really is important that we go over these—"

"Would you please shut up and let me finish," Jon said angrily. He turned to Nesbitt. "Now, tell me what this is all about, in plain English. Why are you firing me?"

Nesbitt shook his head in disgust. "C'mon, Jon, it's pretty obvious. I can't believe you'd send a piece of e-mail like that and think you'd get away with it. I don't know what you—"

"Excuse me, Ted," Chuck Nakayama interjected. "I think that's really not on the agenda for the meeting today. Let's confine our comments to—"

"Chuck, look," Nesbitt said, glaring, "I told you before, if I feel it's necessary to deviate from your little script, or whatever you want to call it, then I will. I'm the manager here, and—"

"I'm sorry, Ted," Nakayama said calmly, "but as the representative from Legal, I need to advise you that—"

"Hey, if you and Barbara want to wait out in the hall, that's fine with me," Nesbitt said. "But this is my office and my meeting, and I'm going to say what I like. Is that clear?"

Nakayama nodded, and looked down at his yellow pad.

Nesbitt turned back to Jon. "Okay, Jon, you asked for plain English. Here's plain English. The e-mail you sent to Francine was repulsive. I know you've had your differences with her, but that's no excuse for what you wrote. You don't threaten a colleague. You don't use the language you did with a colleague. We've known each other for a lot of years now, Jon, and I frankly still can't believe you'd be stupid enough to do something like this. But you did. And it's inexcusable. And that's why I'm firing you."

"What?" Jon blurted out, completely bewildered. "What are you talking about? E-mail to Francine? What kind of e-mail?"

Nesbitt shook his head. "Jon, I'm amazed you'd have the gall to try and play dumb."

"Play dumb?" Jon asked. "I must just be dumb. Because I don't have the faintest idea of what you're talking about. I've never sent any threatening or obscene or who knows what other kind of e-mail to Francine, or to anybody else. This whole thing is ludicrous, that's what it is."

"You know, Jon," Nesbitt said, "I'm even more disappointed now, if that's possible. Because I thought you'd at least have the class to acknowledge your mistake and apologize. Not that apologizing would save your job. It's too late for that."

"I'm not apologizing," Jon said angrily. "This is absurd. I have nothing to apologize for." He stared at Nesbitt. "Ted, please, you know me. You have to know that this is crazy. I wouldn't send e-mail like that."

"Jon, give it up," Nesbitt said with disgust. "We're not talking about some anonymous note slipped under someone's door. This was an electronic mail message sent by you. There's no disputing it."

"What do you mean there's no disputing it?" Jon asked. "I'm disputing it. I'm telling you, I didn't send that e-mail."

"What are you suggesting? That someone else sent the e-mail?"

Jon hadn't thought that far ahead. He'd focused on what he knew hadn't happened. And on what he knew he hadn't done. But what had happened? And who had done it?

"Yes," Jon said quietly, "that's what I'm suggesting. I didn't send that e-mail, so it must have been someone else."

"This is pathetic," Nesbitt said. "I feel like I'm going to throw up." He looked over at Barbara Hanover. "Okay, why don't you go over the benefit stuff."

"No," Jon said. "I'm not finished. I want to see this e-mail. I want to—"

"Jon, you got caught with your hand in the cookie jar," Nesbitt said in exasperation. "The Megasoft Security people have been investigating this all day. They have undeniable proof that the e-mail was sent not only from your account, but from your own office computer. The pass card record shows you were in the building. The video from the hall security camera shows you walking into your office five minutes before the message was sent and leaving fifteen minutes after. No one else entered or left your office. There's no room for alibis, Jon. I spent an hour going over all of this with Burt Seely, and—''

''Burt Seely?'' Jon asked, surprised.

''Yeah, he's the head of security,'' Nesbitt said. ''Very thorough guy. He's—''

''Setting me up,'' Jon said, just as the thought occurred to him. It all made perfect sense now. They weren't going to kill him. They were just going to discredit him. Make him into some kind of kook. The one who got fired for threatening a colleague. Clearly a little unbalanced. Definitely disgruntled. In any case, not someone to be believed.

''Ted, this is a setup,'' Jon said. ''I'm being framed.''

Nesbitt sighed. ''Jon, I'm going to make a suggestion to you, and I really hope you'll consider it carefully. I think you need to get some help. Some counseling or something. Because—''

''You don't understand,'' Jon interrupted. ''I was the only witness to a murder on Monday night. I saw a Megasoft employee gunned down in the parking garage. Now there's a cover-up going on, and Burt Seely is involved in—''

''Jon, I don't know what's happening with you,'' Nesbitt said slowly, ''but you need help. Professional help. If you're doing drugs, you better deal with it. Because you're messing up your whole life with this.'' He shook his head. ''I don't know what else to say. Barbara?''

She gazed uneasily at Jon, the way people do at lunatics and wild animals. ''Yes, well, let's go through the medical benefits. Your coverage will continue until—''

But Jon wasn't listening. Again and again, his thoughts drifted back to the accusation against him. Surely there was some way to refute this lie. He searched for a gap in the account, some glaring oversight to which he could point. But he could think of none.

The evidence against him was digital, binary. Yes or no. True or false. There were no shades of gray.

"Okay, let's sce," Hanover said, leafing through her notes, "I've touched on the medical benefits, the profit sharing, and the stock options. That's it for me." She looked over at Nesbitt. "We usually have the question and comment time now, but I guess we went into that before."

"Have anything else to discuss, Jon?" Nesbitt asked.

"No," Jon replied, getting to his feet, "I think I've heard enough."

13

☆ ☆ ☆ ☆ ☆

Jon sat in the dark, listening to the hum of the refrigerator. Slumped on the sofa in his living room, he gazed out the window as the sky faded from a brilliant orange to a murky black. He thought about eating, or just moving, but it seemed like too much effort. When the phone rang, he just sat there, waiting for the machine to pick up. By the twentieth ring, when he finally remembered that the answering machine was broken, he still didn't feel like getting up. He felt numb. The anger was gone, if only temporarily, and he found himself not feeling much of anything. Except maybe a vague sadness, a sense of loss.

It had been six years since he'd moved three thousand miles from home to take the job with Megasoft. It started as a lark, as an adventure. A crazy stunt that he would talk about someday. The time he lucked into a job at Megasoft. He never expected it to last. After all, what did he know about computer software? After a few months, he assumed, he'd be filling out applications for law school. On to a second career. But, much to his surprise, it hadn't turned out that way. He'd stayed. He'd survived. He'd even flourished.

Now the ride was over. As abruptly and unexpectedly as it had begun. And Jon found himself unable to believe what had happened. It was like when the lights came up after a good movie, and people abandoned their seats reluctantly, unwilling to let go of something that had seemed so real. Jon didn't want Megasoft to end. Not yet. He just wasn't ready.

The doorbell rang, and Jon decided not to answer. Whatever

they were selling, he didn't need. And he wasn't in the mood to sign any petitions or subscribe to any newspapers. Go away, he thought, I gave at the office.

But the doorbell continued to ring. And then Jon heard knocking, followed by pounding.

"Jon, c'mon, I know you're in there. I saw your car downstairs." It was Kenny Alden.

Jon briefly considered not answering the door. He really wanted to be left alone. But finally he roused himself from the sofa and opened the door.

"Bud," Kenny said, "I'm really sorry." He was holding a cardboard box. "This is the stuff from your office. Those bozos were all set to toss it out. They said you didn't want it. But I figured, well—" He looked past Jon into the apartment. "Hey, you gonna invite me in or what? I picked up some Thai food on the way. Your favorite place."

Jon tried to smile. He wanted to be cheery, magnanimous. But he didn't feel that way. "I'm sorry. Come on in." He flicked on the lights in the foyer, squinting in the sudden brightness.

Kenny set down the box near the door, and pulled out a bag with the food. "Where do you keep the plates?" he asked, heading toward the kitchen.

Jon followed him. "Oh, let me get—"

"No, you go sit down," Kenny told him, turning on the lights. "This is a catered meal. Have a seat. I've been here before. I'll figure it out."

"All right." Jon walked over to the table. It was too much work to be gracious tonight. He sat down. "So I guess you heard," he called out to the kitchen, stating the obvious.

"Yeah, I heard," Kenny said, balancing the food on one arm and the plates and silverware on the other. He put everything down on the table. "Everyone heard. TedN sent some e-mail around."

Jon nodded.

Kenny went back into the kitchen and opened the refrigerator. "Milk," he said, shaking his head. "All you've got is milk. Jeez, Jon, how do you live like this?" He filled two glasses with water.

"Someone also forwarded your e-mail," Kenny said, putting down the glasses on the table. He took a seat. "Looks like you got pretty pissed off at Francine. Not that I blame you. She definitely has that effect on people."

"Kenny, I didn't send that e-mail. It wasn't me."

Kenny looked up from his plate. "Say what?"

"That e-mail wasn't from me. It wasn't mine."

"What do you mean, it wasn't from you? Like it was a prank or something?

"No, I don't think it was a prank. I think I was set up."

"Set up?" Kenny raised his eyebrows. "You're saying that someone else sent it to make you look bad?"

"That's what I'm saying."

Kenny looked at Jon for a second. "Jon, you know, what you say to me isn't going to go any further than this room. I mean, you can level with me. I'm not going to run off to TedN and—"

"Kenny, I am leveling with you. I'm telling you, I didn't send that e-mail. I was framed."

Kenny put down his fork. "I want to believe you. I really do. But, I don't know, it just looks like—"

"Looks like what? Like I'm some raving lunatic? Like I'm totally flying off the—"

"Jon, I didn't say that. It's just that this setup thing, I don't know. Why would someone want to set you up like that?"

Jon pushed away his plate. "Because I saw something I wasn't supposed to."

"Saw something? What did you see?"

"A murder, Kenny. That's what this is all about."

Kenny looked at Jon uneasily. "You're not kidding me, are you?"

Jon shook his head.

"That's what I was afraid of," Kenny said. He stared at his plate, thinking it over. Then he looked up. "Okay, I'm not sure I even want to know about this, but why don't you tell me anyway."

"Remember Monday night, when we were working late?"

"Yeah."

"Well, nothing's been the same for me since then," Jon began. And then he told Kenny everything he could remember. From the murder to his firing. When Jon finished, Kenny sat there in silence, hunched over the table with his hand under his chin.

Finally, Kenny sat back and took a deep breath. "Jon, I don't know what to say. This is scary stuff. Weird, scary stuff."

"Tell me about it."

"Let me ask you a couple of things."

"Go ahead."

"For starters, the police. Shouldn't they be all over this thing? Someone got killed in Woodside. That's a big deal."

"Look at it from their perspective, Kenny. There's no body, there's no crime scene, there's no evidence. Megasoft Security says they don't know anything about it. And the one guy who says he was a witness is now just some crazy ex-employee. It's not the kind of situation they rush to investigate."

Kenny nodded. "You're right. Doesn't look too good." He drummed his fingers on the table. "Why do you think this Kaminski got killed? You don't buy that whole business about the drugs and all?"

"No way," Jon replied, "at least not the story Seely was trying to sell me. The pieces just don't fit. Kaminski was this CIA guy. Somehow, I don't see him retiring from the CIA so he could move out to Seattle to deal drugs with the locals. That doesn't work. Whatever Kaminski was involved with probably got him killed. But I don't think it was drugs."

"When you talked to Seely," Kenny asked, "did he say—"

The phone rang. Jon looked at his watch. Damn. It was already almost seven o'clock. He'd forgotten all about meeting Karen at six. She was probably calling now.

Jon ran into the kitchen to grab the phone.

"Hello?"

"Yes, hello, Mr. Goodman," said the caller, whose voice Jon recognized instantly. The elusive Detective Carroll.

"I'm sorry, hold on a sec," Jon said, jiggling the handset, "let me switch phones. The battery's dying on me here." He put his hand over the receiver, and gestured Kenny over to the phone in the living room. "Pick up the phone," he mouthed.

"Hi, sorry about that," Jon said into the phone after Kenny was on the line. "This is Jon."

"Mr. Goodman, we spoke yesterday morning. Do you remember?"

"Yeah, I remember. But I don't think I caught your name."

"My name isn't important, Mr. Goodman. I wouldn't be worrying about that if I were you."

"What would you be worrying about, then?"

"If I were you, Mr. Goodman, I'd be worrying about keeping a low profile."

"Why's that?"

"Well, you connect the dots, Mr. Goodman. You got a little too curious there. And now I hear you're out of a job. Isn't that right?"

"Yeah, that's right. Tell me something, do you work for Burt Seely?"

"I think you're not listening, Mr. Goodman. Because I'm telling you that you don't want to go asking so many questions. It didn't help your career too much, I'd say. And if you keep at it, Mr. Goodman, it's not going to be very good for your health."

"What's that supposed to mean?"

"I'm told you're a very smart guy, Mr. Goodman. I'm going to let you figure that one out all by yourself."

And before Jon could say another word, there was a click. The line was dead.

"This is totally creepy," Kenny said, putting down the phone. "Who was that guy?"

"He's the one who called me yesterday morning and said he was from the Woodside police."

Kenny sat down on the sofa. "Jon, you've got to be careful. You heard that guy. He basically threatened to kill you. Maybe you should just split. Take off somewhere for a while. Anywhere but here. Because you don't want to sit around waiting for them to come get you."

"Kenny, if these guys want to find me, they will. I'm not going to be able to run away from them. At least, not for long."

"What's the alternative? What else can you do?"

"I can try to put together the pieces of the puzzle. I've got all these random clues, but I really have no idea what's going on. I know some guy got killed. I know his name and that he used to work for the CIA. And I know there are a bunch of people who are desperate to keep this all quiet. That's it. That's all I know for sure. But if I can find out what Kaminski was working on, if I can find out who he was working for, then I've got a shot at putting together the puzzle. Because then I'll know why he got killed, and who did it."

"Jon, don't take this the wrong way or anything, but do you really think you're going to be able to figure that out? I mean, you're no secret agent. You're not some private eye. This isn't TV, with a guaranteed happy ending. You start snooping around some more, and you may end up like that Kaminski guy."

"You're right," Jon said. "There might not be a happy ending. But think about it, Kenny. Will these guys let me walk around forever knowing what I know? They're not stupid. Getting me out of Megasoft just buys them some time. I'm still a risk, an unknown quantity for them. As long as I'm alive."

The doorbell rang, and Kenny jumped out of his seat.

Jon smiled, for the first time in hours. "Jeez, Kenny, calm down. I think I know who it is."

He went to the door and squinted into the peephole. "Looks pretty safe to me, Kenny," he said, opening the door.

"I can't believe it," Karen said, shaking her head. "You stood me up."

"Karen, I'm really sorry," Jon said as he ushered her in. "I just totally lost track of the time. I had a surprise waiting for me back at the office."

"I was worried about you," she said, taking off her coat. "I waited there for half an hour. I tried to call, but the phone just rang and rang. So I—" She looked at him. "What kind of surprise?"

Jon took a deep breath. "Well, I—"

"Oh, you must be Kenny," Karen said to Alden, who was coming out of the living room. "I've heard a lot about you." She extended her hand. "I'm Karen Grey."

Kenny shook her hand. "Heard a lot about me?" He looked at Jon. "You should be careful, Jon here tends to exaggerate. What'd he tell you?"

"Sorry, a journalist has to protect her sources," she said. Then she smiled. "I only heard good things, if that's what you're asking."

"Thanks, bud," Kenny said to Jon.

"Any time," Jon replied. He led the way into the living room.

"Why don't we sit down in here." He turned to Karen. "We've got some cold Thai food. I can pop it in the microwave if—"

"I'm fine, Jon. I ate before." She looked around the apartment. "Hey, you've got a nice place here."

"Thanks. Sorry it's kind of on the messy side. If I'd known—"

"Please," she said, "I left the white gloves at home. Anyway, I'm sorry, I cut you off before. You said you had some kind of surprise at the office?"

"It wasn't a very pleasant surprise either. They fired me."

Karen leaned so far forward she almost toppled off the sofa. "What?"

Jon nodded. "That was my reaction, too. They called me into this meeting when I got back to the office, and, boom, that was it."

"I'm amazed," Karen said. "I'd think these guys would be smarter than that. You've got a classic whistleblower case here."

"No, they were pretty smart about it," Jon said. "They claimed I sent this wacko, threatening e-mail to a woman I work with."

"So you're not just a whistleblower," Karen said. "You're some frightening, deranged whistleblower."

"Exactly."

"How totally sleazy. But what did they say when you denied it? Couldn't someone else just send e-mail in your name?"

"Well, it's not that easy," Jon said. "Everyone has a password, so it's pretty difficult to get into someone's account."

"But not impossible," Kenny said. "Definitely not impossible."

"I agree," Jon said. "I just mean that, ordinarily, it never happens. This isn't a common occurrence or anything like that."

"So if the mail really could have been sent by someone else," Karen said, "and you absolutely deny sending it, aren't they standing on kind of shaky ground?"

"No, there's more," Jon replied. "They told me Burt Seely from Megasoft Security investigated this, and—"

"Wait, Burt Seely is that liar I talked to on the phone?"

"One and the same."

"So what did this Burt Seely's investigation turn up?"

"Well, the electronic mail system keeps track of where messages are sent from. And they claim that this one was sent from my office computer. So they checked the video from the security camera in the hall. And, very conveniently, there I am going into my office a few minutes before the e-mail was sent. Myself and no one else."

"I think I underestimated them," Karen said. "Very slick."

"That's for sure," Jon said.

All three of them sat in silence.

"Jon," Karen finally said, "I know you're not going to like this, but I'm wondering whether you're getting in over your head. Maybe you should just try to get out of here for a while and—"

"That's what Kenny was telling me before. But I can't run away from these guys, Karen. Wherever I go, they'll find me eventually."

"Sure I can't change your mind?"

"No, my mind's made up." He checked his watch. 7:12. "So do you still want to go with me?"

She raised her eyebrows. "Do you really think that's wise now?"

"To tell you the truth, probably not. But I don't think I have much choice. Because I just have this feeling that if I don't figure out what happened to Kaminski, the same thing's going to happen to me."

Karen thought about it. She was sure she was making a big mistake. "Okay, if you want to go, let's get it over with."

"Where are you going?" Kenny asked.

"Kaminski's office," Jon replied.

"Want some company?"

Jon hesitated. He didn't want to get Kenny involved in this. But he still wasn't sure how they were going to get into Building 9. Kenny's skills would come in handy. "Maybe you could help us out."

"Whatever I can do, bud."

14

☆ ☆ ☆ ☆ ☆

Jon sat in the car, and watched Karen and Kenny disappear into the building. His building. He'd had something like ten different offices in six years, but always in this building. He could close his eyes and visualize the lobby, with skylights and lush plants so green they looked liked plastic. The long corridors, where high-decibel shouting matches about arcane product features were interrupted by impromptu games of Frisbee. The expansive neon-striped cafeteria, open for breakfast, lunch, and dinner, with an espresso bar during the day and unlimited free soft drinks around the clock. Since college, he'd spent most of his waking hours in this building. This was his home. And it felt so very strange now to be sitting on the outside, barred from ever entering again, watching through the windows as Megasoft toiled on into the night without him.

They were walking down the hall, on the way to Kenny's office.

"This looks like Malcolm campaign headquarters," Karen said. Most of the office doors on the corridor were plastered with AMERICA IS MALCOLM COUNTRY posters.

"If you had a bumper sticker for some other candidate, I don't think you'd want to park out front," Kenny said. "You'd probably get your tires slashed."

"Are you serious?"

Kenny smiled. "Nah, we're all nerds here. But we are pretty intense about JackM."

Karen paused at a bulletin board with a PRESIDENT JACKM banner across the top. "What are all these sign-up sheets for?"

"All kinds of campaign stuff. Publicity, rallies, fund raising. Every building has its own committee. I bet ninety percent of the company is volunteering, one way or another."

"How about you?"

"Oh, yeah. I've been doing some programming for the Web site. Everyone is totally into it. I mean, finally here's a candidate you can be psyched about. JackM isn't some sleazebag politician. He's definitely not in it for the money. And he's not into all of this label crap. You know, like you're either liberal or conservative. He'll be practical about it. He's going to run the country the same way he runs this company. And that's why he's going to be an awesome President."

"People around here must have been pretty shaken up by the assassination attempt," Karen said, following Kenny down the hall.

"We were all watching that interview in the cafeteria when it happened. JackM's office is right across the courtyard, so right away everyone was sprinting over there to see what happened. EricT, he's a buddy of mine, he swears he saw one of the terrorist guys running out the door. I was standing in the driveway in front of the building when they brought out Jack on a stretcher. Here it was eleven-thirty at night, and there must have been a thousand of us, all Megasoft people, standing in a crowd outside. Everyone was stunned. We just couldn't believe it. And he looked terrible when they brought him out. I thought for sure that it was all over. That we'd lost him.

"I never went home that night. And a lot of people who had already gone home came back to work. We were all standing around in the hall, in the cafeteria, watching TV, checking out what was on the Web, trying to find out how Jack was. Every fifteen minutes there was a different rumor. That he was fine. That he was dead. That he was in surgery. Finally, around five in the morning, we got e-mail from one of the VPs saying that Jack was going to make it. You could basically hear a rumble across the whole campus as the news spread from building to building. The reaction was pretty amazing."

Kenny flipped on the lights in his office.

"So does JackM have your vote?" he asked.

Karen smiled. "Actually. . ."

He playfully buried his face in his hands. "Oh, no."

"Sorry, my family's been voting for Democrats since Franklin Roosevelt. My grandfather would turn over in his grave if I changed now."

"Well, at least you're not voting for that Republican goon."

Kenny took out his wallet, and pulled out his Megasoft ID and Jon's driver's license. He opened the lid of the scanner on his desk and placed both of the cards onto the glass.

"Let me have your license a sec," he said.

Karen handed it to him, and he put it next to the other cards. He closed the lid, and a minute later, they were looking at images of the cards on Kenny's computer screen.

She watched the screen as he slightly shrunk the license photos to match the size of his Megasoft ID photo. Then he made two onscreen copies of his ID, replacing his photo with Jon's on one card and Karen's on the other. He typed "Tim Schmidt" on Jon's card and "Jill Alexander" on Karen's.

"How are you going to make cards from this?" Karen asked.

"We've got a color laser printer."

"Are you sure it'll look real enough?"

Kenny looked up from the screen. "Remember when they changed the $100 bill a few years ago, to make it harder to counterfeit? It was these new color laser printers they were worried about."

They watched as the first ID slid out of the printer. "I swear," Kenny said, "you could print money on these things, the copies are so good."

"Mr. Schmidt, you're on the list," the guard in the Building 9 lobby was saying to Jon, "but I don't see any Jill Alexander." He was young, in his early twenties, with a crew cut and a wispy blond mustache. He wore a blue blazer that was several sizes too large for him.

"I don't understand that," Karen said huffily. "I'm the one who made the arrangements. I told them there'd be two of us, Tim and myself."

"Ma'am, I'm not arguing with you on that. It's just that there are certain rules I've—"

"Look, we're already running late," Karen said. "I don't have time for this. I've got kids at home and—"

"Let me see your ID again."

Karen held up her wallet. The ID was beneath a murky plastic holder. She prayed that he wouldn't ask her to take it out.

The guard sighed. "Okay, why don't you just sign in here," he said, pointing to a clipboard on the reception desk.

Jon held the glass door open for Karen, then they walked up the stairs to the second floor.

"Way to go," he whispered to Karen.

At the top of the stairs, they found themselves at the intersection of three rather dim corridors.

"Have any idea where we're going?" Karen asked.

Jon pulled a piece of paper from his pocket. "The office number is 207." He didn't see a sign. "Let's try down here to the left."

The first office they came to was 249. Then 248. And 247.

"At least the numbers are going the right way," Karen said. "It's probably down at the end."

They kept walking. All of the offices were dark. None had nameplates on the doors. Finally, they were at the end of the corridor.

"Must be around the next corner," Jon said. "The last office here is 210."

But when they turned the corner, they were at the beginning of another long corridor. The first office was marked 250. The next, 251. And then 252.

"Wait, what happened?" Karen asked. "Where's 207?"

"I don't know. All the Megasoft buildings have these bizarre floor plans."

Karen looked back around the corner. "This place is like a maze."

"It's JackM's design. Supposedly, this way, more people get window offices. Well, let's just go down to the end here, and—"

A tall man in a blue suit rounded the corner and stopped abruptly, finding Jon and Karen blocking the hall.

"Excuse me," he muttered, glaring at them.

"Sorry," Jon said, stepping aside.

The man brushed by them and started down the hallway. Then he suddenly wheeled around. "You people lost or something?" he asked, eyeing them suspiciously. "What are you doing here?"

"We're from hardware support," Jon replied. "Got a repair call over here. You know, maybe you could point us in the right direction." He pulled a computer printout from his pocket. "We're looking for 207. Which way is that?"

The man squinted at Jon. "What's the number?"

"207."

"I think you're mistaken, friend," the man said in a distinctly unfriendly tone. "There's no one in 207. It's empty."

"Actually, Mr. Block mentioned something about that in his e-mail."

"Block approved this?"

Jon nodded. "Apparently, the employee who originally requested the repair was transferred or—"

"Transferred. The employee in 207 was transferred."

"Right, transferred. But Mr. Block said he wanted the repair done anyway. So—"

"Okay, why don't you follow me. I'm over in that neighborhood myself."

Karen smiled. "Thanks. I was afraid we'd be walking around here all night."

The man said nothing. He just glowered at her, then turned to go down the hall.

As the man turned, Jon caught a glimpse of him in profile. He looked familiar somehow, Jon thought. But from where? The man's features were unremarkable. He was thin, and had dark hair parted neatly on one side. It was hard to pin down an age. Maybe around forty, Jon guessed. As they walked down the hall, Jon stared at the back of the man's head, trying to place him. What seemed so familiar about him? The man's posture, for one thing. And the way he walked. Jon listened to the steady beat of the man's footsteps on the carpet. It made Jon feel uneasy. He wasn't sure why. Then the man coughed. It sounded almost like a short bark.

Instantly, Jon found himself transported back two nights. To the empty garage. Terrified. Pressed against a concrete pillar. Straining to hear what was happening. The footsteps. The cough. Just what he'd heard. Now, watching the man in front of him walk down the corridor, Jon felt a chill. He had no doubt. This man was the killer.

Jon's pulse raced. The sweat beaded on his forehead. If Jon recognized the killer, did the killer recognize him? No, it wasn't possible, Jon tried to convince himself. At least, not from the garage. The killer hadn't known Jon was there. Not then. But now he certainly knew. Maybe he'd even seen a picture of Jon. The witness. The loose end. Jon swallowed hard. If he'd been recognized, where was the man leading them?

"Gee, is this all the Center for Technology Policy?" Karen asked the man.

He looked back over his shoulder. "That's right," he said without much enthusiasm.

"Must be an interesting place to work."

"You could say that."

"Are you a researcher over here?"

"Researcher?" the man asked, as if hearing the word for the first time. "Uh-huh."

They came to the end of one corridor, and made a sharp right onto another, even darker than the first. As they turned, the man suddenly reached into the breast pocket of his jacket. For a gun? Jon gasped and instinctively grabbed Karen's arm. In an instant, her head snapped toward him. At the same time, out of the corner of his eye, Jon saw the man's hand shoot out from inside the jacket.

And, in the hand, Jon saw a handkerchief. An ordinary white cotton handkerchief, which the man used to wipe his nose.

Karen looked at Jon quizzically. He shrugged, and kept on walking. Halfway down the corridor, the man stopped at an office door.

"Here's 207," he said.

"Thanks so much," Karen said. "We would have been—"

"No problem," the man said brusquely over his shoulder, continuing down the corridor. Then he rounded a corner and was gone.

Jon flipped on the light in the office, Karen followed him in.

"What was that all about back there?" she whispered.

He closed the office door. "I thought he had a gun."

"A gun?" Karen asked, confused. She looked at his face. "Are you okay, Jon? You look like you just saw a ghost."

"Not a ghost. A murderer."

"You think he was—"

"Know. I know he was the gunman."

"But I thought you never really got a good look at him."

"It's true," Jon said. "I didn't. I only got a glimpse from the side."

"So how can you be so sure?"

"Because I heard him. The way he walked. And that cough. It was a strange sound. Like a dog barking or something. At least, that's what it sounded like to me."

Karen looked uneasily toward the closed door. "Jon, let's get out of here. If he knows who you are, I don't think we want to be in here."

"I agree," Jon said. "But he would have done something if he recognized me. He wouldn't have just—"

"Jon, maybe he's going for help right now. Or going to get his gun. Who knows? But I really don't want to find out."

"You're right," Jon said, looking around the office. There was nothing out of the ordinary. A desk, a computer, two chairs, a bookcase, and a filing cabinet. "You're totally right. He may be coming back. But we're already here. Let's just take a quick look. Please?"

"Okay, two minutes. Then we go."

"All right," Jon said, opening the desk drawers, "you've got a deal." He gestured to the filing cabinet. "Maybe take a peek in there."

Karen opened the cabinet drawers. "Nothing. How about the desk?"

"No, empty. So's the bookcase." Jon sat down at the desk, and turned on the computer. There was a loud beep.

"Shhh," Karen said, startled.

"Sorry, it does that by itself when it starts up. Okay, let's take a look at what's on the hard drive."

"What are the chances they left—"

"Damn."

"What?" Karen asked.

"There's nothing here. The drive's pretty much empty. Someone was very thorough."

Karen looked at her watch. "C'mon, then, let's go. That guy may decide to come back."

He turned off the computer. "Okay, let's get out of here."

Jon went to the office door and listened. Silence. He opened the door a crack, and peeked outside. Nothing. Jon flicked off the lights, swung open the door, and stepped into the hall. All clear. He gestured to Karen to follow. She pulled the door closed behind her.

"How do we get out of here?" Karen asked.

"Good question." He peered down the long, dark corridor. "I think we need to make a left at the—"

There was the squawk of a walkie-talkie from around the next corner. And several pairs of footsteps, coming closer.

"Back in there?" Karen whispered, pointing to Kaminski's former office.

Jon shook his head. "Maybe they're looking for us." He tried the door across the hall. It was locked.

"How about this one?" Karen asked, moving to the office next to Kaminski's. She turned the knob. The door opened. "Jon, c'mon. In here." When Jon was inside, she quietly pressed the door closed.

The footsteps from the hall grew louder, then stopped near the door.

"All right, here's 207." It was a man's voice.

Someone knocked on Kaminski's office door.

"Hello, anyone in there?" called out another man's voice. "Megasoft Security."

There was the sound of a door opening.

"Nah, no one's in here." The walkie-talkie squawked. "Base, this is Unit 4A, over." He paused for a garbled reply. "We're at 207, and we don't see anyone up here." He paused for the response. "Okay, roger that, base. 4A out."

"False alarm?" asked the first voice.

Kaminski's office door snapped closed.

"Probably. But you know Mr. Donnelly. Everyone looks suspicious to him."

There were footsteps in the corridor again, moving away from the door.

"That Donnelly is some piece of work. Never smiles. Never has two words to say to you. And, don't quote me on this or anything, but I think the man is paranoid as hell. He's got us on these wild-goose chases every other night."

"Herb, he must be doing something right. They say he's General Constanza's right-hand man. A real big cheese, I hear. I was talking to—"

Jon and Karen pressed their ears against the door, but they couldn't hear anything else. And then the footsteps gradually faded to silence.

"Did you get all that?" Karen whispered.

"Not everything, but a lot of it."

"So was Donnelly the guy we saw?"

"It sounded that way."

"Ever hear that name before?"

"No, but if he works for Constanza, he must be pretty high up, don't you think?"

"That would make sense. Are you totally positive that the guy we saw was the killer?"

"I am," Jon said. "I don't know how, but I just am. The sounds brought everything back. The footsteps. That weird little cough. You know, I really did see him in the garage for a split second. But it was from the side. And that wasn't enough to remember, somehow. Then tonight, when I saw him from the same angle again, right away I knew I'd seen him before."

"So if this Donnelly guy was the gunman, and he works for Constanza, do you think Constanza was in on the murder somehow?"

"Maybe," Jon replied, taking a step back to open the office door. "I really don't know that much about—"

Jon tripped on something in the dark, and fell backward with a crash.

"Jon, are you okay?"

He coughed. "Fine. It's just dusty down here. Turn on the lights."

Karen fumbled in the dark, running her hand along the wall until she found the switch. She flicked it on.

The office was nearly identical to Kaminski's. No computer, but the standard desk, bookcase, and two chairs. The office was empty, except for a cardboard box on the floor.

Jon stood up, and dusted himself off.

"Is this what you tripped on?" Karen asked, bending down to the look at the box.

"Yeah, kind of a bad place to leave it, right in the middle of the floor."

"Jon, what's the office number next door again?"

"207. Why?"

Karen pointed to a label on the top flap. "That's what this is marked. 9-207." She pulled back the flap and looked inside. "Books. Just some books."

"Think these were Kaminski's?" Jon asked.

"Could be." Karen pulled out a few of them. "Well, I'll tell you one thing, these aren't exactly light bedtime reading, that's for sure." She handed them to Jon.

"Centers of Power: American Government in the Twentieth Century," Jon read on the spine of one book, before turning to another. *"Propaganda and Disinformation: Use and Misuse."* He looked at a third. *"The Modern Presidency."*

"Jon, look at this," Karen said, holding open the inside cover of a book. "There's an inscription."

Jon squinted to make out the handwriting. *"Walt,"* he read, *"You probably could have written this yourself."* He looked up at Karen. "Can you make out the signature?"

She took another look. "It's just initials. It says, *P.C.*"

"As in Pete Constanza?"

"Now that would be interesting, wouldn't it?"

"It sure would. What's the book, anyway?"

Karen flipped to the title page. *"A Definitive History of Guerrilla Warfare,"* she read. "Sort of a strange book to give as a gift, isn't it?"

"To say the least." Jon flipped to the front of the book again. "But the inscription makes it pretty clear that Kaminski wouldn't have found it strange at all. *You probably could have written this yourself.* So was that Kaminski's specialty in the CIA? Guerrilla warfare?''

''He was in Vietnam,'' Karen said. ''That would certainly teach you something about guerrilla warfare.''

''Vietnam,'' Jon said, thinking it over. He put the book down. ''Is that where Kaminski and Constanza knew each other from?''

''They were over there at the same time.''

''Burt Seely, too. And you figure that, if Constanza knew Kaminski, so did Seely.''

''But what's a high-tech company want with these guys? Seems like a little too much firepower for industrial espionage. Besides, what would this Kaminski guy know about computers or software?''

''Not much, I bet. He just seems like a fish out of water at Megasoft.''

''The thing I'm wondering,'' Karen said, ''is whether Constanza and Seely knew about Kaminski's murder in advance. Or are they just covering it up after the fact?''

''So this Donnelly guy is a rogue, who just takes it upon himself to kill Kaminski? Then Constanza and Seely protect him for some reason? I don't buy it.''

''No, neither do I. It doesn't make sense.'' Karen looked at her watch. ''Jon, we should go. We don't want to run into Donnelly again.'' She flicked off the lights, then slowly opened the door. ''It's clear.'' She followed Jon outside, and pulled the door closed behind them.

''Think any of these other doors are open?'' Jon asked.

''There's only one way to find out,'' Karen replied, testing the knobs. They were all locked.

''All right,'' Jon said, ''let's get out of here.'' They started down the corridor. ''You know, Kaminski's office was really a disappointment. I thought for sure there'd be something left in there. Especially on the computer. It's easy to miss things on computers.''

''That's why they were probably careful about it. I bet they erased anything that was even remotely related to his work. That's what I would have done. Just keep on typing that *delete* command until—''

''I didn't even think of that,'' Jon said, stopping abruptly. ''Karen, we have to go back.''

''Didn't think of what?''

"How they erased the files. I just assumed they re-formatted the hard disk. But maybe they really didn't."

"What do you mean, re-formatted the hard disk?"

"That erases every single piece of information on the hard disk. It lets you start over with a clean slate."

"If they didn't do that, what did they do?"

"Exactly what you said. Use the *delete* command."

"What's the difference?"

"The computer usually keeps track of your files in a kind of card catalog, like in a library. When you delete a file, it really isn't erased. The card is just thrown away."

"So you think Kaminski's files could still be on the hard drive?" Karen asked.

"There's a chance." He turned to go back to Kaminski's office.

"Wait, you want to go back there now?"

"We may not get another chance, Karen."

Karen sighed. "All right."

They retraced their steps to Kaminski's office.

"I'll make this quick," Jon said, closing the office door behind them. He turned on the lights, sat down behind the computer, and flipped on the power switch. When the blinking cursor appeared, he typed *undelete,* then sat back. After a few seconds, a short list appeared on the screen.

"Bingo," Jon exclaimed.

"Bkgrnd, Contacts, Misc, Vanguard," Karen read from the screen. "What are those? Files?"

"No. You see the 'D' next to each one? That means it's a directory, a collection of files." He studied the information on the screen. "Oh, well," he said.

"What's wrong?"

"Only one of the directories is still readable."

"What happened to the others?" she asked.

"They got written over," Jon replied. "When the computer made new directories, it put them where the old ones used to be. It's kind of like building a new house on the same spot where there used to be an old house. Once the new house is finished, you'd never know anything else had ever been there."

"Which directory is left?"

Jon moved his finger down the screen. "Just this one called *Vanguard.* Let's see what files are in there." He typed a command, and the screen was instantly filled with another list.

"Budgsum.doc, memo7.doc, mtgagend.doc," Karen read off the screen.

"They're word processing files," he said. "We should be able to read them. Let me just run the word processor." He pressed a few keys.

There was a loud beep from the computer.

"Great, they erased the word processor," Jon muttered.

"So how are we going to look at those files?"

"We're not. At least not right now." He started opening up desk drawers.

"What are you looking for?" she asked.

"A floppy disk, so I can make a copy of the files. But I don't see any disks in here." He drummed his fingers on the desk, thinking it over. "Maybe I could just copy the files to some other machine on the network, then Kenny can get them for us later."

The computer beeped.

"What's wrong?" Karen asked.

"They canceled my network password."

"C'mon, Jon. We need to get out of here."

"All right," Jon said, turning off the power. "It's a shame I can't take the whole computer with me." He got up, and started for the door. Then he had an idea. "I can't take the whole computer, but I can take the hard drive."

He snapped open the computer case, and peered inside. After a few seconds of fierce tugging, his hand reappeared with a small metal box and some trailing cables.

They were standing next to Karen's car, across the street from Jon's apartment.

He wanted to kiss her. There was something about her that excited him in a way no one else ever had. She had this presence, this confidence about her that he found incredibly sexy. She was smart and she knew it. He liked talking to her. And being with her. And just looking at her. It made his heart race. His eyes darted downward for an instant. God, she really did have a nice—

"I guess I should head home," she said.

"You know, if you want, I could follow you in my car. In case you're still spooked about—"

"Jon, I told you. I'll be fine."

She was wondering whether he was going to kiss her. She saw that look in his eyes, and she wasn't doing anything to discourage him. He intrigued her. She couldn't figure him out. He seemed fiercely independent, but also a little lonely. He was serious, but actually pretty funny. And he had a very cute butt.

A car sped by them on the dark street. They watched the red taillights fade in the distance.

"You didn't see that green minivan tonight, did you?" she asked.

He shook his head. "No brown car?"

"Not that I noticed."

"Maybe they got bored," he said, trying hard to smile.

She looked down the street warily. "Or maybe they're on to new cars."

His smile evaporated. He decided to change the subject. "So you really think this Kaminski thing is related to the campaign?"

"Well, at the very least, it's related to Constanza. You heard that security guy tonight. According to him, Donnelly is Constanza's right-hand man. So if Donnelly really was the gunman Monday night, I think the General's got some explaining to do."

"We'll know for sure about Donnelly tomorrow," Jon said. "Kenny's working on it for me."

"How's he doing that?"

"Actually, you figured this out yesterday. Kenny's just doing the legwork. The gunman used a pass card to get back into the building. Unless someone's doctored those records, there's a computer somewhere that knows exactly who went into the building on Monday night."

Karen smiled. "Very clever."

"And tomorrow, I'll get Kenny to give us a hand installing that hard drive from Kaminski's office. I want to know what's in those files."

She nodded. "I'm going to call my editor in New York tomorrow.

We definitely could use some help. Maybe he could send in some reinforcements. "

"That would be great."

"Yeah."

They couldn't think of anything else to say, so they just stood there in the mist, face to face, a few feet apart.

In the moonlight, her eyes sparkled, her lips glistened.

He wanted to kiss her. He was going to kiss her. He was about to kiss her.

Then he chickened out and looked at his watch.

"It's getting late," he said, already regretting what he hadn't done.

Thursday, October 26

☆ ☆ ☆ ☆ ☆

15

☆ ☆ ☆ ☆ ☆

Karen sat on the sofa in her loft, bathed in the flickering bluish light of a TV infomercial about a miracle stain remover, watching through the wall of windows as the pinks and purples and oranges of a rising sun lit up the dark sky behind the skyscrapers.

Counting sheep hadn't helped. And warm milk hadn't helped. And half a teaspoon of fat-free, sugar-free, taste-free plain vanilla frozen yogurt hadn't helped. And half a quart of super premium chocolate-fudge ice cream hadn't helped.

She just couldn't get back to sleep.

The Megasoft story was worrying her. At first, she had been excited. It sounded like the kind of story that made careers—or rehabilitated them, at least. It was the break she thought she needed. Now, she was having doubts. In all the stories she'd reported, she'd never been followed before. She'd never felt her personal safety at risk. Suddenly, the stakes seemed too high.

She wondered whether she'd been the reason why Jon had been fired. After all, what had he really done? Told off that Burt Seely? That couldn't have been enough to provoke them. But when they found out he'd been talking to a reporter, that very likely pushed them over the edge.

Karen felt sick at the thought: Had she destroyed Jon's career in order to save her own?

He was a sweet guy. He was different from the men she'd met in New York. On the surface, he was all hip and high-tech. Two days, two black T-shirts. And all the computer talk. But he was also old-fashioned somehow. Like the way he'd been too shy to kiss her last night. She smiled when she thought about that.

And she was still smiling when she finally drifted back to sleep.

A thud at her front door woke her again. The paperboy. She hated when he did that.

The TV was still on. She watched a much too cheerful weatherman bounce around in front of a colorful map. Outside, it was brighter. She looked around for a clock. 6:37. The night was over. She pulled herself up from the sofa.

In the kitchen, she set up the coffeemaker and dropped two pieces of whole-wheat bread into the toaster. Then she retrieved the newspaper from her doorstep and put it on the table.

Sipping her coffee, she didn't even notice the story right away. She scanned the headlines without much interest. Then one headline caught her eye. SEC INVESTIGATES INSIDER TRADING. Front page, left side, above the fold. She took a bite of toast and started reading.

Midway through the first sentence, she started to choke. Coughing, eyes tearing, she finally managed to swallow the toast. Then she shoved aside her coffee mug and spread out the newspaper.

> A Seattle-based correspondent for *Business World* magazine is the target of an investigation of alleged insider trading, according to senior officials at the Securities and Exchange Commission. Trading stock on advance knowledge of *Business World* articles, they claim, the reporter made more than $100,000 in illegal profits. Sources at the SEC said the reporter is Karen Grey, a long-time *Business World* employee.

Karen felt like she'd been punched in the stomach, like the wind had been knocked out of her. All she could hear was the sound of her own heart pounding. It felt like it was going to jump out of her chest.

Her first impulse was to pack a bag. To throw some clothes in her suitcase and get on the first plane. She had no idea where she would go. South America? Asia? Where the hell did fugitives flee to these days anyway?

Karen, get a grip, she told herself. Calm down. Think this through. But all she could think was that her life was over.

She felt pure rage. She knew what this was all about. They were trying to discredit her. They were trying to destroy her.

Then she felt pure fear. If they could do this to her, and do it so quickly, what else could they do? What else were they planning to do?

She rested her head on the newspaper and began to sob, watching her tears dissolve the harsh black ink.

16

☆ ☆ ☆ ☆ ☆

It was a pleasant dream, and Jon really didn't want to wake up. But the phone rang loudly, incessantly, at last jarring him from sleep.

"Hello," he said groggily into the receiver.

"Jon, it's Karen."

He was still half asleep. "Karen, how's it going?"

"I'm sorry. I woke you up, didn't I?"

"No. Well, kind of. What time is it?"

"A little after seven."

"That's okay," Jon said, fibbing. "I had to get up anyway."

"I wouldn't have called, but I was just so shocked when I saw it."

"Saw what?"

"The newspaper. The *Seattle Chronicle.* Do you get it?"

"Yeah, yeah, I do." He yawned. "But I haven't—"

"Tell you what. Why don't you go grab the paper. I'll wait."

Jon sighed. He wanted to go back to sleep. "Sure, hold on a minute," he said, putting down the phone and flipping on the light next to his bed. He creakily swung out of bed, and padded to the front door. Wearing only underwear, he shivered in the cold morning air as he threw the door open and scooped up the newspaper.

"Okay," he said, sitting down on the edge of the bed, "what am I looking for?"

"It's there on the front page."

He glanced at the headlines. Nothing caught his eye. "Where on the front page?"

"Jon," she said, irritated, "it's on the left, at the very top of the page."

He looked at the headline. He still didn't get it. "SEC INVESTIGATES INSIDER TRADING," he read aloud. "Is that the one you mean?"

"Read the story."

"All right, let's see," he said, angling the paper to get more light.

He only got through the first paragraph. "Karen, this is incredible."

"I opened the paper this morning, and there it was," she said. "It just took me totally off guard."

"I'm so sorry, Karen. This is my fault. I'm the one who—"

"Jon, don't be silly."

"It's true, though. If I hadn't gotten you involved, this never would have happened."

There was a long pause. "It looks really bad, doesn't it?" she asked quietly.

"Well, yeah, but we both know what's going on here. Yesterday, they got me out of the way. Now they're trying to do the same thing with you. They think they're going to shut us up this way."

"Or at least make it so no one will listen."

"Karen, don't worry, we'll find someone to listen. I'm sure that—"

There was a clicking sound on the line.

"Oh, sorry, Jon. That's my call waiting. Hold on a sec."

Jon picked up the paper and skimmed the rest of the story. The details were sparse. SEC officials claimed that Karen had traded the stock of several high-tech companies just before articles about them appeared in *Business World*. The magazine had over a million readers, so an extremely positive or negative article about a company often affected its stock price. According to the officials, Karen illegally used her position at *Business World* to find out about such articles before publication. She then allegedly bought or sold stock based on this information.

Staring at the story on the front page, Jon felt uneasy. It just seemed so authentic, so solid. Maybe he and Karen really wouldn't be able to convince anyone to listen to them. Then what? Even if they could unravel the mystery of Kaminski's murder, would it make a difference? Jon put down the paper and pulled the blanket on his bed around him.

There was another clicking sound on the phone.

"Jon?" It was Karen. She was crying.

"Karen, what's wrong?"

She didn't answer at first. "I'm sorry," she finally said. "I'm really sorry." Then she continued to cry.

"Who was that?" he asked. "What happened?"

After a minute, Karen could speak again. "He told me to hire a lawyer," she said breathlessly.

"Karen, who told you to hire a lawyer?"

"My editor in New York. That's who called. He just fired me."

17

☆ ☆ ☆ ☆ ☆

"It was really sweet of you to come over," Karen said, giving Jon a hug. "I know, I look like a mess." Her face was puffy, and her eyes red from crying.

"Karen, you look fine," Jon said, trying not to stare. He took a seat at the table.

She backpedaled toward the kitchen. "I know you don't do coffee. Can I get you some orange juice?"

"That would be good."

"Jon," she called out from the kitchen, "you know, I could make you some eggs or something, if you want. Or I've got some English muffins or—"

"Karen, it's okay. Really. I grabbed a bagel on the way out the door. I'm not here for breakfast."

"I'm sorry," she said, setting a glass of orange juice and a cup of coffee on the table. "I get fired and suddenly I'm the happy homemaker." She sat down. "I'm just in a weird mood."

"Don't worry about it," he said. "I'm still feeling pretty strange myself. After I woke up this morning, it took me a while to remember that I wasn't going to work today. I was already making lists of things I had to get done and all. Then it hit me."

Karen took a sip of coffee. "I don't know how you wake up without this stuff. I guess I'm totally addicted to caffeine." She took another sip. "You know, it's amazing how your job just becomes your life after a while. I mean, it becomes your whole identity. Karen Grey, the *Business World* reporter. That's how I think of myself. I bet that's how people who know me think of me. I guess that's pretty stupid. What am I now, Karen Grey, the ex–*Business World* reporter? I don't think I can make a career out of that."

"How long were you at *Business World?*" Jon asked.

"Seven years. I never thought I'd work there that long. My first job out of college was at this sleepy little suburban newspaper in Connecticut. I lasted about six months. I was just bored out of my mind. All I did was cover school board meetings and shopping center openings. To this day, I get the creeps every time I drive into a shopping center.

"It was pretty awful. I'd have to interview these sleazo local politicians. These guys with polyester suits and bad toupees. And they were totally shameless. They'd be wearing these huge, solid gold wedding bands, and they'd ask me out. Oh, I'm separated, they'd tell me. I'm divorced, but I still wear the ring. Yeah, right. Give me a break."

Karen took another sip of coffee. "So, anyway, I hated working at this newspaper. I think I started sending out résumés after the first week. I must have sent out two hundred résumés. And you know how many responses I got?"

Jon shook his head.

"None. Not a single one. Looking back now, I guess I shouldn't have been so surprised. I mean, I had a degree in journalism and exactly one week's experience in the real world. But, at the time, I was devastated. I wanted to be this great investigative reporter, and here I was stuck covering school board meetings. I didn't know what to do. Then I got lucky. The journalism department at my college invited me back for this panel discussion. What a joke. At this point, I had about four months' experience at this dinky newspaper, and suddenly I'm supposed to share my wisdom with students. Well, obviously, I didn't have too much wisdom to share. But it worked out that one of the other panel members was this older alum from *Business World.* And wouldn't you know it? They were looking for someone. So I went down to New York to talk to the editors. And, amazingly, they hired me. I felt like I'd been rescued. Plucked from a raft in the middle of the ocean."

"A happy ending," Jon said. "Until now, at least."

Karen bit her lip. "Not exactly."

"What do you mean?"

"Things were going along pretty well for a while. After three years, they made me a section editor. I was the youngest one ever. It was a big deal. I had this huge office. I had eight people working for me. I was pretty impressed with myself." She shook her head. "But all good things must come to an end, right?"

"What happened?" Jon asked.

"Paul Halladay. That's what happened. I was his editor."

Jon vaguely remembered the name. It had been a big story about a year or two ago, he thought. "Was that the thing with the cigarette company?"

"Yup, that's the one. Paul brought me a great story. The widow of a tobacco executive had discovered a filing cabinet full of company documents in her basement. This stuff proved one of the cigarette companies knew how dangerous its products were as far back as the early '50s. We ran that story on the cover for two weeks. 'The Cigarette Papers: A *Business World* Investigation.' God, what a story.

"Of course, there was one small problem. Paul hadn't gotten the documents from any widow. He'd waltzed right into the company's headquarters and stolen them."

"But that wasn't your fault."

Karen smiled sadly. "I happen to agree with you, but that's not what my bosses thought. They said that I hadn't supervised him adequately. He was a year out of college. I should have been double-checking everything he did." She sighed. "Maybe I should have been watching him more closely. Maybe I should have insisted on meeting his source, but he told me that she insisted on being anonymous."

"You must hate this Halladay guy," Jon said.

"It's not so simple." She looked out the window for a moment. "No, I don't hate him. He thought he was doing something good. As far as he was concerned, the guys who ran the cigarette companies were murderers. And he was collecting evidence of their crimes. What he didn't understand, though, is you can't break the law to do that."

"The cigarette company sued, right?"

"For $500 million. The magazine settled out of court. I think we ended up paying something like $15 million. It's still a big secret. And we agreed to run an apology on the cover and give them the first twenty pages inside to tell their side of the story. It was a total fiasco. In every way possible.

"Of course, Paul they got rid of on day one. That was easy. But I was a harder case. I know a lot of people at *Business World* thought I'd been in on the whole thing. They just couldn't believe that I'd been such a sucker. But management was afraid to fire me. The lawyers told them that it would make our case even weaker. Better that it had been one loose cannon rather than some staff conspiracy. So they were stuck with me. And that's how I got transferred out here last year. Just because they had to keep me on the payroll didn't mean they had to look at me every day."

"I don't get it," Jon said. "Why would you want to work for people like that? Why didn't you look for a job somewhere else?"

"I tried," she said. "You don't know how hard I tried. But no one was interested. People I'd known in the business for years wouldn't even return my calls. As far as they were concerned, I was either lying or incompetent. And either way, they weren't hiring."

She picked up the newspaper from the table and stared at the front page. "This removes any doubt. Now they know for sure. Karen Grey is a liar. And an inside trader. And who knows what else. *Business World* can finally wash its hands of me. They all can. I'll never work again in journalism. No one in his right mind would ever hire me."

Tears welled in her eyes and she looked away, pressing her lips together, trying hard not to cry.

Jon took her hand. "Karen, you can fight this thing. You didn't do anything wrong. It doesn't have to end this way."

Then she started to cry. Just a trickle, and then a gusher. She buried her face in her hands, sobbing.

"Jon, you don't understand," she said, wiping her tears with a napkin. "You just don't understand. This is the end. There's nothing I can do."

"That's not true," he said. "Your editor was right. You should get a lawyer and—"

"Jon, I did it," she said, sobbing, "I did it. I'm guilty of what they say."

"What?"

Karen gripped his hand tighter. "I did it. I'm guilty. That's the truth."

Jon looked down at his orange juice. He couldn't think of anything to say.

They both sat in silence.

"Are you surprised?" Karen finally asked.

He took a deep breath. "I guess I am."

"I know it was a crazy thing to do, but—"

"Karen, it's none of my business. You don't have to explain it to me."

"No, I know that," she said. "But I want to explain it. I'm not proud of it, if that's what you're thinking."

"I wasn't thinking that."

"It just kind of happened. I know that sounds completely phony. How could it just happen? But it did. Right after I came out here last year, I stumbled across this tiny biotech company in Seattle. They basically had no money, but they had this incredible gene therapy under development. The founder was this academic guy with lots of grandiose dreams, but not too much management experience. So the venture capital firms didn't take him seriously.

"Well, I knew some of these venture capital people from all the reporting I'd done about biotech and software and all that. So I got them together with this company. I convinced them it was an incredible opportunity. To make a long story short, they eventually helped take this company public. They offered me the chance to buy some stock at the insider's price. And I thought to myself, if I hadn't gotten involved, the deal never would have happened. So I bought the stock. Then, before the initial public offering of the stock, I wrote about the company. It was a fair piece, but it was definitely flattering. I knew it would help the stock price. And it did. And I never told my editor about the stock I bought."

"Wait," Jon said, "are you sure that's even insider trading? I mean, maybe it's a little unethical, but is that really illegal?"

"I don't know," she replied. "Maybe if that's the only thing I'd done, I'd feel differently about this. But it didn't stop there. I saw a chance to make some money, to be independent. After what had happened to me, I never wanted to have the rug pulled out from under me again. So I took a chance. Just a few times since then.

They were all companies I really believed in. I mean, I didn't just randomly choose a company, buy the stock, then write this glowing article. Nothing like that. I'd pick companies that I thought were doing something important, something worthwhile, and I'd invest in them."

She looked down. "I'm not complaining. I knew what I was doing. I took a chance, and I got caught. Now, would I have gotten caught if I hadn't gotten mixed up in this thing with Megasoft? I don't know. Maybe eventually. Maybe never. But I—"

The phone rang.

"Hello?" She listened for a few seconds, then covered the receiver.

"A reporter," she whispered to Jon, before speaking into the phone.

"No, I'm sorry," she said. "I don't have any comment."

18

☆ ☆ ☆ ☆ ☆

Jack Malcolm sat alone in the small room backstage, cradling a Styrofoam cup of hot tea and collecting his thoughts. His throat hurt from talking too much. The last thing he felt like doing was giving another speech. He took a sip of tea, savoring the taste of the honey.

But Malcolm wasn't going to skip this speech. It had become a Megasoft tradition. Once a year, all 25,000 Seattle-based employees abandoned their offices for a morning and gathered at the Sportdome. Megasoft had held its first company meeting, Malcolm remembered, in a booth at the local International House of Pancakes. That was when the headcount was four, including Malcolm and his wife, who handled the accounting part-time. Now the Sportdome, a vast concrete cavern with a green plastic football field, was the only place in Seattle big enough to hold everyone.

Megasoft had grown larger and faster than Malcolm had ever imagined. And it was continuing to grow. Every Monday morning, new hires arrived on campus for orientation. Nibbling on muffins and Danish, they'd sit in the darkened auditorium and watch the slide show, jotting notes about medical benefits and company policies. They'd watch an inspirational video, complete with uplifting music and nuggets of corporate wisdom. Then, after a brief question-and-answer session, they'd file out from the auditorium, ready to be shepherded across the campus to begin their Megasoft careers.

For many years, Malcolm had stopped by to greet these new employees, to welcome them to the Megasoft family. Jack and Ruth

Malcolm were childless, and in many ways, he had adopted the company as his extended family. He'd dote on new arrivals with fatherly pride. "You are truly the best and the brightest," he'd tell them. "We are lucky to have you." A few years back, though, Malcolm had stopped attending the orientation sessions. At the time, he'd told the Human Resources people that his schedule had just gotten too crowded. He didn't have the time. But reflecting on it now, as he read over his remarks to the company meeting, another explanation flickered into consciousness. He didn't much respect the people Megasoft was hiring these days.

Too many of them were followers, flunkies. Timid souls who yearned only for regular hours and a steady paycheck. They never would have considered Megasoft in the early days. And Megasoft never would have considered them. Back then, joining the company was an adventure, a leap of faith. You had to believe in the vision. The idea of a *personal* computer had only recently been science fiction. And even as those first crude, underpowered, overpriced PCs were trickling off the assembly lines, it wasn't really clear anyone would want to buy them. Sure, the hobbyists would snap them up. But they were the same folks who dabbled in ham radio and soldered together Heathkit stereos in their spare time. No, Malcolm and his little flock had a different vision: the personal computer as a consumer item, as commonplace in homes as telephones and TVs.

Unfortunately, no one knew how to make that dream a reality. The software business hadn't come with an instruction manual. There were no obvious parallels, no clear precedents. So they made up the rules as they went along. They improvised, they failed, they tried again. Nowadays, there were policies and procedures and guidelines and regulations at Megasoft for everything. You couldn't order a pencil without referring to some handbook. The type of person Malcolm had hired when the company headquarters was over a pizzeria wouldn't last a day at the modern Megasoft.

Sipping his tea, Malcolm closed his eyes and tried to compose a mental list of his first employees. Where in the company were they now? He kept tally as the faces appeared before him. Retired. Retired. Retired. Retired. Malcolm opened his eyes with the answer. They weren't in the company anymore. Their tiny stakes in an uncertain venture had made them rich beyond belief. High risk, high reward. They'd realized their original vision, and now there was no place for them at Megasoft.

The old vision had long since given way to a new one: the personal computer as a replacement for the telephone and the television. Some industry luminaries talked about an "information appliance" for the home, but Malcolm didn't like the term. It was too narrow, too abstract. It made the thing sound like a high-tech encyclopedia, Malcolm thought. *Information* was just a small part of it. The new vision placed the personal computer at the very center of people's lives. They'd shop by PC, pay the bills by PC, learn by PC, work by PC, vote by PC, entertain themselves by PC. And Megasoft would make it all possible. The company's software would be the medium in which this new digital society flourished. That was Malcolm's vision.

He'd spent four years assembling the building blocks. The first step had been the acquisition of CalFirst Bancorp, the nation's third largest bank. Malcolm regarded his lumbering new competitors in the retail banking industry with undisguised scorn. "We're going to eat their lunch," he'd predicted. And Megasoft had. In a move that surprised the competition, the company had immediately sold or closed half of CalFirst's branch offices. There were no smiling tellers when you banked Megasoft-style. No potted plants. And no lines, for that matter. Because the millions of consumers who now banked with Megasoft did so in the privacy of their own homes, via personal computer. There was rarely any need to visit the bank. Megasoft had even begun to close CalFirst's ATM sites, because the personal computer was now also a cash machine. Before heading out the door to go shopping, consumers just inserted their Megasoft "stored value" card in the PC and added some dollars. In three years' time, the Megasoft DollarCard had become almost as widely accepted as the actual greenback.

Megasoft's second big acquisition had been Video-Communications, Inc., the largest cable TV provider. Malcolm had announced the VCI deal at the company meeting two years ago, he recalled. The memory made him grit his teeth. He'd been sitting in this very same little room, getting ready to go out and share the good news, when a call came in from the investment bankers.

VCI's chairman was having second thoughts. The price wasn't high enough. Furious, Malcolm had been tempted to scrub the whole deal. There were other cable companies to buy. But then he'd calmed down and thought the thing through. With five minutes to go before the big announcement, Malcolm boosted his bid by $200 million. VCI accepted. At the time, the Wall Street analysts had chortled at Malcolm's last-minute capitulation. The consensus was that Megasoft had seriously overpaid for VCI. Two years later, though, no one was chortling. Because it was clear that VCI had been a bargain.

Around the time of the VCI purchase, the Internet had begun to experience a second spurt of explosive growth. In the first growth spurt, fueled by the World Wide Web, millions of educated, upper-income Americans had used their $2,000 personal computers to surf the Net via telephone lines. But the Internet still wasn't a truly mass medium, for two main reasons: PCs were too expensive and phone lines were too slow. The Japanese electronics companies provided a solution to the first problem. Mostly left on the sidelines during the first personal-computer revolution, the Japanese rushed to introduce the first $300 PCs. These bare-bones machines were designed exclusively for Internet use. Cheap and easy-to-use, they were enormously popular.

Megasoft's VCI subsidiary provided the solution to the speed problem that had previously held back the Internet. Standard telephone lines, made of copper, were very narrow information pipes. You couldn't fit very much through such pipes at one time. In contrast, the coaxial cables used to deliver TV service were very wide pipes indeed. "It's the difference between drinking from a straw and drinking from a fire hose," Malcolm liked to say. It was a difference consumers were willing to pay for. Pictures and sounds that had previously taken minutes to appear on the computer screen, now appeared in the blink of an eye. Megasoft OneWire service made it possible for consumers with $300 PCs to receive full-screen video through the Internet. It also allowed them to make inexpensive worldwide phone calls via the Internet, completely bypassing traditional long-distance and local telephone carriers. Suddenly, the old-line TV networks and phone companies were in jeopardy. They were dinosaurs, Malcolm thought, on the eve of extinction.

"Jack?"

Malcolm looked up from his papers. It was Herb Abernathy, the campaign press secretary. "Is it time already?"

"Yup. You're on next."

Joined by four burly bodyguards, they walked down a dimly lit tunnel to the mouth of the huge sports arena. A young woman with a walkie-talkie held them there, waiting for the cue.

"Remember," Abernathy whispered, "we've got the media here this year. You're not just talking to a company crowd. So let's try to stick to our message."

Looking straight ahead, straining to hear the public-address announcer, Malcolm nodded slightly.

The arena was now dark, with only the red exit signs and the dim lights on the stairs visible. Malcolm took a deep breath when he heard the announcer say, "Our founder and the next President of the United States, JackM." The crowd roared, and Copland's *Fanfare for the Common Man* erupted from the speakers. A rainbow of laser light flashed through the darkness.

The usher received the cue over her walkie-talkie, and Malcolm and his bodyguards strode into the arena. A narrow spotlight illuminated Malcolm as he made his entrance. The roar from the crowd was deafening. Malcolm slowly advanced down the center aisle toward the podium, pausing every few rows to shake hands. His security team gently pushed him forward.

As the last bars of Copland's fanfare echoed in the arena, Malcolm mounted the stairs to the podium, turning to wave to the crowd. High above the photogenic blue backdrop, three gigantic video screens made his broad smile visible to every seat in the house. When he finally arrived at the transparent glass lectern, he paused, waiting for the applause to end. But the crowd continued to cheer.

"Thank you," he said, raising his hands for silence. "Thank you very much." He was looking out on a sea of 25,000 identical black T-shirts, each imprinted with the yellow Megasoft OneWire logo. The cheering went on.

There was something so inefficient about all of this, Malcolm thought as he was grinning and nodding. Giving speeches was inefficient. Politics was inefficient. You knew what had to be done, and instead of just doing it, you first had to convince the people in the T-shirts. No matter what idiots they were. Like some high-school popularity contest, for God's sake. How ironic, Malcolm thought. He'd never won any popularity contests in high school, and now here he was vying for first place in the biggest popularity contest of them all. They'd respected him in high school. Named him "Most Likely to Succeed" in the senior yearbook. But the "Most Popular" title had gone to someone else. Malcolm had never been a backslapper. He wasn't the hail-fellow-well-met kind of guy. Even in high school, though, his indomitable drive, his unflinching sense of purpose had been evident. He had decided early on that he wanted to be a scientist. There was a certain purity to the field that attracted him. It held out the hope of finding not just satisfactory explanations, but the truth itself. Instead of shades of gray, there were clear patches of black and white. Science was wondrously logical and efficient. Politics was neither.

After high school in Boulder, science had led Malcolm across town to a scholarship at the University of Colorado. Eight years later, at twenty-six, he'd become the youngest tenured professor in the history of the physics department. Physics captivated Malcolm. It offered the most fundamental answers, he thought. Malcolm had become an enormously successful academic, consistently winning research grants from the most prestigious national funders. It was a satisfying career, and Malcolm had never thought he'd do anything else. Then, out of the blue, a friend had asked for some help writing a statistics program for one of the first personal computers. It was the kind of computer that arrived with a bunch of loose parts and a photocopied instruction manual. Hardly a pretty sight. But Malcolm was hooked—by the technology, crude though it was, and by the business world, in which he'd previously had little interest. At heart, Malcolm was fiercely competitive, and he found the marketplace a far more exciting arena than the laboratory. Within a year, he had resigned his post at the university to found Megasoft.

"Twenty-five years ago," Malcolm read from the teleprompter as the applause in the Sportdome finally faded, "Ruth and I moved to Seattle to begin a great adventure. We arrived here with little more than the clothes on our back and some vague dreams of how the personal computer might change the world.'' Malcolm fingered his tweed jacket and smiled. ''I know some people will say that I'm still wearing those same old clothes.'' Then, as the laughter died down, he added, ''But, my friends, twenty-five years later, no one will dispute the fact that, together, you and I have changed the world and made those dreams come true.''

In unison, 25,000 people in black T-shirts rose from their seats to cheer.

19

☆ ☆ ☆ ☆ ☆

"So how was it?" Jon asked immediately.

"Oh, you know how these things are," Kenny replied, trying hard to sound nonchalant. He sat down on the sofa in Jon's living room.

"Lots of demos, I guess. Just the usual stuff, right?"

"Pretty much."

This was the first company meeting Jon had missed in six years with Megasoft. The company meeting was always a big deal. It was a chance to find out what your peers were up to. All the cool things they were working on that the rest of the world wouldn't know about for months or years more. Jon remembered hearing about Megasoft OneWire for the first time at a company meeting, long before the service was officially announced or the rumors even hit the trade press. It made you feel like you were part of something larger than your own little project. Megasoft was more than just a company. It was a community of shared values and shared goals. The company meeting reinforced that somehow. You'd see 25,000 people playfully jeering when a competitor's name was mentioned. Or laughing at the same inside joke. And then you'd know that you were in this thing together. You were all on the same team. It was Megasoft against the world, and you suddenly liked the odds better than ever.

The company meeting charged you up for another year of long hours and late nights. It gave you a certain momentum, Jon thought. So much of the Megasoft experience involved sitting alone in front of a computer. You wrote code alone. You sent e-mail alone. For most of the year, the Megasoft community was more virtual than actual. Then, for a few hours on an October morning, the virtuality became actuality. The arcane project code names and the terse e-mail addresses magically materialized as real human beings. You'd finally get to see people who worked on the other side of the campus, but might as well have lived on the other side of the globe for as often as you'd seen them. From the parade of presenters, you could discern who was out and who was in. Who were the has-beens and who were the rising stars. Presenting at the company meeting was always a harbinger of good things to come. A few months before TedN was promoted to VP of systems, Jon remembered, he'd given a keynote presentation. That was a sure sign Nesbitt was in favor with JackM. At this year's meeting, for the first time, Jon had been slated to give a demo. It wasn't one of the leadoff demos, but it wasn't at the very end of the meeting either. It would have marked Jon as someone to watch, as a solid contender for bigger assignments in the future. But it hadn't worked out that way. Now he was nobody at Megasoft.

"So did TedN give the Hollywood demo?" Jon asked.

"Just a really quick one. We didn't hit all the points you were going to."

We? Jon was surprised. He hadn't been planning to take Kenny with him on stage. "You got to—"

Kenny looked down. "Yeah, Ted called me last night and asked whether I'd help him out. Because, you know, he—"

"Sure, I understand." But Jon didn't. He felt betrayed.

"Jeez, I'm really sorry, Jon. I probably should have said I was busy or something."

"For the company meeting?" Jon shook his head. "No, don't be crazy. You couldn't have gotten out of it." Yes, life goes on, Jon thought. Just because you lose your job, doesn't mean that everyone else stops working, too.

"Anyway," Kenny said, eager to change the subject, "I was able to get in and look at the data."

Jon looked at him blankly, still thinking about the company meeting. Data? What was Kenny talking about? Then he remembered. "The pass card data?"

"Yeah. It was actually pretty hard to get to. They have it on this completely separate computer, pretty isolated from the corporate network."

"So what'd you do?" Jon asked.

"A little social engineering."

"Social engineering? What do you mean?"

"You know all those computers I broke into in high school? All of them supposedly totally airtight and secure? How do you think I did it?"

Jon shrugged. "I don't know. You're a good programmer. I guess you changed the security software or something like that."

"Nope, hate to shatter your illusions, but you're wrong. That's not what great hackers do."

"What do they do, then?"

"Social engineering," Kenny replied. "They hit on the weakest link in the chain. And that's people. If there were no people involved, computers would be way more secure. But people are involved, and they're the weakest link. By far. Because with people involved, you need to have passwords. Everyone gets a password. Even the guy who runs the whole computer system. And you just have to cross your fingers and hope that no one gives away a password. Because once a hacker has a password, he's got a foothold. He's in there."

"Why would anyone give out his password?" Jon asked.

"Because most people are amazingly trusting," Kenny replied. "They're gullible, really. That's what it comes down to."

"So, what do you do, just call the system administrator on the phone and ask for his password?"

"That's how I broke into the NSA computer."

"You're telling me that you just called some guy at the National Security Agency, at this top-secret government lab or whatever it was, and asked for his password? Yeah, right."

"That's what the judge said, too, when he sentenced me," Kenny said. "So, to prove it to him, I went with him into his chambers, picked up the phone, and called the system administrator for the Federal courthouse. And guess what? In two minutes, I had the password and I was able to log into the judge's computer."

It's a lucky thing this kid isn't a professional con man, Jon thought. We'd all own a piece of the Brooklyn Bridge. "So how do you convince these people to tell you their password?"

"Easy," Kenny replied. "Okay, first thing is, you need to listen to the person you're calling. I mean, really listen. How they answer the phone, the way they talk. The dumb little joke they make. Because you want to sound just like them. You want them to think you're one of them. If they answer the phone, 'engineering section,' you say you're from the 'administration section,' or something like that. Use the same words they use. The same tone. That's key."

"Then what?"

"Now that they think you're one of them, you just create a situation, maybe a little crisis, that they can help you with. Because most people are basically very helpful. That's rule number one. If you need some help, and it's not too much trouble for them, they're not going to let you down.

"Take last night, case in point. You asked me to get this info on the pass cards. First of all, I have to figure out where they keep it. And you can't just call up Megasoft Security and ask them that. So, you know that security guy who's always patrolling around in our building at night?"

"Tony?"

"Yeah, Tony. Nice guy. Likes to talk about football. So I happen to be in the hall when he comes around last night and we start talking. Just shooting the breeze. Then, as we're talking, my pass card just happens to accidentally slip out of my pocket and fall on the floor."

"You mean you dropped your pass card on the floor."

"Yup," Kenny said, "but Tony isn't thinking that. Anyway, suddenly the conversation just happens to turn to pass cards. When Megasoft first started using them. How they work. And, yes, where they store the data. You know, the funny thing is, I didn't even have to ask Tony that. He volunteered it. You know why? Because everyone wants to be an expert on something. I don't care if you're a brain surgeon or a carpenter. It's the same thing. You want everyone to think you know what you're doing. And given half a chance, you're going to try to prove it. Last night, all I did was give Tony his chance.

"The rest was easy. After talking to Tony, I know exactly where to call. All I have to do is create the right situation on the phone, and that password is mine for the asking. So I call this security operations center Tony was kind enough to tell me about. As soon as the guy answers the phone, I start acting all frantic. I'm calling from the admin center in Building 14, I tell him, and my boss is going to kill me. I'm supposed to finish this report for him by tomorrow, but I just did the stupidest thing. I erased the password to the computer I need to use. And then I blab on for a minute, working in all the jargon Tony used. Well, the guy on the other end finally cuts me off, and tells me to calm down. It's all right. You know why?''

Jon nodded. ''Rule number one. Most people are basically very helpful.''

''Very good,'' Kenny said. ''Anyway, the guy puts me on hold for a minute, then comes right back with the password. And, I'm telling you, he feels like a hero. Because he thinks he just saved someone's butt.'' Kenny pulled a computer printout from his pocket.

''So you found the name?''

He tapped on the printout. ''According to this, at 1:38 on Tuesday morning, a Megasoft employee entered Building 9 from the parking garage. Some guy by the name of Charles—''

''Donnelly,'' Jon interrupted.

Kenny looked up from the paper, frowning. ''Hey, if you knew the name, why'd you make me go through all this?''

''When I asked you last night, I didn't know the name.''

''How'd you figure it out since then?''

''Karen and I saw the guy last night in Building 9.''

''No way.''

''It was weird,'' Jon said. ''I didn't recognize him at first. Because, Monday night, I only saw him for a second. Then I was behind the pillar, just listening. And, you know, it was really the sound last night that jogged my memory. This weird cough he had. Then I knew right away it was the same guy.''

''Wait, I don't get it,'' Kenny said. ''Where'd you see him last night?''

''Karen and I were wandering around, looking for Kaminski's office. Believe it or not, this Donnelly comes along and helps us find it. Then he calls Security on us. Told them we looked suspicious. And I guess he was right."

"What did Security do?" Kenny asked.

"Nothing. We were already out of Kaminski's office by the time they got there."

Kenny shook his head. "You better be careful, Jon. You don't want to toy with these guys. You already saw what this Donnelly is capable of."

An image of Kaminski lying in a pool of blood on the garage floor came to Jon. He tried to think about something else, but he couldn't. The grisly scene wouldn't leave him. Jon wanted it to be like something you saw at the movies. It scared you for the moment, but then you could barely even remember it later on. But this was different. It was lurking, lingering. It was real. It wouldn't go—

"Bud, are you still with me?"

Jon focused back on Kenny. "I'm sorry. What were you saying?"

"I asked whether you and Karen found anything in Kaminski's office."

"No, they cleaned it out, except for—"

Jon stopped.

"Except for what?" Kenny asked.

"I almost forgot," Jon said. He reached under the sofa and pulled out a small metal box with cables attached. "Want to give me a hand installing this?"

"What is it?"

"The hard drive from Kaminski's computer."

Kenny examined the drive. "Sure, we can—"

The doorbell rang.

"That must be Karen," Jon said. He looked to the door, and then back again at Kenny. He wanted to talk to Karen. Alone. How was he going to do this gracefully?

"I'll get that," he said. "Hey, why don't you go ahead and try installing that? I'll be right with you."

Kenny headed for the bedroom.

Jon opened the front door and was surprised to see Karen looking so composed. She was dressed casually, in jeans and a blazer.

He gave her a hug, noticing up close how nice her perfume smelled.

"Are you doing okay?"

She didn't quite smile, but she didn't frown either. "Better than before."

He closed the door behind her.

"Did you have lunch yet? I've got some leftover Thai—"

"No, thanks, I'm fine. I haven't had any appetite today."

"I could understand that. Hear anything else?"

She shook her head. "I unplugged my phone."

"That was brave."

"I heard enough bad news for one day. I decided to let it just sink in for a while." She looked into the living room. "Is Kenny here yet?"

"He's trying to install Kaminski's hard drive in my computer."

"Perfect timing, then."

"Karen, you know, if you're not into doing this today, I totally—"

"No, I want to get back to work."

Kenny was just connecting the last cable. He looked up from the computer.

"Hey, Karen. I hear you two had quite an adventure last night."

"Thanks to your ID cards. We never would have gotten in there without them."

"No problem." He snapped the lid of the computer back into place. "I think we're all set."

Jon flipped on the power. The computer beeped, then the various drives began to whir.

"What's on the drive?" Kenny asked.

"Just some word processing files, I think. We couldn't tell last night. There was no word processor on the drive to read them."

"I'm surprised they left anything on the drive at all. You'd think they would have erased everything."

"Actually, they tried," Jon said. "I had to use the *undelete* command to get these back."

"That was smart. I would've figured they just re-formatted the whole drive."

"I guess someone was careless," Jon said. "Or didn't know any better." He started typing.

"What's in that *Vanguard* directory?" Kenny asked, looking over Jon's shoulder.

"That's what we were wondering last night," Karen said.

Jon opened the word processor. "All right, let's take a look at this *budgsum.doc* file," he said. After a few seconds, a title page appeared. *"Project Vanguard Budget: An Overview,"* Jon read from the screen.

"Project Vanguard?" Kenny asked. "I don't think that's a Megasoft project. At least, not one I've ever heard of."

"Me either," Jon said. "Let's look at the rest of it." He pressed a key, and another page came into view.

> The attached spreadsheet details the current Project Vanguard budget, including expenditures for both personnel and materiel. Except under circumstances approved personally by General Constanza, all payments will be made in cash or equivalent. All project accounting will be centralized at the Center for Technology Policy. In no event, however, will project monies or activities appear in CTP budgets, records, or reports.
>
> It must be emphasized that the accompanying budget is subject to change during the lifetime of the project. Previous experience with military/political operations indicates the high probability of unexpected scenarios that involve considerable cash outlays. We must be prepared for such situations, and flexible in our ability to shift resources as needed.
>
> Project Vanguard must remain entirely covert in nature. Any breach of security will certainly doom the project to failure. In addition, such a breach will likely cause a catastrophic outcome for all participants. As a result, the sources and methods of funding for the project must be carefully disguised.

"This is totally incredible," Karen said. She tapped on the screen. "Look at this stuff. 'Military/political operations.' 'Entirely covert in nature.' I think we know one thing for sure. This definitely isn't about technology policy."

"Who's funding this?" Jon asked. "Megasoft? The government? And what's the deal with Constanza? I mean, the man is a candidate for vice president of the United States, and according to this, here he is running some secret military operation, or whatever this Project Vanguard is.''

Kenny studied the screen. ''Where's the spreadsheet with the budget?''

Jon tried to turn to the next page, but the computer beeped in response. End of file.

''Maybe it's in another file,'' Kenny said.

Jon went back to the directory listing and opened the next file, *memo7.doc.* The computer beeped again. The file was protected with a password. He tried typing in Kaminski's name as the password. The computer's reply was curt and quick. Access denied. ''Well, I guess we're not reading *memo7.doc.*''

Kenny looked around Jon's desk. ''Got a floppy disk somewhere?''

''Sure,'' Jon said, opening the top drawer. ''Why?''

''Do me a favor and make a copy of that file. I want to bring it into the office. I'm pretty sure I can get into it.''

''How are you going to do that? You need to know the password.''

''Yeah, just like Megasoft Mail,'' Kenny replied. ''Don't worry. I've got a friend who works on Megasoft Write. He owes me one.'' Kenny slipped the disk into his pocket.

Jon turned back to the screen and opened the last file in the directory, *mtgagend.doc.*

PV Meeting Agenda: September 25

1. Cincinnatus field visit, Idaho training center (Walt)
   Readiness determination for Woodside operation, October 10
   Contingency plans for post-October 10 activities
2. Update on latest version of *meganet.sys* (Al)
   Anticipated changes
   Development schedule
3. Staffing issues (Pete)

''Cincinnatus field visit?'' Kenny said. ''These guys are terrorists. Or at least they're pretty friendly with some terrorists.''

Karen's eyes lingered for a few seconds on ''Woodside operation'' before she made the connection. ''What day was the assassination attempt?''

''Two weeks ago on Tuesday,'' Kenny replied.

''October 10,'' Jon said, and suddenly it was instantly clear to him. ''Constanza is trying to kill his own running mate. That's what this is all about.''

''Wait,'' Kenny said, ''what's Constanza without JackM?'' The answer occurred to him immediately. ''Duh. Pete Constanza is president of the United States.''

''He's president with a very convenient enemy,'' Jon said. ''It sounds like he's got these Cincinnatus guys on the payroll. He'll look like a real hero when he shuts them down once he gets in office.''

Karen frowned. ''Jon, why shut them down?''

''What do you mean?''

''Like you said, they're a very convenient enemy. Why not keep them around? Whenever President Constanza's approval rating goes down a few points, he can bring them out. You know, stage some phony attack, then a few days later score some equally phony victory against terrorism. The media would eat it up. General Constanza to the rescue. What a story.''

Then Jon thought of an even more chilling scenario. ''Or what if Constanza uses the terrorists as an excuse, as a smoke screen.''

''A smoke screen for what?'' Kenny asked.

''For making big changes,'' Jon replied. ''Think about it. If you throw people off balance enough with these terrorist attacks, maybe all of sudden they're willing to consider things they wouldn't otherwise. Maybe they don't complain as loudly when you limit their rights. Or you take away their property. Because it's for their own good. It's for their own protection.''

''You're talking about fascism,'' Karen said.

''That's what you usually call it when some general takes over the country.''

''So what do we do?'' Kenny asked.

As he thought about Kenny's question, Jon was embarrassed to find that his first impulse was to do nothing. He wanted the whole thing to go away. It was an imposition. The truth was, he just wanted his job back. He wanted his life back. He felt like a total slime for thinking it, but he realized that he would be willing to sweep the dirt back under the rug if that's what it would take to put this behind him. But then he thought about the people who'd taken away his job and screwed up his life, and he knew that they would never let him walk away. Not with the stakes so high.

"I don't know what we should do," Jon said. "Who do we go to? The police? They didn't believe me when I reported a murder. What are they going to say when I call back and say that General Constanza is plotting a coup? I guess we could try the FBI or the CIA or something like that. But we don't know the scope of this. I don't want to sound totally paranoid, but Kaminski worked for the CIA. Maybe he was still working for them when he got killed. Maybe the CIA is funding this Project Vanguard.

"What I'm saying is, we just don't know enough yet. And we don't have any evidence. All we've got are a couple of computer files. You could forge this stuff in five minutes on any computer. It'll be our word against Constanza's. No one's going to believe us. Not the police. Not the FBI. Not the press. Not even the conspiracy theorists. They'll all think we're nuts."

"Unfortunately," Karen said, "you're probably right." Then she stared at the screen again. "You know, I don't understand something here. What's this *meganet.sys* thing?"

Kenny shrugged. "I don't get that either. It's just this standard Megasoft programming file that ships with the operating system. A hundred million PCs have a copy of it. It gives you access to all the OneWire functionality. We use it in Hollywood to let people send and receive video clips across the network. It's no big deal. That's why it's so weird that it was on the agenda for their meeting."

Jon read the agenda. "This says there's some kind of updated version of *meganet.sys*. Kenny, know anything about that?"

"No, those files are always changing. The only time I pay attention is when the stuff I need doesn't work right. Then I send flame mail so they'll fix it. But I can look into it. I think EricT knows someone over in the OneWire group."

Kenny looked at his watch. "Jeez, I'm late for a meeting." He got up to go. "I'll call you two later on."

He was already at the front door when Jon called out to him. "Kenny?"

"What, bud?"

"Just be careful."

"Don't worry," Kenny replied as the door closed behind him.

But Jon couldn't stop worrying

"He's still on the same conference call?" Karen was saying into the phone. She was sitting on the sofa in Jon's living room, desperately trying to find someone to listen to their story. How hard could it be? She was a journalist, after all. She knew dozens of people in the news business. Someone had to listen.

"C'mon," she pleaded, "you told me that two hours ago. This is the third time I've tried him today. If he doesn't want to talk to me, at least he could have the courtesy to—"

She heard a click. "I can't believe it," she muttered, slamming down the phone. "She hung up on me."

Jon crossed the reporter's name off the list. "Who is this guy anyway?"

"I used to work with him at *Business World.* Now he's at one of the competitors. He probably thinks I'm calling for a job."

"That's okay," Jon said, trying to sound hopeful, "we've still got some other names here." But not too many, he thought. He silently tallied the results. After three solid hours of calling, Karen had managed to have a real conversation with exactly one editor, who listened politely and then advised her to take some time off.

Karen slumped back into the sofa. She wasn't going to make any more calls today. Why bother? No one was listening. They probably wouldn't have talked to her a week ago anyway, she thought. After the whole Halladay "Cigarette Papers" debacle, she was certain that her reputation couldn't sink any lower. Now, she knew better. If the Pulitzer people started handing out a prize for the least respected journalist in America, Karen knew she'd be a shoo-in.

"Jon, I'm scared," she said. "We're in over our heads, and I feel like we're all alone. Who's going to help? Who do we turn to? Right now, I don't think I could get a high-school newspaper to listen to our story."

He tried to think of something reassuring to say, but nothing came to mind. He had to agree with her. No one was going to listen to them. No one except—

"Maybe we should go straight to JackM," he heard himself saying out loud. "Maybe he'd listen."

Karen sat up. There was a chance. They had nothing to lose. "Think you could get in to see him?"

Jon shrugged. "I really don't know. I'm not exactly a popular guy at Megasoft at the moment."

Then he had an idea. "Bruce Kroll," he mumbled.

"What?"

"Bruce Kroll. He's this programmer I know. His girlfriend works for JackM. She's one of his secretaries. I wonder if she'd do me a favor."

Jon picked up the phone to find out.

20

☆ ☆ ☆ ☆ ☆

"Charlie, I'm kind of in a hurry here," Peter Constanza said, standing behind his desk, tossing papers into an open attaché case. "Can this wait until tomorrow?"

Charles Donnelly took a tentative step into the office. "Actually, General, I don't think we want to wait that long."

Constanza looked up. "Is that so?"

Donnelly nodded.

"All right, come on in for a minute," Constanza said. He pointed to the office door. "Shut that, will you?"

"Sure," Donnelly said, closing the door behind him.

Constanza picked up a thick loose-leaf binder from his desk. "This thing must weigh ten pounds," he said, trying to wedge it into the attaché case. "I'm gonna get a hernia carrying this junk around."

"What is that?" Donnelly asked.

"A briefing book. Another little treat from the idiots Malcolm has running his campaign. I must get a new one of these on my desk three times a week. And they're all the same. Polls, polls, polls. Want to know what Jane Doe in Peoria, Illinois thinks about dog doo on the sidewalk?" He tapped the binder. "It's in here, Charlie. Tabulated, computed, analyzed, and summarized. With plenty of nice color pictures, in case you can't read too well. Which I guess is a real possibility, considering the bozos we've got in Congress. I'm telling you, these political consultants are total scam artists.

You know how much Malcolm is paying one of these guys for this nonsense?''

Donnelly shook his head.

''Believe it or not,'' Constanza said, ''two-hundred thousand bucks a month. What a rip-off. My twelve-year-old granddaughter could tell you this stuff.'' He opened the binder, and flipped through the pages. ''Okay, let's see. All right, here's a real insight. *Most voters believe violent criminals should be severely punished.* Right. Just in case I wasn't sure of that. I mean, I was thinking maybe we'd give ice-cream sundaes to violent criminals. Well, thank God this poll saved me from a blunder like that.'' He laughed and closed the binder.

''Anyway, General, I—''

''Malcolm's people sent over one of these political hacks yesterday,'' Constanza said, rearranging the papers in the attaché case. ''A television consultant. You should have seen this guy. Hair down to his shoulders. Two earrings. I wouldn't let this guy clean my limo. And he wants to give me advice on how to come across better on TV. Amazing.

''The whole thing's a charade, Charlie. I was talking to one of Malcolm's campaign folks a few days ago, and he was all worried about the polls, about momentum, about the commercials, and on and on. I just wanted to say to him, you fool, you don't understand. This election is decided. It's over. I already know who's going to be sitting in the Oval Office in January. But, hey, we don't want to spoil their fun now, do we, Charlie?''

Donnelly smiled. ''No, sir.''

Constanza tried to close the attaché case, but it wouldn't shut. He sighed, and started taking out papers. ''No, we don't want to shatter these idiots' illusions about the democratic process. It would demoralize them. Couldn't have that. God forbid they knew how little they're affecting the outcome of this election.''

''General, the reason I—''

''Jeez, this isn't going to work,'' Constanza said, dumping the contents of the attaché case onto the desk. Then he started to put the papers back into the case. ''You know, come to think of it, the political consultants aren't so bad compared to the journalists. Especially these TV news people. Complete morons. They spend so much time on the hair spray and the make-up, they don't have any time to think of decent questions. You should hear some of the nonsense they waste my time with. I was down in Phoenix last week doing this local news show, and you know what the first question was? Not the economy. Not crime. Not education. This so-called journalist asked me what my favorite flavor of jellybeans is. That's right, jellybeans. She actually asked me about jellybeans. What did she think, I'm running for vice president of a candy factory?

"It's no wonder this country is a mess today. People turn on the news and they hear about jellybeans. And they don't know any better, because the schools are so bad. Half the kids who get a high-school diploma can barely read. How competitive can America be when the only thing these kids are qualified to do is flip burgers? There's no such thing as a fast-food superpower. The country that makes the cars and the electronics and everything else is the country that's the superpower. And pretty soon, that's not going to be us anymore. We're slipping. We're falling behind. And what's Congress doing about it? What's the president doing about? Nothing. Absolutely nothing. They're fiddling, and Rome is burning.

"That's what this is all about, Charlie. That's why Project Vanguard exists. Some people would call us subversives, but we're not. You know what we are? We're patriots. Our system is broken. Democracy isn't working. And, by God, we're going to fix it. We're going to make things right." Constanza looked at his watch. "Is the limo here?"

"In the garage, sir," Donnelly replied.

"Good." Constanza smiled. "Not that I'm particularly eager to get to the airport. I find these campaign trips unbearable. Repeating the same drivel twenty times a day. Shaking hands. Slapping backs. Kissing babies. No wonder why we have no leaders in this country. We run elections like we're choosing TV game-show hosts. Just smile wide, read the cue cards, and you're in. I'm telling you, it's a disgrace." He snapped shut the attaché case. "Okay, finally. Now you've got my undivided attention, Charlie. So what's the crisis of the day?"

"We had some uninvited visitors here last night, General."

Constanza sat down. "What kind of visitors?"

"The Kaminski witness and the reporter."

"You mean that Goodwin guy?"

"Goodman," Donnelly replied, nodding.

"How'd they get in here?" Constanza asked. "Don't we have any security in this place?"

"We do, sir, but they got by us. The guard downstairs thought they were technicians from the repair department. So he let them in."

Constanza frowned. "You've got to be kidding me. Some kid with a walkie-talkie and a flashlight is our only line of defense against intruders?"

"They were on his list, sir. At least Goodman was. Or actually some name he made up."

"Charlie, sit down," Constanza said, pointing to a chair. "I'm not following you, and I'm about to get very angry, so I'd appreciate if you could explain this to me. From the beginning."

"Well," Donnelly said, "I saw these two technicians wandering around last night, looking for Kaminski's office. Naturally, I was suspicious. So I called Security to check it out. They told me these two were on their entry list and all, but I still had them go up to the office to verify. By the time they got there, the technicians were already gone.

"I just had a bad feeling about it, so I brought it up with Alan this morning. That's when I found out what really happened. Turns out Alan got this e-mail from a technician about Kaminski's computer. Some nonsense about needing a new hard drive or something like that. Alan gets all worried that the technician is mentioning Kaminski, so he gives him permission to do the work. Told me he didn't want to raise suspicions.

"The thing Alan didn't realize, which I found out with one phone call, is that the e-mail was a fake. There's no technician by that name. When I had Burt look at the security video this morning, he picked out Goodman right away. And we immediately put two and two together. Goodman sent the e-mail."

Constanza sighed. "I knew Block was wrong for this. He's a bureaucrat to the bone. You drop a paper clip and he jumps." The general leaned back in his chair. "What's the damage here? Was there anything in Kaminski's office for them to find?"

''No, sir. We were very thorough about that on Monday night.''

''Okay, so at least they didn't get anything. I would—''

''They actually did take something from the office, sir, and that worries me.''

''What did they take?''

''The hard drive from Kaminski's computer.''

''Why'd they take that? Was there anything on it?''

''No, we erased everything.''

''Well, could be nothing. But, you know, it's my experience that people only steal valuable things.''

''That's what worries me,'' Donnelly said.

''All right, Charlie, let's assume the worst. That there were still some Project Vanguard documents on the hard drive. Obviously, that would be a disaster for us. We need to respond quickly.''

''Burt and I are looking into—''

''Charlie, whatever you do,'' Constanza said, standing up, ''I want it done now. If we need to eliminate these two, make it happen. That's an order.''

21

☆ ☆ ☆ ☆ ☆

Jon unlocked the front door and flipped on the lights in the foyer.

"How come you have a key to Kenny's apartment?" Karen asked.

"He used to lock himself out about twice a week," Jon replied, closing the door behind them. "So the superintendent started charging Kenny fifty bucks every time he had to send someone out to open the door. That's when I became the designated door opener. Now Kenny calls me at two o'clock in the morning when he gets locked out."

"You know, you're like a big brother to him."

"Sort of," Jon said. "I mean, I'm older than him. But, you know, the truth is, he usually gives me better advice than I give him. He's a smart guy. And not just about computers. That's really just the least of it."

Karen walked into the living room. "This place is kind of Spartan." At one end of the room, there was a futon on the floor. And at the other end, resting on a cardboard box, there was a huge television. Bare white walls provided the backdrop. "Why doesn't he buy himself some furniture?"

Jon shrugged. "I don't know. Kenny is Kenny. He likes it this way, I guess."

"Maybe he can't afford to buy anything."

"Karen, that's definitely not it," Jon said. "He makes more than I do."

"Really?"

"Really. Good programmers make big bucks. And Kenny's one of the best."

"So why does he live this way?" Karen asked.

"Ask him that."

"I don't want to hurt his feelings."

"Karen, you're not going to hurt his feelings. Believe it or not, he's actually proud of the stuff he's got."

She looked around the apartment. "What stuff?"

"Let's see. The two-thousand-dollar TV set. The motorcycle. Oh, yeah. And a couple of snowboards."

"But no furniture," she said.

"He's not into furniture. Or food. You know what the staples of his diet are?"

"What?"

"Fruit Loops, Kraft macaroni and cheese, and Coca-Cola."

"Well, he's certainly unique."

"That's what I'm telling you. Kenny is Kenny."

Jon remembered the first time they'd met. He'd been working on 3-D graphics software at the time. Out of the blue, he received some flame mail from this programmer he didn't know, working on a different project, telling him how totally brain-dead the current version of the software was. It was bloated, slow, ugly, confusing. The list went on and on. Jon sent back a one-line reply: *So how would you make it better?* There was no response for two days. Then, Jon arrived at his office on the third morning, and found some long-haired kid in a tie-dyed T-shirt sleeping on the floor. It smelled like he hadn't bathed in a few days. And, in fact, he hadn't. For two days, Kenny Alden had been programming around the clock, racing to answer Jon's e-mail challenge. Roused from sleep, he presented Jon with a floppy disk. This is ten times better than the stuff you have, he told Jon. But when Jon looked at the software, he disagreed. No, he told Kenny, this is a hundred times better. When he finally got Kenny out of his office, Jon headed straight for TedN, and convinced him to transfer Kenny to his team. They'd been working together ever since.

Kenny was Megasoft at its very best, Jon thought. He had a childlike absorption in the technology. He could spend hours immersed in some programming puzzle, his fingers tapping at the keyboard in staccato bursts of motion. It wasn't a job for him; the money didn't seem to register with him. Jon suspected that Kenny would work at Megasoft for nothing, if he had to. Maybe he would even pay to work there. Megasoft was the center of the software universe, and Kenny wanted to be there. He loved being an insider. He loved knowing JackM personally, going to the JackM review meetings, getting the occasional piece of e-mail from JackM. Malcolm was the high priest of software, all-knowing and all-powerful, and Kenny was a zealous disciple. The business of software held no allure for Kenny. He didn't care about the marketing plans or the quarterly financial numbers. Megasoft wasn't a business for Kenny. Steeped in legend and ritual, it was more like a religion.

The phone rang. Jon checked his watch on the way to the kitchen. Almost midnight. It was probably Kenny. Late as usual.

"Hello."

"Bud, it's me. I'm really sorry. This took a lot longer than I thought."

Jon covered the mouthpiece and whispered "Kenny" to Karen, who had come in from the living room. "So are you leaving now?"

"In a few minutes, if you can wait. Is Karen with you?"

"Karen's here. We can wait. Find anything interesting?"

"Uh-huh. Especially on that *meganet.sys* thing. Pretty incredible, actually. I started to send you e-mail about it a minute ago, then I realized you probably aren't on the system anymore."

"Nah, they canceled my account," Jon said.

"That's what I figured. Anyway, I called the guy in OneWire that EricT knows, and he couldn't tell me anything. As far as he knows, OneWire isn't doing any work with the Center for Technology Policy. So that was a dead end. I couldn't think of anything else to do, so just for the hell of it, I pulled a copy of the latest version of *meganet.sys* off the OneWire server."

"Where'd you get the password for the OneWire server?"

"EricT's friend. He didn't have a problem with it. Well, the source code for *meganet.sys* is like a million lines long, but I just start reading through it. And that's when I found the interesting stuff. It's totally undocumented. I mean, it's completely buried in there. I was lucky to—" Kenny paused. "Jon, hold on."

Jon heard Kenny open his office door and say good night. Then the door snapped shut.

"Sorry," Kenny said. "EricT was heading out. Where was I?"

"The source code for *meganet.sys*. The undocumented stuff."

"Oh, yeah. So I—" Kenny stopped. "Wait, before I forget. I can't believe I didn't tell you this right away. Remember that file from the hard drive? The one with the password?"

"Yeah. Did you get into it?"

"Uh-huh. And I think I know why Kaminski got killed. He was blackmailing Constanza."

"Blackmailing him? With what?"

"This video. Kaminski wanted a million bucks for it."

"What kind of video?" Jon asked.

"I don't know. The memo didn't say. Maybe some kind of kinky sex tape. You know, something that would embarrass Constanza, I guess. But it could be anything. I really have no—" There was some noise in the background. "Got someone at the door again. Wait a sec."

Jon heard Kenny put the phone down and swing the door open. He heard Kenny say, "Hi, what can I do for you?"

Then Jon wasn't sure what he was hearing. There was a crash, a thud. All of a sudden, Kenny was back on the phone screaming, "Jon, help—"

There was a click.

"Kenny!" he shouted into the phone. "Kenny!"

Then all he could hear was a dial tone.

"Jon, what happened?" Karen was saying. "What happened?"

He wasn't listening. He was feverishly dialing Kenny's office.

One ring. Two rings. Three rings.

"C'mon, Kenny, pick up the phone. Pick up the phone."

Four rings. Five rings.

Then the voice mail system answered.

"This is Kenny," the recorded voice said breezily. "You know what to do."

There was a long beep, then complete silence.

"Jon, what is it?"

He let the phone drop to the floor.

"Something happened to him," he said, already on the way to the door. "We've got to get over there."

As soon as they pulled out of the parking lot, Jon saw the green minivan in his rearview mirror.

"What do we do?" Karen asked.

"Hold on," Jon said.

This time of night, the traffic was light. He suddenly spun the steering wheel to the left, sending his little orange car over the double yellow line. The tires squealed as he made a tight U-turn on the wet pavement. Then he floored the accelerator.

Karen was pushed back into her seat. She twisted around to look out the rear window. "I don't think they're—"

And then she watched the minivan make a screeching U-turn of its own.

"Jon, they're behind us!"

"I see, I see," he said, peeking into the rearview mirror.

Karen watched as the minivan gained on them.

"Faster!" she shouted above the roar of the engine.

Jon glanced at the speedometer. He had the gas pedal down all the way, but he couldn't get the needle past 70 mph. It was an old car. He knew he couldn't outrun them.

At the first big intersection, he made a hard right turn. The rear end of the car skidded out. He fought to keep the car on the road.

Now they were on a highway. A blur of brightly lit shopping centers and fast-food restaurants and gas stations and car dealerships were whizzing by them.

The minivan was only a few car lengths behind them.

He eased up on the accelerator.

"Jon, what are you doing?"

He looked in the rearview mirror. All he could see was the front end of the minivan.

Karen was staring into her side mirror. She saw an arm stretch out the passenger window of the minivan. She squinted to see what—

"He has a gun!"

The minivan was just a few feet away.

Jon abruptly jerked the wheel to the right, sliding into the next lane. Then he stomped on the brake pedal with all his weight.

The minivan flew by them on the left.

They skidded to a stop in front of a bank.

Karen pointed to the narrow passage beside the drive-through window. "Go in there," she said.

Jon turned the wheel and tapped on the gas.

The car stalled.

He fumbled to turn the key in the ignition. There was a wheezing sound, but the engine didn't start.

He tried again. Nothing.

"Please," he said, "not now. Not now!"

Karen craned her neck. She could see the minivan turning around.

"They're coming!"

He counted to three, then he twisted the key again.

The engine roared to life.

Jon stepped on the gas, and guided the car past the bank's drive-through window. Now they were in the mostly empty parking lot of a supermarket.

He cut across the lot diagonally, then made a quick left turn into the dark alley behind the supermarket. He weaved around the trucks that were parked at the store's loading docks. At the end of the alley, he made a right, onto a residential street.

When they were deep in the maze of the suburban neighborhood, Karen finally stopped checking her side mirror.

"I think we lost them," she said.

Ten minutes later, they were parking in a used-car lot. Behind the lot, beyond the dense woods, was the Megasoft campus.

Jon turned off the motor, and rested his forehead on the steering wheel.

"Oh my God," he murmured. "Oh my God."

Karen sat there completely frozen, staring straight ahead. She was seriously questioning her own sanity. How had she gotten involved in something like this? That man had a gun. A gun! She was used to getting hung up on. She could get used to getting fired. But getting shot at was something entirely different. It was a matter of life and death. It was just off the scale.

In that moment, she decided that she had to get away. With or without Jon. If he wanted to come, that was fine. But if he didn't, she would leave him behind. She wasn't going to stick around and get killed.

Jon sat back in his seat and slowly exhaled.

He was torn. On one hand, he desperately wanted to find out what had happened to Kenny. On the other hand, he was now more scared than he'd ever been in his entire life. His emotions swung back and forth like a pendulum. Stay. Go. Stay. Go.

"Okay," he finally said, pulling the keys from the ignition.

"Okay what?"

"Let's go find Kenny."

It wasn't the answer she wanted to hear. She didn't say anything.

He waited. And waited.

She said nothing.

"Please," he said, "I need your help." He took her hand. "I need you."

Her head said no. Instantly. It was an easy decision. She'd be crazy to go.

But her heart wasn't so sure. She felt the warmth of Jon's hand. She saw the fear in his eyes. He did need her. How could she abandon him now?

Karen opened the car door and stepped with a soft crunch onto the gravel.

Then, with the flashlight from the glove compartment, they made their way through the trees.

Of the dozens of large square windows in the two-story concrete building, only a handful were lit. The blacktop out front, moistened by a light rain, emptied of cars, glistened in the darkness. The wet air smelled like soil and pine needles. Alone in a corner of the parking lot sat Kenny's silver motorcycle.

They peeked out from behind the trees. It was quiet. They didn't see anyone.

"I don't know," Karen said. "Maybe they're waiting for us. Maybe we shouldn't risk it."

"Karen, I have to go in there. I have to see for myself." He stepped onto the pavement. "You can stay here, if you want," he said, hoping that she wouldn't make him go alone.

She hesitated for a moment, then followed him.

"Thank you," he said, putting his arm around her shoulders.

He headed for the lobby, then remembered that he no longer had a pass card for the door. He veered off the slate path onto the muddy grass.

"Is there another door back there?" Karen asked as they circled around the building.

"No, but that's where Kenny's office is." When they turned the corner, he pointed to the single bright white square amid a long row of black windows on the first floor.

They snaked their way through the shrubs to the base of Kenny's window. Standing on his toes, grabbing onto the windowsill, Jon was just barely able to see into the office.

First he noticed that a can of Coca-Cola had been overturned on the desk, creating a brown puddle on the carpet below. Then he noticed that a bookcase had been toppled, scattering an assortment of programming manuals and cereal boxes. Then he noticed that Kenny was gone.

He smashed his fist against the sealed glass.

"Where is he?" Jon nearly shouted. "What did they do to him?"

"Jon, let's go," Karen whispered. "We shouldn't be here."

"You bastards!" he screamed at the top of his lungs. His voice echoed in the empty courtyard. "I'll kill you! Do you hear me? I'll kill every last one of you!"

Karen grabbed his arm so hard he almost fell over.

"Listen to me," she said. "We're leaving now."

The tears were still streaming down his cheeks as she dragged him back into the woods.

22

☆ ☆ ☆ ☆ ☆

"I'm here all night, so you two take your time," the waitress at Denny's told them when they sent her away for the third time. At one o'clock in the morning, they weren't at Denny's for the pancakes. It was the only place in Woodside that was open late. It was a haven. They were sitting at the back of the restaurant, away from the windows, near the rest rooms. The kind of table nobody wanted. But they'd requested it. They were scared to go home. So they sat there on the orange vinyl seats, under a flickering fluorescent light, clutching each other's hands across the table.

Karen stroked Jon's right hand, which was swollen.

"How does it feel?" she asked. "Maybe we should get some ice for it."

"No, it's fine, really. I just bruised it." He flexed his hand a few times. "That was pretty stupid of me. I'm lucky I didn't break the glass. I don't know what I was thinking."

"You were thinking about your friend."

"If I'd been thinking about him, I never would have let him get involved. All I was thinking about was me. That's why this happened."

"Jon, listen to me. Kenny is an adult. He chose to get involved. You're not responsible for him. You're his friend. You care about him. But you're not his guardian angel."

Jon wasn't listening. Guilt and anger and fear swirled around inside him. He was replaying Kenny's visit the previous night. But this time he sent Kenny away. Didn't tell him anything. He was thinking about Seely and Donnelly and Constanza and all the other faceless conspirators, murderers, terrorists. Whoever they were, whatever the hell they were doing. And he was picturing Kaminski. The rivers of blood. The pallid flesh of death. It felt like a nightmare, and he just wanted to wake up. To rub his eyes and to stretch his arms and to go back to his life. Because this didn't feel like his life at all.

"I hope you don't mind," Karen said, pulling a pack of cigarettes out of her purse. "I really need one of these."

Jon stared at the cigarettes.

"I'm sorry," she said, "are you totally repulsed? I almost never smoke anymore. It's just that—"

"Could I have one?" Jon asked quietly.

"What?"

"Could I have a cigarette, please?"

"*You* smoke?"

Jon looked down and ran a hand through his hair. "No, well, I mean, not for a long time. Not since college."

She handed him a cigarette. "Here I thought I was corrupting you with the moo shu pork," she said, giving him a light.

A faint smile fluttered to his face. "Freshman year in college, I used to go up on the roof of the dorm in the middle of night and smoke. This was in New Hampshire, in the dead of winter. The wind would howl and the snow would blow and I would stand there by myself shivering. I could barely hold on to the cigarette, my hands were so cold. But it was beautiful up there. If it was clear, the stars were incredible. The sky was so black and the stars were so bright. And it was quiet. Absolute silence. Like I was the only one in the world. I'd stay there until the cigarettes ran out or I just got too cold.

"I was so miserable freshman year. My high-school girlfriend went to college in California. At first, we'd call each other every night and just talk and talk. That lasted about a month. Then of course she found someone else. But I couldn't get over it. I couldn't move on. I thought I was going to marry her. I thought she was the only one I'd ever love." He shook his head and smiled. "It's embarrassing how dumb I was. But what do you know when you're eighteen years old?"

He took a long drag on the cigarette, then slowly exhaled. "All through college, I always wanted to be somewhere else. I was there, but I was just going through the motions. I never felt committed. I never felt like I was part of anything. I was an English major, but I didn't have any passion for it. It was just some major. I played lacrosse, but I never got into the whole jock thing. I wasn't a team player. I was always on the outside. Then, I moved out here after college. I knew it was a total fluke that I got the job. I had no idea how long I'd last. But I was determined to make things different. I wanted to care. I wanted to give a hundred percent. And I had to work at it. Because I'd spent so much time not caring, I'd almost forgotten what it was like to be committed to something.

"I'm not saying that every day at Megasoft has been this totally fulfilling experience. There are plenty of things I don't like about Megasoft. But, mostly, I've felt like I've finally found a place I belong. It's a weird place in a lot of ways. A unique place. There are an amazing number of smart people at Megasoft. Starting at the top. I have a lot of respect for Jack Malcolm. What he's accomplished. The way he's still involved in things. Sometimes I get irritated with all the name dropping. JackM said this and JackM did that. But, you know, the truth is, I'm pretty proud that I get to see him on a regular basis."

Jon slid over an ashtray and snuffed out the cigarette. "I'm talking like I still work there," he said, watching the last wisps of smoke curl through the air. "God help me, I don't know what I'm going to do."

The waitress came back for the fourth time. "Made up your minds yet?"

They opened the shiny, plastic-coated menus and surveyed the overly optimistic pictures.

"I'll have the French toast," Jon said.

"Bacon or sausage with that, hon?"

He hesitated for a second. Then, with a little smile at Karen, he said, "Bacon. And I'll take a cup of coffee, too."

"Sounds good," Karen said, handing her menu to the waitress. "I'll have the same."

The waitress finished scribbling on her pad, tucked the menus under the arm of her blue double-knit polyester dress, and headed for the kitchen.

"When you feel like the end is near," Jon said, "you're suddenly a lot less concerned about cholesterol and caffeine."

"Do you really feel like the end is near?"

"A lot more than I did on Monday morning, I'll tell you that." He sat there, playing with the silverware. "I don't know. I don't know what to think."

"I feel like we need to do something," Karen said. "Anything. We can't just sit around waiting for them to come for us."

"How about the stuff we found on the hard drive? What can we do with it?"

"Jon, honestly, I don't think anyone is going to believe us. Even if we had some real evidence, it would still be a pretty wild story. Look, if someone came to me at *Business World* with this story, with absolutely no evidence, I probably wouldn't even bother looking into it. I mean, what's the responsible, journalism-school thing to do? Call up General Constanza and ask whether he has any plans to kill his running mate? No one's going to do that."

Jon nodded. "Should we go to the police about Kenny?"

"We could file a missing-person report or whatever they call it. But what are they going to do? Put his picture on milk cartons? Anyway, it looks like they're already letting Donnelly get away with murder."

Jon thought about Kaminski again, and then about Kenny. He'd been trying not to think about it, but the question kept coming back. "Do you think Kenny's still alive?" he asked.

Karen bit her lip and looked away. "Yes," she finally said, so softly that he could barely hear. "Yes, I do."

"Then we're going to find a way to get him back."

She thought it over. "Okay, let's look at this like a kidnapping. There are two obvious things we need to know. First of all, who are the kidnappers? Who do we negotiate with? And second, what do they want? What will they take in exchange for Kenny?"

"The first part is easy," Jon said. "We're just going to assume it's Constanza and Donnelly and Seely. Now, I don't think that General Constanza himself is holed up somewhere, with a gun to Kenny's head. But I bet he knows about this. I bet Donnelly and

Seely know. So we'll treat them like the kidnappers. We'll deal directly with them."

"I agree," she said. "That makes sense. Now the question becomes, what do we have that they want? What can we trade?"

Jon shrugged. "Us. They want us. But there's no way they're going to take the two of us and let Kenny go."

"No, that won't work."

They sat there in silence. Karen lit another cigarette. Jon absent-mindedly picked up a little plastic container of strawberry jam from the table, and started reading the ingredients.

The waitress set down two cups of coffee.

Jon took a sip. It tasted awful, but he really needed to stay awake. He added some milk, then poured in three packets of sugar. Much better.

"You know," Karen said, "maybe we can learn something from Walter Kaminski."

"What do you mean?"

"Think about what Kenny told you on the phone, about the memo with the password. He said that Kaminski was trying to blackmail Constanza with some kind of video."

"Right."

"Let's assume that's the reason why Donnelly killed Kaminski. To stop him from blackmailing Constanza. Anyway, what I'm getting at is, this video must have been pretty damaging to Constanza."

"True," Jon said.

"Why don't we use the same bargaining chip?" Karen asked. "Why don't we tell them we have the video?"

He put down his coffee. "Karen, aren't you forgetting a couple of things?"

"Like what?"

"Like the fact that we don't know what's on the video."

"They don't know that."

"Or the fact that we don't even have the video."

She blew a stream of smoke toward the ceiling. "You got any better ideas?"

He hated to admit it, but he couldn't think of anything else.

* * *

Jon moved his finger down the names in the phone book. ''Here he is. 'Seely, Burt R.,' on Mercer Island. It has to be the same guy, don't you think?''

''Definitely,'' Karen said. ''It's not like his name is John Smith. There can't be that many.''

He balanced the book on the shelf beneath the pay phone, then took the receiver off the hook. ''You're sure we shouldn't wait?'' he asked, checking his watch. ''It's three o'clock in the morning.''

''Jon, remember, we want to catch them off balance. We want to shake them up. Put some pressure on them.''

Jon nodded, and dialed the number.

''Hello?'' It was a woman's voice, heavy with sleep.

''Burt Seely, please.''

''Who's calling?'' the woman asked, sounding less sleepy and more annoyed.

''Jon Goodman.'' When there was no immediate reply, he added, ''From Megasoft.''

''Oh, from Megasoft,'' she said, as if that made it all right to call at three o'clock in the morning. ''Just a minute.''

Jon heard her muffled explanation. Then he heard a man clear his throat.

''Burt Seely.''

''Mr. Seely, this is Jon Goodman.''

''Mr. Goodman, it's the middle of the night. I hope you have a hell of a good reason for waking me up.''

''I want Kenny Alden back.''

''What? What are you talking about?''

''You heard me. I want Kenny Alden back. I know you have him. And I want him back.''

''Mr. Goodman, I don't know what you're talking about. I don't know who this Kenny Alden is. I have no idea why you're calling me about him. And let me tell you something else, Mr. Goodman. If you ever call me again at home at this hour of the morning, I'm reporting you to the police. This is harassment, and I—''

''We have Kaminski's video.''

"What did you say?" Seely asked.

"I said we have Walter Kaminski's video. And if you don't release Kenny Alden, we're releasing the video."

"Where did you get—" Seely caught himself. "What kind of video are you talking about?"

"The kind that isn't going to be very helpful to Project Vanguard, okay?"

There was a long pause. "Mr. Goodman, I'm thinking maybe we should get together, just the two of us, and talk this through, man to man. What do you say?"

"Let Kenny go. Then we'll talk."

"Mr. Goodman, I'm really not in a position to—"

"Listen to me. You let him go by noon today. Or else the whole world watches that video. Your choice."

"There's no way I can meet that deadline," Seely said. "I need to speak to—"

"I don't care. You have until noon."

"In that case, Mr. Goodman, I'm going to have to get back to you. Where can I reach you?"

"I'll be in touch," Jon said, hanging up.

Friday, October 27

☆ ☆ ☆ ☆ ☆

23

☆ ☆ ☆ ☆ ☆

He'd considered not showing up at all. He knew he was crazy to show his face again on campus. But a phone call wouldn't have been the same. He wanted to look JackM straight in the eye. That was the only way Jon was going to convince him.

Bruce Kroll's girlfriend had let Jon in a side door, so he could avoid the main reception desk in the lobby. He didn't want to meet any Megasoft Security people today. Now he was sitting in her office, waiting for her to clear things with Jack.

He was feeling a little self-conscious. A few discreet sniffs confirmed that he was the source of the unpleasant odor. He smelled like cigarettes and sweat. He'd tried to wash up in the men's room at Denny's, but what he really needed was a hot shower and a change of clothes. There was mud on his jeans and maple syrup on his flannel shirt. On Thursday morning, facing his first full day of unemployment, he had decided not to shave. Now, rubbing his ample stubble, he wished he had. It was a little past ten o'clock in the morning, and he was having trouble keeping his eyes open. But there was no time to sleep.

For years, Jon had wished for this meeting. Daydreamed about it. A one-on-one session with JackM. Over six years, he'd met JackM dozens of times. But never alone. He'd always been part of a group. Sometimes, Jon had been the star presenter, talking JackM through the demo. Answering the technical questions that TedN preferred not to take. But he'd never really conversed with JackM. Never exchanged ideas or even made small talk. Of his peers, Jon didn't know anyone who had. JackM's door was always open. That was the company lore. Any employee could stop by to chat. The reality, though, was that few dared venture over that threshold. Aside from project review meetings, most communication with JackM was conducted through electronic mail.

E-mail was pure communication, unhindered by time-consuming social niceties. You said what you meant in e-mail. It was blunt, direct, telegraphic. There was no subtlety. If you didn't like something, you said so. Unequivocally. *This is brain-dead. This is the stupidest thing I've ever heard.* If your feelings were easily hurt, you didn't last very long at Megasoft. The only concession to nuance in e-mail was the occasional appearance of "emoticons," which were odd little faces cobbled together from punctuation marks. When you tilted your head to the left, :-) was supposed to convey the sender's frivolity, :-(his displeasure, and ;-) his ironic intent.

E-mail at Megasoft was rarely private. A message sent to a single recipient was often forwarded to many others, without the sender's knowledge or permission. To get the discussion started, the forwarder might preface the message with a comment like: *FYI. Personally, I think this whole idea sucks.* Soon, the original sender's mailbox was overflowing with uninvited responses. And the flame war had begun. Full of righteous indignation, the original sender replied en masse to his critics, at the same time broadening the distribution list to include some supporters. As foes and friends replied and forwarded and carbon copied, the boundaries of the battle ever enlarged.

Still, few flame wars lasted more than a single day, which seemed to be the community's collective attention span. After hundreds or even thousands of messages had been sent, passions would subside. Either that, or JackM would intervene. With a terse message like, *Take this off-line,* he could instantly end electronic hostilities. He generally wasn't involved in flame wars, even though the fortunate recipients of his personal messages invariably forwarded them to others. But, then again, no one forwarded JackM's messages with snide comments.

The closest Jon had ever come to an actual conversation with JackM was via e-mail. After the first project review for Hollywood, Malcolm sent e-mail to Jon with a question on some arcane technical point. Jon scrambled to find the answer, and quickly assembled it into a few paragraphs of densely packed information. Within an hour, Jon had JackM's reply: *Okay. Good demo.* Pleased, he e-mailed the reply and his thanks to Kenny Alden, who had helped him research Malcolm's question. Happy to get a secondhand JackM message, Kenny then forwarded it to a few friends, who in turn forwarded it to their friends. By lunchtime, people were patting Jon on the back in the cafeteria. *Way to go, Jon. Very cool, dude.* For a few days, the entire Hollywood team basked in the reflected glory.

This was not the meeting with JackM that Jon had long hoped for. In his daydreams, Jon was summoned to Malcolm's office unexpectedly. *Son, I've had an eye on you,* Malcolm would begin. He'd review Jon's many contributions to the corporation, including Jon's successful stewardship of the Hollywood project. Then he'd explain that Megasoft was facing a stiff challenge in a particular area, and he needed a savvy manager to head up the company's efforts. Would Jon be his man? Rehearsing the scene, Jon had decided that he would pause contemplatively for a moment, appearing to carefully weigh the decision. Then he would—

"Jon?"

He opened his eyes. It was Carol, Bruce Kroll's girlfriend.

"Jack's free now."

"Thanks." He felt a little unsteady on his feet when he got up. He was angry at himself for dozing off. He wanted to be sharp, clearheaded, in control. But he was feeling groggy. This was going to be a disaster, he told himself.

He tried to keep his head down as he followed Carol to Malcolm's office. Every open doorway on the long corridor seemed to harbor a potential threat. He just needed to—

"There's Goodman," he heard a loud voice say.

He froze. What should he do? Run? Which way?

Then he felt a hand on his back, and he turned to see two marketing guys he'd worked with on Astro, the project before Hollywood.

"Dude," one of them said, "long time, no see."

"Hey, Kevin," Jon said, trying not to seem surprised. He shook hands with them, and noticed that his hand was shaking. "Mike, man, how's it going?"

"Just the same old. You know how wretched the life of a poor marketing slime is. How's by you?"

So they hadn't heard, Jon realized.

"Nothing too exciting," he said, backing away from them. He gestured to Carol. "I'm late for this meeting, but we should do lunch sometime."

Kevin laughed. "Do lunch sometime," he repeated derisively. "Mike, do you think he's blowing us off or what?"

"I'll call you," Jon said, following Carol down the hall. "I promise."

JackM's office looked larger than Jon remembered. In the past, it had always been filled to capacity with people. Now it was empty, except for Malcolm, who was sitting at a little computer table behind his plate-glass desk. With his back to the door, facing a floor-to-ceiling window with a panoramic view of the Cascades, he sat staring at a computer monitor.

"Am I interrupting?" Jon asked, as he walked the considerable distance from the door to Malcolm's desk.

There was no reply. Malcolm was typing, banging on the keys with such force that the table quivered.

Jon stood at one of the chairs in front of Malcolm's desk. A long minute went by.

"Jack, is this a bad time?"

Without turning around, without missing a keystroke, Malcolm said, "Have a seat. I just want to finish this."

"Sure, no problem," Jon said. He was surprised to see that Malcolm's desk was covered with paper. Piles and piles of it. At project review meetings, there was rarely more than a mug of coffee on the desk. JackM was famous for working without notes.

Finally, Malcolm swiveled around in his tall, leather-backed chair. He was wearing a denim shirt and a Western-style string tie. He immediately pulled off his reading glasses, which Jon hadn't seen before.

"So there's no misunderstanding," Malcolm began, "I want to tell you straight off that I'm not going to overrule TedN on personnel matters. TedN runs the show in his division, and he makes the decisions. I'm not going to start second-guessing him. That's not how I treat my managers. If you made this appointment hoping to get your job back, I'm telling you right now, you're wasting your time. You clear on that?''

Jon nodded. He knew he had to interrupt at some point, to say what he had to, but for now it was easier to listen.

''Let me give you some advice, Jon. How old are you? Twenty-six, twenty-seven?''

''Twenty-eight.''

''Fine, twenty-eight. The point is, you're just starting out. You've got a lot of years ahead of you. If I were you, I'd take this as a learning experience. Look, there's no way around it. You screwed up. I'm sure you know that. So learn from it. You're a smart guy, and now you know you have a weakness in the people skills department. So fix it. Take some courses. Read some books. You can learn this stuff. And, this way, the next time you run into a situation like that, you don't just fly off the handle. You have a strategy. You have some knowledge behind you. That's the way to go.''

Jon found himself agreeing. Listening to Malcolm, he almost believed that he had done something wrong. A minor offense, to be sure. And he should have known better. But now JackM was absolving him. Sending him off to say ten Hail Mary's. Jon wished that it could be so simple.

Malcolm leaned forward, ready to get up. ''Well, I've got a pretty full calendar today, Jon. If that's all—''

''No,'' Jon said. ''I, uh—'' He wasn't sure where to start. ''I'm not here about my job. About getting fired. I mean, it's related to that. It's the reason for it, really.'' He stopped again. ''I'm sorry, I'm not making much sense. I didn't get any sleep last night.''

''Take your time,'' Malcolm said, sitting back. ''No rush.''

''Jack, there's something going on that you need to know about.'' Jon couldn't think of any other way to say what he had to, so he said it directly. ''Peter Constanza is trying to kill you.''

''He's what?'' Malcolm asked incredulously.

''Trying to kill you. He was behind the assassination attempt.''

24

☆ ☆ ☆ ☆ ☆

''What did he say?'' Karen asked, before Jon had even closed the car door.

''Not that much,'' Jon said, sliding behind the wheel. ''He mainly asked questions. Who Kaminski was. Who he worked for. Why the police weren't investigating the murder. That kind of thing. And about Constanza and Project Vanguard. What proof we had. To tell you the truth, I have no idea whether he believed me or not. He seemed to listen pretty carefully. He even took notes, which I'd never seen him do before. But, for all I know, he might have thought I was a raving lunatic. I didn't show him any evidence. All I had was a wild story.''

''How did you leave it?''

Jon shrugged. ''He said he'd look into it. Starting with Kaminski, I guess. And I told him that I'd let him know if we found anything else. Like Kaminski's video. He asked me what I thought Kaminski was blackmailing Constanza with. I told him that without seeing the video, it was impossible to know. And that's really how we left it. He told me to stay in touch. Let him know where we were. Which I guess is a good sign. Or maybe it's not. Maybe he was just trying to get me out of the office.''

''Jon, c'mon, you did the best you could. If something happened to Malcolm, and you had never even tried to warn him, you wouldn't forgive yourself. So you did what you had to. Now it's up to him.''

''But if he doesn't believe me, he's not going to do anything about it.''

"Okay, say he doesn't believe you. Thinks you're a total nut. I bet even then you've planted a seed of doubt about Constanza. Because now if Malcolm runs across something out of the ordinary, he's going to remember this. And that's worth a lot."

Jon wasn't so sure. He felt like he'd botched the assignment. He hadn't convinced Malcolm. He hadn't accomplished anything. But he didn't want to think about the meeting anymore. JackM was going to have to take care of himself. Kenny Alden, though, was another story. Kenny was depending on him, and Jon didn't want to screw up again.

He started the engine, and shifted into reverse.

"Where to?" Karen asked.

"We need to find a phone."

"Burt Seely's office."

"This is Jon Goodman. I'd like to speak to Burt Seely." He closed the door of the phone booth to block out some of the road noise.

"What's this in reference to, Mr. Goodman?"

"I think he'll know why I'm calling."

"Just a moment."

Jon was trying to figure out what to do if Seely insisted on proof. If he wanted to see a copy of the video before he made any deals.

"Mr. Goodman?"

"Yes."

"This is Burt Seely. I'm afraid I need some more time. Preferably another day. I'm just not able to move on this as fast as—"

"I'm not negotiating. You can't have another day. You can't have another hour. You release Kenny or we release the video. Those are the options."

"I understand that, Mr. Goodman. And, honestly, if there were any way for me to speed up this process, I—" There was a muffled voice in the background. "Mr. Goodman, let me put you on hold a minute."

Listening to the canned music, Jon felt uneasy. Were they trying to trace the call? How long would that take to do? The phone booth, with its glass walls, made him feel especially vulnerable. He was at a gas station, at the corner of a busy intersection. He felt like an easy target. But they'd be crazy to try anything here, he told himself. There were cars and people everywhere. A hundred witnesses. He looked over at Karen, who was sitting in the orange Volkswagen. She raised her eyebrows. He shrugged. He didn't know what was happening.

Then Seely was back on the line.

"Mr. Goodman?"

"I'm still here."

"I'll meet you at your apartment at three o'clock."

"What?"

"Your apartment at three o'clock. Be there." Suddenly, Seely wasn't sounding very obsequious.

How stupid did Seely think he was? It was obviously a trap. "No, I don't think so," Jon replied. "We can talk on the phone just fine."

"If you want your little reunion, Mr. Goodman, you'll be there at three."

Jon didn't like Seely's tone of voice. "Hey, Burt. Listen up. I don't think you're in a position to make any demands. Unless you want to be watching that video on the six o'clock news."

"Mr. Goodman, I'm very busy right now. I don't have time for this. I'll see you at three."

"No you won't. That's not acceptable."

"You know what, Mr. Goodman? I really don't care what you think is acceptable or not. I'll see—"

"Hello?" Jon shouted into the phone. "Hello? Are you listening to me? Because it sure sounds like you're forgetting that we have the video and we're prepared to—"

"Mr. Goodman, you don't have squat. And you don't have a choice. You be there at three and we'll talk."

Then Seely slammed down the phone.

25

☆ ☆ ☆ ☆ ☆

"Jon, please, don't do it," Karen pleaded. "Don't go in there."

They were parked across the street from Jon's apartment complex, which looked like most of the other rental properties in suburban Woodside. Winthrop Square had six low-rise buildings with outdoor stairwells.

"No, Seely is right," Jon said wearily. "I don't have a choice. I don't have anything to bargain with. They know I don't have the video. Kenny probably told them."

"Jon, don't you see? He's bluffing. He can't know for sure whether you have the video, no matter what Kenny says. The minute you walk in there, you're eliminating any doubt."

"Karen, nothing's going to happen. We talked this over already. First of all, you're staying out here. So you'll be safe. And I'm not going in there alone. I'll do it just the way I said. I'll tell the guy in the rental office that I got locked out. So he'll go with me. Look, I bet I can even think of some excuse to get the superintendent to go, too. I'll say there's a flood. So they'll both be my witnesses. I'm telling you, there's no way Seely will take a chance and try something in broad daylight with all those people around."

Karen shook her head. "You're tired, Jon. You're not thinking clearly. And you're making a big mistake."

She's probably right, Jon thought as he got out of the car.

* * *

Walking to the rental office, it occurred to Jon that he'd been planning to move from Winthrop Square for about five years now. He'd found the apartment on his first day at Megasoft, signed a lease on the spot, and lived there ever since. There was really nothing wrong with the apartment. It was a decent size for a one-bedroom. Except for the year when he had a neighbor whose musical tastes ran to heavy metal, it was pretty quiet. And it was convenient to Megasoft. Driving leisurely, the commute took about seven minutes. Late for a meeting, Jon could make the trip in under five. So there was no great pressure to move. Jon just felt as if he should. But, somehow, he never got around to it.

Every few weeks, he methodically went through the listings in the Sunday paper, circling the most promising ones. Then, feeling as if he'd accomplished something, as if he'd taken an important first step, he put the paper down and resolved to make the calls on Monday. But he never called. On Monday, he was too busy. There was always a spec to write. Or a JackM review to prepare. Or a job candidate to interview. And by Friday, he was too tired. It had been a long week and he wasn't going to waste Saturday apartment hunting. So the weeks turned into months. And the months into years. And, six years later, he was still living at Winthrop Square.

It was the same with the painting class. For about four years, Jon had been meaning to sign up for one. He'd always wanted to learn how to paint with watercolors. There was something about the vibrancy of the colors that attracted him. At the beginning of every academic semester, he picked up a catalog from the local adult-ed center and folded down the pages with the painting classes. Sometimes, he went as far as filling out the registration form. But he never registered. He intended to. He planned to. He promised to. But he didn't. Instead, when the deadline had safely passed, he vowed to sign up next semester. Eight semesters later, though, Jon still didn't know how to paint with watercolors.

Work expands to fill the available time, and Jon's work at Megasoft had expanded to fill his life. It was an easy, all-purpose excuse for not doing other things. When he wasn't actually working, he was going to work, preparing for work, thinking about work, recovering from work. Virtually everyone Jon knew worked at Megasoft. When he got together with them, wherever they went, whatever they did, they inevitably talked about work. It was what they had in common. And for Jon, increasingly, it was all he knew. Megasoft defined the boundaries of his world. It was as if he had moved to another country, with its own language and customs and history. There were no rules against spending time with foreigners. It was just easier to spend time with people who spoke the language.

Now, walking through Winthrop Square, Jon found it hard to believe that six years had passed since he'd moved in. It didn't seem like that long. What had he been doing for six years? He wondered whether he had squandered precious time. For years, he had been delaying, deferring. A wife, a family, a house, a life. He had assumed that there would always be time. Years and years. Now, suddenly, he found himself measuring the future in minutes. Opening the door to the rental office, he had a feeling that he wouldn't be living at Winthrop Square much longer.

"Thanks," Jon said as the rental agent unlocked the apartment door. "Sorry to make you walk over here. I really appreciate it." He checked his watch. It was a few minutes past three.

It was just the two of them. The superintendent was out to lunch, so Jon shelved the flood story. Anyway, he hadn't been exactly sure how he was going to explain the miraculous evaporation of the water. Instead, Jon mentioned that the apartment needed a fresh coat of paint. The rental agent, a heavyset man who always had an open box of donuts on his desk, reluctantly agreed to have a look.

Jon gingerly pushed open the door, not knowing what to expect. He reached inside to flip the light switch.

"I think the bathroom is probably in the worst condition," he said in a loud voice, just to have something to say. If there were unexpected visitors inside, he wanted them to know he wasn't alone.

From the foyer, Jon didn't see anyone. It was quiet. With the rental agent close behind, he headed down the hall to the bathroom. He turned on the light.

"You see, near the sink and around the tub," he said from the hallway, while peering over his shoulder into the bedroom.

"The painters do closets, right?" Jon called out, walking into the bedroom and pulling open the closet door. There was no one lurking.

The decor in Jon's apartment was decidedly eclectic. Over six years, he'd assembled the kind of variety usually associated with tag sales. In the bedroom, the night table was Mission-style, the dresser Colonial, and the bookcase plywood-and-concrete-block.

Jon walked back down the hall, leaving the rental agent to inspect the bedroom. "You know, the kitchen really isn't in such great shape either," he said, turning on the overhead lights. It was empty. Just the same stack of dirty dishes he'd left unwashed on Thursday morning.

Heading for the living room, Jon tried to think of a reason for the rental agent to stay longer. It was only five past three. Who knew when Seely would show up? And now that Jon thought about it, he didn't know what he was going to do to keep the rental agent around when Seely did show up. Karen was right. This whole thing was incredibly stupid. He was tired and he was making mistakes.

Jon changed his mind. He wasn't staying. He'd walk out with the rental agent, get back into the car, and drive away. He was a fool to have come.

"The living room is fine," Jon called to the rental agent, who was in the kitchen. "The painters won't need to—" He stopped. Out of the corner of his eye, Jon thought he saw something in the living room. The high back of a sofa blocked his view. With the blinds closed, the room was dark. And the light switch was on the other side of the room. Jon froze, waiting for the rental agent to catch up to him.

"I guess it would help if we had some light in here," he said when the rental agent came around the corner. Jon plunged into the darkness, making his way to the light switch. He braced himself and flipped the switch.

In the first few seconds, he saw nothing. The room was as he had left it. Some magazines piled on the coffee table. All the pillows on the sofa pushed to one side. Everything seemed to be in order. Then Jon lowered his eyes, and caught a glimpse of something through the wood frame of the coffee table. He took a step toward the center of the room.

That was when he could clearly see two bare feet, toes pointing in the air, between the coffee table and the sofa. He took two more steps, and saw who was sprawled on the carpet.

Wearing a pair of torn jeans, naked from the waist up, with a belt around his left arm and a syringe in his right hand, it was—

"Kenny," he whispered.

There was no reply.

"Kenny!"

There was no movement.

Jon shoved aside the coffee table with such force that it toppled over on its side. He knelt on the carpet beside his friend.

"Kenny, can you hear me?"

He grabbed Kenny's shoulders. The skin was pale and cold.

"C'mon, wake up!" he pleaded. "Kenny, wake up!"

Kenny stared at the ceiling. A thin line of dark blood trickled from his left arm.

Jon let go of Kenny's shoulders. The head rolled slightly to the right, so that the lifeless eyes now looked up at Jon.

"No!" Jon wailed. "No!"

Kenny's unblinking eyes stared at him unmercifully, accusing him, reproaching him. How could you let this happen to me?

"I'm sorry, Kenny," he babbled. "I'm so sorry."

Jon felt hot. He was sweating. He stood up and the room began to spin around him. He had to get outside. To the fresh air. It was too hot in here. Too hot.

He had the sensation that his own body was leaving him. He felt himself floating away, and he saw his body left behind below. Now he was watching the whole scene from high above. He saw himself standing over Kenny's lifeless form. Touching Kenny's cold, cold skin. Then, gradually, the picture he was seeing got smaller and smaller. Fuzzier and fuzzier. He fought to keep the picture in focus. But it kept fading and fading. Slipping away. And then the picture was black.

"Jon? Can you hear me?"

Jon opened his eyes. He squinted. It was bright. He was looking up at Karen. He moved his hands and rubbed against the carpet. He was lying on the floor.

"How do you feel?"

He tilted his head a bit to the left and saw the underside of a table. His coffee table, he thought. There was a lot of activity going on around him. Lots of shoes moving past his head.

"Jon?"

He wondered why he was lying there. His head hurt. Everything seemed kind of hazy. He'd gone to meet Seely. He was walking around with the rental agent. Then, then—

"Kenny," he said, rolling his head to the left. Through the legs of the table, he saw Kenny, waxy and motionless.

"No, no," Karen said, putting her hand in front of Jon's eyes. "You don't want to see that."

Jon looked back at her. "What happened to me?"

"The guy from the rental office said you passed out. He's the one who called the ambulance." She brushed Jon's hair away from his forehead. "You have quite a bump here."

He lifted his hand and touched his forehead. It hurt. "How did I get this?"

"From the table."

The thought of his head hitting the wood table made him feel queasy. He tried to sit up, but a hand held him back.

"Not so fast, big fella," said a voice he didn't recognize. "Why don't you just take it easy down there for a minute." He looked to his right and saw a ruddy-faced man with a mustache. A paramedic in a blue windbreaker. Then the man was talking to Karen, as if Jon couldn't hear. "Well, he's around pretty quickly. Doesn't sound like he was out for very long. That's a good sign. Chances are, he came in here, saw the body, and just fainted. The only thing to worry about is that he conked his head on the table on the way down. So, just to be safe, we're going to take him over to the hospital, and let them check him out for a concussion."

Saw the body and fainted. Jon repeated that to himself. He was having trouble concentrating. The body? Kenny's body? As the mental fog lifted, he found himself doubting what he'd just seen.

"Karen?"

She was kneeling beside him. "Feel a little better?"

"A little." Jon tried to focus, to collect his thoughts. "Karen, is Kenny—" He stopped. He couldn't bring himself to say the word.

Karen looked at him, her eyes welling with tears. She nodded, almost imperceptibly.

Jon began to cry. Then he shut his eyes tight, wanting desperately for this nightmare to end.

26

☆ ☆ ☆ ☆ ☆

"Mr. Goodman, looks like you were pretty lucky," the doctor said, examining the X-ray.

Jon was sitting on a gurney in a curtained-off area of the emergency room. He was holding Karen's hand, which felt warm and reassuring.

"No skull fracture here, as far as I can tell," the doctor continued. "When the radiologist comes in tonight, he'll double-check, but I don't think he's going to find anything." He took one last look, then pulled the X-ray from the light box.

"As I said, this kind of thing can be pretty frightening for the patient, but really, medically, it's not a huge deal. I'd like to keep you here overnight for observation, but that's because you hit your head, not because of the fainting. This is a classic case of what we call vasovagal syncope, which translated into everyday language—"

Jon wasn't listening. He couldn't stop thinking about Kenny. One sickening image haunted him. The unmoving body. The cold gray skin. And the piercing, blaming eyes. He must have hated me in the end, Jon thought. Reviled me. I was his friend, and I let this happen to him.

Jon's eyes welled with tears. He bit his lip. He didn't want to cry. Not here. Not now. He had to get a grip. He had to think clearly, or else they were going to kill him, too.

"You're sure he doesn't have a concussion?" Karen was asking.

"He's definitely doing fine now," the doctor replied, "but we need to watch him. That's the only way to be certain. So he'll stay the night, and if there are no problems, he'll be out of here first thing in the morning. Good as new.'' He patted Jon on the shoulder, and turned to go.

But Jon didn't want to spend the night. He'd be a sitting duck for Seely and the others. ''You know, actually,'' he said, ''I'd prefer to go home now. I think I'd get a lot more rest that way.''

''I really wouldn't recommend that, Mr. Goodman,'' the doctor said. ''Why take the chance? We're talking about one night. They'll take you upstairs, you can watch some TV if you want, put your feet up and relax. If you're feeling okay in the morning, they'll discharge you at eight. Honestly, I'd advise you to—''

''Thanks, but I'm going to pass. I'll be—''

''Jon,'' Karen said, ''I agree with him. You really should—''

''Karen, I'll just feel more—''

''You know,'' the doctor said, edging toward the curtain, ''why don't I let you two discuss this. I'll be right back. But, Mr. Goodman, if you want my advice, if it were me, I'd spend the night. It's your—''

The curtain was jerked open, and a bald man in a rumpled plaid sport jacket walked in. ''Forgive me for eavesdropping, but if I were you, Mr. Goodman, I'd listen to the doctor. Because I'm going to give you a choice. You can spend the night in the hospital or you can spend the night in jail.''

''Excuse me, who are you?'' the doctor asked. ''This is a private area.''

The man pulled out a badge. ''Detective Vic Oppenheim, Woodside PD. If you're finished in here, doctor, I have some questions for Mr. Goodman.''

The doctor glared at Oppenheim, but didn't protest. ''If you decide to stay over, Mr. Goodman, have one of the nurses find me.'' Then he was gone.

Oppenheim looked at Karen. ''Ma'am, if you don't mind, I'd like to speak to Mr. Goodman alone.''

''Actually, since you ask, I do mind. And, what's more, I don't think this is an appropriate time to bother Mr. Goodman with questions. He's had a pretty serious injury, and—''

''I'm sorry,'' Oppenheim interrupted, ''I didn't get your name, ma'am.''

"Karen Grey, *Business Wo*—" She caught herself. "I'm a journalist."

He stared at her for a few seconds, then made the connection. "Are you the Karen Grey I read about in the *Chronicle* yesterday?"

"Yes, I am."

"I see." He pulled out his notepad and started writing. "And, Ms. Grey, what's your relation to Mr. Goodman?"

"I'm a friend. What's this about, anyway?"

Oppenheim finished making a note and looked up. "I have no objection to your staying, Ms. Grey. But I'm the one asking the questions. This is official police business, ma'am. As a member of the press, I'm sure you understand what that means."

"I wouldn't want to interfere with your official business," Karen said coolly, "but I think Mr. Goodman is entitled to know why he's being questioned."

"He's being questioned, Ms. Grey, although I've yet to have the opportunity to ask him a single question, because someone died from a drug overdose in his apartment. And considering that our search of the crime scene turned up a rather considerable quantity of controlled substance, I think Mr. Goodman has some serious explaining to do. In your professional opinion, Ms. Grey, wouldn't you agree?"

Karen ignored the sarcasm. "What kind of controlled substance?"

"Heroin. But I think you haven't been listening. Because I told you that if you wanted to stay—"

"This is crazy," Jon said. "Heroin? You've got to be—"

"Jon," Karen said, "don't say another word. You're not talking to this guy without a lawyer present."

Oppenheim turned around and yanked closed the white curtain. Then he moved closer to them.

"Look," he said, lowering his voice to barely more than a whisper, "you don't have to tell me anything. That's your right. But I think you need my help, Mr. Goodman. And I could certainly use yours."

Jon and Karen exchanged glances. Where was Oppenheim going with this?

"You think I don't remember you?" the detective asked Jon. "I know who you are. You called me Tuesday morning with that wild story. Like I told you then, I thought you were kidding me. A buddy of mine on the Seattle force is always messing with me that way. So I didn't give it another thought.

"Then, Tuesday afternoon, I get a call from Jerry Hayes at Megasoft. Totally out of the blue. Hadn't talked to him in years. When he was a cop in Woodside, he never gave me the time of day. Now, all of a sudden, he's my pal, asking how my kids are doing, how's my golf game. And, the whole time, I'm asking myself, what's he really calling me for? Then he just happens to bring up your name. Jonathan Goodman. And suddenly I realize that maybe it wasn't a joke after all.

"Well, Jerry launched into this whole convoluted explanation of why I shouldn't pay any attention to you. The whole thing was ridiculous. It was classic Jerry. He always thought he was a lot smarter than the rest of us. Like he was too good for police work or something.

"Anyway, he got me curious about this thing. So when I hung up the phone, I went downstairs and looked over the logbook. And, sure enough, there's a call at 1:49 in the morning on Tuesday from Megasoft. Possible shooting. Two cars dispatched. Then, three minutes later, there's a second call from Megasoft, saying it was all a big mistake. Just some kids shooting water pistols. So the two cars were recalled.

"I didn't know what to think, and I was too busy on Tuesday and Wednesday to look into it any further. But yesterday I had some time, so I decided I'd talk to whoever made that call from Megasoft on Tuesday morning. But when I went to check the logbook again, I couldn't find the entry. It hadn't been crossed out or whited out or even ripped out. This is a bound book I'm talking about, not a looseleaf binder. And the entry was gone. It simply didn't exist anymore. Someone had rewritten a hundred pages by hand just so that entry wouldn't be there. Very strange."

Oppenheim's story was starting to sound depressingly familiar to Jon. Tantalizing clues and vanishing evidence. But maybe Oppenheim could help them. At least he might believe them.

"I tried to call you today at work, Mr. Goodman," the detective said. "And that's when I found out you'd been fired. Then, not two hours later, I'm standing over a corpse in your living room. A textbook overdose. And then I'm finding a stash of heroin. A textbook drug seizure. But you know what? I'm not as stupid as Jerry Hayes thinks. The only place you find textbook examples is in a textbook. It was all too perfect. I mean, we couldn't find any fingerprints on the belt around this kid's arm. He wasn't wearing rubber gloves. In fact, I couldn't find a single glove in the whole apartment. So how'd he tighten the belt without touching it? And there were no prints on the bag of heroin he supposedly opened. That doesn't happen in the real world. No way."

Listening to Oppenheim talk, Karen felt increasingly optimistic. They'd found a friend, she thought. They'd found someone they could trust.

"Like I said before," Oppenheim continued, "you don't have to talk to me. I'm going to investigate this, with or without your help. But I have a feeling you know a lot more about this than I do. And it sure would be a lot easier if I started off by knowing what you know."

With one quick look at each other, Jon and Karen instantly decided to tell Oppenheim everything. It was their only hope. They took turns narrating as Oppenheim scribbled copious notes.

When he finished writing, Oppenheim looked up and shook his head in astonishment. "Jeez, this is incredible." He paged through his notes. "Let me make sure I understand this. You say your friend Kenny was able to look at the pass card records, and that's how you're sure the killer was this guy Donnelly?"

"That, and the fact that I recognized him when I saw him Wednesday night," Jon replied.

"And Donnelly works for Peter Constanza?"

Karen nodded. "I called the Center for Technology Policy, and they told me that his title is senior analyst, reporting directly to General Constanza "

Oppenheim made one last note, then tucked his pad into his jacket. He pulled a card out of his pocket and wrote a number on the back. "That's my home phone," he said, handing the card to Jon. "I want you to call me there tomorrow."

"So I'm free to go?" Jon asked.

"Actually, you're under arrest," Oppenheim said.

Jon's jaw dropped.

"I'm sorry, but with all that heroin in your apartment, I have to arrest you. That's the law."

"Wait," Karen said, "but—"

Oppenheim held up his hand. "Now, I have to go out front and make a phone call. I'm leaving you here on your honor. Understand?"

He jerked open the white curtain.

"You two take care of yourselves," he whispered before walking away.

"Are you sure you're up to driving?" Karen asked before handing back Jon's keys.

"I'm fine," he said. Actually, he felt a little lightheaded, but he couldn't tell whether it was from hitting his head or lack of sleep.

It was already rush hour when they pulled out of the hospital parking lot. For once, Jon was pleased to see so many cars on the road. Maybe all the traffic would make his bright orange convertible less conspicuous. He drove the few blocks to the highway with one eye on the rearview mirror. No sign of the green minivan from last night.

"How long a drive is it to Snowdon Falls?" Karen asked.

"Probably about an hour," he said, merging onto the highway, "if the traffic isn't too bad."

Karen looked at her watch. Almost six o'clock. She tried to figure out how many hours she'd been awake, but doing the arithmetic made her even more drowsy. She hadn't slept at all Thursday night, and Wednesday night she'd gotten just a couple of hours of sleep. No wonder why she was so tired.

"Think we can trust Oppenheim?" Jon asked.

"I hope so. I mean, he wouldn't have let you go if he were working for them."

"True."

"I'm more afraid that one lone cop isn't going to be able to do much. But at least it feels like we have someone on our side now."

They were crawling along, bumper to bumper. There was a sea of red taillights ahead. Jon was having trouble keeping his eyes open. It felt warm in the car. He rolled down his window a few inches.

Karen turned on the radio.

"—shocked coworkers at Megasoft," the announcer was saying. "They say the twenty-one-year-old programmer had no history of drug use. The occupant of the apartment, Jonathan Goodman, a former Megasoft employee, is wanted by the police for questioning in connection with the fatal overdose. In other news—"

Jon was instantly wide awake. "Can you believe this? They won't let me alone."

"That's why we have to get out of here," Karen said. "It's only going to get worse."

Sitting there in the middle of a traffic jam, Jon had the feeling that the whole world was watching him. The drug dealer who killed his best friend. He slid down in his seat, willing himself to be invisible.

27

☆ ☆ ☆ ☆ ☆

"Did you get Malcolm?" Karen asked, when she was out of the shower. She was wearing a white terry robe with a Snowdon Lodge logo on the pocket.

Jon was lying on the bed. "No, he was already gone for the day, so I just left a message. I said he could reach us here at the hotel until tomorrow midday. After that, we probably weren't going to be in Snowdon."

"Well, I feel a little better," Karen said. "At least someone knows where we are now. If they come spirit us away in the middle of the night, maybe Malcolm will send someone after us." She walked over to the glass door that opened onto a ground-floor terrace. She watched the Snowdon River race by, in the final yards before its dizzying drop to the bottom of Snowdon Falls. There was a steady, soothing roar as the water made the 270-foot trip down ragged rock. A cloud of mist, illuminated by floodlights, rose from the falls in the darkness.

"I think we're pretty safe for tonight," Jon said. "We're out in the boondocks, the middle of nowhere. This definitely isn't the first place they're going to look for us."

He lay on his back, staring at the ceiling, thinking about Kenny Alden. He'd seen the body, he knew Kenny was dead, but it still seemed unreal. He didn't want to believe it. Death was for old people. Like relatives who lived far away, who you never knew very well anyway. It was for strangers. Like Walter Kaminski, or the unfamiliar names in the obituary column. It was sad and sobering and completely abstract. It was only a vague, inadequate preview of the death of someone you cared about. He realized that, until now, he had never lost anyone he cared about. Facing this first loss, he found his emotions unpleasantly selfish. The grief he felt was not as much for Kenny as it was for himself. Jon thought about all the small ways that their lives had become intertwined. Kenny had been more than just a friend to Jon. He had been a soul mate, an alter ego. Jon had grown up without siblings, so he wasn't sure how it felt to have a brother. In Kenny, though, he thought he had come as close to having a brother as he ever would. Now that brother was gone, and there was a gap in Jon's life, an empty space that he rubbed against like a missing front tooth.

Karen sat down next to him on the bed and gently touched his forehead. "How does it feel?"

"Not bad. It looks worse than it is."

"You don't feel dizzy or anything like that, do you? The doctor said that was one of the symptoms of a concussion."

"No, I feel fine."

"You heard him say that you're not supposed to take any aspirin for forty-eight hours, right?"

"Yes."

"You know, there's a gift shop in the lobby. I bet I can get you some Tylenol or something like that, if you want. He said Tylenol was okay. Maybe you'll feel better."

"I don't want any Tylenol."

She nodded. "Well, why don't I let you rest?" She started to get up, but Jon reached out for her hand.

"Wait, could you just sit here with me for a while?"

"Sure."

He held her hand on his chest. He watched her watching him, and he tried to think of the right words. Some way of explaining, connecting. He struggled against the silence, but none of the words felt right.

Minutes passed. Then, gradually, his mind quieted, and the words slipped away, and he was content to watch her watching him.

Her hair was still wet, and it glistened in the light. She smelled like coconut shampoo. Her lips were soft and pink and full. When their eyes met, he pulled her toward him, and pressed his lips against hers.

He kissed her hungrily, breathlessly, as his hands wandered her velvety skin. She broke off the kiss to open up her robe, and then he felt her against him, warm and naked and alive.

In the moonlight, Karen quietly slid out of bed and sat in a chair by the window. She glanced at the red numbers on the desk clock. 3:07. Jon was sleeping peacefully, and she watched his chest slowly rise and fall with each breath. The sheet had slipped off his bare shoulders. One of his arms snugly encircled his pillow, while the other reached out to Karen's side of the bed.

She was remembering how it felt to be enveloped by him, momentarily melding two bodies as one. She felt exhilarated. And uncertain. She was suspicious of her own feelings. They had been thrown together by chance. Would the attraction last only as long as the danger?

The danger. Karen felt a chill, and pulled her knees tight against her chest. She thought about Kenny. He was just a kid, murdered in cold blood. It was senseless, depraved. What kind of animals were they dealing with? If Constanza were really involved in this, the man must be a psychopath. He clearly would do anything to get his way. And if he could control armies of terrorists, if he could murder his way to the White House, how could Karen and Jon escape? Where would they go? Who would help them?

Karen considered the possibilities. She knew only a handful of people in Seattle, none well enough to rely on now. Her closest friends were in New York, but she was hesitant to involve them. Jon had gotten his friend involved, and look what had happened to Kenny. Her parents, who lived in Miami, would help in any way they could, she knew. But that would be the first place Seely's men would look. No, better that her parents knew nothing. She decided that Oppenheim was really their best hope. Maybe their only hope. And she still wasn't sure whether they could even trust him.

She was feeling sleepy again, so she crawled back into bed. As she drifted off to sleep, one more name popped into mind. It was an unlikely choice, the oddest of comrades, but she didn't care. He owed her, so maybe he would help.

Saturday, October 28

☆ ☆ ☆ ☆ ☆

28

☆ ☆ ☆ ☆ ☆

In Jon's dream, he was back in his office at Megasoft. It was just as he remembered it. A brown simulated wood desk, piled with papers. Two guest chairs, upholstered in muted cranberry. A tall steel bookcase, filled with loose-leaf binders and lucite mementos from projects past. A framed Olympic skiing poster on the wall. Jon was eating cold pizza from a greasy cardboard box on the desk. He was staring at the computer monitor, watching the cursor blink, but he wasn't exactly sure why. He knew he was supposed to be working. It was late, past midnight, and he had to finish. But what was it he had to finish?

As he ate the pizza, he kept trying to remember. Just when he thought he had finally remembered, he forgot again. He moved aside the pizza box, and started searching through the papers on the desk. No matter how hard he squinted, though, he found that he couldn't read the type. The words were too blurry. Then there were two knocks on the wall. Kenny? Jon got up so quickly that he pushed the rest of the pizza onto the carpet. He stepped over the gooey mess, and walked out into the hall. It was dark. He didn't see Kenny's office. There was only a blank wall. He walked back to his office, but now he couldn't see it either. Jon decided that he must be in the wrong building, so he continued down the hall to the exit. It was cold outside, and Jon noticed that he was wearing shorts. He really should go home and change. He looked around the parking lot for his car. As Jon was standing there, Kenny Alden pulled up on his silver motorcycle. Jon started to ask Kenny how he could be there if he was dead, but Kenny cut him off. He said that he was flying to Casablanca in the morning and had to get to sleep. He didn't have time to talk. Jon took a step closer to the motorcycle, and reached out to touch Kenny. But the motorcycle was already rolling away. Kenny twisted around and said he'd send e-mail from Casablanca. Before Jon could say a word, Kenny disappeared in the darkness.

Jon awoke to the sound of Karen's voice.

"Who's there?" she asked.

He looked around and saw that she wasn't in bed anymore. She was at the door.

"Room service," was the muffled reply to her question.

He checked the clock radio on the nightstand. It was 6:04. Kind of early for breakfast, he thought.

"I think you have the wrong room," Karen said. "We didn't order any room service."

Jon pulled the blanket over his head. He was going back to sleep.

"It's the weekend special. Complimentary breakfast."

"Hold on. I just got out of the shower."

Then Karen was standing over him.

"Jon, wake up," she whispered.

He took the blanket off his head. It didn't look like she'd just gotten out of the shower. She was already dressed.

"I don't want breakfast now," he said sleepily.

"They're not here with breakfast."

"What?"

"I can't see who it is. The peephole is blocked. But when I looked under the door, I saw four pairs of shoes. It doesn't take four people to deliver breakfast."

Now Jon was awake.

Karen turned on the table lamp next to the bed. "C'mon, put on your clothes."

While he scrambled to step into his jeans, she went back to the door. "Just a minute," she called. "Be right with you."

"What are we going to do?" Jon asked, sitting at the foot of the bed, tying his shoes.

"We'll go out the terrace."

"What if they have people out there, too?"

"Have a better idea?" she asked.

"No, but—"

"Jon, we don't have time to debate this. If we—"

The door popped open, held back only by an inside chain.

"Let's go," Jon shouted.

He slid open the glass door to the slate patio. They stepped over the low bushes at the perimeter, onto a vast lawn that sloped down to the Snowdon River. The sun was just rising, and its dim orange light barely penetrated the dense fog. Snowdon Falls thundered invisibly in the distance.

They ran to the left, looping around the hotel toward the parking lot. Within fifty yards, though, they made out two figures, advancing toward them in the fog.

"Can you see who they are?" Karen asked, stopping.

"No, but at six o'clock on Saturday morning, I bet they're not out for a stroll in the fog."

"Let's head back the other way."

"Toward the falls?" Jon asked.

Karen started to run in the opposite direction. "There's a path alongside the falls. We can take it down to the bottom."

Jon followed, but suddenly there were three more figures ahead. He stopped.

"What do we do?" he asked, huffing and puffing.

Karen had her hands on her hips, trying to catch her breath. "I don't know. They have us surrounded."

Jon took her hand. "This way," he said, and headed down the hill.

"Jon, that's the river down there."

"We don't have a choice," he said, quickening the pace.

At the bottom of the hill, they stood at the railing, watching the Snowdon River thrash against the concrete retaining wall below. Huge logs lost by upstream lumber mills pounded against the rocks. To the right, they could see the water meet the sky, as it flew out over the falls. To the left, pressed against the railing, there was a flimsy wooden concession stand, its weathered shutters padlocked closed.

Jon tugged on the padlocks, but they didn't budge.

"They're coming," Karen cried, pointing to the top of the hill.

"Hold on to me," he said, throwing one leg over the railing.

She grabbed onto his arm. "Jon, are you crazy? What are you doing?"

"We'll hide behind the stand. They won't see us back there."

"Back *where?* There's just a railing."

"And a ledge. We'll stand on the ledge. Like this." He swung his other leg over the railing.

Karen looked over the railing. There was a thirty-foot drop to the river. She shook her head. "I don't know."

Jon slowly sidestepped toward the stand. "Look, this isn't that hard. Just hold on to the—"

His foot slipped off the ledge. He teetered backward for an instant, over the water, then managed to pull himself forward. He clung to the railing, terrified. "No big deal," he finally said, trying to appear calm. But he was lying. He was so scared that he didn't know whether he could take another step. "It's just a little slippery. Be careful."

Karen looked back over her shoulder one last time, watching the dim figures make their way down thc hill. Then she took a deep breath and put her leg over the railing. She started to swing over the other leg, but stopped midway.

"Jon, I can't do this," she said, watching the water race by below.

"Karen, don't look down. Look the other way. Keep your eyes on the hill."

She nodded. "I'll try." Gripping the railing with white knuckles, she swung over the other leg.

"That was the hardest part," Jon said, starting to sidestep again toward the stand. "Now we're just going to take tiny steps. Nice and easy." He tried to follow his own advice and look only straight ahead.

They sidestepped their way to the center of the stand, then waited, their bodies pressed tightly against the railing and each other.

"How did they find us so quickly?" Jon whispered. He wanted to think about something other than the raging waters below.

"I don't think anyone followed us last night. We were pretty careful."

"Could they have traced your credit card or something like that?"

"No, remember, I paid in cash."

"Then I don't get it," he said. "Besides the guy at the front desk, no one knew we were here."

Karen started to agree, and then thought it over. "Actually," she said, "no one but Jack Malcolm."

Jon looked at her. "Are you really suggesting that he tipped them off somehow?"

"I guess I am," she replied somewhat hesitantly, knowing what the reaction would be.

"Karen, that's crazy. I don't believe that."

"How do you explain the way they found us so quickly?"

He didn't answer right away. There had to be a perfectly reasonable explanation, he knew. One that didn't involve JackM.

"Maybe they're tapping his phone," Jon finally said, not at all convinced that it was a good answer. But he felt like he had to say something.

"That's possible," Karen said diplomatically. She really didn't think so, but this wasn't the time to get into—

The stand shook violently, and they heard someone on the other side.

"This thing is locked up tight," a man said. "I don't see anybody down here."

There was an inaudible reply from a walkie-talkie.

Clinging to the rail, Jon and Karen waited silently.

Jon was still trying to think of reasons why Karen had to be wrong about JackM. There was no way he was involved. No way.

Listening to the roar of the falls, though, Jon heard a nagging refrain.

"What if she's right?" the gurgling water seemed to ask. "What if she's right?"

29

☆ ☆ ☆ ☆ ☆

Malcolm was fuming. He had zero tolerance for incompetence. And this was a major screw-up.

"What do you mean they got away? I told you exactly where they were."

Constanza shrugged. "Jack, what can I tell you? I wasn't there. Seely sent fifteen men. It should have been a piece of cake. But apparently there was a lot of fog. It was early in the morning. Some signals got crossed. These things happen." He shifted his chair in front of Malcolm's glass desk. "Look, I'm not explaining it away. We blew it. We failed. It was my operation, and I accept full responsibility for the outcome."

Malcolm was tempted to press him further, but he knew it wasn't any use. Constanza had slipped into his Pentagon mode. Blathering on about accepting responsibility when it was clear that he was trying hard to distance himself from a mess. Some days, he had no patience for Constanza. The endless war stories. The whole military mindset. Constanza might be a good leader, Malcolm thought, but he wasn't much of a manager. He had no conception of the bottom line, of how much things really cost. He treated Malcolm's money like some Congressional appropriation, to be spent in full by budget year's end, no matter what. Constanza had already blown a hundred million bucks on Project Vanguard, and there was no end in sight.

But Malcolm needed Constanza. Running a military operation was different from running a business. The initial idea had been

Malcolm's, but he couldn't have accomplished it alone. Constanza helped make the idea a reality. He supplied the know-how, the contacts, the practical information. When the Cincinnatus team needed a rocket launcher or a helicopter, Constanza made it happen. He knew people all over the world. Soldiers, spies, arms dealers. An informal, international fraternity of which Constanza was a member in good standing. It was an affiliation that opened doors. But Malcolm had found that there was also a downside. Constanza's associates were thoroughly apolitical, reserving their primary allegiance for their Swiss bank accounts. Walter Kaminski was a perfect example. He was talented, but greedy. After a career spent drawing middling government pay, he'd seen a chance to cash in. To make some easy money. But it hadn't been so easy. His little blackmail scheme had blown up in his face. Now Kaminski was dead, and they were still scrambling to clean up the mess he'd made.

"Okay, this morning is history," Malcolm said, trying to sound conciliatory. "It's behind us. The question now is, what are we doing to resolve this thing? Because I don't want this lingering. It's a distraction. We've got a lot of other stuff to worry about."

"Jack, I totally agree. And we're going to get this wrapped up as quickly as we can. I promise you. We've got a lot of resources on this. Not only our own. Chances are, the cops are going to pick up these two before we do. There's a warrant out on Goodman for drug possesion. They're not going to get very far."

"What happens when the cops take them into custody? Do we have contingency plans for that?"

"If these two wind up in jail, they'll be like fish in a barrel. We'll pluck them out in a minute. And I don't mean to downplay this at all, but what do they really have anyway? Nothing. Goodman told you that himself. They don't have a shred of evidence. Now, don't get me wrong. I'm as concerned as you are that they know what they do. That's why we need to get rid of them. But, honestly, they're not in a position to do anything."

Malcolm always felt uneasy when Constanza sounded so upbeat. It was another one of those military tics of his. Putting on the happy face for the commanding officer. Malcolm wasn't reassured.

"Do we know any more about what the Alden kid found out?"

"Jack, I don't think he found out anything. You know this computer stuff a lot better than I ever will, but they tell me that this *meganet.sys* file has hundreds of thousands of lines of programming code. For him to have found anything, it would have been like finding a needle in a haystack. He didn't even know what he was looking for. And if he did happen to stumble onto something, it's a moot point now. Because he's not around to tell anyone."

Malcolm was about to send Constanza away when he thought of one more thing. "What's happening with Kaminski's video? Any other copies turn up?"

"Nope," Constanza replied. "And Burt hasn't left too many stones unturned. Personally, I don't think there were any other copies. I knew Walt Kaminski for thirty-five years, and he was the most arrogant son of a bitch you'd ever want to meet. I bet the thought never occurred to him that we'd find the copy he had. So I don't think we have anything to worry about."

Malcolm nodded politely, but he'd already made up his mind. He wasn't taking any chances on the video.

30

☆ ☆ ☆ ☆ ☆

"Maybe this one's broken," Jon said.

They were at a cash machine in the shopping center across the street from Kenny's apartment. It was almost noon. They'd abandoned Jon's car at the hotel, and taken the bus back to Woodside.

Karen moved over to the next machine. She inserted her card, punched in her PIN code, pressed the key next to $250, and waited.

After a long delay, the same message appeared. *Transaction not available to this account.*

"That's weird," she said.

Jon took out his wallet. "Let me try my card."

A minute later, he was staring at an identical screen. *Transaction not available to this account.*

Karen peeked over at the cash machine she'd tried first. A woman with two young children was using it now.

"Excuse me," Karen called to her, "I think these aren't working."

The woman looked up from the screen. "No, actually this one's fine."

They watched as she pulled a wad of bills from the cash dispenser.

Jon and Karen looked at each other.

"Uh-oh," Jon said.

Karen suddenly noticed the video camera mounted above the cash machines. She ducked her head.

"C'mon," she whispered, "let's go."

They walked out into the parking lot.

"What are the chances that was a coincidence?" Jon asked.

"Zero," she replied.

He looked in his wallet. He only had $31 left. "How much do you have?"

Karen opened her purse and took out her wallet. "Twelve bucks. And two credit cards."

"I've got a couple of credit cards, too. But if they managed to cancel my cash card, I bet they did the same thing to my credit cards."

"Have any checks with you?"

"No. How about you?"

She shook her head. "I never carry my checkbook."

Jon leaned back against a parked car and sighed. "You know what? We're screwed."

"I don't see anyone up there," Jon whispered, peering up the outdoor stairwell to Kenny's apartment.

"Jon, all of a sudden, I have a bad feeling about this. Maybe we should go."

He hesitated. Maybe she was right. But, then again, without the key to Kenny's motorcycle, they weren't going to get very far.

"Karen, it'll take me thirty seconds. I know exactly where the key is."

She craned her neck, trying to see the top of the stairs. Then she nodded. "Okay, thirty seconds."

They walked up the steps.

At Kenny's door, Jon paused before inserting the key. He listened a moment. It seemed quiet.

Karen looked around nervously. "Jon, I don't think we want to stand around out here."

He unlocked the door and opened it a crack. He peeked inside, Nothing unusual. He pushed the door open all the way and went inside, with Karen close behind him.

The apartment looked just as they had left it Thursday night. The lights were on in the living room and the kitchen. The phone that Jon had dropped was still on the floor.

"It doesn't look like anyone's been here," Karen said.

Jon went into the kitchen and opened a drawer. The key was exactly where he'd thought. He put it in his pocket.

When he looked up, he glimpsed a box of Fruit Loops on the counter. Jon had an image of Kenny hunched over his computer keyboard, with the cereal box balanced on his lap. It was hard for Jon to believe that he would never see that again. Looking around the kitchen, he expected Kenny to walk in any minute and—

Jon heard what sounded like a gunshot.

"Karen!" he shouted, running into the living room.

He didn't see her right away.

"Karen!"

Then he saw her by the window, with her hand on her chest. She looked ashen.

"Are you okay?"

She nodded. "Just scared."

"What was that?"

Karen pointed across the room. "The front door," she said, a little short of breath. "It slammed."

He put his arms around her. "God, we're going to drive ourselves crazy."

Megasoft was just a ten-minute walk from Kenny's apartment. Once on campus, they kept to the secluded running trails that meandered through the woods.

They cautiously scanned the parking lot from behind the trees. It was surprisingly full for a Saturday, nominally a day off from work. But this was a Megasoft parking lot, and the Megasoft work ethic was well known. Kenny's motorcycle sat forlornly in a corner of the lot, its silver paint shimmering in the hazy sun.

The motorcycle was only fifty yards away, but it looked like a mile to them. To get there, they'd need to walk directly through the center of the parking lot, in broad daylight. They'd be completely exposed.

"I wish we could just rent a car," Jon said.

Karen stepped onto the asphalt. "We're here," she said. "Let's get it over with."

They walked quickly, but not too quickly. They didn't want to attract attention.

Halfway to the motorcycle, they heard a car coming up from behind them. As the car passed, Jon looked up for a brief instant and accidentally made eye contact with the driver.

It was Francine. She'd seen him. He was positive.

"Damn!" he muttered, hastening their pace.

"What?"

"That woman in the car. I know her, and she saw me."

"Jon, calm down. She's probably not—"

"Karen, you don't understand. That was Francine. She's a nut. She hates me. I bet she's already on the phone to Megasoft Security."

"Wait, you mean the same Francine who—"

"Understand now?"

"Oh God."

They finally got to the motorcycle.

Jon handed Karen the key. "Are you sure you know how to ride one of these?"

"Relax. I was riding motorcycles way before I ever drove a car."

She got on first and started up the bike.

"How did you learn to ride?" Jon asked.

"My older brother. He was a total biker fanatic in high school, so he taught me. I was kind of a tomboy, and I used to hang around with him and his friends. They thought it was hysterical, this girl riding a motorcycle."

"You were a tomboy?" Jon asked, swinging his leg over the seat.

"I think my parents were afraid I was going to grow up to be a mud wrestler or whatever it is tomboys are supposed to grow up to be."

The image of Karen as a tomboy briefly brought forth a smile, which instantly evaporated when he saw the red Megasoft Security truck out of the corner of his eye. It was turning into their aisle.

"Let's go!" he shouted. "They're already here."

"Who?"

"Security. C'mon!"

Karen found the bike hard to maneuver with two people on it.

She was still trying to get out of the parking spot when the red truck screeched to a stop behind them.

They were startled by the booming voice from the loudspeaker. "Get off the motorcycle now. And keep your hands where we can see them."

In the distance, they heard sirens.

Karen twisted around to see behind them. The truck blocked the back of the parking spot. There was no way to get past it.

If they couldn't go back, they would go forward. She aimed the bike between the two parked cars in front of them, then gave the engine some gas.

The motorcycle flew through the narrow gap. The left handlebar slammed into one car's side mirror, snapping it off. Karen held on tight, keeping the bike on course.

She leaned right when they were past the cars, but saw another red truck waiting for them at the end of the aisle. She jerked the handlebars to the left, heading in the opposite direction.

Jon had his arms clenched around her waist. He was afraid he was going to fall off.

They roared down the aisle, making the first left. Karen accelerated toward the exit. She checked her rearview mirror. Two red trucks were right behind them.

At the exit, she made a left. They were now on the road that hugged the perimeter of the campus.

Jon turned around. The trucks were gaining on them.

"Faster, Karen!"

She accelerated as they went into a curve.

Then, back on a straightaway, she looked down the road. A hundred yards ahead, she saw three more red trucks blocking the way. In her mirror, she saw the trucks behind them.

They were trapped.

"Hold on tight!" she shouted.

Karen turned the handlebars to the right and sent the motorcycle over the curb, into the woods. She mowed through ten yards of dense brush before she found the running trail. Then she made a sharp left onto the wooded path.

The trees whizzed past them as they roared through the forest.

A few minutes later, they were back on the gravel at the used-car lot. Karen stopped the bike for a minute to catch her breath.

"Are you okay?" Jon asked.

"I'm just scared. I'm not used to—"

They heard the harsh whine of a motor through the trees. Maybe it was just a lawn mower, Jon thought. Or maybe Megasoft Security was still looking for them.

"C'mon," he said, "we better move."

31

☆ ☆ ☆ ☆ ☆

Jon carefully read the article from beginning to end for a second time, then threw the newspaper on the table.

He was at the Woodside Mall, sitting at the back of the food court, facing the wall, trying to be inconspicuous. When he turned around to see what was keeping Karen, he noticed that an elderly woman in a green raincoat appeared to be staring at him. He quickly turned away, and kept his eyes focused on the table.

He studied the photo of himself in the newspaper. It was six years old, taken on his first day at Megasoft. His hair had been longer, and his face had been a little thinner, he thought. But the photo pretty much looked like him. Anyone who saw it would recognize him. The drug dealer responsible for his own friend's fatal overdose. That's who he was now. It was in the newspaper. It was on the local TV news. It was going to be in his obituary. This was his fifteen minutes of fame.

Karen put down the plastic tray with the food.

She watched Jon unwrap the cheeseburger he'd ordered. "You're not going to get sick from that, are you?"

"I'm not feeling so great anyway," he said. He was tired and irritable. Wiping his face with a napkin, he felt three days' growth of beard. It itched. He needed to shave. Then he glanced again at the newspaper photo, and realized that he wouldn't be shaving again anytime soon. For that matter, he wouldn't be driving his car again anytime soon. He wouldn't be going back to his apartment anytime soon. He wouldn't be doing just about anything he used to do. His entire life had been hijacked.

"I know you don't want to hear it," Karen was saying, "but it makes the most sense. I'm telling you, all the pieces fit."

"Well, I don't buy it," he said. "You're talking about coincidences. That's all."

"No, I think it's more than that. You won't believe it because you have this blind faith in the guy. That's why you won't even consider the possibility."

"Bull. I considered the possibility. I just don't agree. Everything we know points to Constanza."

"Jon, listen to me. This morning, how could they have possibly found us so quickly, if Jack Malcolm didn't tell them? And yesterday, why did Seely seem so nervous at first about our having the video, then suddenly become so sure that we didn't have it? The only thing that happened between the two calls is that you went and told Malcolm that we didn't have the video. That's how Seely found out."

"You don't know that," Jon said testily. "You're guessing. You're speculating. That's it." He started to take a bite of his cheeseburger, then abruptly took it away from his mouth. "And I don't have blind faith in Jack Malcolm. That's unfair. I just don't believe he'd be involved in something like this. Do you really think that he was involved in planning an assassination attempt on himself? Because that's what you're implying. If he's working with Constanza, and Constanza is funding Cincinnatus, then that means Malcolm arranged to have himself killed. Is that what you're saying?"

"No," Karen said, "he didn't arrange to have himself killed. He arranged to make it look like he almost got killed. There's a big difference."

"Karen, c'mon, the night of the assassination attempt, there were a hundred witnesses. They're all part of this huge conspiracy?"

"Not necessarily. It was like they were all watching a magic show, but didn't know. It was an illusion, and they believed it."

"And the doctors at the hospital? They were all fooled, too? They couldn't tell the difference between ketchup and blood?"

"Who said anything about blood?" Karen asked. "There wasn't any blood. He supposedly had internal injuries. The bullets all hit his bulletproof vest. That should have been the tip-off. This was the friendliest assassination attempt in history. A terrorist shoots at Malcolm with a submachine gun from three feet away, and misses his head six times? Every bullet landed smack in the center of Malcolm's bulletproof vest. Isn't that just a little too tidy, a little too convenient?''

''They didn't know he was wearing a bulletproof vest.''

''Jon, think about it for a second. You're arguing that Constanza planned the assassination attempt, right?''

''Right.''

''Well, how could he of all people not know about Malcolm's security arrangements? He's the man's running mate. He would know if Malcolm wore a bulletproof vest. Besides, if Constanza really wanted to kill Malcolm, why would he try to do it during some national TV interview? He has total access to Malcolm. He knows his schedule, his travel plans. He could arrange to kill him anytime he wanted to. Anyway, it doesn't make sense that he'd try to kill him before the election. He would wait until after Malcolm got into office. Otherwise, what guarantee would Constanza have that he'd become president?''

''But what does Malcolm get out of faking his own assassination? Some sympathy? Big deal. It wouldn't be worth the risk.''

''Jon, if you were behind in the polls the way he was, it would be worth the risk. In a week, he went from ten points behind to ten points ahead. All because of the assassination attempt. It made him more than just another rich guy who wants to be president. It created a whole myth around him. Single-handedly fighting against the terrorists. Almost dying because of his convictions. Then nearly coming back from death to lead us. Believe me, that kind of PR is worth the risk.''

But . . .

But what? Jon couldn't think of any more objections. He was still absolutely certain, though, that Malcolm wasn't involved.

Absolutely certain? He reconsidered. Well, pretty certain. Somewhat certain. Not uncertain.

Then Jon started getting queasy. He was overcome with nausea. It was either the cheeseburger or the sickening feeling that what Karen said made a lot of sense.

* * *

The salesman in the computer department at Sears wouldn't let them alone.

"Do you two have kids yet?"

"No," Jon said, hoping to end the conversation right there.

"Well, you're planning on a family eventually, right?"

"I don't know. We're not—"

"You see, what I'm getting at here is, this is a wonderful PC for the whole family. Even if that's just the two of you at the moment. That's fine. No kids required. Because this—"

"You know," Karen interrupted, "I think we'd just like to look around for a while and—"

"Sure, no problem. Take your time. Now, I don't want to pressure you in any way, but keep in mind that the sale we've been advertising does end today. It's an incredible deal. You save twenty percent on any PC, and you also get a free trial of Megasoft OneWire for three months. Honestly, I don't think you're going to find a better—"

"Great, thanks for your help," Jon said.

Spotting some better prospects across the showroom, the salesman handed Jon his business card and excused himself.

"How does this back-door thing work?" Karen asked, watching Jon type at the keyboard.

"A friend of Kenny's did some of the programming for Megasoft Mail. To make the program easier to test, he left a way to get into the mail system without a password."

"You think you can look in Kenny's mailbox this way?"

"I'm pretty sure."

"How about Malcolm's or Constanza's?"

"Should work the same—"

Malcolm's voice blared from stereo speakers. "Son, you just haven't thought this through!"

The salesman looked over at them from the other side of the showroom, but quickly went back to giving his spiel to an attentive family of four.

"Shhh," Karen whispered, staring at the grainy picture of Malcolm on the screen. "Turn that down."

"Sorry, I forgot."

"What was that?"

"Some hacker humor," Jon replied, not finding it at all amusing this time. The carefree hacker spirit suddenly seemed sadly naive. He thought about his last conversation with Kenny, who had been so proud to have cracked the code, to have solved the puzzle. For two days, Jon had been turning over in his head what Kenny had said about *meganet.sys.* Then the words had come to him, as if he was hearing them on tape. *I started to send you e-mail about it.* That's what Kenny had told him. *I started to send you e-mail about it.* Did that mean Kenny had actually typed out a message? Or had he just been thinking about it? Jon intended to find out.

"Should we try Malcolm's account first?" Karen asked. "That might clear up a lot."

"All right."

She watched over his shoulder as he logged in to Malcolm's account. There was a long pause after he finished typing.

"What's taking so long?" she asked.

"I don't know. We should have seen the new screen by—"

The computer beeped, and an error message appeared. *Incompatible version.*

"What's that mean?" Karen asked.

"Haven't got a clue. Let me try again." After a minute, the same message appeared. *Incompatible version.*

"Try Constanza's account."

"Okay." A flurry of typing produced the same result. *Incompatible version.* Jon tried to log in to Seely's account. Then he tried Donnelly's. And finally Block's. *Incompatible version.*

"Looks like someone closed the back door," Karen said.

"Slammed it in my face. I guess they figured out how I sent that message to Block about Kaminski's hard drive."

He made one last attempt. Kenny's account. He held his breath waiting.

Incompatible version.

"Damn."

"There isn't any other way to get in?" she asked.

"Not that I know of," Jon said. Unlike Kenny, he thought, who would have known ten other ways into the e-mail system.

"Why can't you try logging in to Kenny's account directly, without going through this back door?"

"Because I don't know his password."

"Then guess."

"Karen, I can't just guess his password. It's not like it's one of five choices. It could be anything."

"Not anything," she said. "It's something Kenny would have thought of. And you knew him better than anyone else did. If anyone can guess it, you can."

He knew it was a stupid idea, but he really didn't feel like arguing. So he exited the back door, and logged in as KennyA. The cursor blinked patiently on the password line, waiting for an answer. Jon didn't know where to begin.

"Well?" Karen said.

"Karen, really, I have no idea. Like I said, it could be anything."

"Just give it a try."

He typed in "Hollywood." The computer beeped. *Log-in failed. Invalid address and/or password.* So he tried "Woodside." And then "snowboard." And then "JackM." And then "Toy Town." And then "FoamBlaster." And then "Cal Tech." And then "Fruit Loops." The computer's response was the same every time. *Log-in failed. Invalid address and/or password.*

"Go on," Karen urged. "Try some more."

He shook his head. "This is silly. I'm not going to—" He stopped in mid-sentence.

"Not going to what?" she asked.

Jon didn't know why, but he found himself thinking about what Kenny had said in the dream. That he was flying to Casablanca. Impulsively, he typed in "Casablanca," and crossed his fingers.

Log-in failed. Invalid address and/or password.

"Casablanca?" Karen asked. "What made you try that?"

He shrugged. "I don't know. It was just this running joke we had. He was always making fun of me for insisting that Bogart never really says—" He stopped talking, and entered, "Play it again, Sam." After a few seconds, the screen changed.

Welcome to Megasoft Mail. You have 16 unread messages, 1 unsent message, and 247 saved messages.

He was stunned. "That's amazing. What are the chances of guessing that?"

"It's just like I told you," she said. "You knew Kenny better than anyone else did."

For a fleeting moment, Jon wanted to believe in ghosts. Because he had the uncanny feeling that he couldn't have guessed the password on his own. It had been so easy. Too easy. Then he decided that there had to be a perfectly rational explanation for what had happened. Wasn't there always?

Karen tapped on the screen. "Let's take a look at that one unsent message."

Jon typed a command. After a few seconds, the message appeared on the screen.

To: JonGo
From: KennyA
Subject: meganet.sys, version 3.0

Some weird stuff here. Found about a dozen functions that aren't documented in the reference files. As far as I can tell, these are the basic ones:

redirectStream
storeStream
packageStream
retrieveStream
deleteStream

Looks like they're part of a new scripting language. Commands sent from OneWire Central are carried out by the PC that receives them. Totally bypasses all the security features in OneWire, including encryption. Example: before an e-mail message is encrypted and sent, allows OneWire Central to instruct the PC to save an unencrypted copy and forward it later. Pretty much works the same way with telephone conversations. Can be saved and forwarded, or monitored in real-time. If PC equipped with microphone or video camera, even possible for OneWire Central to turn these on and record. In general, any files on hard drive can be vacuumed up and transmitted back.

Everything is completely transparent to the end user. Your

hard drive might whir a little more, but you really wouldn't have any idea something different is going on.

Maybe I'm wrong, but this sure looks like a surveillance system to me. OneWire = Big Brother?

EricT's friend told me that this new meganet.sys is supposed to be rolled out in early November.

By the way, I was able to read the file from Kaminski's hard drive. Turns out that he had a video they wanted. Have an idea who he might have given a copy to.

—Kenny

P.S. remote [JackM:zip]. I'll explain later. Gotta go now.

Jon looked up from the screen. "This is incredible."

"And frightening," Karen said. "Jon, everyone I know either has OneWire service or is about to sign up."

"Right now, the OneWire people say they're into a quarter of the households with computers. By the end of next year, they're aiming for half."

"Do you think Kenny could have gotten it wrong? Misunderstood the programming code or that kind of thing?"

"I doubt it," Jon replied. "He was the best programmer I ever met. Everyone else used to go to him when they ran into a problem."

"Even if Kenny was right, I can't believe they could get away with this. With all those millions of customers, someone would notice. Someone would find out for sure."

"How?" Jon asked. "There'd be nothing to notice. The hard drive on your PC is always going on and off. That's not going to tell you anything. You wouldn't be suspicious until the police came in the middle of the night to take you away. By then, it'd be too late."

"But some people would examine the software, figure out how it works," she said.

"Karen, it's not like a car. You can't look under the hood and see how the parts fit together. This is software. It's just thousands and thousands of instructions, and there's no easy way to know what the instructions are, or who wrote them, or what their purpose is. Ever look on the hard drive of your PC? There must be a thousand files with names like *meganet.sys*. You never think to scrutinize every file. You just accept that everything works. And then you connect your PC to a network like OneWire, and you assume that you're in control of what's flowing back and forth. But you really have no idea. You didn't write the software. You don't know what the instructions are. The truth is, it's entirely out of your hands."

"What if you don't upgrade to the new version of the software?"

"You don't have a choice," Jon replied. "If you get OneWire service, *meganet.sys* is updated automatically whenever there's a new version available. Once you're connected to the network, you don't have any control over what's on your PC."

"Kenny got it right," Karen said. "This is like Big Brother."

"Sort of. But did you ever read *1984?* This is a lot different from what Orwell was thinking of. With OneWire, you're not going to have a huge screen in your living room with a picture of Big Brother staring at you. You won't even know that Big Brother is watching. It'll be this silent, secret spying. I'd call it Little Brother. It looks over your shoulder all the time. Follows you around. Then snitches on you when you do something you're not supposed to."

"But, Jon, do you really think they have the resources to spy on everyone? On a hundred million households, or however many there are? That seems pretty impossible."

"They don't have to spy on a hundred million households. A few thousand would be enough. They could just target the people who have the money or the power to make waves. Top business people. Politicians. Journalists. Academics. They're the ones who already have computers anyway. They're the people who probably already have OneWire."

"How are we going to convince anybody of this?" she asked. "What evidence do you show to prove it?"

"I don't know," he said. "It was a total fluke that Kenny got to see the computer code in the first place. They're not going to make the same mistake twice."

"Even if we had a copy of the code," Karen said, "how convincing would that really be? Because, face it, there are only a handful of people out there who could read the code and actually understand it. The rest of us are just going to have to take some so-called expert's word for it."

"And you know what would happen then," Jon said. "The other

side would hire twenty experts who completely disagreed with our experts. They'd say that all this stuff is in place to allow OneWire to provide better customer support. To make it easier to diagnose technical problems from the central office. Or some nonsense like that. And there'd be no way to prove that's a lie. Because the technology is neutral. It's not inherently good or bad. It all depends on what it's used for. It's no different from a knife. You can use a knife to kill someone. Or you can use it to cut your steak. So when you see a knife, you can't know in advance what its purpose is. All you know is its potential."

Karen nodded. "Anyway, the fact is that we don't have the computer code, and there's no chance we're going to get it. Which gives us absolutely no credibility. Look, I know how the news business works. Journalism today is all about sound bites and labels. And you know what our labels are? Disgraced former *Business World* reporter and disgraced former Megasoft employee. We're going to end up sounding like those kooks who used to argue that adding fluoride to the drinking water was some kind of Commie plot. Or the nuts who claim that we never landed on the moon, that it all took place in a TV studio. We'll be lucky to get this story into the supermarket tabloids next to the Elvis sightings and the fudge brownie diet."

"What do we do?" Jon asked.

"The video is the best lead we have. From what Kenny said, it's the one piece of evidence that would give us some leverage."

Jon studied Kenny's e-mail message again. *Have an idea who he might have given a copy to.* "What was Kenny thinking? Who would Kaminski have trusted with a backup copy?"

"A lawyer? A friend with a safe-deposit box? Those are the obvious candidates. But we really don't know enough about Kaminski to make an educated guess."

"We should talk to his daughter again," Jon said. "Maybe she could put us in contact with some of his friends."

"Jon, it didn't sound like they were close enough that she'd know any of his friends."

"Now that I think about it, you're probably right. Here Kaminski lived twenty minutes away from his daughter, and they hadn't found time to get together since last summer. Sure doesn't seem like she'd be the person he'd confide in."

"Definitely not," Karen said. "Until the week before he died, she didn't even have a decent photo of the guy. Her own father. Remember she mentioned that? What a tragedy that they—" Karen's voice suddenly trailed off.

"Karen?"

She didn't answer. She was staring off into the distance.

"Karen?"

"She has it," Karen whispered, nodding slowly.

"What?"

"He sent her a copy."

"What makes you say that?"

"Jon, don't you remember? She had a picture of him because he sent her one last week. He hadn't talked to her since last summer and, the week before he's killed, he just happens to send her a box of photo albums and—"

"Videos," Jon said. "The home movies he transferred to tape."

"Right."

"But wouldn't she have watched the videos by the time we talked to her?"

"I doubt it," Karen said.

"Why?"

"Because she told us that she didn't own a VCR."

"Let's go," Jon said.

Before logging out of Megasoft Mail, he printed a copy of Kenny's message and tucked the paper into his pocket.

The salesman intercepted them as they headed for the door.

"So you folks ready to buy the OneWire package?" he asked.

"Thanks," Karen replied, "but I think we're going to pass."

32

☆ ☆ ☆ ☆ ☆

Herb Abernathy stuck his head into his office.

"Jack, excuse me. Charlie Donnelly's here."

Malcolm looked up from the papers he'd spread out on Abernathy's desk. He'd made himself at home.

"Fine. Send him over." He checked his watch. Three-fifteen. "Are the TV people here yet?"

"They're setting up in your office now. We should be ready to roll in about a half hour or so." He turned to go, then hesitated. "You're sure you don't want to run through your lines one more time?"

"Positive," Malcolm said before returning to his papers. Abernathy was competent, but he worried too much, Malcolm thought. It was irritating.

"What do you have for me today, Charlie?" he asked when Donnelly came into the office.

Donnelly closed the door and took a seat. "After the election, I think the Speaker of the House is going to be very easy to get along with."

"Why's that?" Malcolm asked.

"Well, he does represent a pretty conservative Congressional district. I think his constituents might be kind of disappointed if they found out that Mr. Family Values himself cheats on his wife."

"Where'd that little gem come from?"

"Fortunately for us," Donnelly said, "the Speaker is a big fan of electronic banking. Pays all his bills on-line. Turns out that about two years ago, he paid a few bills from some urologist in the D.C. area. Over five years, it was the only time he ever paid a doctor. Which got us wondering. I mean, he's a congressman. He definitely has medical insurance. Why's he paying for this out of his own pocket?''

''So you checked with Amerifax,'' Malcolm said.

''You got it. He was being treated for gonorrhea. I guess he thought that if he didn't file an insurance claim, there wouldn't be any record.''

Malcolm smiled. ''And here I thought we overpaid for Amerifax. It was worth every penny.'' Amerifax had originally been a provider of credit reports. As a Megasoft subsidiary, Amerifax had also become a leading clearinghouse of medical records, serving the largest insurance companies.

''We're really just getting started with the research,'' Donnelly said. ''With all the slimeballs you've got in Washington, I figure this is only the beginning. And, obviously, when we get the OneWire modifications in place, we're going to have access to a whole new world of data.''

''Is there a revised schedule yet for the OneWire roll-out?''

''The network upgrade is supposed to be finished by the first week of November.''

''Shame we couldn't have gotten the thing up and running sooner. You're going to have a couple of million on-line voters this year for the first time. We definitely could have finessed the vote counts a little.''

''It sure is easy to stuff an electronic ballot box,'' Donnelly said.

''You bet.'' Malcolm laughed, and repeated a line from his campaign stump speech. ''As president, I intend to make the convenience of on-line voting a reality for all Americans, regardless of where they live or how much they make.''

''Wait till the next election,'' Donnelly said, getting up from his chair.

''Yup.''

Donnelly opened the office door. ''Will you have some time for me on Tuesday?''

''Check with Herb. I know I'm in Chicago on Monday. I think I'll be back here Tuesday morning.''

Donnelly nodded and closed the door behind him.

Thinking it over, Malcolm decided that he was actually pleased that the OneWire upgrade wasn't ready yet. This way, he was going to have to win the votes on his own. Convince millions of nitwits to walk into the voting booth and affirm that he was the best man for the job. That would make the victory sweeter. In the long run, Malcolm saw OneWire as an edge, an advantage. It wasn't going to solve all of his problems, but it would make governing easier. He knew that the changes he planned would spark fierce opposition. OneWire would allow him to push aside the critics and move ahead quickly. He didn't want to get bogged down in endless debate, in business as usual.

A radical transformation required radical means. The press and the politicians might not understand that, but the historians of the future would. They would laud Malcolm for leading a second American revolution, peaceful and bloodless, but just as important as the first. The Information Age demanded a different form of government. Not democracy, but meritocracy. Not the chaotic, inefficient rule of the masses, but the wise guidance of the brightest minds. To survive in the twenty-first century, that was what America needed. And as America's first electronic monarch, that was what Malcolm intended to provide.

There was a knock at the door.

"Come on in."

It was Abernathy.

"Jack, they're all set up in your office. Whenever you're ready."

33

☆ ☆ ☆ ☆ ☆

Ellen Kaminski's living room looked like a tornado had ripped through it. Crumpled papers and broken pottery littered the carpet. The paintings on the walls were askew. The fabric covering the sofa was slashed open.

"Believe it or not," she said, "this is an improvement over last night when I got home. I've been cleaning up since eight o'clock this morning."

The rest of the house didn't look any better. In the kitchen, there were pots and pans all over. Even the cabinet under the bathroom sink had been emptied onto the floor.

"I think we know what they were looking for," Karen said.

Ellen raised her eyebrows. "What could I possibly have that these people would want?"

"The package your father sent you last week."

"You're telling me that they destroyed my house for a crummy box of photos? These guys are sickos."

"Where's the package?" Jon asked.

"In my bedroom, I think. Let's go take a look."

They followed her up the stairs.

"I'm pretty sure I left the box right here," she said, patting the top of her dresser. But there was no box. On the floor, she rummaged through her scattered possessions. "No, I don't see any of the albums down here."

"Could you have left the package anywhere else?" Karen asked.

"Maybe the other bedroom. I use it as my office." She walked across the hall to a smaller room.

The contents of a filing cabinet had been dumped on the floor. They searched through the debris, but didn't find anything.

"I guess you were right," Ellen said, walking down the stairs. "They wanted the package."

"Looks like we're a day late," Jon said.

"Ellen, any chance that your father sent videos to some other relative?" Karen asked.

"No, I doubt—" She stopped. "Videos?"

"The home movies."

"Oh, I'm sorry, I forgot about those. When you mentioned the package, I just assumed you were talking about the photo albums. I could still have the videos."

"Where do think they might be?" Jon asked.

"The freezer."

"Pardon?"

"The freezer. I have a neighbor who's a camera buff, and he once told me that film keeps better in the freezer. I figured that I wasn't going to be watching those movies anytime soon, so I stuck them in the freezer."

In the kitchen, Ellen opened the freezer door, moved aside a few boxes of frozen vegetables, and pulled out a plastic bag with two videotapes inside.

"Maybe this is a mistake," Karen said, as Jon closed the apartment door behind them. "They could be watching Kenny's place, thinking we'd come back here."

"We're not going to be here long. I promise."

"What if there's ten hours of video on these?" she asked, holding up the plastic bag with the tapes. "Even if we fast-forward, it's going to take forever."

"That's why I wanted to use V-File," he replied, flipping on the lights in the bedroom.

"What's V-File?"

"The last piece of software Kenny wrote. It's kind of a souped-up VCR."

There was a futon on the floor, with wrinkled sheets shoved to one side. A clock-radio with large red numbers sat on the carpet nearby, flashing 12:00. The walls were bare. In the corner, there was a desk covered with a tangle of cables and computer components.

"What is all this stuff?" Karen asked, as Jon sat down at the desk.

"It's the prototype for Hollywood. That's the project we were working on. When it's done, it's all supposed to fit in one box. It'll look just like a VCR." He pressed the power button. After some beeps and a short delay, the hard drive began to whir. Then two computer monitors slowly lit up, displaying information about the system status. Finally, the initial V-File screen appeared on one of the monitors. A college football game flickered onto the other monitor.

"Is that a TV picture?" Karen asked.

"Yeah, this is plugged into OneWire." He turned up the sound and flipped through the channels. Sports. Cooking. Sports. Movie. News.

"Leave on the news," Karen said. "Maybe we'll hear something about us."

"Okay." He inserted the two videotapes into side-by-side slots. There was a steady whine as the tapes spun.

"What's it doing?" she asked.

"Segmenting. It scans the tape, and figures out where scenes begin and end. It'll take a minute."

The sun was setting, and Jon watched a square of golden light on the wall gradually fade. Even with the TV on, the apartment seemed unnaturally quiet, he thought. It was a painful silence. Listening to the whine of the tape decks, he could almost make out Kenny's voice. He could almost hear Kenny's laugh. He strained to hear more, but he couldn't. Almost was the best he could do. He stared at the pile of dirty laundry next to the futon, T-shirts and baggy drawstring pants in the vivid colors Kenny had favored. It was easy for Jon to imagine the clothes on their owner, snowboarding down a mountain or motorcycling through a pouring rain. Just lying there in a heap, though, the clothes looked as if they had died, too.

A beep brought Jon's attention back to the monitor. V-File had finished the segmenting. He pressed a key, and the TV news disappeared from the other monitor. After a few seconds, a checkerboard of moving pictures filled the screen.

"What are we looking at?" Karen asked.

"These are all the scenes on the first tape. Each one of these little squares shows a scene."

"A lot of this stuff must be pretty old," she said. "It's in black and white."

"These definitely look like home movies. A bunch of people standing around a Christmas tree. A couple of different shots of a guy carving a turkey."

"Could that be Kaminski?"

Jon squinted at the screen. "No, I don't think so." He pointed to another square. "Maybe over here, though." He typed a command, and the scene filled the screen. A man held a little girl's hand. "Yeah, that's Walter Kaminski."

"And I think that's Ellen with him," Karen said.

"I can't tell." Jon switched back to the checkerboard, and tapped on a different square. "This one is Ellen, for sure." A young woman in a satiny dress accepted a corsage from a young man in a tuxedo.

"Are we looking at everything that's on this tape?" Karen asked.

He nodded. "Nothing interesting here. Let's try the other tape." He pressed a few keys, and a new checkerboard appeared on the screen.

Karen looked over the squares. A few scenes at the beach. A wedding. A barbecue. "This is just more of the same. I don't think there's anything here."

Jon scrutinized the images, searching for some significance, some connection. But he couldn't find any. These were clearly old home movies. Nothing more.

He leaned back and sighed. "It made so much sense. Kaminski had this incredibly valuable video he wanted to protect. He doesn't see his daughter for months and months, doesn't talk to her, then the week before he's killed, what does he just happen to send her? Videos. Tell me, how could that be a coincidence?" Jon shook his head. "Maybe Kaminski messed up. Maybe he sent her the wrong tape. Or maybe—"

"Jon, what's wrong with this square?" She pointed to the last one at the bottom right of the screen, which was filled with static.

"That's just a bug," Jon said. "I've seen that before. I guess Kenny never got around to fixing it."

"It looks like there's a green arrow under the static. What's that?"

Jon leaned closer. "What's happening is that V-File is treating the end of the tape as a scene. But the end of the tape is blank, so we're seeing the static."

"What's the arrow for?"

"It shouldn't be there. You're only supposed to see it when there are more scenes to display."

"Well, try to show more scenes," Karen said.

"All right," Jon said, as he pressed a key, "but I'm telling you, it's only a bug. There aren't any other—"

A single new square appeared in the upper left of an otherwise black screen. In crisp color, it wasn't a home movie. It was Jack Malcolm sitting behind his glass desk.

"That's the assassination attempt," Karen said. "Start it over again."

Jon typed a command to enlarge the square.

Malcolm suddenly looked to one side and the camera panned to show a man with a black ski mask advancing, gun in hand. The assailant stepped to the edge of the desk, then pointed the gun at Malcolm's chest.

"Okay, the blanks get fired here," said an off-camera voice. "Go on."

Malcolm grimaced and slumped back. His chair rolled for a few feet, teetered for an instant, but didn't tip over. Malcolm sat up and began to laugh uproariously.

"Folks, I think I need a chair without wheels," he said when he stopped laughing. "Because I don't want to roll backward. I want to topple backward. I want to be sprawled on the—"

The scene ended abruptly, and the square looped back to the beginning, with Malcolm at his desk.

They sat watching it again and again, from beginning to end, until Jon finally pressed a key that brought the TV news back to the screen.

"The bastard," Jon muttered. "The lying bastard." He turned to Karen. "You were right."

"Jon, I'm sorry. I know how much—"

"God, I'm so stupid," he said. "I should have known. I never should have trusted him. You hit it on the head before. I had this idiotic blind faith in him. Like a child. Our hero, JackM. Our great visionary leader. I believed it. I really did. I was just another sucker. If I had kept my eyes open, maybe Kenny would still be alive."

Jon felt disoriented, as if some basic point of reference, like the sun or the moon, had disappeared. He was lost. For six years, he'd been navigating relative to a mirage, a fiction. The cult of JackM. Jon had been a card-carrying member. But JackM was a fraud. And Kenny was dead. Jon wanted justice.

"He's not getting away with this. This is the end for him."

"We have the evidence to stop them now," Karen said. "They killed Kaminski because they knew this would destroy them if it got out."

Jon nodded, and glared at the smiling image of Malcolm that had just appeared before him on the TV news.

"Turn up the sound," Karen said.

"—pulling ahead dramatically," the news anchor said, "now with a lead of twelve points. In his Woodside office this afternoon, Mr. Malcolm was in high spirits as he took a break from campaigning to help Federal investigators re-create the failed assassination attempt against him."

The news video showed Malcolm grimacing and slumping back. His chair rolled for a few feet, teetered for an instant, but didn't tip over. Malcolm sat up and began to laugh uproariously.

"Look at this," Karen said. "I can't believe this. He's not re-creating the assassination attempt. He's re-creating Kaminski's video."

Jon just sat there staring, too stunned to say a word.

On screen, Malcolm had stopped laughing. "Folks, I think I need a chair without wheels. Because I don't want to roll backward. I want to topple backward. I want to be sprawled on the floor."

"It's the same," Karen whispered in horror. "Word for word. The same damn thing."

The news anchor appeared on screen again.

"In case you're wondering, Mr. Malcolm got his wish. The Secret Service found a different chair. And on the second try, he found himself exactly where he wanted to be. Sprawled on the floor." The anchor smiled. "I'll be back with more news in—"

"You idiot!" Karen shouted at the face on the screen. "He's using you. He's using the media. Can't you see?"

All Jon could feel was rage. Kaminski's video was worthless now. Malcolm had slithered away.

Jon stood up, grabbed onto the desk with both hands, and flipped it over. Everything crashed to the floor.

"C'mon," he said, "we're getting out of here."

They found a pay phone at a gas station a few blocks away from Kenny's apartment.

Jon took a business card out of his wallet and dialed the number on the back.

"I hope Oppenheim is home," Karen said.

On the third ring, a woman answered.

"May I speak to Detective Oppenheim, please," Jon said. There was a lot of noise in the background. It sounded like they were having a party.

The woman hesitated. "Who's calling, please?"

"My name is Jonathan Goodman. Detective Oppenheim asked me to call him at home today. Is this Mrs. Oppenheim?"

"No, no, this is his sister-in-law. Could you hold on a minute, please?"

He heard another woman's voice, but he couldn't make out what she was saying.

"Is he there?" Karen asked.

Jon shrugged.

The sister-in-law was back on the line. "Sorry about that. Things are a little crazy around here right now. Look, I'm sorry to be the one to tell you, but Vic was in an accident this morning."

The color drained from Jon's face. They were counting on Oppenheim.

"An accident?"

"What kind of accident?" Karen whispered.

Jon held up his hand. He was trying to listen.

"—don't know what happened exactly. The police think he fell asleep behind the wheel."

"How is he doing now?"

There was a long pause.

"He passed away," she said quietly. "They rushed him to the hospital, but. . ."

She didn't say any more, and she didn't need to. Jon felt embarrassed for not understanding right away.

"I'm so sorry," he said. "I—"

Then he didn't know what else to say. There was an awkward silence.

"Please accept my condolences," he finally mumbled.

The woman thanked him and politely ended the call.

Jon stood there frozen with the phone in his hand. He was stunned.

"Condolences?" Karen asked incredulously. "For Oppenheim?"

He nodded slowly and hung up the phone. "She said he died in a car accident this morning. He supposedly fell asleep behind the wheel."

"Oh God."

Karen barely knew Oppenheim, but the tears welled in her eyes anyway. He had been their last hope. Who could they turn to now?

Jon felt dazed. And responsible. He'd been the one who called Oppenheim. He was the one who got Oppenheim involved. And killed. Just like Kenny.

He slumped against the phone booth and closed his eyes.

Karen tugged his arm. "Let's go. We shouldn't be standing out here."

Jon opened his eyes. "Go where? We have thirty-four bucks left. That's not going to get us too far."

"We only have to get to Oregon."

"Why Oregon?"

"I know someone in Portland we can stay with."

"A friend?"

"Not exactly," she said, heading for the motorcycle.

* * *

Halfway to Portland, they stopped at a roadside diner.

When their sandwiches arrived, they ate in silence, watching the cars pass by on the highway.

Karen thought about what she was leaving behind. Everything but the clothes on her back. She'd spent a lifetime accumulating possessions, all of which she was now abandoning. When she'd walked out of her loft two days ago, it had never occurred to her that she wouldn't be back. Now she visualized the clothes and the books and the photos and the furniture and the various mementos, and wondered what she would have taken with her, had she known.

She surprised herself with the unsentimental answer.

More underwear.

At the moment, that was all she needed. The rest suddenly seemed superfluous. She could live without it.

She reached across the table and took Jon's hand. For now, she felt content with what she had.

Jon held her hand, and felt reassured. For days, he had been playing "if only" games in his head. If only he'd gone home five minutes earlier on Monday night. If only he'd gone along with the cover-up. If only he hadn't told Kenny anything.

But there was one thing he didn't regret.

Meeting Karen.

Sometimes he felt guilty about having gotten her involved. He knew his motives had been purely selfish. But he couldn't imagine being where he was, doing what he was doing, all alone. Without her, he was certain that he wouldn't have gotten this far. They would have already found him and killed him.

Holding Karen's hand, Jon felt calm. He didn't know what was going to happen to them. He had no idea what they were going to do. With Karen nearby, though, he felt confident despite the long odds. At the very least, they'd be together.

The waitress put the check on the table. $12.53.

Jon pulled out his wallet and put thirteen dollars on the table. So now they were down to twenty-one dollars between them.

Then he hesitated. How could he leave a tip of 47 cents? He dropped another dollar on the pile. That left them a nice even twenty bucks for their nest egg.

Shoving his wallet back into his pocket, Jon felt a folded-up piece of paper. He took it out and put it on the table.

"What's that?" Karen asked.

"The e-mail from Kenny that I printed out."

She unfolded the paper and started reading.

Two minutes later, she was still reading the brief message.

"What's so interesting?" Jon asked.

"The postscript," Karen replied. "Have any idea what he was talking about?"

Jon took back the paper and read the e-mail again.

P.S. remote [JackM:zip]. I'll explain later. Gotta go now.

"What's that mean?" she asked.

He shrugged "I'm not sure." He put down the paper. "The 'JackM:zip' part sounds like the Megasoft Mail back door."

"You mean the thing we tried from Sears? That they shut down?"

"Exactly. You just log in as JackM, then use the Woodside ZIP code as the password."

"Why would he tell you about that again in this message?"

"I don't know."

Karen studied the postscript. "What do you think this word 'remote' means?"

"It usually means a way to connect to the network when you're out of the office. You know, from home or from some hotel room."

"Maybe he's telling us about some way to connect to OneWire from outside."

Jon sat up. "A back door into OneWire?"

Karen nodded.

"Now wouldn't that be interesting?" he asked.

34

☆ ☆ ☆ ☆ ☆

It was almost midnight when Karen knocked on the apartment door.

"I hope I have the right address," she whispered, checking the apartment number again in her little black book. She'd copied the address off a Christmas card last year. Now she was wishing that she'd sent a card back.

The apartment was on the top floor of an old, three-story tan brick building. It was just off the main boulevard of the trendy, renovated Hawthorne district in southeastern Portland, where sushi bars and funky coffeehouses were fast replacing run-down mom-and-pop stores.

When the door finally opened, Karen thought she had the wrong apartment. In the dim light, she didn't immediately recognize the shirtless man with a brown beard standing in the doorway. But when he threw his arms around her and she smelled his cologne and felt his hands on her back, she knew she was in the right place.

"What are you doing here?" he said, releasing her.

"It's a long story," she replied. "When'd you grow the beard?"

"After I moved out here." He stroked his cheek with the back of his hand. "I look pretty different, huh?"

"Yeah, you do." But his eyes gave him away, she thought. They were the bluest eyes she'd ever seen.

"I got tired of people recognizing me."

"Well, I almost didn't." It looked like he worked out now, she noticed. And the earring was new. He didn't have that when she was going out with him.

"I definitely recognize you," he said, brushing away a few strands of hair from her face. "You look great."

Karen smiled radiantly.

Jon moved a step closer and put his arm around her shoulders.

"I'm sorry," she said. "This is my friend, Jon Goodman."

My friend? Kind of vague, Jon thought, as he held out his hand.

"Hi, I'm Paul Halladay."

"Nice to meet you," Jon said as they shook hands.

Jon had to force himself to smile, because he already didn't like this guy.

"So Malcolm faked the assassination attempt," Paul said, "and he's actually funding the terrorists?"

"He and Constanza are in on it together," Jon replied.

They were sitting in Paul's living room. The 1960s yellow bean bag chairs and purple lava lamp were balanced by the decidedly modern personal computer on a desk in one corner.

Karen had mixed feelings about seeing Paul again. At some level, there was still an undeniable attraction. When they were going out, no one in the office was supposed to know about it. She was his boss, and she was afraid of all the raised eyebrows. The stealth made the whole thing more exciting. She delighted in the contrast between their professional coolness during the day and their passionate warmth at night.

Eventually, though, there was gossip. And when the Cigarette Papers controversy erupted, her colleagues were unsympathetic. After all, if she'd been sleeping with the guy, how couldn't she have known where he'd gotten the papers?

She felt betrayed by what Paul had done. There was no getting around that. It had derailed her career. But she couldn't assign him all of the blame. If she hadn't been involved with him, she probably would have asked more questions. She probably would have insisted on talking to his source. And for those lapses, she had no one to blame but herself.

Karen had found it hard to stay angry at Paul. She knew him

too well for that. He hadn't acted maliciously. He was a zealot. He was determined to prove how evil the cigarette companies were. No matter what the method. Because he unflinchingly believed that the ends justified the means.

She distinctly remembered the last time she'd seen him, the day after he'd been fired. He came to say goodbye to her in the office. He'd cleaned out his apartment and packed up his car. He was double-parked downstairs. Everyone was staring at him as he made his way to her office. "I just want to tell you I'm sorry," he said, "but I think you already know that." Then he embraced her and kissed her on the cheek and he was gone. A few weeks later, she'd had one brief, awkward phone conversation with him, but that was it. There was nothing more to say.

"If you can get me some evidence," Paul was telling Jon, "I can put it on the air. We're just a little UHF station, not part of any of the networks. But we've got 20,000 people in greater Portland watching our news every night."

"Karen," Jon said, "did you hear that?"

She'd gotten up. She couldn't sit anymore.

"Yeah, all we need now is some evidence." She was standing next to Paul's desk. She looked down and saw the OneWire user's guide. "Paul, do you have OneWire?"

"I signed up a few weeks ago. It's a really good deal." Then he added sheepishly, "Well, at least I thought it was, before I knew that Big Brother was going to be watching me."

"Mind if I give it a try?" Karen asked.

"Go ahead," Paul replied.

She flipped on the power switch.

A minute later, they were staring at the OneWire welcome screen.

"I need to type in my password here," Paul said.

"No, we're going to log in as someone else," Karen replied. Next to *User,* she typed JackM. "Jon, what's the Woodside ZIP code?"

She typed in the five numbers.

The computer responded immediately. *Invalid user and/or password.*

"What's the ZIP code again?" She tried once more.

Invalid user and/or password.

Karen slumped back in the chair. "I knew this sounded too good to be true."

Jon dug into his pocket for the copy of Kenny's e-mail. He read the last line again. *P.S. remote [JackM:zip]*. What else could that mean?

Then something at the top of Kenny's message caught his eye. "Karen, switch over to the file navigator."

She changed screens.

"Go to the OneWire directory."

She pressed the arrow keys a few times.

"Now tell me the version number of that *meganet.sys* file."

"Version 2.01," she read from the screen.

"Maybe that's the problem." He showed her Kenny's e-mail. *Subject: meganet.sys Version 3.0*

"The new version is 3.0," he said. "This machine is running the old version."

"How do I upgrade?" Paul asked.

"You don't," Jon replied. "OneWire does it automatically."

Karen was reading Kenny's message. "Jon, he says right here that it's not going to be upgraded until early November."

"I guess we have to wait," Paul said.

"By then," Karen said, "Jack Malcolm is going to be president-elect."

"What a scary thought," Jon said. "If only there were some way to stop him."

Karen turned off the computer. "Right now," she said, "he looks pretty unstoppable."

The lights were off in the living room and Paul's bedroom door was closed.

Jon shifted uncomfortably on the sofa bed. The mattress was too soft.

"You can't sleep either?" Karen whispered.

"Nah."

"Long day."

"That's for sure."

"This morning at Snowdon Falls, I thought they had us. But we got away. Then, when we were watching that video of Malcolm, I thought we had them. I really did. But they got away. And then Oppenheim. . ." She sighed. "I feel like we were on a roller coaster today."

"I'm still in shock about Malcolm," Jon said. "On the one hand, I know the truth about him now. But on the other hand, I want it not to be true. I know that sounds crazy, but—"

"He meant a lot to you."

"And even more to Kenny. That's what I keep thinking about. Kenny was a total fanatic when it came to JackM. In his mind, the man could do no wrong. And for all we know, Malcolm might have been the one who told them to kill Kenny. Wouldn't that be sick?"

"I really don't understand why Malcolm is doing this," Karen said. "He's one of the richest men in the world. You'd think that would be enough. What does he want so badly, that he's willing to murder all these people to get?"

Jon thought about it for a while. "I don't know," he finally said. "Power? Is that what Malcolm wants? I have no idea. No matter how much some people have, it's not enough for them."

Karen rested her head on Jon's shoulder. "Right now, I have what I want."

Jon wasn't going to say anything, but as he lay there, the question gnawed at him.

"Why didn't you tell me the whole story? I mean, about him?" he said, jerking his head toward Paul's closed door.

She didn't answer right away.

"Maybe because I wasn't very proud of how I behaved. Maybe because that's ancient history, as far as I'm concerned. That was then, and this," she said as she lifted her head to kiss him, "is now."

Election Night: Tuesday, November 7

☆ ☆ ☆ ☆ ☆

35

☆ ☆ ☆ ☆ ☆

When the cheering in the ballroom finally subsided, Malcolm began to speak.

"My friends, I've just received a call from the president—"

There were scattered boos from the crowd.

He held up his hands. "No, no, please. Tonight's a night for being gracious. This has been a hard-fought campaign, but it's behind us. Now's the time for us to come together as a nation."

There was a roar of approval.

Malcolm shuffled his note cards. "Both the president and Governor Duncan have been kind enough to call and offer their congratulations on our victory today. The president pledged to do his best to ensure a smooth transition to a Malcolm administration." He grinned. "Malcolm administration. I like the way that sounds."

The applause was deafening.

"I was also pleased to receive a call earlier this evening from the Speaker of the House, who promised to work with us in a positive and constructive manner. I am grateful for his support, and in the days and weeks ahead, I will seek to win the support of the entire Congressional leadership.

"I intend to fulfill the promises I have made to you during this campaign. It will not be easy. Some of our opponents attempt to intimidate us through violent acts. But we will not be intimidated. As president, I will do everything in my power to end the violence and restore order to our land. I believe. . ."

* * *

Jon felt like throwing something at the television. Watching Malcolm declare victory made him feel sick. Malcolm had been ahead in the polls for weeks, but Jon had held on to the slim hope that there would be some miraculous upset. Now there was no hope. It was President-elect Malcolm.

He got up from the sofa. He felt restless. He'd been sitting around this living room for too long.

"Where are you going?" Karen asked.

It was just the two of them tonight. Paul was working late.

"I just want to see if there's anything new on the tape," he said, walking over to the computer.

On Sunday night, for the first time, they'd been able to use the OneWire back door. Version 3.0 was finally in place.

"Jon, no one's going to be there tonight. All you're going to see is more video of an empty office."

So far, they hadn't been able to look into the offices of Malcolm or Seely. Maybe the system upgrade wasn't finished, Jon thought. But they did have a clear view of Constanza's office.

He rewound the tape, then fast forwarded through the last few hours. Karen was right. More pictures of a dark office.

She was looking over his shoulder. "You've got to be patient," she told him. "The trap is set. Now all we need is the rat."

From the top of the stairs, Malcolm waved one last time to the crowd on the tarmac, then he turned and boarded his jet.

Herb Abernathy was standing in the doorway.

"Welcome aboard, Mr. President-elect."

There was a hearty round of applause from the campaign staff gathered in the first cabin.

Malcolm grinned. "Thank you, Herb. Thank you all. It's too late at night for making speeches, so I just want to thank each one of you for your help. This is your victory tonight as much as it is mine. And I promise never to forget that."

He moved through the cabin triumphantly, shaking hands and slapping backs.

Abernathy followed him into the private quarters at the rear of the plane, and handed him a binder.

"Here's your speech at the Capitol tomorrow."

Malcolm had wanted to get a good night's sleep at home, but the staff had convinced him to fly through the night to Washington. He was going to appear with a bipartisan group of Congressional leaders. A nice symbolic gesture on the day after his victory.

He dropped the binder on a table and took off his suit jacket. Then, with a yawn, he sunk into a wide leather seat by the window.

"Mind if we go over the speech in the morning? I'm exhausted."

"No, no, that's fine."

"Good, I'm going to get a few hours of sleep then."

Abernathy paused at the door to the main cabin. "Jack?"

He looked up. "Yeah?"

"Congratulations."

Malcolm smiled. "Thanks, Herb. You did a hell of a job. Thanks for everything."

Abernathy nodded, then closed the door behind him.

Malcolm sat there alone in the darkened cabin, savoring the silence.

For a week now, he'd been confident that he was going to win the election. All the polls had placed him in the lead. But it wasn't until he heard the president's voice on the phone tonight, conceding defeat, that the victory seemed real.

President Malcolm. It did have a nice ring to it. He pictured himself meeting with foreign dignitaries in the Oval Office. Signing legislation out in the Rose Garden. Striding up to the podium as the band played *Hail to the Chief.*

But that wasn't what this was all about. It wasn't a matter of ego. It was a matter of putting America back on course. In January, Malcolm was going to hit the ground running. The whirlwind of activity he planned for his first Hundred Days would make Roosevelt's pale in comparison.

The plane began to taxi out to the runway. Malcolm fastened his seat belt.

Now that the campaign was over, he intended to close down Cincinnatus. The terrorists had served their purpose. OneWire was all the edge he needed now. Besides, he'd never felt comfortable with the violence, with the loss of life. That hadn't been his idea. He thought it would have been enough to just blow up the Statue of Liberty or something like that. There was no need to kill anyone. But Constanza had derided that approach, calling it naive. He'd insisted that Cincinnatus wouldn't be taken seriously if there were no casualties. So, reluctantly, Malcolm let Constanza do it his way.

No longer, though. There would be no more violence. It had been a promise of Malcolm's in the campaign, and he intended to keep it.

Constanza was a problem. He could cause trouble, if Malcolm wasn't careful. He had a big mouth, and big ambitions. He had to be kept busy, out of the way. Malcolm would load him up with the usual vice presidential fare. Chairing useless presidential commissions. Attending ridiculous ecological conferences in third-world countries. If Malcolm played his cards right, Constanza would find some reason to step down after his first term as vice president. Let the general retire and play with his grandchildren. The country would be better off.

The plane accelerated down the runway, then lifted off into the air.

Malcolm watched out the window as the plane climbed into the night sky. He could see a highway far below. He could see a grid of streetlights.

The plane banked gently to the left.

A flash of light on the ground caught Malcolm's eye. He stared for a second, but didn't see anything else, so he shifted his gaze toward the distant brightness of downtown Seattle.

Then he noticed a streak of light below. It was rapidly tracing a steep, upward sloping arc. Toward the plane.

His pulse quickened as he wondered whether it could be a—

The light arrived suddenly, silently. Then it exploded, and the sound was unimaginably loud.

"Turn it up!" Karen shouted.

Jon fumbled to find the volume button on the remote control.

"—erupted in a fireball shortly after takeoff," the news anchor was saying. "Seconds before the explosion, witnesses on the ground say they saw what appeared to be the launching of a surface-to-air missile. We go now to Eric—''

The anchor stopped and pressed a finger against his earpiece. ''No, I'm sorry. We'll have that report in a moment. First, this breaking news. We've just received a fax that purports to be a communication from the New Society of Cincinnatus, the terrorist group. According to this fax—and let me emphasize that the authenticity of this document is unconfirmed—the Cincinnatus organization is claiming responsibility for a missile attack tonight on the aircraft of President-elect Jack Malcolm.''

He briefly looked off camera. ''Okay, we're going now to our correspondent Eric Shields, who joins us live from Seattle.'' He turned to face a large monitor. ''Eric, what can you tell us?''

''Bob, as you can see behind me, firefighters are attempting now to control the raging flames that have engulfed a portion of the fuselage of Mr. Malcolm's airplane. I say a portion because it appears that the wreckage from the plane is scattered over an extremely wide area.''

''Eric, any survivors so far?''

''No, and of course it's too early to say for sure, but I'm afraid that the prospects don't seem very good at this point, Bob. This really was a horrific crash.''

''Eric, thank you.'' The anchor looked back at the camera. ''If you're just joining us, a plane carrying President-elect Jack Malcolm has crashed in—''

Jon turned down the volume.

''Oh my God,'' he said. ''This is wild.''

''You know, right now,'' Karen said, ''I'm not even sure whether to believe it or not. Is this for real? Or is this like the assassination attempt?''

''Wait, are you serious? You really think they could fake a plane crash?''

''If you'd told me last month that Malcolm faked the assassination attempt, I would have thought you were nuts. Now. . .'' She just shrugged.

''Well, if Malcolm survived, we'll know soon enough.''

''True.''

"But what if he didn't?" Jon said. "What if Cincinnatus really did shoot down his plane?"

"Jon, Malcolm runs Cincinnatus. I don't think—"

"No, Malcolm and Constanza run Cincinnatus. Maybe Constanza really was planning to get rid of Malcolm."

"But Malcolm was in on the assassination attempt," Karen said. "We know that. We saw proof of that."

"That was before the election, when Constanza still needed Malcolm to win. Now it's after the election. Now, without Malcolm, the general is suddenly the president."

Karen slumped back into the sofa. "At this point, I don't know what to hope for. Either way, whether Malcolm is alive or dead, whether it's President Malcolm or President Constanza, the country is still screwed."

Wednesday, November 8

☆ ☆ ☆ ☆ ☆

36

☆ ☆ ☆ ☆ ☆

The news conference was held in the same Seattle hotel where Jack Malcolm had celebrated his victory a little more than twelve hours before. Folding chairs had been hastily arranged on top of the confetti from the previous night's celebration. The ballroom was still ringed by red, white, and blue streamers.

As journalists filed into the room, hotel employees were struggling to pull down the AMERICA IS MALCOLM COUNTRY! banner that stretched across the stage.

A few minutes past noon, a somber Peter Constanza, dressed in a dark blue suit, walked across the empty stage to a lectern in the center. He pulled a stack of note cards from his jacket pocket and placed them on the lectern.

"A little over an hour ago, I was informed that the search for survivors from the crash of President-elect Jack Malcolm's aircraft had been concluded. All passengers aboard the plane, including my dear friend—"

Constanza's voice cracked. He stopped and pressed his lips together.

"I'm sorry," he whispered. Then he tried again. "All passengers aboard the plane, including my dear friend Jack Malcolm, are now presumed to have perished."

He looked down at his note cards for a moment, then continued.

"This is a national tragedy. We have been robbed of a great leader by a band of craven outlaws. Mere words fail to express the profound grief and the immense outrage that I feel today.

"To the American people, I pledge to carry on Jack Malcolm's vital work, with all my energy and all my heart. And to the terrorists who dare to call themselves patriots, I pledge to continue Jack Malcolm's fight against you.

"Despite what our adversaries might believe, the wheels of American government will continue to turn. Pursuant to the Twenty-Fifth Amendment to our Constitution, I will soon nominate a new vice president. And on January twentieth, I promise that the Constanza administration will be ready to fulfill its responsibilities."

Constanza slid his note cards back into his pocket.

"I'll take a few questions now," he said quietly. He pointed to a woman in the first row.

"Sir, are we positive that this crash was indeed the result of a missile attack? Should we take the Cincinnatus claims at face value?"

"We do have radar information that indicates the presence of a missile," Constanza said. "Beyond that, for security reasons, I don't think it would be appropriate for me to comment further."

He pointed to a man in the back.

"General, don't you think it's premature to invoke the Twenty-Fifth Amendment? Under the Constitution, until the Electoral College votes, you have not yet officially been elected vice president. Now that Mr. Malcolm is deceased, are you certain that the Electoral College will vote for the Malcolm-Constanza ticket?"

"The American people elected us last night," Constanza replied. "I'm not concerned about the Electoral College."

Then he noticed that an aide had walked onto the stage.

"I'm sorry," the general said. "That's all the time we have for questions."

Jon looked at his watch. 2:35. He'd been going back to the computer every five minutes. He double-checked the VCR they'd set up on the desk, making sure that it was still recording. He wanted to be certain that they were getting everything on tape.

Karen was on the sofa, watching the nonstop TV news coverage of the Malcolm plane crash and its aftermath.

"See anyone?" she called.

"Just his secretary, I think," Jon said, peering into the computer monitor. He saw a desk with a keyboard in the foreground, a high-back leather chair behind it, and a window looking out on the Megasoft campus in the background.

"It was only for a second," he said. "She came in and put some papers on—"

A hand appeared on the screen and grabbed the back of the chair, which was pulled away from the camera.

"Karen!"

Seconds later, they were staring at an image of a smiling Peter Constanza.

"You slime," Karen hissed at the screen. "We've got you."

Constanza leaned back in his chair and put his feet up on the desk.

"Charlie," he began, "all in all, not a bad day."

Across the street from the apartment building, Burt Seely was sitting in the passenger seat of a white van.

He pulled off a pair of headphones.

"Okay, she just hung up the phone," he said to the driver, a young man with a military haircut and a blue windbreaker. "They should be out any minute now. They're heading for her friend at the TV station. With some kind of video about Constanza."

"Video, sir?"

"That's what she said. A video about Constanza. I don't know what's on it, but I want it. And I want them."

He unplugged his headphones and tossed them on the back-seat. "Listen, when they first pull out, I want you to keep your distance. This area is too crowded. I don't want a million witnesses."

"Yes, sir."

Seely stared out the window. "The General's still on my case about the screw-up at Snowdon Lodge. If we botch this, I'll never hear the end of it. So take it easy. Let's not make any mistakes. We were lucky to find them. I don't want to lose them again."

"How were they located, sir?"

"Calling-card records. Last night, the reporter charged a call to her card. The two of them have been smart about not trying to use their credit cards, so she must have forgotten. Or not realized,

I guess. People don't understand that everything they do these days winds up in a computer file somewhere.''

Seely pulled a gun out of his shoulder holster and placed it on the floor beside him. ''Call the other unit and confirm that they understand their orders. We're not taking any chances this time. It's shoot to kill.''

37

☆ ☆ ☆ ☆ ☆

Jon felt almost giddy as he walked out of the apartment. He was grinning. Constanza wasn't going to get away with it, after all.

"Have the tape?" Karen asked before she closed the door.

He patted his jacket pocket. "Right here."

As they went down the stairs to the street, Karen glanced at her watch. 3:48. Plenty of time. "Paul said that if we get to the station by five-thirty, he'll put the video on the six o'clock news."

The motorcycle was parked at the curb in front of the building.

"Great," Jon said. "It's only a fifteen-minute ride over there."

She smiled and tossed him the key to the motorcycle. "Your turn."

He laughed. "Are you sure? Kenny only let me ride this thing once."

"What happened?"

"I forgot how to stop. We nearly went under a tractor trailer."

"C'mon, get on. I'll teach you. It's easy. Just like riding a bicycle."

Jon got on the motorcycle and started up the engine.

"Not bad," Karen said, getting on behind him. She put her arms around his waist, then kissed him on the back of his neck.

"Hey, I like your teaching style already."

"I'm a big believer in positive reinforcement."

"Hold on," Jon said, as he gently nudged the bike forward onto the street.

"That's it. Nice and easy."

He slowly guided the motorcycle to the corner of Hawthorne Boulevard, then stopped.

"Good braking," Karen said.

"That's the one thing I learned in my first—"

As Jon looked to the left, about to make a right turn onto Hawthorne, he spotted a familiar face. He turned his head in time to lock eyes for an instant with Burt Seely, in the passenger window of a white van.

"It's Seely!" he shouted.

"What?"

"Across the street, in the van. It's Burt Seely."

"Jon, go!"

He edged the bike forward, but the traffic on Hawthorne was too heavy. He couldn't turn.

There was a screech to their left as the white van pulled away from the curb.

"Jon, c'mon!"

But none of the cars whizzing by on Hawthorne would let him in.

The van swerved in front of them, diagonally blocking the crosswalk.

Jon pulled the handlebars to the right, gave the engine some gas, and jumped the curb.

Now they were flying along the sidewalk on Hawthorne, under awnings, past store windows. A bakery. A dry cleaner. A hardware store. A coffeehouse.

"Watch out!" Karen cried.

Jon leaned to the left, narrowly missing a woman with a baby carriage.

An elderly man dropped his bag of groceries on the pavement when he saw the motorcycle coming, pressing his body against the window of a hair salon. The front tire of the motorcycle crushed the grocery bag.

Karen looked to her left. The white van had turned onto Hawthorne, and was now nearly parallel with them, just beyond the parked cars.

At the corner, Jon flew out into the crosswalk, nearly hitting a taxi, then turned hard left, onto Hawthorne Boulevard.

He weaved in and out of the traffic, keeping one eye on the rearview mirror.

Seely's van kept pace, no more than a few car lengths behind.

The TV station was still more than a mile away, on the other side of the Willamette River, just across the Hawthorne Bridge.

It would be a straight shot, except that Hawthorne Boulevard became a one-way street a few blocks before the bridge.

One way going the wrong way. Jon would have to make a right on Twelfth, a left on Madison, then another left and right back onto Hawthorne.

He'd have to slow down to make all those turns. It would make them sitting ducks.

He checked the mirror. The white van was close behind, and gaining.

As Jon neared Twelfth, he made his decision. He wouldn't turn right. He was going straight.

"Jon, no! It's one way!"

"I know!" he shouted.

The motorcycle hopped the median and plunged into the oncoming traffic.

Jon swerved to avoid a bus, then steered to the far right. He kept the bike close to the parked cars on his right, trying to stay away from the cars speeding by in the opposite direction on his left.

Karen twisted around in her seat.

"Jon, they're not following. Take it easy."

He slowed down, and concentrated on keeping the motorcycle on course. It was unnerving to ride against the traffic.

Cars were honking at him. On the sidewalk, pedestrians were shouting.

At the next intersection, Hawthorne Boulevard became two-way again.

As Jon hopped another median, he looked to the right and saw a blue pickup truck turning onto Hawthorne. He eased up on the gas and let the truck turn onto the street ahead of him.

Then he saw a hand reach out the passenger window of the truck. There was a gun in the hand.

He jerked the handlebars to the left, and moved into the center lane. Just as they got to the Hawthorne Bridge, he roared by the truck on its left.

Jon nervously scanned the other cars on the bridge. Suddenly, they all seemed threatening. How many of them were working for Seely?

"Pick it up!" Karen shouted as they went across the bridge.

The truck had moved into the far left lane and was closing in on them.

Jon gave the engine more gas. The needle on the speedometer passed 60. Then 70. He was afraid to go any faster. He was having trouble controlling the motorcycle.

Then he heard an explosion, and felt something whiz by his head.

"Jon, they're shooting!"

He accelerated and swerved to the left, cutting off the truck.

They were almost over the bridge.

"Get to the right," Karen said. "We need to make the first right."

But he couldn't. In the mirror, he could see the truck close behind him on his right. Turning right would give them a clear shot.

At the end of the bridge, he made a left. He forgot how fast he was going and had to fight to keep the bike upright.

"Where are you going?" Karen shouted.

"I don't know."

The truck had fallen back a bit, now about twenty yards behind them.

At the first big intersection, Jon made a hard right. He had to turn around somehow and get to the TV station.

Up ahead, he saw a sign for Washington Park. He looked in his mirror. The truck was coming up fast. He had to do something.

With squealing tires, he made a right into the park.

At the far end of a nearly empty parking lot, Jon spotted a chain-link gate with a wide gravel road beyond. A man in green coveralls was closing the gate.

The man jumped out of the way as Jon threaded the motorcycle through the narrow opening. He sped down the gravel road, which cut through dense trees.

Seconds later, the truck followed, ripping through the chain-link gate.

They were now on the perimeter of a large Japanese garden.

Jon looked for some place to turn. The truck was on his tail. He didn't want to give them a clear—

The sound of a gunshot made him jump. His hands involuntarily jerked the handlebars, nearly toppling the bike.

Then he saw a narrow asphalt path leading into the Japanese garden. He leaned right, flying into the turn at high speed.

Just yards behind, the truck followed, mowing down the vegetation on both sides of the path.

The path opened onto a rock garden, with carefully manicured shrubs intermingled with small, irregularly shaped boulders.

Jon veered onto a slate path, which followed the contour of a lily pond. He checked his mirror. The truck was still—

Another gunshot rang out, startling a flock of birds and sending them into the air.

"Jon, the bridge!" Karen shouted.

Ahead, a little wooden bridge crossed the pond.

He swerved left onto the steeply arched bridge. He could feel the structure sag under the weight of the motorcycle.

At the top of the arch, Jon realized that he had been going too fast, and was shocked to find the motorcycle launched into midair.

The rear tire landed first, smashing down on the thin wooden planks near the end of the bridge. It took all of Jon's strength to hold on to the bike when the front tire hit the ground.

Karen turned around in time to see the truck reach the top of the bridge. It seemed to hang there for an instant, suspended in time.

Then, with barely a sound, the whole bridge collapsed.

In his rearview mirror, Jon watched the truck crash through the flimsy wood beams into the pond below.

A few minutes later, he stopped the motorcycle near the park exit and turned off the motor.

Then they both just sat there, too stunned to speak.

"How did they find us?" Jon finally asked.

"I don't know. We've been so careful."

He looked at his watch. It was just a few minutes after four.

"We'll drop the tape off with Paul, then we'll get back on the road. Maybe we can head down the coast to California. I've got friends in San Francisco."

Karen had a bad feeling about the TV station. "What if they know where Paul works? What if they're waiting for us there?"

"Look," Jon said, "they obviously figured out we've been staying with Paul. They may know where he works. But there's absolutely no way they know about the Constanza tape. They're not going to be expecting us to run to the TV station right now. They'll think that we're on our way out of town."

Karen nodded. She knew they had to get the tape on the air. And Paul was their best hope for that.

"Okay," she said, "let's go."

Jon pulled the key out of the ignition.

"From now on," he said, handing her the key, "you drive."

38

☆ ☆ ☆ ☆ ☆

They parked the motorcycle a few blocks away from the TV station, and walked the rest of the way. Each time a car passed, Karen tensed, half expecting a hand with a gun to appear in the window. Jon scanned the street for Seely's white van, but didn't see it.

The station was in a boxy modern building, with two huge satellite dishes and a CHANNEL 25 BRINGS IT HOME! billboard on the roof.

In the lobby, Jon gave the receptionist their names and told her they were visiting Paul Halladay. She said that he was expecting them, and showed them on a floor plan where to find him.

"So far, so good," Karen said as they got on the elevator.

Jon took her hand. "A few more minutes, and this whole thing will be over."

They got off at the third floor and followed the receptionist's directions, walking to the end of a long corridor.

Karen knocked on a door marked CONTROL ROOM 2.

A moment later, Paul appeared at the door.

"Hey," he said simply, holding the door open for them.

They walked into the darkened room, which had a bank of TV monitors on one wall. Each of the monitors had a different picture. A basketball game. A weather map. A reporter holding a microphone. A talk show. Below the monitors was a complex array of electronic equipment, mounted horizontally.

"We've got the Constanza tape," Karen said.

Jon pulled the videocassette out of his jacket. "It's pretty incredible stuff."

Then the lights came up and they heard a voice behind them.

"I'm sure the general would love to see that," Burt Seely said. He was holding a gun.

"You," he said, pointing the gun at Paul, "got a VCR in here to play that?"

Paul nodded.

"Mr. Goodman, give him the tape."

Jon handed it to Paul.

"Fine," Seely said. "Now show us what's so incredible."

Paul rolled a chair over to the control panel, then sat down and inserted the tape into a slot. He pressed a few buttons. All of the monitors went black.

A few seconds later, an image of General Constanza flickered onto the monitors. He was sitting in his office, with the Megasoft campus visible through the window behind him.

"Charlie," he began, "all in all, not a bad day."

The four of them watched the video for a minute without saying a word.

"Jesus Christ," Seely finally blurted out, "how'd you record him like this?"

"The same way he was going to record everyone else," Jon said.

"OneWire?" Seely asked.

"That's right."

Seely smiled and continued to watch the monitors. "Very clever, Mr. Goodman. I have to admit that. But not clever enough. Because I promise you that no one else is ever going to see this tape."

There was pounding on the door.

Seely motioned to Paul. "Answer that. Whoever it is, get rid of them."

Paul got up from his chair and went to the door, opening it just a crack.

"Halladay, what are you, crazy?" a man was screaming. "You just cut into Oprah. They're gonna fire both of us. Get Constanza off the air and put Oprah back on. Now!"

"What?" Seely shouted, as he slammed the door shut. "You're playing this thing on the air? You sneaky son of a—"

Karen gave Paul's empty chair a vicious kick, rolling it into Seely's knee. Seely gasped and instinctively clutched his knee.

Jon shoved Seely's head against the wall, and wrestled the gun away from him. Then he got him in a headlock, and pressed the barrel of the gun against Seely's temple.

"You bastard," Jon whispered, with his finger on the trigger. "Is this what you did to Kenny? How does it feel?"

Jon's forearm pressed so hard against Seely's neck that the man could barely breathe.

"Please," Seely mouthed.

"I'll show you all the mercy you showed my friend," Jon seethed. His finger pulled against the trigger.

"Jon, no!" Karen cried. "Don't do it."

For an instant, his finger trembled, millimeters away from firing the gun. He felt enraged, consumed with hatred. Seely had killed Kenny. Now he was going to kill Seely.

Then the madness passed.

Maybe it was the way that Karen looked at him, pleading with him to do the right thing. Or maybe it was because Jon couldn't stand to think of himself as a murderer.

He relaxed his trigger finger and let Seely drop to the floor.

Jon wasn't going to kill anyone. There already had been enough killing.

One Week Later:
Wednesday, November 15

☆ ☆ ☆ ☆ ☆

39

☆ ☆ ☆ ☆ ☆

The image on the TV wasn't the usual broadcast quality. It looked more like home video, grainy and slightly out of focus. Superimposed across the bottom of the screen was a blue title: *Courtesy of Channel 25 News, Portland, OR.*

There was a desk with a keyboard in the foreground, a high-back leather chair behind it, and a window looking out on a lush green landscape in the background.

A hand appeared on the screen and grabbed the back of the chair, which was pulled away from the camera.

Then a smiling Peter Constanza sat down.

Constanza leaned back in his chair and put his feet up on the desk.

"Charlie," he began, "all in all, not a bad day."

"Yes, sir," Donnelly replied.

"To tell you the truth, I was worried that our old Cincinnatus boys were going to screw up the missile launch. First they wanted to use one of those handheld Stinger things, and I knew that wasn't going to work. The range is way too short. So I told Seely to get hold of some of those new compact Chinese SAMs. With one of those babies, you can blow a plane out of the sky at 20,000 feet."

"You gotta have the right tools, sir."

Constanza nodded. "That's what I'm always saying. Use the right tool and the job is easy. Poor old Jack didn't have a chance."

He twisted his face into a mock serious expression. "My dear friend, Jack Malcolm." Then he laughed uproariously. "Jeez, what a relief to have him out of the way."

He looked through some papers on his desk. "Any of this stuff urgent?"

"Not really, sir. Just some prep work for the transition. Recommendations on Cabinet appointments. That sort of thing."

Constanza dropped the papers. "There's plenty of time for that stuff. I'm not moving into the White House till January." He cleared his throat. "By the way, did you hear that reporter at the news conference? You know, that nonsense about the Electoral College. What do you make of that?"

"I know Walt Kaminski looked into that," Donnelly replied. "He said we were taking a risk getting rid of Malcolm so soon. But you know how Walt was. Always sweating the details."

"Yeah, a real worrywart. I just thought it would be cleaner to take Malcolm out on day one. It made the whole thing a lot more dramatic. It gives us the crisis mentality I want. Don't you think?"

"Absolutely, sir."

Constanza waved his hand dismissively. "I'm not going to give this Electoral College crap a second thought. It's some weird historical thing. It's a rubber stamp. They wouldn't dare—"

"Are they still playing our Constanza video on the news?" Karen asked, peeking at the TV. She'd just gotten out of the shower, and was drying her hair with a towel.

They were back at Snowdon Lodge for a few days, tired of facing the reporters who were camped out at their apartments. The hotel room was lit up by bright morning sun.

Jon clicked off the TV with the remote.

"The Electoral College just got done voting," he said.

"And?"

"They voted for Constanza."

Karen stared at him, dumbfounded.

"What?" she shouted. "How could they—"

Then he had his arms around her.

"Karen, calm down. It's a joke. I'm kidding."

She smiled. "Who'd they really vote for?"

"The president. They returned him to office."

"Good." She tossed the towel back into the bathroom. "Did I hear the phone when I was in the shower?"

"Hey, I almost forgot. That was the Woodside DA's office. They're not filing any charges against me on the drug thing."

"What happened?"

"No evidence. Maybe Oppenheim did me a favor and flushed it down the toilet or something. I guess I'll never know. But wherever that heroin is, the police don't have it."

"So I won't be visiting you in prison?"

"Nope."

She kissed him lightly on the lips. "And here I was already looking forward to the conjugal visits."

"Why wait?" he asked, as they fell back on the bed.

Epilogue

☆ ☆ ☆ ☆ ☆

Charles Donnelly is serving a life sentence for the murder of Walter Kaminski.

Burt Seely entered into a plea-bargain agreement in connection with manslaughter charges arising from the death of Kenny Alden. He received a sentence of 25 years to life.

Peter Constanza was convicted of violating Federal arms importation statutes. Released on bail while appealing the conviction, he fled the country. His current whereabouts are unknown.

Paul Halladay is a producer at National Public Radio in Washington, D.C. He is the author of a book on the Malcolm presidential campaign, *Ulterior Motive,* which spent 17 weeks on the *New York Times* best-seller list.

Karen Grey Goodman settled her insider-trading case with the Securities and Exchange Commission. She agreed to return $136,854 in illegal profits, and paid a $20,000 fine. She is a business correspondent for CNN.

Jonathan Goodman was awarded $8.2 million by a jury in his wrongful-termination suit against Megasoft Corporation. He donated $1 million to the California Institute of Technology, endowing the Kenneth G. Alden Memorial Scholarship. He is the co-founder and president of a Silicon Valley start-up developing Internet security software.

The Goodmans live with their twin daughters, Rachel and Sharon, in the San Francisco Bay area.

Megasoft Corporation continues to offer OneWire service. According to a recent press release, the latest version of the software has "enhanced personal privacy safeguards."

Your Turn

Thanks for reading this far. I'm curious to hear what you think about the book. You can reach me by e-mail at megasoft@ibm.net. (I'm looking forward to reading your comments, but if my mail pile gets too high, please understand that I might not be able to reply.)

—Daniel Oran

P.S. If you liked *Ulterior Motive,* please recommend it to a friend!